CLASSICS OF HUMOUR

CLASSICS
OF
HUMOUR

Edited by Michael O'Mara

with illustrations by

Donald Rooum

CONSTABLE LONDON

This edition first published in Great Britain 1976 by
Constable and Company Ltd
10 Orange Street London WC2H 7EG
Copyright © Book Club Associates 1976

ISBN 0 09 461440 7

Set in Photon Baskerville
Printed in Great Britain by
REDWOOD BURN LIMITED
Trowbridge & Esher

CONTENTS

Acknowledgments   vii

Introduction   ix

J B MORTON ('Beachcomber')
Big White Carstairs and the M'Babwa of M'Gonkawiwi   1

CHARLES DICKENS
The Dancing Academy   10
The Great Winglebury Duel   17

O HENRY
One Thousand Dollars   33
Jeff Peters as a Personal Magnet   39

A G MACDONELL
The Cricket Match   46

KATHERINE MANSFIELD
The Modern Soul   61

FLANN O'BRIEN
The Brother   70

FRANK O'CONNOR
Song Without Words   84

EDGAR ALLAN POE
The System of Doctor Tarr and Professor Fether   92

DAMON RUNYON
Blood Pressure   109
Romance in the Roaring Forties   122

SAKI (H H MUNRO)
The Lost Sanjak   134
The Mouse   140

SOMERVILLE and ROSS
   The Holy Island   145

JAMES THURBER
   The Dog That Bit People   161
   The Remarkable Case of Mr Bruhl   168
   The Day the Dam Broke   175

MARK TWAIN
   The Notorious Jumping Frog of Calaveras County   181
   Blue-Jays   187

EVELYN WAUGH
   Mr Loveday's Little Outing   192
   Period Piece   200

OSCAR WILDE
   The Canterville Ghost   208

P G WODEHOUSE
   The Rummy Affair of Old Biffy   234
   Comrade Bingo   256

ACKNOWLEDGMENTS

Thanks are due to the following for permission to use copyright material:

The literary estate of Damon Runyon and Constable and Company Limited for the stories, *Blood Pressure* and *Romance in the Roaring Forties*; A D Peters and Company Limited for *Mr. Loveday's Little Outing* and *Period Piece* by Evelyn Waugh, *Song Without Words* by Frank O'Connor, the chapter from *England Their England* by A G Macdonell; John Farquharson Limited for *The Holy Island* by Somerville and Ross; The estate of P G Wodehouse for *Comrade Bingo* and *The Rummy Affair of Old Biffy*; Mrs Helen Thurber and Hamish Hamilton Limited for *The Dog That Bit People*, *The Day the Dam Burst* and *The Remarkable Case of Mr Bruhl*; J B Morton and the Daily Express for *Big White Carstairs*; Granada Publishing Ltd and Evelyn O'Nolan for *The Brother*.

For Paula

INTRODUCTION

In this anthology of twenty-five stories I have tried to bring together some of the finer elements of humorous prose in modern times. The stories have been selected to present as broad a range as possible of the many shades of humour which have passed in and out of vogue over the past one hundred and fifty years or so. From the light-hearted Wodehouse through the whimsical Thurber to the acid observations of Saki and Waugh a great deal of ground is covered, but these authors do share one thing central to this collection: the ability to make us laugh.

I have also tried to strike a balance between the familiar and the out of the way, so that even the connoisseur should be introduced to a few entirely new stories as well as renewing acquaintances with old favourites. The unfamiliar should include the pieces by Somerville and Ross and Flann O'Brien and the humour, out of character, of Edgar Allan Poe and Katherine Mansfield. On the other hand, 'The Cricket Match' by A G Macdonell and Waugh's 'Mr Loveday's Little Outing' should be, at least to the over forties, the most familiar of all.

Those of you who note that, although this is a modern anthology, none of the stories included is less than twenty years old, may draw your own conclusions. It does seem, however, that there is little room for the humorous short story these days. Many of the magazines that once published humour are now defunct or only publish satire of a topical and short-lived nature, and the catch phrase among book publishers today is 'humour doesn't pay!' I suppose television comedy and the humorous film now fill this need in most people.

But perhaps you, like me, still find the world created by a Runyon or Wodehouse a more personal and civilized retreat from harsh reality. If so, do enjoy the stories that follow, and pass the word along.

The splendid illustrations in this volume are all by Donald Rooum, except for those in the three Thurber stories which are, of course, the unmistakable work of Thurber himself.

Michael O'Mara
1976

J B MORTON
(b. 1893)

Although J B Morton has written many books of humour, biographies, and histories he is best known as 'Beachcomber' of the *Daily Express*. His zany world, populated by Dr Strabismus (whom God Preserve) of Utrecht, Justice Cocklecarrot, The Filthistan Trio, and Dr Smart-Allick of Narkover, has been a refuge from reality since 1924. The following material appeared as Britain prepared for the coronation of George VI

Big White Carstairs and the M'Babwa of M'Gonkawiwi

BIG WHITE CARSTAIRS has been busy preparing a list of the names of African chieftains who might be invited to attend the Coronation celebrations in England. The most picturesque personality on the list is the Yubwa of Yubwabu, who stamps all his letters with the skull of a warrior dipped in boiling dirtibeeste's-milk cheese, and has thick hair on the soles of his feet.

His grandfather travelled 4,000 miles through dense jungle to meet Livingstone near the Victoria Falls. After a journey of eight months he arrived at the meeting-place, only to find that he had missed Livingstone by fourteen minutes. He ran after him, but was too tired to go far, and so he and Livingstone never met.

Livingstone was told the story years later at a reception given by Lady Berrington. He laughed a good deal.

If the Coronation festivities include a processional march of the representatives of the Empire, will the M'Babwa of M'Gonkawiwi be included? And will he insist on being accompanied by Ugli, the witch-doctor and perhaps by Jum-Jum, the sacred crocodile? A special committee of M.P.s is meeting at the House of Commons to consider these questions.

There is a feeling in some quarters that if one curious potentate and his entourage are to be honoured, then the claims of others must be considered. And that brings us to the fascinating question of what is to be done with the Wug of Noonooistan and his Holy Apes, Buruwo and Buruwa; with the Baffomi of Gopahungi; with the Padalu of

Pokmo; with the Hereditary Snevelinka of Ridolulu and his Dancing Bear; with the Bhopi of Sliwiziland; with Mrs. Elspeth Nurgett, M.B.E., and her corps of Swuruhi Girl Guides; with the yellow harbourmaster at Grustiwowo Bay; with Hijiwana, the Queen of the Waspidili pigmies; and with Plakka, the roving ambassador of the Nopi of Buttabuttagatawni.

A message from Big White Carstairs has reached the Colonial Office. It says that the M'Babwa of M'Gonkawiwi insists on marching through London, so that people may see him. His party which will accompany him on the march, is to include Jum-Jum the sacred crocodile, Ugli the witch-doctor, eighteen wives, thirty-eight devil dancers, forty-one pigmies, a sorcerer, an astrologer, four idol carriers, six head-hunters, a dwarf wrestler, the Zimbabwe Wanderers cricket team, the Umpopo United football team, Mrs. Roustabout, the missionary, the old tribal hedgehog, a mad spearman, a baboon, a herd of dirtibeeste, and a native actress.

The M'Babwa said, 'Ufganoola.'

2

The M'Babwa of M'Gonkawiwi, who has hitherto taken no part in the controversy which is raging over his visit to England, broke his silence yesterday with a strong expletive much used by his tribe. When Carstairs told him that the Great White Mother Over the Sea might not be too pleased to welcome Ugli the witch-doctor and Jum-Jum the sacred crocodile, the M'Babwa said, 'Ufganoola.' A rough translation of this would be, 'I hope you and your Great White Mother may be roasted over a slow fire of dirtibeeste's wool.' He later insisted on bringing his team of devil dancers, his eighteen wives, his magicians, and his pigmy poisoners. Carstairs at once cabled to the Colonial Office as follows:

M'Babwa threatening bring devildancers wives magicians poisoners stop what action advised stop.

The Colonial Office cabled back:

Impossible include poisoners magicians wives devildancers in official welcome stop must come as private tourists stop.

There has been a spirited correspondence between Big White Carstairs and various Government departments on the subject of the visit for the Coronation of his Serene Highness the M'Babwa of M'Gonkawiwi, M'Gibbonuki, M'Bobowambi, Zimbabwe, and the Wishiwashi hinterland, comprising Wowo, Nikiwawa, Wibbliwambi, M'Hoho, M'Haha, M'Tralala Zogomumbozo, Moponambi, Nambipambi, and Sockemondejaw.

In answer to the application for an invitation, the Colonial Office wrote to Carstairs:

. . . We have been unable to find some of the places mentioned as being under the jurisdiction of his Serene Highness on any map. Nor have we been able to trace a ruler with such a title as the M'Babwa claims. Is the M'Hoho mentioned in your report the M'Hoho near Zumzum or the M'Hoho near Wodgi? Should he travel as the ruler of the places mentioned he will be allotted a seven-and-sixpenny seat in Shepherd's Bush. If, on the other hand, he travels as Mr. Posworth, we can promise him nothing nearer than Slough High Street. The suggestion that he should bring with him a tribal witch-doctor and a sacred alligator is not favourably viewed. There is no accommodation for witch-doctors or animals, though doubtless the latter could be temporarily accommodated at Whipsnade, and the former in Bond Street, in the parlour of Mme La Zophitella, star-gazer. . . .

Carstairs replied:

. . . Of the utmost importance not to offend the M'Babwa. Discontent among the

3

tribes in his territory might mean a rising of the Slobga pygmies and the Ushawiri head-hunters. Could not the sacred crocodile be held up at the Customs until a doctor's examination had certified some infectious disease? As to the witch-doctor, why not get him into some Mayfair set? Plant him on the rich women as a new craze. They've never met anyone who can foretell the weather from the entrails of a goat. . . . Most of the M'Babwa's possessions are not on any map yet, but the M'Hoho mentioned is the one near Wodgi. . . . You can't put him as far off as Slough. There'd be a rising here . . .

The Colonial Office has just been thrown into as fine a state of panic as ever seized a flock of Limousin sheep by another despatch from Big White Carstairs.

It appears that the M'Babwa of M'Gonkawiwi has assimilated huggermugger and helterskelter and hotcherypotchery a certain amount of Western usage – just enough to make things awkward for everybody. He has, for instance, determined to travel to England as plain 'Mr. Hurst,' while his wives have been saddled with the names of English football teams, such as Oldham Athletic, Sheffield Wednesday, and so forth. Ugli, the witch-doctor, is to travel as Herr Goethe, and Jum-Jum, the sacred crocodile, as Fido. Carstairs has pointed out that this is not the right procedure for the occasion. But the M'Babwa is as stubborn as a Numidian goat. Furthermore he insists on wearing his cricket cap (Zimbabwe Wanderers) while in England.

Yesterday Miss Whelkstone (Soc., Wriggleminster) asked the Minister of Transport whether the system of lights applied to sacred crocodiles. The Minister replied that he did not anticipate that the crocodile would be allowed to go out unaccompanied. Major Thruster (Con., Thostlehampton-with-Buckett) said he thought foreign visitors would get a very queer idea of the Empire if they found the hotels and restaurants filled with the magicians and devil dancers of dubious potentates. The Home Secretary, or someone made up to look like him, said that His Majesty's Government had never at any time contemplated filling hotels and restaurants with magicians or devil dancers. There would, at most, be a round dozen, and arrangements were being made to shove them on to the Boy Scout organisations.

Miss Wilkinson: Shame!
Miss Rathbone: Yes, shame!
The Speaker: Will you two ladies kindly stop talking rubbish?

Mr. Hatt (Lib., Pomphbury): In the event of the M'Babwa of M'Gonkawiwi seeing fit to include cannibals in his suite, will the Board of Trade give an undertaking that no foreign visitors will be eaten?

Miss Rathbone: Are they to eat the English, then?

Miss Wilkinson: Yes, are they to eat the English, then?

No answer was given.

AT THE BOARD OF AGRICULTURE AND FISHERIES

Memo:

What is all this about an African chief and his crocodile? What are we supposed to do?

Memo:

It's a sacred crocodile. I don't see where we come in.

Memo:

What do you mean – 'sacred'?

Memo:

I don't know. I suppose they worship it.

Memo:

If so, it comes under the Established Church. Better pass all this correspondence on to the Home Office.

Mrs. Wretch, supported by the P.E.N. Club, Auntie Edna's International Pacifists, Mr. Aldous Huxley, Mrs. Wurfie, and the Neo-Liberal League, is making a last frantic appeal to the Home Office to keep the M'Babwa of M'Gonkawiwi out of England. From a photograph in her posession she has established the fact that he wears a black shirt. But Big White Carstairs has cabled: 'That is not a shirt stop it is his chest stop.' Mrs. Wretch, however, is still convinced that he is a Fascist, and that his mission is to annoy Professor Laski, and to carry on secret propaganda against the National Liberal Club.

Unless the Home Office can be persuaded to act, the M'Babwa will arrive in England shortly.

The following statement was made in the House yesterday with reference to the M'Babwa of M'Gonkawiwi:

Unless our dusky cousin from overseas intends to appear in London naked to the waist, the blackness of his chest should not give offence to that progressive and enlightened part of our population which, very naturally, sees in this colour an or-

5

ganised international menace to progressive Liberalism and enlightened Marxism.

Dear Sir,

Much as I love our great British Empire — I had a cousin once who was rescued from drowning by an Australian — I do not see why the M'Babwa of M'Gonkawiwi should be given facilities for seeing the Coronation when so many white people will not be able to see it. Furthermore, by extending hospitality to an animal and a witch-doctor, we are carrying democracy to absurd lengths.

I learn that an official of the R.S.P.C.A. has objected to the sacred crocodile Jum-Jum being lodged in an aquarium, where it would have to mix with ordinary animals. It is further pointed out that much cruelty is needed to train a crocodile to be sacred, and the suggestion is that if the beast comes to London it should be looked after by a Mrs. Gespill, whose lodging-house in the Camberwell Road is a haven for creatures of the deep, including the toothless shark from Dumeira, captured by Rear-Admiral Sir Ewart Hodgson during manoeuvres in the Red Sea.

Asked yesterday whether the M'Babwa of M'Gonkawiwi, etc., had a seat reserved for him at the Coronation, Mr. Ramsay MacDonald said: 'What we have to do is, at present, according to what we can do, is to see that in the allocation of seats, that is, of seats for various people at the Coronation, is to see that the seats are sufficient. The question of the M'Babwa being allowed to have his crocodile Jum-Jum next to him is a question which must be decided by those who are competent to make such a decision, that is, by those who have the competent authority to make a decision on this matter. Such decisions can only be made by the people who can make decisions of this sort in such matters, not otherwise. What we have to do is to see that this is done, or to see that somebody does it, who can do it, in such a matter, I think.'

Mrs. Borgholz asked to-day in the House whether it is a fact that the chest of the M'Babwa of M'Gonkawiwi is really black, and if this is not Fascist propaganda designed to prevent the British public from knowing that he wears a black shirt. It is suggested in progressive quarters that Miss Wilkinson and Miss Rathbone and Canon Ball should make a journey of investigation to find out to what extent Fascism is prevalent among the M'Gonkawiwi tribes.

A sad voice interposed: 'But who will pay for the trip?'
Another voice replied, 'The Moujiks, Ltd., Travel Agency.'

The affair of Carstairs, the M'Babwa, and the Colonial Office has reached such gross proportions that the Colonial Office has ceased attempting to push the whole thing on to the Board of Agriculture and Fisheries, on the plea that Jum-Jum, the sacred crocodile, is a beast to be dealt with by that department.

Meanwhile Carstairs has received the following letter from Lady Cabstanleigh:

Dear Major Carstairs,

I trust you will forgive the liberty I am taking, but a mutual friend of ours, young Hoofe of the Colonial Office crowd, tells me there is some hitch about one of your local big pots bringing his witch-doctor to England. I understand the fellow's name is Ugli. Is he more of a witch than a doctor or vice versa? Well, I thought I might help you all out by putting the fellow up while he's here. What does he eat and drink? Will he have dress clothes? I suppose he's not utterly savage — not that one really cares, but there'll be a sort of bishop in the house, and I don't want any exorcism stuff. And I hope he can behave decently. I mean, I've never forgotten that Rumanian gipsy singer who bit the neck off a magnum of Yquem 1904. By the way, I suppose he's plumb black. If he's yellow I shall unload him on to Sybil, who loves 'em yellow ever since she was rescued from a snake by a Chinese chef. But it turned out to be jaundice. Forgive me for bothering you. . . .

Carstairs has replied to Lady Cabstanleigh's offer to accommodate the witch-doctor:

Dear Lady Cabstanleigh,

I'm afraid the witch-doctor Ugli would be rather a handful for you. He chants incantations all night, picks his teeth with his spear, and lights bonfires whenever he can. One does one's best, but all one's efforts to make him change for dinner have so far failed. He simply doesn't seem to understand, and, under his influence, even the M'Babwa himself won't go beyond a dinner jacket and a black tie. He seems to think a white tie is some sort of symbol of the domination of the white races — as indeed it is. For these reasons I hesitate to put him on to you. And he might start sacrificing one of the ladies to Bok, the headless god of the Boopi jungle. And then the bishop you spoke of would have to intervene, I suppose. And you couldn't have the papers getting hold of a story of human sacrifice at Cabstanleigh Towers. I'm rather inclined to get him into some quiet hotel in Kensington, where the retired Army and Naval officers might be able to manage him . . . . I understand that the Galashiels Aquarium has offered to house Jum-Jum, the sacred crocodile, temporarily.

Professor Roosch, Tollemache Professor of Comparative Folk-Lore at Oxford, has written to the Colonial Office to point out that the housing of the sacred crocodile Jum-Jum in the Galashiels Aquarium would most certainly be resented all along the lower Poopoo, and might start a Garumpi, or holy crocodile war, since Jum-Jum is supposed to be a kind of deity. To which the Galashiels Aquarium replied that they already have a sacred codfish from Bali and that it is treated just like any other cod, except that on the occasion of the first full moon after August Bank Holiday it is exchanged for a dwarf jelly-fish in the Bodmin Aquarium, according to a proviso in the will of the donor, Captain Marabout.

Carstairs landed at Southampton from the *Megatherium* yesterday morning. He was met by his mother, and motored straight to his home near Brocklehurst. His mother said, in an exclusive interview, 'I am so glad to have my son home again.

'It is so good to have him back. Naturally I am delighted to have him back home again, and to see him again. It is so good to see him back that I am overjoyed to have him with me once more, and to have him back again, so that I can have him home again.

'I am so glad to see him back again, and so glad that he is home once more. It is so good to have him back, and to see him home again once more. I am delighted to have my son back home, and to see him again. It is so good to see him back home, and I am delighted to have him back.

'Naturally I am very glad to have him with me once more, and to see him back. And I am overjoyed to be able to have him home with me again, and to see him once more, now that he is back home again with me. It is so good to have him back home again and to see him back.'

Carstairs said, 'Everyone has been most frightfully decent, and I must say I think everybody's been awfully good.

'Naturally I am fearfully glad to be back home again with my mother, and to see her again, now that I am back home again once more. It is so good to see her again, now that I am back home, and I'm naturally pretty pleased to be back again, so that I can see her now that I am home again with her once more.

'It is frightfully good to be home again with my mother, so that I can see her, and I am awfully glad to see her now that I can be back home again with her again.'

CHARLES DICKENS
(1812–1870)

The two pieces that follow are from *Sketches by Boz* which began appearing in the *Old Monthly Magazine* in 1833 when Dickens was only twenty-one years of age. This series of satirical sketches ran for two years and was immediately followed by *The Posthumous Papers of the Pickwick Club*, better known as *Pickwick Papers*, which firmly established the young author's popularity.

The Dancing Academy

OF all the dancing academies that ever were established, there never was one more popular in its immediate vicinity than Signor Billsmethi's, of the 'King's Theatre'. It was not in Spring-gardens, or Newman-street, or Berners-street, or Gower-street, or Charlotte-street, or Percy-street, or any other of the numerous streets which have been devoted time out of mind to professional people, dispensaries, and boarding-houses; it was not in the West-end at all – it rather approximated to the eastern portion of London, being situated in the populous and improving neighbourhood of Gray's-inn-lane. It was not a dear dancing-academy – four-and-sixpence a quarter is decidedly cheap upon the whole. It was *very* select, the number of pupils being strictly limited to seventy-five, and a quarter's payment in advance being rigidly exacted. There was public tuition and private tuition – an assembly-room and a parlour. Signor Billsmethi's family were always thrown in with the parlour, and included in parlour price; that is to say a private pupil had Signor Billsmethi's parlour to dance *in*, and Signor Billsmethi's family to dance *with*; and when he had been sufficiently broken in in the parlour he began to run in couples in the Assembly-room.

Such was the dancing academy of Signor Billsmethi when Mr. Augustus Cooper, of Fetter-lane, first saw an unstamped advertisement walking leisurely down Holborn-hill, announcing to the world that Signor Billsmethi, of the King's Theatre, intended opening for the season with a Grand Ball.

Now, Mr. Augustus Cooper was in the oil and colour line – just of age with a little money, a little business, and a little mother, who, having managed her husband and his business in his lifetime took to managing her son and *his* business after his decease; and so, somehow or other, he had been cooped up in the little back parlour behind the shop on week-days, and in a little deal box without a lid (called by courtesy a pew) at Bethel Chapel, on Sundays, and had seen no more of the world than if he had been an infant all his days; whereas Young White, at the Gas-fitter's over the way, three years younger than him, had been flaring away like winkin' – going to the theatre – supping at harmonic meetings – eating oysters by the barrel – drinking stout by the gallon – even stopping out all night, and coming home as cool in the morning as if nothing had happened. So Mr. Augustus Cooper made up his mind that he would not stand it any longer, and had that very morning expressed to his mother a firm determination to be 'blowed,' in the event of his not being instantly provided with a street-door key. And he was walking down Holborn-hill thinking about all these things, and wondering how he could manage to get introduced into genteel society for the first time, when his eyes rested on Signor

An unstamped advertisement walking leisurely down Holborn-hill

11

Billsmethi's announcement, which it immediately struck him was just the very thing he wanted; for he should not only be able to select a genteel circle of acquaintance at once out of the five-and-seventy pupils at four-and-sixpence a quarter, but should qualify himself at the same time to go through a hornpipe in private society, with perfect ease to himself, and great delight to his friends. So he stopped the unstamped advertisement – an animated sandwich, composed of a boy between two boards – and having procured a very small card with the Signor's address indented thereon, walked straight at once to the Signor's house – and very fast he walked too, for fear the list should be filled up, and the five-and-seventy completed before he got there. The Signor was at home, and, what was still more gratifying, he was an Englishman! Such a nice man – and so polite! The list was not full, but it was a most extraordinary circumstance that there was only just one vacancy, and even that one would have been filled up that very morning, only Signor Billsmethi was dissatisfied with the reference, and being very much afraid that the lady wasn't select, wouldn't take her.

'And very much delighted I am, Mr. Cooper,' said Signor Billsmethi, 'that I did *not* take her. I assure you, Mr. Cooper – I don't say it to flatter you, for I know you're above it – that I consider myself extremely fortunate in having a gentleman of your manners and appearance, sir.'

'I am very glad of it too, sir,' said Augustus Cooper.

'And I hope we shall be better acquainted, sir,' said Signor Billsmethi.

'And I'm sure I hope we shall too, sir,' responded Augustus Cooper. Just then the door opened, and in came a young lady with her hair curled in a crop all over her head, and her shoes tied in sandals all over her legs.

'Don't run away, my dear,' said Signor Billsmethi; for the young lady didn't know Mr. Cooper was there when she ran in and was going to run out again in her modesty, all in confusion-like. 'Don't run away, my dear,' said Signor Billsmethi, 'this is Mr. Cooper – Mr. Cooper, of Fetter-lane. Mr. Cooper, my daughter, sir – Miss Billsmethi, sir, who I hope will have the pleasure of dancing many a quadrille, minuet, gavotte, country-dance, fandango, double-hornpipe, and farinagholkajingo with you, sir. She dances them all, sir; and so shall you sir before you're a quarter older sir.'

And Signor Billsmethi slapped Mr. Augustus Cooper on the back as if he had known him a dozen years, – so friendly; and Mr. Cooper bowed to the young lady, and the young lady curtseyed to him, and

Signor Billsmethi said they were as handsome a pair as ever he'd wish
to see; upon which the young lady exclaimed, 'Lor, pa!' and blushed
as red as Mr. Cooper himself – you might have thought they were both
standing under a red lamp at a chemist's shop; and before Mr.
Cooper went away it was settled that he should join the family circle
that very night – taking them just as they were – no ceremony nor nonsense of that kind – and learn his positions, in order that he might lose
no time and be able to come out at the forthcoming ball.

Well; Mr. Augustus Cooper went away to one of the cheap shoema-
kers' shops in Holborn, where gentlemen's dress-pumps are seven-
and-sixpence, and men's strong walking, just nothing at all, and
bought a pair of the regular seven-and-sixpenny, long-quartered,
town mades, in which he astonished himself quite as much as his
mother, and sallied forth to Signor Billsmethi's. There were four other
private pupils in the parlour: two ladies and two gentlemen. Such nice
people! Not a bit of pride about them. One of the ladies in particular,
who was in training for a Columbine, was remarkably affable, and she
and Miss Billsmethi took such an interest in Mr. Augustus Cooper,
and joked and smiled, and looked so bewitching, that he got quite at
home and learnt his steps in no time. After the practising was over,
Signor Billsmethi, and Miss Billsmethi, and Master Billsmethi, and a
young lady, and the two ladies, and the two gentlemen, danced a quadrille – none of your slipping and sliding about but regular warm
work, flying into corners, and diving among chairs, and shooting out
at the door, – something like dancing! Signor Billsmethi in particular,
notwithstanding his having a little fiddle to play all the time, was out
on the landing every figure, and Master Billsmethi, when every body
else was breathless, danced a hornpipe with a cane in his hand, and a
cheese-plate on his head, to the unqualified admiration of the whole
company. Then Signor Billsmethi insisted as they were so happy, that
they should all stay to supper, and proposed sending Master Billsmethi for the beer and spirits, whereupon the two gentlemen swore,
'strike 'em wulgar if they'd stand that;' and they were just going to
quarrel who should pay for it, when Mr. Augustus Cooper said he
would, if they'd have the kindness to allow him – and they *had* the
kindness to allow him; and Master Billsmethi brought the beer in a
can, and the rum in a quart-pot. They had a regular night of it; and
Miss Billsmethi squeezed Mr. Augustus Cooper's hand under the
table; and Mr. Augustus Cooper returned the squeeze and returned
home too, at something to six o'clock in the morning when he was put
to bed by main force by the apprentice, after repeatedly expressing an

uncontrollable desire to pitch his reverend parent out of the second-floor window, and to throttle the apprentice with his own neck-handkerchief.

Weeks had worn on, and the seven-and-sixpenny town-mades had nearly worn out, when the night arrived for the grand dress-ball at which the whole of the five-and-seventy pupils were to meet together for the first time that season, and to take out some portion of their respective four-and-sixpences in lamp-oil and fiddlers. Mr. Augustus Cooper had ordered a new coat for the occasion – a two-pound-tenner from Turnstile. It was his first appearance in public; and after a grand Sicilian shawl-dance by fourteen young ladies in character, he was to open the quadrille department with Miss Billsmethi herself, with whom he had become quite intimate since his first introduction. It *was* a night! Every thing was admirably arranged. The sandwich-boy took the hats and bonnets at the street-door; there was a turn-up bed-stead in the back parlour, on which Miss Billsmethi made tea and coffee for such of the gentlemen as chose to pay for it, and such of the ladies as the gentlemen treated; red port-wine negus and lemonade were handed round at eighteen-pence a head, and, in pursuance of a previous engagement with the public-house at the corner of the street, an extra potboy was laid on for the occasion. In short, nothing could exceed the arrangements, except the company. Such ladies! Such pink silk stockings! Such artificial flowers! Such a number of cabs! No sooner had one cab set down a couple of ladies, than another cab drove up and set down another couple of ladies, and they all knew, not only one another, but the majority of the gentlemen into the bargain, which made it all as pleasant and lively as could be. Signor Billsmethi in black tights, with a large blue bow in his buttonhole, introduced the ladies to such of the gentlemen as were strangers: and the ladies talked away – and laughed they did – it was delightful to see them.

As to the shawl-dance, it was the most exciting thing that ever was beheld; there was such a whisking, and rustling, and fanning, and getting ladies into a tangle with artificial flowers, and then disentangling them again; and as to Mr. Augustus Cooper's share in the quadrille, he got through it admirably. He was missing from his partner now and then certainly, and discovered on such occasions to be either dancing with laudable perseverance in another set, or sliding about in perspective, apparently without any definite object; but, generally speaking, they managed to shove him through the figure, until he turned up in the right place. Be this as it may, when he had finished a great many ladies and gentlemen came up and complimented him very much, and said they had never seen a beginner do any thing like it before; and Mr. Augustus Cooper was perfectly satisfied with himself, and every body else into the bargain, and 'stood' considerable quantities of spirits and water, negus, and compounds, for the use and behoof of two or three dozen very particular friends, selected from the select circle of five-and-seventy pupils.

Now, whether it was the strength of the compounds, or the beauty of the ladies, or what not, it did so happen that Mr. Augustus Cooper encouraged, rather than repelled, the very flattering attentions of a young lady in brown gauze over white calico who had appeared particularly struck with him from the first; and when the encouragements had been prolonged for some time, Miss Billsmethi betrayed her spite and jealousy thereat by calling the young lady in brown gauze a 'creeter,' which induced the young lady in brown gauze to retort in certain sentences containing a taunt founded on the payment of four-and-sixpence a quarter, and some indistinct reference to a 'fancy man;' which reference Mr. Augustus Cooper, being then and there in a state of considerable bewilderment, expressed his entire concurrence in. Miss Billsmethi, thus renounced, forthwith began screaming in the loudest key of her voice at the rate of fourteen screams a minute; and being unsuccessful, in an onslaught on the eyes and face, first of the lady in gauze and then of Mr. Augustus Cooper called distractedly on the other three-and-seventy pupils to furnish her with oxalic acid for her own private drinking, and the call not being honoured, made another rush at Mr. Cooper, and then had her stay-lace cut and was carried off to bed. Mr. Augustus Cooper, not being remarkable for quickness of apprehension, was at a loss to understand what all this meant, till Signor Billsmethi explained it in a most satisfactory manner by stating to the pupils that Mr. Augustus Cooper had made and confirmed divers promises of marriage to his daughter on divers occasions, and had now basely deserted her; on which the indignation of the pupils became universal and as several chivalrous gentlemen inquired rather pressingly of Mr. Augustus Cooper, whether he required any thing for his own use, or, in other words, whether he 'wanted any thing for himself,' he deemed it prudent to make a precipitate retreat. And the upshot of the matter was, that a lawyer's letter came the next day, and an action was commenced next week; and that Mr. Augustus Cooper, after walking twice to the Serpentine for the purpose of drowning himself, and coming twice back without doing it, made a confidant of his mother who compromised the matter with twenty pounds from the till, which made twenty pounds four shillings and sixpence paid to Signor Bills-methi, exclusive of treats and pumps; and Mr. Augustus Cooper went back and lived with his mother, and there he lives to this day; and as he has lost his ambition for society, and never goes into the world, he will never see this account of himself and will never be any the wiser.

The Great Winglebury Duel

THE little town of Great Winglebury is exactly forty-two miles and three quarters from Hyde Park corner. It has a long, straggling, quiet High-street, with a great black and white clock at a small red Town-hall, half-way up – a market-place – a cage – an assembly-room – a church – a bridge – a chapel – a theatre – a library – an inn – a pump – and a Post-office. Tradition tells of a 'Little Winglebury' down some cross-road about two miles off; and as a square mass of dirty paper, supposed to have been originally intended for a letter, with certain tremulous characters inscribed thereon, in which a lively imagination might trace a remote resemblance to the word 'Little,' was once stuck up to be owned in the sunny window of the Great Winglebury Post-office, from which it only disappeared when it fell to pieces with dust and extreme old age, there would appear to be some foundation for the legend. Common belief is inclined to bestow the name upon a little hole at the end of a muddy lane about a couple of miles long, colonised by one wheelwright, four paupers, and a beer-shop; but even this authority, slight as it is, must be regarded with extreme suspicion, inasmuch as the inhabitants of the hole aforesaid concur in opining that it never had any name at all, from the earliest ages down to the present day.

The Winglebury Arms in the centre of the High-street, opposite the small building with the big clock, is the principal inn of Great Winglebury – the commercial inn, posting-house, and excise-office; the 'Blue' house at every election, and the Judges' house at every assizes. It is the head-quarters of the Gentlemen's Whist Club of Winglebury Blues (so called in opposition to the Gentlemen's Whist Club of

17

Winglebury Buffs, held at the other house, a little further down); and whenever a juggler, or wax-work man, or concert-giver, takes Great Winglebury in his circuit, it is immediately placarded all over the town that Mr. So-and-so, 'trusting to that liberal support which the inhabitants of Great Winglebury have long been so liberal in bestowing, has at a great expense engaged the elegant and commodious assembly-rooms, attached to the Winglebury Arms.' The house is a large one, with a red brick and stone front; a pretty spacious hall ornamented with evergreen plants, terminates in a perspective view of the bar, and a glass case, in which are displayed a choice variety of delicacies ready for dressing, to catch the eye of a new-comer the moment he enters, and excite his appetite to the highest possible pitch. Opposite doors lead to the 'coffee' and 'commercial' rooms; and a great wide, rambling staircase, – three stairs and a landing – four stairs and another landing – one step and another landing – half a dozen stairs and another landing – and so on – conducts to galleries of bedrooms, and labyrinths of sitting-rooms, denominated 'private,' where you may enjoy yourself as privately as you can in any place where some bewildered being or other walks into your room every five minutes by mistake, and then walks out again, to open all the doors along the gallery till he finds his own.

Such is the Winglebury Arms at this day, and such was the Winglebury Arms some time since – no matter when – two or three minutes before the arrival of the London stage. Four horses with cloths on – change for a coach – were standing quietly at the corner of the yard, surrounded by a listless group of post-boys in shiny hats and smock-frocks, engaged in discussing the merits of the cattle; half a dozen ragged boys were standing a little apart, listening with evident interest to the conversation of these worthies; and a few loungers were collected round the horse-trough, awaiting the arrival of the coach.

The day was hot and sunny, the town in the zenith of its dullness, and with the exception of these few idlers, not a living creature was to be seen. Suddenly the loud notes of a key-bugle broke the monotonous stillness of the street; in came the coach, rattling over the uneven paving with a noise startling enough to stop even the large-faced clock itself. Down got the outsides, up went the windows in all directions; out came the waiters, up started the ostlers, and the loungers, and the post-boys, and the ragged boys as if they were electrified – unstrapping, and unchaining, and unbuckling, and dragging willing horses out, and forcing reluctant horses in, and making a most exhilarating bustle. 'Lady inside, here,' said the guard. 'Please to alight, ma'am,'

18

said the waiter. 'Private sitting-room?' interrogated the lady. – 'Certainly, ma'am,' responded the chambermaid. 'Nothing but these 'ere trunks, ma'am?' inquired the guard. 'Nothing more,' replied the lady. Up got the outsides again, and the guard, and the coachman; off came the cloths, with a jerk – 'All right' was the cry; and away they went. The loungers lingered a minute or two in the road, watching the coach till it turned the corner, and then loitered away one by one. The street was clear again, and the town, by contrast, quieter than ever.

'Lady in number twenty-five,' screamed the landlady. – 'Thomas!'

'Yes, ma'am.'

'Letter just been left for the gentleman in number nineteen. – Boots at the Lion left it. – No answer.'

'Letter for you, sir,' said Thomas, depositing the letter on number nineteen's table.

'For me?' said number nineteen, turning from the window, out of which he had been surveying the scene we have just described.

'Yes, sir, – (waiters always speak in hints, and never utter complete sentences) – yes, sir, – Boots at the Lion, sir – Bar, sir – Missis said number nineteen, sir – Alexander Trott, Esq., sir? – Your card at the bar, sir, I think, sir?'

'My name *is* Trott,' replied number nineteen breaking the seal. 'You may go, waiter.' The waiter pulled down the window-blind, and then pulled it up again – for a regular waiter must do something before he leaves the room – adjusted the glasses on the sideboard, brushed a place which was *not* dusty, rubbed his hands very hard, walked stealthily to the door, and evaporated.

There was evidently something in the contents of the letter of a nature, if not wholly unexpected, certainly extremely disagreeable. Mr. Alexander Trott laid it down and took it up again, and walked about the room on particular squares of the carpet, and even attempted, though very unsuccessfully, to whistle an air. It wouldn't do. He threw himself into a chair and read the following epistle aloud:

'Blue Lion and Stomach-warmer,
    Great Winglebury.

'*Wednesday Morning.*

'Sir,

'Immediately on discovering your intentions, I left our counting-house, and followed you. I know the purport of your journey; – that journey shall never be completed.

'I have no friend here just now, on whose secrecy I can rely. This

19

shall be no obstacle to my revenge. Neither shall Emily Brown be exposed to the mercenary solicitations of a scoundrel, odious in her eyes, and contemptible in every body else's: nor will I tamely submit to the clandestine attacks of a base umbrella-maker.

'Sir, – from Great Winglebury Church, a footpath leads through four meadows to a retired spot known to the townspeople as Stiffun's Acre (Mr. Trott shuddered). I shall be waiting there alone, at twenty minutes before six o'clock to-morrow morning. Should I be disappointed of seeing you there, I will do myself the pleasure of calling with a horsewhip.

'Horace Hunter.

'PS. There is a gunsmith's in the High-street; and they won't sell gunpowder after dark – you understand me.

'PPS. You had better not order your breakfast in the morning till you have seen me. It may be an unnecessary expense.'

'Desperate-minded villain! I knew how it would be!' ejaculated the terrified Trott. 'I always told father, that once start me on this expedition, and Hunter would pursue me like the wandering Jew. It's bad enough as it is, to marry with the old people's commands, and without the girl's consent; but what will Emily think of me, if I go down there, breathless with running away from this infernal salamander? What *shall* I do? What *can* I do? If I go back to the city I'm disgraced for ever – lose the girl, and what's more lose the money too. Even if I did go on to the Brown's by the coach, Hunter would be after me in a post-chaise; and if I go to this place, this Stiffun's Acre, (another shudder) I'm as good as dead. I've seen him hit the man at the Pall-mall shooting gallery, in the second button-hole of the waistcoat five times out of every six, and when he didn't hit him there, he hit him in the head.' And with this consolatory reminiscence, Mr. Alexander Trott again ejaculated, 'What shall I do?'

Long and weary were his reflections as burying his face in his hands, he sat ruminating on the best course to be pursued. His mental direction-post pointed to London. He thought of 'the governor's' anger, and the loss of the fortune which the paternal Brown had promised the paternal Trott his daughter should contribute to the coffers of his son. Then the words 'To Brown's' were legibly inscribed on the said direction-post, but Horace Hunter's denunciation rung in his ears; – last of all it bore, in red letters, the words 'To Stiffun's Acre;' and then Mr. Alexander Trott decided on adopting a plan which he presently matured.

First and foremost he despatched the under-boots to the Blue Lion and Stomach-warmer, with a gentlemanly note to Mr. Horace Hunter, intimating that he thirsted for his destruction and would do himself the pleasure of slaughtering him next morning without fail. He then wrote another letter, and requested the attendance of the other boots – for they kept a pair. A modest knock at the room-door was heard – 'Come in,' said Mr. Trott. A man thrust in a red head with one eye in it, and being again desired to 'come in,' brought in the body and legs to which the head belonged, and a fur cap which belonged to the head.

'You are the upper-boots, I think?' inquired Mr. Trott.

'Yes, I am the upper-boots,' replied a voice from inside a velveteen case with mother-of-pearl buttons – 'that is, I'm the boots as b'longs to the house; the other man's my man, as goes errands and does odd jobs – top-boots and half-boots I calls us.'

'You're from London?' inquired Mr. Trott.

'Driv a cab once,' was the laconic reply.

'Why don't you drive it now?' asked Mr. Trott.

'Cos I over-driv the cab, and driv over a 'ooman,' replied the top-boots, with brevity.

'Do you know the mayor's house?' inquired Trott.

'Rather,' replied the boots, significantly, as if he had some good reason to remember it.

'Do you think you could manage to leave a letter there?' interrogated Trott.

'Shouldn't wonder,' responded boots.

'But this letter,' said Trott, holding a deformed note with a paralytic direction in one hand, and five shillings in the other – 'this letter is anonymous.'

'A – what?' interrupted the boots.

'Anonymous – he's not to know who it comes from.'

'Oh! I see,' responded the rig'lar, with a knowing wink, but without evincing the slightest disinclination to undertake the charge – 'I see – bit o' sving, eh?' and his one eye wandered round the room as if in quest of a dark lantern and phosphorous-box. 'But I say,' he continued, recalling the eye from its search, and bringing it to bear on Mr. Trott – 'I say, he's a lawyer, our mayor, and insured in the County. If you've a spite agen him, you'd better not burn his house down – blessed if I don't think it would be the greatest favour you could do him.' And he chuckled inwardly.

If Mr. Alexander Trott had been in any other situation, his first act

21

'If you've a spite agen him, you'd better not burn his house down'

would have been to kick the man down stairs by deputy; or, in other words, to ring the bell, and desire the landlord to take his boots off. He contented himself, however, with doubling the fee and explaining that the letter merely related to a breach of the peace. The top-boots retired, solemnly pledged to secrecy; and Mr. Alexander Trott sat down to a fried sole, maintenon cutlet, Madeira, and sundries, with much greater composure than he had experienced since the receipt of Horace Hunter's letter of defiance.

The lady who alighted from the London coach had no sooner been installed in number twenty-five, and made some alteration in her travelling-dress, than she endited a note to Joseph Overton, esquire, solicitor, and mayor of Great Winglebury, requesting his immediate attendance on private business of paramount importance – a summons which that worthy functionary lost no time in obeying; for after sundry openings of his eyes, divers ejaculations of 'Bless me!' and other manifestations of surprise, he took his broad-brimmed hat from its accustomed peg in his little front office, and walked briskly down the High-street to the Winglebury Arms; through the hall and up the staircase of which establishment he was ushered by the landlady, and a crowd of officious waiters, to the door of number twenty-five.

'Show the gentleman in,' said the stranger lady, in reply to the foremost waiter's announcement. The gentleman was shown in accordingly.

The lady rose from the sofa; the mayor advanced a step from the door, and there they both paused for a minute or two, looking at one another as if by mutual consent. The mayor saw before him a buxom richly-dressed female of about forty; and the lady looked upon a sleek man about ten years older, in drab shorts and continuations, black coat, neckcloth, and gloves.

'Miss Julia Manners!' exclaimed the mayor at length, 'you astonish me.'

'That's very unfair of you, Overton,' replied Miss Julia, 'for I have known you long enough not to be surprised at any thing you do, and you might extend equal courtesy to me.'

'But to run away – actually run away – with a young man!' remonstrated the mayor.

'You would not have me actually run away with an old one I presume,' was the cool rejoinder.

'And then to ask me – me – of all people in the world – a man of my age and appearance – mayor of the town – to promote such a scheme!' pettishly ejaculated Joseph Overton; throwing himself into an armchair, and producing Miss Julia's letter from his pocket, as if to corroborate the assertion that he had been asked.

'Now, Overton,' replied the lady, impatiently, 'I want your assistance in this matter, and I must have it. In the lifetime of that poor old dear, Mr. Cornberry, who – who – '

'Who was to have married you, and didn't because he died first; and who left you his property unencumbered with the addition of himself,' suggested the mayor, in a sarcastic tone.

'Well,' replied Miss Julia, reddening slightly, 'in the lifetime of the poor old dear, the property had the incumbrance of your management; and all I will say of that is, that I only wonder *it* didn't die of consumption instead of its master. You helped yourself then: – help me now.'

Mr. Joseph Overton was a man of the world, and an attorney: and as certain indistinct recollections of an odd thousand pounds or two, appropriated by mistake, passed across his mind, he hemmed deprecatingly, smiled blandly, remained silent for a few seconds; and finally inquired, 'What do you wish me to do?'

'I'll tell you,' replied Miss Julia – 'I'll tell you in three words. Dear Lord Peter – '

'That's the young man, I suppose – ' interrupted the mayor.

'That's the young nobleman,' replied the lady, with a great stress on the last word. 'Dear Lord Peter is considerably afraid of the resentment of his family; and we have therefore thought it better to make the match a stolen one. He left town to avoid suspicion, on a visit to his friend, the Honourable Augustus Flair, whose seat, as you know, is about thirty miles from this, accompanied only by his favourite tiger. We arranged that I should come here alone in the London coach; and that he, leaving his tiger and cab behind him, should come on, and arrive here as soon as possible this afternoon.'

'Very well,' observed Joseph Overton, 'and then he can order the chaise, and you can go on to Gretna Green together, without requiring the presence or interference of a third party, can't you?'

'No,' replied Miss Julia. 'We have every reason to believe – dear Lord Peter not being considered very prudent or sagacious by his friends, and they having discovered his attachment to me – that immediately on his absence being observed, pursuit will be made in this direction: to elude which, and to prevent our being traced, I wish it to be understood in this house, that dear Lord Peter is slightly deranged, though perfectly harmless; and that I am, unknown to him, waiting his arrival to convey him in a postchaise to a private asylum – at Berwick, say. If I don't show myself much, I dare say I can manage to pass for his mother.'

The thought occurred to the mayor's mind that the lady might show herself a good deal without fear of detection; seeing that she was about double the age of her intended husband. He said nothing, however, and the lady proceeded –

'With the whole of this arrangement, dear Lord Peter is acquainted: and all I want you to do is, to make the delusion more complete by giving it the sanction of your influence in this place, and assigning this as a reason to the people of the house for my taking the young gentleman away. As it would not be consistent with the story that I should see him until after he has entered the chaise, I also wish you to communicate with him, and inform him that it is all going on well.'

'Has he arrived?' inquired Overton.

'I don't know,' replied the lady.

24

'Then how am I to know?' inquired the mayor. 'Of course he will not give his own name at the bar.'

'I begged him, immediately on his arrival, to write you a note,' replied Miss Manners; 'and to prevent the possibility of our project being discovered through its means, I desired him to write anonymously, and in mysterious terms to acquaint you with the number of his room.'

'God bless me!' exclaimed the mayor, rising from his seat, and searching his pockets – 'most extraordinary circumstance – he *has* arrived – mysterious note left at my house in a most mysterious manner, just before yours – didn't know what to make of it before, and certainly shouldn't have attended to it. – Oh! here it is.' And Joseph Overton pulled out of an inner coat-pocket the identical letter penned by Alexander Trott. 'Is this his lordship's hand?'

'Oh yes,' replied Julia; 'good, punctual creature! I have not seen it more than once or twice, but I know he writes very badly and very large. These dear, wild young noblemen, you know, Overton – '

'Ay, ay, I see,' replied the mayor. – 'Horses and dogs, play and wine – grooms, actresses, and cigars, – the stable, the green-room, the brothel, and the tavern; and the legislative assembly at last.'

'Here's what he says,' pursued the mayor; '"Sir, – A young gentleman in number nineteen at the Winglebury Arms, is bent on committing a rash act to-morrow morning at an early hour. (That's good – he means marrying.) If you have any regard for the peace of this town, or the preservation of one – it may be two – human lives" – What the deuce does he mean by that?'

'That he's so anxious for the ceremony, he will expire if it's put off, and that I may possibly do the same,' replied the lady with great complacency.

'Oh! I see – not much fear of that; – well – "two human lives you will cause him to be removed to-night. – (He wants to start at once.) Fear not to do this on your responsibility: for to-morrow, the absolute necessity of the proceeding will be but too apparent. Remember: number nineteen. The name is Trott. No delay; for life and death depend upon your promptitude." – Passionate language, certainly. – Shall I see him?'

'Do,' replied Miss Julia; 'and entreat him to act his part well. I am half afraid of him. Tell him to be cautious.'

'I will,' said the mayor.

'Settle all the arrangements.'

'I will,' said the mayor again.

'And say I think the chaise had better be ordered for one o'clock.'

'Very well,' cried the mayor once more; and ruminating on the absurdity of the situation in which fate and old acquaintance had placed him, he desired a waiter to herald his approach to the temporary representative of number nineteen.

The announcement – 'Gentleman to speak with you, sir,' induced Mr. Trott to pause half-way in the glass of port, the contents of which he was in the act of imbibing at the moment; to rise from his chair, and retreat a few paces towards the window, as if to secure a retreat in the event of the visitor assuming the form and appearance of Horace Hunter. One glance at Joseph Overton, however, quieted his apprehensions. He courteously motioned the stranger to a seat. The waiter after a little jingling with the decanter and glasses, consented to leave the room; and Joseph Overton placing the broad-brimmed hat on the chair next him, and bending his body gently forward, opened the business by saying in a very low and cautious tone,

'My lord – '

'Eh?' said Mr. Alexander Trott in a very loud key, with the vacant and mystified stare of a chilly somnambulist.

'Hush – hush!' said the cautious attorney: 'to be sure – quite right – no titles here – my name is Overton, sir.'

'Overton!'

'Yes: the mayor of this place – you sent me a letter with anonymous information, this afternoon.

'I, sir?' exclaimed Trott with ill-dissembled surprise; for, coward as he was, he would willingly have repudiated the authorship of the letter in question. 'I, sir?'

'Yes, you, sir; did you not?' responded Overton, annoyed with what he supposed to be an extreme degree of unnecessary suspicion. 'Either this letter is yours, or it is not. If it be, we can converse securely upon the subject at once. If it be not, of course I have no more to say.'

'Stay, stay,' said Trott, 'it *is* mine; I *did* write it. What could I do, sir? I had no friend here.'

'To be sure – to be sure,' said the mayor, encouragingly, 'you could not have managed it better. Well, sir; it will be necessary for you to leave here to-night in a post-chaise and four. And the harder the boys drive the better. You are not safe from pursuit here.'

'Bless me!' exclaimed Trott, in an agony of apprehension, 'can such things happen in a country like this? Such unrelenting and cold-blooded hostility!' He wiped off the concentrated essence of cowardice that was oozing fast down his forehead, and looked aghast at

Joseph Overton.

'It certainly is a very hard case,' replied the mayor with smile, 'that, in a free country, people can't marry whom they like without being hunted down as if they were criminals. However, in the present instance the lady is willing, you know, and that's the main point, after all.'

'Lady willing!' repeated Trott, mechanically – 'How do you know the lady's willing?'

'Come, that's a good one,' said the mayor, benevolently tapping Mr. Trott on the arm with his broad-brimmed hat, 'I have known her well for a long time, and if any body could entertain the remotest doubt on the subject, I assure you I have none, nor need you.'

'Dear me!' said Mr. Trott, ruminating – 'Dear me! – this is very extraordinary!'

'Well, Lord Peter,' said the mayor, rising.

'Lord Peter!' repeated Mr. Trott.

'Oh – ah, I forgot; well, Mr. Trott, then – Trott – very good, ha! ha! – Well, sir, the chaise shall be ready at half-past twelve.'

'And what is to become of me till then?' inquired Mr. Trott, anxiously. 'Wouldn't it save appearances if I were placed under some restraint?'

'Ah!' replied Overton, 'very good thought – capital idea indeed. I'll send somebody up directly. And if you make a little resistance when we put you in the chaise it wouldn't be amiss – look as if you didn't want to be taken away, you know.'

'To be sure,' said Trott – 'to be sure.'

'Well, my lord,' said Overton, in a low tone, 'till then, I wish your lordship a good evening.'

'Lord – lordship!' ejaculated Trott again, falling back a step or two, and gazing in unutterable wonder on the countenance of the mayor.

'Ha-ha! I see, my lord – practising the madman? – very good indeed – very vacant look – capital, my lord, capital – good evening, Mr. – Trott – ha! ha! ha!'

'That mayor's decidedly drunk,' soliloquised Mr. Trott, throwing himself back in his chair, in an attitude of reflection.

'He is a much cleverer fellow than I thought him, that young nobleman – he carries it off uncommonly well,' thought Overton, as he wended his way to the bar, there to complete his arrangements. This was soon done: every word of the story was implicitly believed, and the one-eyed boots was immediately instructed to repair to number nineteen, to act as custodian of the person of the supposed lunatic

27

until half-past twelve o'clock. In pursuance of this direction, that somewhat eccentric gentleman armed himself with a walking-stick of gigantic dimensions, and repaired with his usual equanimity of manner to Mr. Trott's apartment, which he entered without any ceremony, and mounted guard in, by quietly depositing himself upon a chair near the door, where he proceeded to beguile the time by whistling a popular air with great apparent satisfaction.

'What do you want here, you scoundrel?' exclaimed Mr. Alexander Trott, with a proper appearance of indignation at his detention.

The boots beat time with his head, as he looked gently round at Mr. Trott with a smile of pity, and whistled an *adagio* movement.

'Do you attend in this room by Mr. Overton's desire?' inquired Trott, rather astonished at the man's demeanour.

'Keep yourself to yourself, young feller,' calmly responded the boots, 'and don't say nothin' to nobody.' And he whistled again.

'Now mind,' ejaculated Mr. Trott, anxious to keep up the farce of wishing with great earnestness to fight a duel if they'd let him, – 'I protest against being kept here. I deny that I have any intention of fighting with any body. But as it's useless contending with superior numbers, I shall sit quietly down.'

'You'd better,' observed the placid boots, shaking the large stick expressively.

'Under protest, however,' added Alexander Trott, seating himself, with indignation in his face but great content in his heart. 'Under protest.'

'Oh, certainly!' responded the boots: 'any thing you please. If you're happy, I'm transported; only don't talk too much – it'll make you worse.'

'Make me worse!' exclaimed Trott, in unfeigned astonishment: 'the man's drunk!'

'You'd better be quiet, young feller,' remarked the boots, going through a most threatening piece of pantomime with the stick.

'Or mad!' said Mr. Trott, rather alarmed. 'Leave the room sir, and tell them to send somebody else.'

'Won't do!' replied the boots.

'Leave the room!' shouted Trott, ringing the bell violently; for he began to be alarmed on a new score.

'Leave that 'ere bell alone, you wretched loo-nattic!' said the boots, suddenly forcing the unfortunate Trott back into his chair, and brandishing the stick aloft. 'Be quiet, you mis'rable object, and don't let every body know there's a madman in the house.'

'He *is* a madman! He *is* a madman!' exclaimed the terrified Mr. Trott, gazing on the one eye of the red-headed boots with a look of abject horror.

'Madman!' replied the boots – 'dam'me, I think he *is* a madman with a vengeance! Listen to me, you unfort'nate. Ah! would you? – [a slight tap on the head with the large stick, as Mr. Trott made another move towards the bell-handle] I caught you there! did I?'

'Spare my life!' exclaimed Trott, raising his hands imploringly.

'I don't want your life,' replied the boots, disdainfully, 'though I think it 'ud be a charity if somebody took it.'

'No, no, it wouldn't,' interrupted poor Mr. Trott, hurriedly; 'no, no, it wouldn't! I – I – 'd rather keep it!'

'O werry well,' said the boots; 'that's a mere matter of taste – ev'ry one to his liking. Hows'ever, all I've got to say is this here: You sit quietly down in that chair, and I'll sit hoppersite you here, and if you keep quiet and don't stir, I won't damage you; but if you move hand or foot till half-past twelve o'clock, I shall alter the expression of your countenance so completely, that the next time you look in the glass you'll ask vether you're gone out of town, and ven you're likely to come back again. So sit down.'

'I will – I will,' responded the victim of mistakes; and down sat Mr. Trott and down sat the boots too, exactly opposite him, with the stick ready for immediate action in case of emergency.

Long and dreary were the hours that followed. The bell of Great Winglebury church had just struck ten, and two hours and a half would probably elapse before succour arrived. For half an hour the noise occasioned by shutting up the shops in the street beneath betokened something like life in the town, and rendered Mr. Trott's situation a little less insupportable; but when even these ceased, and nothing was heard beyond the occasional rattling of a post-chaise as it drove up the yard to change horses, and then drove away again, or the clattering of horses' hoofs in the stables behind, it became almost unbearable. The boots occasionally moved an inch or two, to knock superfluous bits of wax off the candles, which were burning low, but instantaneously resumed his former position; and as he remembered to have heard somewhere or other that the human eye had an unfailing effect in controlling mad people, he kept his solitary organ of vision constantly fixed on Mr. Alexander Trott. That unfortunate individual stared at his companion in his turn, until his features grew more and more indistinct – his hair gradually less red – and the room more misty and obscure. Mr. Alexander Trott fell into a sound sleep,

29

from which he was awakened by a rumbling in the street and a cry of –
'Chaise-and-four for number twenty-five!' A bustle on the stairs succeeded; the room-door was hastily thrown open; and Mr. Joseph
Overton entered, followed by four stout waiters, and Mrs. Williamson, the stout landlady of the Winglebury Arms.

'Mr. Overton!' exclaimed Mr. Alexander Trott, jumping up in a
frenzy of passionate excitement – 'Look at this man sir; consider the
situation in which I have been placed for three hours past – the person
you sent to guard me, sir, was a madman – a madman – a raging, rav-
aging, furious madman.'

'Bravo!' whispered Overton.

'Poor dear!' said the compassionate Mrs. Williamson, 'mad people
always thinks other people's mad.'

'Poor dear!' ejaculated Mr. Alexander Trott, 'What the devil do
you mean by poor dear! are you the landlady of this house?'

'Yes, yes,' replied the stout old lady, 'don't exert yourself, there's a
dear – consider your health, now; do.'

'Exert myself!' shouted Mr. Alexander Trott, it's a mercy, ma'am,
that I have any breath to exert myself with, I might have been assassinated three hours ago by that one-eyed monster with the oakum
head. How dare you have a madman, ma'am – how dare you have a
madman, to assault and terrify the visiters to your house?'.

'I'll never have another,' said Mrs. Williamson, casting a look of
reproach at the mayor.

'Capital – capital,' whispered Overton again, as he enveloped Mr.
Alexander Trott in a thick travelling-cloak.

'Capital, sir!' exclaimed Trott, aloud, 'it's horrible. The very recol-
lection makes me shudder. I'd rather fight four duels in three hours if I
survived the first three, than I'd sit for that time face to face with a
madman.'

'Keep it up, as you go down stairs,' whispered Overton, 'your bill is
paid, and your portmanteau in the chaise.' And then he added aloud,
'Now, waiters, the gentleman's ready.'

At this signal the waiters crowded round Mr. Alexander Trott. One
took one arm, another the other, a third walked before with a candle,
the fourth behind with another candle; the boots and Mrs. Williamson brought up the rear, and down stairs they went, Mr. Alexander
Trott expressing alternately at the very top of his voice either his
feigned reluctance to go, or his unfeigned indignation at being shut up
with a madman.

Mr. Overton was waiting at the chaise-door, the boys were ready mounted, and a few ostlers and stable nondescripts were standing round to witness the departure of 'the mad gentleman.' Mr. Alexander Trott's foot was on the step, when he observed (which the dim light had prevented his doing before) a human figure seated in the chaise, closely muffled up in a cloak like his own.

'Who's that?' he inquired of Overton, in a whisper.

'Hush, hush,' replied the mayor; 'the other party of course.'

'The other party!' exclaimed Trott, with an effort to retreat.

'Yes, yes; you'll soon find that out, before you go far, I should think – but make a noise, you'll excite suspicion if you whisper to me so much.'

'I won't go in this chaise,' shouted Mr. Alexander Trott, all his original fears recurring with tenfold violence. 'I shall be assassinated – I shall be – '

'Bravo, bravo,' whispered Overton. 'I'll push you in.'

'But I won't go,' exclaimed Mr. Trott. 'Help here, help, they're carrying me away against my will. This is a plot to murder me.'

'Poor dear!' said Mrs. Williamson again.

'Now, boys, put 'em along' cried the mayor, pushing Trott in and slamming the door. 'Off with you as quick as you can, and stop for nothing till you come to the next stage – all right.'

'Horses are paid, Tom,' screamed Mrs. Williamson; and away went the chaise at the rate of fourteen miles an hour, with Mr. Alexander Trott and Miss Julia Manners carefully shut up in the inside.

Mr. Alexander Trott remained coiled up in one corner of the chaise, and his mysterious companion in the other, for the first two or three miles; Mr. Trott edging more and more into his corner as he felt his companion gradually edging more and more from hers; and vainly endeavouring in the darkness to catch a glimpse of the furious face of the supposed Horace Hunter.

'We may speak now,' said his fellow traveller, at length; 'the postboys can neither see nor hear us.'

'That's not Hunter's voice!' – thought Alexander, astonished.

'Dear Lord Peter!' said Miss Julia, most winningly: putting her arm on Mr. Trott's shoulder – 'Dear Lord Peter. Not a word?'

'Why, it's a woman!' exclaimed Mr. Trott in a low tone of excessive wonder.

'Ah – whose voice is that?' said Julia – ''tis not Lord Peter's.'

'No, – it's mine,' replied Mr. Trott.

'Yours!' ejaculated Miss Julia Manners, 'a strange man! Gracious Heaven – how came you here?'

'Whoever you are, you might have known that I came against my will, ma'am,' replied Alexander, 'For I made noise enough when I got in.'

'Do you come from Lord Peter?' inquired Miss Manners.

'Damn Lord Peter,' replied Trott pettishly – 'I don't know any Lord Peter – I never heard of him before to-night, when I've been Lord Peter'd by one and Lord Peter'd by another, till I verily believe I'm mad, or dreaming – '

'Whither are we going?' inquired the lady tragically.

'How should *I* know, ma'am?' replied Trott with singular coolness; for the events of the evening had completely hardened him.

'Stop! stop!' cried the lady, letting down the front glasses of the chaise.

'Stay, my dear ma'am!' said Mr. Trott, pulling the glasses up again with one hand, and gently squeezing Miss Julia's waist with the other. 'There is some mistake here; give me till the end of this stage to explain my share of it. We must go so far; you cannot be set down here alone, at this hour of the night.'

The lady consented; the mistake was mutually explained. Mr. Trott was a young man, had highly promising whiskers, an undeniable tailor, and an insinuating address – he wanted nothing but valour, and who wants that with three thousand a-year? The lady had this, and more; she wanted a young husband, and the only course open to Mr. Trott to retrieve his disgrace was a rich wife. So, they came to the conclusion that it would be a pity to have all this trouble and expense for nothing and that as they were so far on the road already, they had better go to Gretna Green, and marry each other, and they did so. And the very next preceding entry in the Blacksmith's book was an entry of the marriage of Emily Brown with Horace Hunter. Mr. Hunter took his wife home, and begged pardon, and *was* pardoned; and Mr. Trott took *his* wife home, begged pardon too, and was pardoned also. And Lord Peter, who had been detained beyond his time by drinking champagne and riding a steeple-chase, went back to the Honourable Augustus Flair's, and drank more champagne, and rode another steeple-chase, and was thrown and killed. And Horace Hunter took great credit to himself for practising on the cowardice of Alexander Trott; and all these circumstances were discovered in time, and carefully noted down; and if ever you stop a week at the Winglebury Arms, they'll give you just this account of The Great Winglebury Duel.

O HENRY (William Sydney Porter)
(1862–1910)

O Henry was born in North Carolina but later went to Texas where he became editor of a humorous magazine. He was imprisoned for embezzlement in 1897 and turned to writing while serving his three year sentence. Much of the material for his early stories came from the tales of his fellow prisoners.

One Thousand Dollars

'ONE THOUSAND DOLLARS,' repeated Lawyer Tolman solemnly and severely, 'and here is the money.'

Young Gillian gave a decidedly amused laugh as he fingered the thin package of new fifty-dollar notes.

'It's such a confoundedly awkward amount,' he explained, genially, to the lawyer. 'If it had been ten thousand a fellow might wind up with a lot of fireworks and do himself credit. Even fifty dollars would have been less trouble.'

'You heard the reading of your uncle's will,' continued Lawyer Tolman, professionally dry in his tones. 'I do not know if you paid much attention to its details. I must remind you of one. You are required to render to us an account of the manner of expenditure of this $1,000 as soon as you have disposed of it. The will stipulates that. I trust that you will so far comply with the late Mr. Gillian's wishes.'

'You may depend upon it,' said the young man politely, 'in spite of the extra expense it will entail. I may have to engage a secretary. I was never good at accounts.'

Gillian went to his club. There he hunted out one whom he called Old Bryson.

Old Bryson was calm and forty and sequestered. He was in a corner reading a book, and when he saw Gillian approaching he sighed, laid down his book and took off his glasses.

'Old Bryson, wake up,' said Gillian. 'I've a funny story to tell you.'

'I wish you would tell it to someone in the billiard-room,' said Old Bryson. 'You know how I hate your stories.'

'This is a better one than usual,' said Gillian, rolling a cigarette, 'and I'm glad to tell it to you. It's too sad and funny to go with the rattling of billiard balls. I've just come from my late uncle's firm of legal corsairs. He leaves me an even thousand dollars. Now, what can a man possibly do with a thousand dollars?'

'I thought,' said Old Bryson, showing as much interest as a bee shows in a vinegar cruet, 'that the late Septimus Gillian was worth something like half a million.'

'He was,' assented Gillian joyously, 'and that's where the joke comes in. He's left his whole cargo of doubloons to a microbe. That is, part of it goes to the man who invents a new bacillus, and the rest to establish a hospital for doing away with it again. There are one or two trifling bequests on the side. The butler and the housekeeper get a seal ring and $10 each. His nephew gets $1,000.'

'You've always had plenty of money to spend,' observed Old Bryson.

'Tons,' said Gillian. 'Uncle was the fairy godmother as far as an allowance was concerned.'

'Any other heirs?' asked Old Bryson.

'None.' Gillian frowned at his cigarette and kicked the upholstered leather of a divan uneasily. 'There is a Miss Hayden, a ward of my uncle, who lived in his house. She's a quiet thing – musical – the daughter of somebody who was unlucky enough to be his friend. I forgot to say that she was in on the seal ring and $10 joke, too. I wish I had been. Then I could have had two bottles of brut, tipped the waiter with the ring, and had the whole business off my hands. Don't be superior and insulting, Old Bryson – tell me what a fellow can do with a thousand dollars.'

Old Bryson rubbed his glasses and smiled. And when Old Bryson smiled, Gillian knew that he intended to be more offensive than ever.

'A thousand dollars,' he said, 'means much or little. One man may buy a happy home with it and laugh at Rockefeller. Another could send his wife South with it and save her life. A thousand dollars would buy pure milk for one hundred babies during June, July, and August, and save fifty of their lives. You could count upon a half-hour's diversion with it at faro in one of the fortified art galleries. It would furnish an education to an ambitious boy. I am told that a genuine Corot was secured for that amount in an auction room yesterday. You could move to a New Hampshire town and live respectably two years on it. You could rent Madison Square Garden for one evening with it, and lecture your audience, if you should have one, on the precariousness of the profession of heir-presumptive.'

One Thousand Dollars

'People might like you, Old Bryson,' said Gillian, always unruffled, 'if you wouldn't moralise. I asked you to tell me what I could do with a thousand dollars.'

'You?' said Bryson, with a gentle laugh. 'Why, Bobby Gillian, there's only one logical thing you could do. You can go buy Miss Lotta Lauriere a diamond pendant with the money, and then take yourself off to Idaho and inflict your presence upon a ranch. I advise a sheep ranch, as I have a particular dislike for sheep.'

'Thanks,' said Gillian, rising, 'I thought I could depend upon you, Old Bryson. You've hit on the very scheme. I wanted to chuck the money in a lump, for I've got to turn in an account for it, and I hate itemising.'

Gillian phoned for a cab and said to the driver:

'The stage entrance of the Columbine Theatre.'

Miss Lotta Lauriere was assisting Nature with a powder puff, almost ready for her call at a crowded matinée, when her dresser mentioned the name of Mr. Gillian.

'Let it in,' said Miss Lauriere. 'Now, what is it, Bobby? I'm going on in two minutes.'

'Rabbit-foot your right ear a little,' suggested Gillian critically. 'That's better. It won't take two minutes for me. What do you say to a little thing in the pendant line? I can stand three ciphers with a figure one in front of 'em.'

'Oh, just as you say,' carolled Miss Lauriere. 'My right glove, Adams. Say, Bobby, did you see that necklace Della Stacey had on the other night? Twenty-two hundred dollars it cost at Tiffany's. But of course – pull my sash a little to the left, Adams.'

'Miss Lauriere for the opening chorus!' cried the call-boy without.

Gillian strolled out to where his cab was waiting.

'What would you do with a thousand dollars if you had it?' he asked the driver.

'Open a s'loon,' said the cabby promptly and huskily. 'I know a place I could take money in with both hands. It's a four-story brick on a corner. I've got it figured out. Second story – Chinks and chop suey; third floor – manicures and foreign missions; fourth floor – poolroom. If you was thinking of putting up the cap –'

'Oh, no,' said Gillian, 'I merely asked from curiosity. I take you by the hour. Drive till I tell you to stop.'

Eight blocks down Broadway Gillian poked up the trap with his cane and got out. A blind man sat upon a stool on the sidewalk selling pencils. Gillian went out and stood before him.

35

'Excuse me,' he said, 'but would you mind telling me what you would do if you had a thousand dollars?'

'You got out of that cab that just drove up, didn't you?' asked the blind man.

'I did,' said Gillian.

'I guess you are all right,' said the pencil dealer, 'to ride in a cab by daylight. Take a look at that, if you like.'

'I guess you are all right,' said the pencil dealer, 'to ride in a cab by daylight.'

He drew a small book from his coat-pocket and held it out. Gillian opened it, and saw that it was a bank deposit book. It showed a balance of $1,785 to the blind man's credit.

Gillian returned the book and got into the cab.

'I forgot something,' he said. 'You may drive to the law offices of Tolman & Sharp, at – Broadway.'

Lawyer Tolman looked at him hostilely and inquiringly through his gold-rimmed glasses.

'I beg your pardon,' said Gillian cheerfully, 'but may I ask you a question? It is not an impertinent one, I hope. Was Miss Hayden left anything by my uncle's will besides the ring and the $10?'

'Nothing,' said Mr. Tolman.

'I thank you very much, sir,' said Gillian, and out he went to his cab. He gave the driver the address of his late uncle's home.

Miss Hayden was writing letters in the library. She was small and slender and clothed in black. But you would have noticed her eyes. Gillian drifted in with his air of regarding the world as inconsequent.

'I've just come from old Tolman's,' he explained. 'They've been going over the papers down there. They found a' – Gillian searched his memory for a legal term – 'they found an amendment or a post-script or something to the will. It seemed that the old boy loosened up a little on second thoughts and willed you a thousand dollars. I was driving up this way, and Tolman asked me to bring you the money. Here it is. You'd better count it to see if it's right.' Gillian laid the money beside her hand on the desk.

Miss Hayden turned white. 'Oh!' she said, and again 'Oh!'

Gillian half turned and looked out the window.

'I suppose, of course,' he said, in a low voice, 'that you know I love you.'

'I am sorry,' said Miss Hayden, taking up her money.

'There is no use?' asked Gillian, almost lightheartedly.

'I am sorry,' she said again.

'May I write a note?' asked Gillian, with a smile. He seated himself at the big library table. She supplied him with paper and pen, and then went back to her secretaire.

Gillian made out his account of his expenditure of the thousand dollars in these words:

'Paid by the black sheep, Robert Gillian, $1,000 on account of the eternal happiness, owed by Heaven to the best and dearest woman on earth.'

Gillian slipped his writing into an envelope, bowed, and went his way.

His cab stopped again at the offices of Tolman & Sharp.

'I have expended the thousand dollars,' he said, cheerily, to Tolman of the gold glasses, 'and I have come to render account of it as I agreed. There is quite a feeling of summer in the air – do you not think so, Mr. Tolman?' He tossed a white envelope on the lawyer's table. 'You will find there a memorandum, sir, of the *modus operandi* of the vanishing of the dollars.'

Without touching the envelope, Mr. Tolman went to a door and called his partner, Sharp. Together they explored the caverns of an immense safe. Forth they dragged as trophy of their search a big envelope sealed with wax. This they forcibly invaded, and wagged their venerable heads together over its contents. Then Tolman became spokesman.

'Mr. Gillian,' he said formally, 'there was a codicil to your uncle's will. It was intrusted to us privately, with instructions that it be not opened until you had furnished us with a full account of your handling of the $1,000 bequest in the will. As you have fulfilled the conditions, my partner and I have read the codicil. I do not wish to encumber your understanding with its legal phraseology, but I will acquaint you with the spirit of its contents.

'In the event that your disposition of the $1,000 demonstrates that you possess any of the qualifications that deserve reward, much benefit will accrue to you. Mr. Sharp and I are named as the judges, and I assure you that we will do our duty strictly according to justice – with liberality. We are not at all unfavourably disposed toward you, Mr. Gillian. But let us return to the letter of the codicil. If your disposal of the money in question has been prudent, wise, or unselfish, it is in our power to hand you over bonds to the value of $50,000, which have been placed in our hands for that purpose. But if – as our client, the late Mr. Gillian, explicitly provides – you have used this money as you have used money in the past – I quote the late Mr. Gillian – in reprehensible dissipation among disreputable associates – the $50,000 is to be paid to Miriam Hayden, ward of the late Mr. Gillian, without delay. Now, Mr. Gillian, Mr. Sharp and I will examine your account in regard to the $1,000. You submit it in writing, I believe. I hope you will repose confidence in our decision.'

Mr. Tolman reached for the envelope. Gillian was a little the quicker in taking it up. He tore the account and its cover leisurely into strips and dropped them into his pocket.

'It's all right,' he said smilingly. 'There isn't a bit of need to bother you with this. I don't suppose you'd understand these itemised bets, anyway. I lost the thousand dollars on the races. Good day to you, gentlemen.'

Tolman & Sharp shook their heads mournfully at each other when Gillian left, for they heard him whistling gaily in the hallway as he waited for the elevator.

Jeff Peters As A Personal Magnet

JEFF PETERS has been engaged in as many schemes for making money as there are recipes for cooking rice in Charleston, S.C.

Best of all I like to hear him tell of his earlier days when he sold liniments and cough cures on street corners, living hand to mouth, heart to heart, with the people, throwing heads or tails with fortune for his last coin.

'I struck Fisher Hill, Arkansaw,' said he, 'in a buckskin suit, moccasins, long hair, and a thirty-carat diamond ring that I got from an actor in Texarkana. I don't know what he ever did with the pocket-knife I swapped him for it.

'I was Dr Waugh-hoo, the celebrated Indian medicine man. I carried only one best bet just then, and that was Resurrection Bitters. It was made of life-giving plants and herbs accidentally discovered by Ta-qua-la, the beautiful wife of the chief of the Choctaw Nation, while gathering truck to garnish a platter of boiled dog for the annual corn dance.

'Business hadn't been good at the last town, so I only had five dollars. I went to the Fisher Hill druggist and he credited me for half a gross of eight-ounce bottles and corks. I had the labels and ingredients in my valise, left over from the last town. Life began to look rosy again after I got in my hotel room with the water running from the tap, and the Resurrection Bitters lining up on the table by the dozen.

'Fake? No, sir. There was two dollars' worth of fluid extract of cinchona and a dime's worth of aniline in that half-gross of bitters. I've gone through towns years afterwards and had folks ask for 'em again.

'I hired a wagon that night and commenced selling the bitters on

39

Main Street. Fisher Hill was a low, malarial town; and a compound hypothetical pneumocardiac anti-scorbutic tonic was just what I diagnosed the crowd as needing. The bitters started off like sweet-breads-on-toast at a vegetarian dinner. I had sold two dozen at fifty cents apiece when I felt somebody pull my coat tail. I knew what that meant; so I climbed down and sneaked a five-dollar bill into the hand of a man with a German silver star on his lapel.

'"Constable," says I, "it's a fine night."'

'"Have you got a city licence," he asks, "to sell this illegitimate essence of spooju that you flatter by the name of medicine?"'

'"I have not," says I. "I didn't know you had a city. If I can find it to-morrow I'll take one out if it's necessary."'

'"I'll have to close you up till you do," says the constable.'

'I quit selling and went back to the hotel. I was talking to the landlord about it.'

'"Oh, you won't stand no show in Fisher Hill," says he. "Dr. Hoskins, the only doctor here, is a brother-in-law of the Mayor, and they won't allow no fake doctor to practise in town."'

'"I don't practise medicine," says I, "I've got a State pedlar's licence, and I take out a city one wherever they demand it."'

'I went to the Mayor's office the next morning and they told me he hadn't showed up yet. They didn't know when he'd be down. So Doc Waughhoo hunches down again in a hotel chair and lights a jimpson-weed regalia, and waits.'

'By and by a young man in a blue neck-tie slips into the chair next to me and asks the time.'

'"Half-past ten," says I, "and you are Andy Tucker. I've seen you work. Wasn't it you that put up the Great Cupid Combination package on the Southern States? Let's see, it was a Chilian diamond engagement ring, a wedding-ring, a potato masher, a bottle of soothing syrup, and Dorothy Vernon – all for fifty cents."'

'Andy was pleased to hear that I remembered him. He was a good street man; and he was more than that – he respected his profession, and he was satisfied with 300 per cent profit. He had plenty of offers to go into the illegitimate drug and garden seed business; but he was never to be tempted off of the straight path.'

'I wanted a partner; so Andy and me agreed to go out together. I told him about the situation in Fisher Hill and how finances was low on account of the local mixture of politics and jalap. Andy had just got in on the train that morning. He was pretty low himself, and was going to canvass the town for a few dollars to build a new battleship by popular subscription at Eureka Springs. So we went out and sat on the porch and talked it over.

'The next morning at eleven o'clock, when I was sitting there alone, an Uncle Tom shuffles into the hotel and asked for the doctor to come and see Judge Banks, who, it seems, was the mayor and a mighty sick man.

'"I'm no doctor," says I. "Why don't you go and get the doctor?"

'"Boss," says he, "Doc Hoskins am done gone twenty miles in de country to see some sick persons. He's de only doctor in de town, and Massa Banks am powerful bad off. He sent me to ax you to please, suh, come."

'"As man to man," says I, "I'll go and look him over." So I put a bottle of Resurrection Bitters in my pocket and goes up on the hill to the Mayor's mansion, the finest house in town, with a mansard roof and two cast-iron dogs on the lawn.

'This Mayor Banks was in bed all but his whiskers and feet. He was making internal noises that would have had everybody in San Francisco hiking for the parks. A young man was standing by the bed holding a cup of water.

'"Doc," says the Mayor, "I'm awful sick. I'm about to die. Can't you do nothing for me?"

'"Mr. Mayor," says I, "I'm not a regular preordained disciple of S. Q. Lapius. I never took a course in a medical college," says I, "I've just come as a fellow-man to see if I could be of assistance."

'"I'm deeply obliged," says he. "Doc Waughhoo, this is my nephew, Mr. Biddle. He has tried to alleviate my distress, but without success. Oh, Lordy! Ow-ow-ow!!" he sings out.

'I nods at Mr. Biddle and sets down by the bed and feels the Mayor's pulse. "Let me see your liver – your tongue, I mean," says I. Then I turns up the lids of his eyes and looks close at the pupils of 'em.

'"How long have you been sick?" I asked.

"I was taken down – ow-ouch – last night," says the Mayor. "Gimme something for it, doc, won't you?"

'"Mr. Fiddle," says I, "raise the window shade a bit, will you?"

'"Biddle," says the young man. "Do you feel like you could eat some ham and eggs, Uncle James?"

'"Mr Mayor," says I, after laying my ear to his right shoulder-blade and listening, "you've got a bad attack of super-inflammation of the right clavicle of the harpsichord!"

'"Good Lord!" says he, with a groan. "Can't you rub something on it, or set it or anything?"

41

'I picks up my hat and starts for the door.

'"You ain't going, doc?" says the Mayor with a howl. "You ain't going away and leave me to die with this – superfluity of the clap-boards, are you?"

'"Common humanity, Dr Whoa-ha," says Mr. Biddle, "ought to prevent your deserting a fellow-human in distress."

'"Dr. Waugh-hoo, when you get through ploughing," says I. And then I walks back to the bed and throws back my long hair.

'"Mr. Mayor," says I, "there is only one hope for you. Drugs will do you no good. But there is another power higher yet, although drugs are high enough," says I.

'"And what is that?" says he.

'"Scientific demonstrations," says I. "The triumph of mind over sarsaparilla. The belief that there is no pain and sickness except what is produced when we ain't feeling well. Declare yourself in arrears. Demonstrate."

'"What is this paraphernalia you speak of, doc?" says the Mayor. "You ain't a Socialist, are you?"

'"I am speaking," says I, "of the great doctrine of psychic finan-ciering – of the enlightened school of long-distance, subconscientious treatment of fallacies and meningitis – of that wonderful indoor sport known as personal magnetism."

'"Can you work it, doc?" asks the Mayor.

'"I'm one of the Sole Sanhedrims and Ostensible Hooplas of the Inner Pulpit," says I. "The lame talk and the blind rubber whenever I make a pass at 'em. I am a medium, a coloratura hypnotist and a spirituous control. It was only through me at the recent séances at Ann Arbor that the late president of the Vinegar Bitters Company could revisit the earth to communicate with his sister Jane. You see me peddling medicine on the streets," says I, "to the poor. I don't practise personal magnetism on them. I do not drag it in the dust," says I, "because they haven't got the dust."

'"Will you treat my case?" asks the Mayor.

'"Listen," says I. "I've had a good deal of trouble with medical societies everywhere I've been. I don't practise medicine. But, to save your life, I'll give you the pyschic treatment if you'll agree as mayor not to push the licence question."

'"Of course I will," says he. "And now get to work, doc, for them pains are coming on again."

' "My fee will be $250.00, cure guaranteed in two treatments," says I.

'I sat down by the bed and looked him straight in the eye.'

'"All right," says the Mayor. "I'll pay it. I guess my life's worth that much."

'I sat down by the bed and looked him straight in the eye.

'"Now," says I, "get your mind off the disease. You ain't sick. You haven't got a heart or a clavicle or a funny-bone or brains or anything. You haven't got any pain. Declare error. Now you feel the pain that you didn't have leaving, don't you?"

'"I do feel some little better, doc," says the Mayor, "darned if I don't. Now state a few lies about my not having this swelling in my left side, and I think I could be propped up and have some sausage and buckwheat cakes."

'I made a few passes with my hands.

'"Now," says I, "the inflammation's gone. The right lobe of the perihelion has subsided. You're getting sleepy. You can't hold your eyes open any longer. For the present the disease is checked. Now, you are asleep."

'The Mayor shut his eyes slowly and began to snore.

43

'"You observe, Mr. Tiddle," says I, "the wonders of modern science."

'"Biddle," says he. "When will you give uncle the rest of the treatment, Dr. Pooh-pooh?"

'"Waugh-hoo," says I. "I'll come back at eleven to-morrow. When he wakes up give him eight drops of turpentine and three pounds of steak. Good morning."

'The next morning I went back on time. "Well, Mr. Riddle," says I, when he opened the bedroom door, "and how is uncle this morning?"

'"He seems much better," says the young man.

'The Mayor's colour and pulse was fine. I gave him another treatment, and he said the last of the pain left him.

'"Now," says I, "you'd better stay in bed for a day or two, and you'll be all right. It's a good thing I happened to be in Fisher Hill, Mr. Mayor," says I, "for all the remedies in the cornucopia that the regular schools of medicine use couldn't have saved you. And now that error has flew and pain proved a perjurer, let's allude to a cheerfuller subject – say the fee of $250. No cheques, please; I hate to write my name on the back of a cheque almost as bad as I do on the front."

'"I've got the cash here," says the Mayor, pulling a pocket-book from under his pillow.

'He counts out five fifty-dollar notes and holds 'em in his hand.

'"Bring the receipt," he says to Biddle.

'I signed the receipt and the Mayor handed me the money. I put it in my inside pocket careful.

'"Now do your duty, officer," says the Mayor, grinning much unlike a sick man.

'Mr. Biddle lays his hand on my arm.

'"You're under arrest, Dr. Waugh-hoo, alias Peters," says he, "for practising medicine without authority under the State law."

'"Who are you?" I asks.

'"I'll tell you who he is," says Mr. Mayor, sitting up in bed. "He's a detective employed by the State Medical Society. He's been following you over five counties. He came to me yesterday and we fixed up this scheme to catch you. I guess you won't do any more doctoring around these parts, Mr. Faker. What was it you said I had, doc?" the Mayor laughs, "compound – well it wasn't softening of the brain, I guess, anyway."

'"A detective," says I.

'"Correct," says Biddle. "I'll have to turn you over to the sheriff."

'"Let's see you do it," says I, and I grabs Biddle by the throat and half throws him out of the window, but he pulls a gun and sticks it under my chin, and I stand still. Then he puts handcuffs on me, and takes the money out of my pocket.

'"I witness," says he, "that they're the same bills that you and I marked, Judge Banks. I'll turn them over to the sheriff when we get to his office, and he'll send you a receipt. They'll have to be used as evidence in the case."

'"All right, Mr. Biddle," says the Mayor. "And now, Doc Waughhoo," he goes on, "why don't you demonstrate? Can't you pull the cork out of your magnetism with your teeth and hocus-pocus them handcuffs off?"

'"Come on, officer," says I, dignified. "I may as well make the best of it." And then I turns to old Banks and rattles my chains.

'"Mr. Mayor," says I, "the time will come soon when you'll believe that personal magnetism is a success. And you'll be sure that it succeeded in this case, too."

'And I guess it did.

'When we got nearly to the gate, I says: "We might meet somebody now, Andy. I reckon you better take 'em off, and – " Hey? Why, of course it was Andy Tucker. That was his scheme; and that's how we got the capital to go into business together."

A G MACDONELL

(1895–1941)

Archibald Gordon Macdonell was born in Aberdeen but educated in England at Winchester. His writings include biography, travel books, and mysteries under the pseudonyms of Neil Gordon and John Cameron, but his triumph is *England, Their England*, a Scotsman's commentary on the peculiarities of the Sassenach. The following chapter, on the subject of the Noblest Game, is a perfect example of the art of dead-pan humour.

The Cricket Match

THE CRICKET field itself was a mass of daisies and buttercups and dandelions, tall grasses and purple vetches and thistle-down, and great clumps of dark-red sorrel, except, of course, for the oblong patch in the centre – mown, rolled, watered – a smooth, shining emerald of grass, the Pride of Fordenden, the Wicket.

The entire scene was perfect to the last detail. It was as if Mr. Cochran had, with his spectacular genius, brought Ye Olde Englyshe Village straight down by special train from the London Pavilion, complete with synthetic cobwebs (from the Wigan factory), hand-made smocks for ye gaffers (called in the cabaret scenes and the North-West Mounted Police scenes, the Gentlemen of the Singing Ensemble), and aluminium Eezi-Milk stools for the dairymaids (or Ladies of the Dancing Ensemble). For there stood the Vicar, beaming absent-mindedly at everyone. There was the forge, with the blacksmith, his hammer discarded, tightening his snake-buckled belt for the fray and loosening his braces to enable his terrific bowling-arm to swing freely in its socket. There on a long bench outside the Three Horseshoes sat a row of elderly men, facing a row of pint tankards, and wearing either long beards or clean-shaven chins and long whiskers. Near them, holding pint tankards in their hands, was another group of men, clustered together and talking with intense animation. Donald thought that one or two of them seemed familiar, but it was not until he turned back to the char-à-banc to ask if he could help with the luggage that he realized that they were Mr. Hodge and his team already sampling the proprietor's wares. (A notice above the door of the inn stated that the proprietor's name was A. Bason and that he was licensed to sell wines, spirits, beers, and tobacco.)

All round the cricket field small parties of villagers were patiently waiting for the great match to begin – a match against gentlemen from London is an event in a village – and some of them looked as if they had been waiting for a good long time. But they were not impatient. Village folk are very seldom impatient. Those whose lives are occupied in combating the eccentricities of God regard as very small beer the eccentricities of Man.

Blue-and-green dragonflies played at hide-and-seek among the thistle-down and a pair of swans flew overhead. An ancient man leaned upon a scythe, his sharpening-stone sticking out of a pocket in his velveteen waistcoat. The parson shook hands with the squire. Doves cooed. The haze flickered. The world stood still.

At twenty minutes to three Mr. Hodge had completed his rather tricky negotiations with the Fordenden captain, and had arranged that two substitutes should be lent by Fordenden in order that the visitors should field eleven men, and that nine men on each side should bat. But just as the two men on the Fordenden side, who had been detailed for the unpleasant duty of fielding for both sides and batting for neither, had gone off home in high dudgeon, a motor-car arrived containing not only Mr. Hodge's two defaulters but a third gentleman in flannels as well, who swore stoutly that he had been invited by Mr. Hodge to play and affirmed that he was jolly well going to play. Whoever stood down, it wasn't going to be him. Negotiations therefore had to be reopened, the pair of local Achilles had to be re-called, and at ten minutes to three the match began upon a twelve-a-side basis.

Mr. Hodge, having won the toss by a system of his own founded upon the differential calculus and the Copernican theory, sent in his opening pair to bat. One was James Livingstone, a very sound club cricketer, and the other one was called, simply, Boone. Boone was a huge, awe-inspiring colossus of a man, weighing at least eighteen stone and wearing all the majestic trappings of a Cambridge Blue. Donald felt that it was hardly fair to loose such cracks upon the humble English village until he fortunately remembered that he, of all people, a foreigner, admitted by courtesy to the National Game, ought not to set himself up to be a judge of what is, and what is not, cricket.

The Fordenden team ranged themselves at the bidding of their captain, the Fordenden baker, in various spots of vantage amid the daisies, buttercups, dandelions, vetches, thistle-down, and clumps of dark-red sorrel; and the blacksmith having taken in, just for luck as it were, yet another reef in his snake-buckle belt, prepared to open the attack. It so happened that, at the end at which he was to bowl, the ground behind the wicket was level for a few yards and then sloped away rather abruptly, so that it was only during the last three or four intensive galvanic yards of his run that the blacksmith, who took a long run, was visible to the batsman or indeed to anyone on the field of play except the man stationed in the deep field behind him. This man saw nothing of the game except the blacksmith walking back dourly and the blacksmith running up ferociously, and occasionally a ball driven smartly over the brow of the hill in his direction.

The sound club player having taken guard, having twiddled his bat round several times in a nonchalant manner, and having stared arrogantly at each fieldsman in turn, was somewhat surprised to find that, although the field was ready, no bowler was visible. His doubts, however, were resolved a second or two later, when the blacksmith came up, breasting the slope like a mettlesome combination of Vulcan and Venus Anadyomene. The first ball which he delivered was a high full-pitch to leg, of appalling velocity. It must have lighted upon a bare patch among the long grass near long-leg, for it rocketed, first bounce, into the hedge and four byes were reluctantly signalled by the village umpire. The row of gaffers on the rustic bench shook their heads, agreed that it was many years since four byes had been signalled on that ground, and called for more pints of old-and-mild. The other members of Mr. Hodge's team blanched visibly and called for more pints of bitter. The youngish professor of ballistics, who was in next, muttered something about muzzle velocities and started to do a sum on the back of an envelope.

The second ball went full-pitch into the wicket-keeper's stomach and there was a delay while the deputy wicket-keeper was invested with the pads and gloves of office. The third ball, making a noise like a partridge, would have hummed past Mr. Livingstone's left ear had he not dexterously struck it out of the ground for six, and the fourth took his leg bail with a bullet-like-pitch. Ten runs for one wicket, last man six. The professor got the fifth ball on the left ear and went back to the Three Horseshoes, while Mr. Harcourt had the singular misfortune to hit his wicket before the sixth ball was even delivered. Ten runs for two wickets and one man retired hurt. A slow left-hand bowler was on at the other end, the local rate-collector, a man whose whole life was one of infinite patience and guile. Off his first ball the massive Cam-

The second ball went full-pitch into the wicket-keeper's stomach

bridge Blue was easily stumped, having executed a movement that aroused the professional admiration of the Ancient who was leaning upon his scythe. Donald was puzzled that so famous a player should play so execrable a stroke until it transpired, later on, that a wrong impression had been created and that the portentous Boone had gained his Blue at Cambridge for rowing and not for cricket. Ten runs for three wickets and one man hurt.

The next player was a singular young man. He was small and quiet, and he wore perfectly creased white flannels, white silk socks, a pale-pink silk shirt, and a white cap. On the way down in the char-à-banc he had taken little part in the conversation and even less in the beer-drinking. There was a retiring modesty about him that made him conspicuous in that cricket eleven, and there was a gentleness, an almost finicky gentleness about his movements which hardly seemed virile and athletic. He looked as if a fast ball would knock the bat out of his hands. Donald asked someone what his name was, and was astonished to learn that he was the famous novelist, Robert Southcott himself.

Just as this celebrity, holding his bat as delicately as if it was a flute or a fan, was picking his way through the daisies and thistledown towards the wicket, Mr. Hodge rushed anxiously, tankard in hand, from the Three Horseshoes and bellowed in a most unpoetical voice: 'Play carefully, Bobby. Keep your end up. Runs don't matter.'

'Very well, Bill,' replied Mr. Southcott sedately. Donald was interested by this little exchange. It was the Team Spirit at work – the captain instructing his man to play a type of game that was demanded by the state of the team's fortunes, and the individual loyally suppressing his instincts to play a different type of game.

Mr. Southcott took guard modestly, glanced furtively round the field as if it was an impertinence to suggest that he would survive long enough to make a study of the fieldsmen's positions worth while, and hit the rate-collector's first ball over the Three Horseshoes into a hayfield. The ball was retrieved by a mob of screaming urchins, handed back to the rate-collector, who scratched his head and then bowled his fast yorker, which Mr. Southcott hit into the saloon bar of the Shoes, giving Mr. Harcourt such a fright that he required several pints before he fully recovered his nerve. The next ball was very slow and crafty, endowed as it was with every iota of finger-spin and brain-power which a long-service rate-collector could muster. In addition, it was delivered at the extreme end of the crease so as to secure a background of dark laurels instead of a dazzling white screen, and it swung a little in the air; a few moments later the urchins, by this time delirious with ecstasy, were fishing it out of the squire's trout stream with a bamboo pole and an old bucket.

The rate-collector was bewildered. He had never known such a travesty of the game. It was not cricket. It was slogging; it was wild, unscientific bashing; and furthermore, his reputation was in grave danger. The instalments would be harder than ever to collect, and Heaven knew they were hard enough to collect as it was, what with bad times and all. His three famous deliveries had been treated with contempt – the leg-break, the fast yorker, and the slow, swinging off-break out of the laurel bushes. What on earth was he to try now? Another six and he would be laughed out of the parish. Fortunately the village umpire came out of a trance of consternation to the rescue. Thirty-eight years of umpiring for the Fordenden Cricket Club had taught him a thing or two and he called 'Over' firmly and marched off to square-leg. The rate-collector was glad to give way to a Free Forester, who had been specially imported for this match. He was only a moderate bowler, but it was felt that it was worth while giving him a trial, if only for the sake of the scarf round his wàist and his cap. At the other end the fast bowler pounded away grimly until an unfortunate accident occurred. Mr. Southcott had been treating with apologetic contempt those of his deliveries which came within reach, and the blacksmith's temper had been rising for some time. An urchin had shouted, 'Take him orf!' and the other urchins, for whom Mr. Southcott was by now a firmly established deity, had screamed with delight. The captain had held one or two ominous consultations with the wicket-keeper and other advisers, and the blacksmith knew that his dismissal was at hand unless he produced a supreme effort.

It was the last ball of the over. He halted at the wicket before going back for his run, glared at Mr. Harcourt, who had been driven out to umpire by his colleagues – greatly to the regret of Mr. Bason, the landlord of the Shoes – glared at Mr. Southcott, took another reef in his belt, shook out another inch in his braces, spat on his hand, swung his arm three or four times in a meditative sort of way, grasped the ball tightly in his colossal palm, and then turned smartly about and marched off like a Pomeranian grenadier and vanished over the brow of the hill. Mr. Southcott, during these proceedings, leant elegantly upon his bat and admired the view. At last, after a long stillness, the ground shook, the grasses waved violently, small birds arose with shrill clamours, a loud puffing sound alarmed the butterflies, and the blacksmith, looking more like Venus Anadyomene than ever, came thundering over the crest. The world held its breath. Among the spectators conversation was suddenly hushed. Even the urchins, understanding somehow that they were assisting at a crisis in affairs, were silent for a moment as the mighty figure swept up to the crease. It was the charge of Von Bredow's Dragoons at Gravelotte over again.

But alas for human ambitions! Mr. Harcourt, swaying slightly from leg to leg, had understood the menacing glare of the bowler, had marked the preparation for a titanic effort, and – for he was not a poet for nothing – knew exactly what was going on. And Mr. Harcourt sober had a very pleasant sense of humour, but Mr. Harcourt rather drunk was a perfect demon of impishness. Sober, he occasionally resisted a temptation to try to be funny. Rather drunk, never. As the giant whirlwind of vulcanic energy rushed past him to the crease, Mr. Harcourt, quivering with excitement and internal laughter, and wobbling uncertainly upon his pins, took a deep breath and bellowed, 'No ball!'

51

It was too late for the unfortunate bowler to stop himself. The ball flew out of his hand like a bullet and hit third-slip, who was not looking, full pitch on the knee-cap. With a yell of agony third-slip began hopping about like a stork until he tripped over a tussock of grass and fell on his face in a bed of nettles, from which he sprang up again with another drum-splitting yell. The blacksmith himself was flung forward by his own irresistible momentum, startled out of his wits by Mr. Harcourt's bellow in his ear, and thrown off his balance by his desperate effort to prevent himself from delivering the ball, and the result was that his gigantic feet got mixed up among each other and he fell heavily in the centre of the wicket, knocking up a cloud of dust and dandelion-seed and twisting his ankle. Rooks by hundreds arose in protest from the vicarage cedars. The urchins howled like intoxicated banshees. The gaffers gaped. Mr. Southcott gazed modestly at the ground. Mr. Harcourt gazed at the heavens. Mr. Harcourt did not think the world had ever been, or could ever be again, quite such a capital place, even though he had laughed internally so much that he had got hiccups.

Mr. Hodge, emerging at that moment from the Three Horseshoes, surveyed the scene and then the scoreboard with an imperial air. Then he roared in the same rustic voice as before:

'You needn't play safe any more, Bob. Play your own game.'

'Thank you, Bill,' replied Mr. Southcott as sedately as ever, and, on the resumption of the game, he fell into a kind of cricketing trance, defending his wicket skilfully from straight balls, ignoring crooked ones, and scoring one more run in a quarter of an hour before he inadvertently allowed, for the first time during his innings, a ball to strike his person.

'Out!' shrieked the venerable umpire before anyone had time to appeal.

The score at this point was sixty-nine for six, last man fifty-two.

The only other incident in the innings was provided by an American journalist, by name Shakespeare Pollock – an intensely active, alert, on-the-spot young man. Mr. Pollock had been roped in at the last moment to make up the eleven, and Mr. Hodge and Mr. Harcourt had spent quite a lot of time on the way down trying to teach him the fundamental principles of the game. Donald had listened attentively and had been surprised that they made no reference to the Team Spirit. He decided in the end that the reason must have been simply that everyone knows all about it already, and that it is therefore taken for granted.

Mr. Pollock stepped up to the wicket in the lively manner of his native mustang, refused to take guard, on the ground that he wouldn't know what to do with it when he got it, and, striking the first ball he received towards square leg, threw down his bat, and himself set off at a great rate in the direction of cover-point. There was a paralysed silence. The rustics on the bench rubbed their eyes. On the field no one moved. Mr. Pollock stopped suddenly, looked round, and broke into a genial laugh.

'Darn me —' he began, and then he pulled himself up and went on in refined English, 'Well, well! I thought I was playing baseball.' He smiled disarmingly round.

'Baseball is a kind of rounders, isn't it, sir?' said cover-point sympathetically.

Donald thought he had never seen an expression change so suddenly as Mr. Pollock's did at this harmless, and true, statement. A look of concentrated, ferocious venom obliterated the disarming smile. Cover-point, simple soul, noticed nothing, however, and Mr. Pollock walked back to the wicket in silence and was out next ball.

The next two batsmen, Major Hawker, the team's fast bowler, and Mr. Hodge himself, did not score, and the innings closed at sixty-nine, Donald not-out nought. Opinion on the gaffers' bench, which corresponded in years and connoisseurship very closely with the Pavilion at Lord's, was sharply divided on the question whether sixty-nine was, or was not, a winning score.

After a suitable interval for refreshment, Mr. Hodge led his men, except Mr. Harcourt who was missing, out into the field and placed them at suitable positions in the hay.

The batsmen came in. The redoubtable Major Hawker, the fast bowler, thrust out his chin and prepared to bowl. In a quarter of an hour he had terrified seven batsmen, clean bowled six of them, and broken a stump. Eleven runs, six wickets, last man two.

After the fall of the sixth wicket there was a slight delay. The new batsman, the local rate-collector, had arrived at the crease and was ready. But nothing happened. Suddenly the large publisher, who was acting as wicket-keeper, called out 'Hi! Where's Hawker?'

The words galvanized Mr. Hodge into portentous activity.

'Quick!' he shouted. 'Hurry, run, for God's sake! Bob, George, Percy, to the Shoes!' and he set off at a sort of gallop towards the inn, followed at intervals by the rest of the side except the pretty youth in the blue jumper, who lay down; the wicket-keeper, who did not move; and Mr. Shakespeare Pollock, who had shot off the mark and was well ahead of the field.

But they were all too late, even Mr. Pollock. The gallant Major, admitted by Mr. Bason through the back door, had already lowered a quart and a half of mild-and-bitter, and his subsequent bowling was perfectly innocuous, consisting, as it did, mainly of slow, gentle full-pitches to leg which the village baker and even, occasionally, the rate-collector hit hard and high into the long grass. The score mounted steadily.

Disaster followed disaster. Mr. Pollock, presented with an easy chance of a run-out, instead of lobbing the ball back to the wicket-keeper, had another reversion to his college days and flung it with appalling velocity at the unfortunate rate-collector and hit him in the small of the back, shouting triumphantly as he did so. 'Rah, rah, rah!' Mr. Livingstone, good club player, missed two easy catches off successive balls. Mr. Hodge allowed another easy catch to fall at his feet without attempting to catch it, and explained afterwards that he had been all the time admiring a particularly fine specimen of oak in the squire's garden. He seemed to think that this was a complete justification of his failure to attempt, let alone bring off, the catch. A black spot happened to cross the eye of the ancient umpire just as the baker put all his feet and legs and pads in front of a perfectly straight ball, and, as he plaintively remarked over and over again, he had to give the batsman the benefit of the doubt, hadn't he? It wasn't as if it was his fault that a black spot had crossed his eye just at that moment. And the stout publisher seemed to be suffering from the delusion that the way to make a catch at the wicket was to raise both hands high in the air, utter a piercing yell, and trust to an immense pair of pads to secure the ball. Repeated experiments proved that he was wrong.

The baker lashed away vigorously and the rate-collector dabbed the ball hither and thither until the score – having once been eleven runs for six wickets – was marked up on the board at fifty runs for six wickets. Things were desperate. Twenty to win and five wickets – assuming that the blacksmith's ankle and third-slip's knee-cap would stand the strain – to fall. If the lines on Mr. Hodge's face were deep, the lines on the faces of his team when he put himself on to bowl were like plasticine models of the Colorado Canyon. Mr. Southcott, without any orders from his captain, discarded his silk sweater from the Rue de la Paix, and went away into the deep field, about a hundred and twenty yards from the wicket. His beautifully brushed head was hardly visible above the daisies. The professor of ballistics sighed deeply. Major Hawker grinned a colossal grin, right across his jolly red face, and edged off in the direction of the Shoes. Livingstone, loyal to his captain, crouched alertly. Mr. Shakespeare Pollock rushed about enthusiastically. The remainder of the team drooped.

But the remainder of the team was wrong. For a wicket, a crucial wicket, was secured off Mr. Hodge's very first ball. It happened like this. Mr. Hodge was a poet, and therefore a theorist, and an idealist. If he was to win a victory at anything, he preferred to win by brains and not by muscle. He would far sooner have his best leg-spinner miss the wicket by an eighth of an inch than dismiss a batsman with a fast, clumsy full-toss. Every ball that he bowled had brain behind it, if not exactness of pitch. And it so happened that he had recently watched a county cricket match between Lancashire, a county that he detested in theory, and Worcestershire, a county that he adored in fact. On the one side were factories and the late Mr. Jimmy White; on the other, English apples and Mr. Stanley Baldwin. And at this particular match, a Worcestershire bowler, by name Root, a deliciously agricultural name, had outed the tough nuts of the County Palatine by placing all his fieldsmen on the leg-side and bowling what are technically known as 'in-swingers'.

Mr. Hodge, at heart an agrarian, for all his book-learning and his cadences, was determined to do the same. The first part of the performance was easy. He placed all his men upon the leg-side. The second part – the bowling of the 'in-swingers' – was more complicated, and Mr. Hodge's first ball was a slow long-hop on the off-side. The rate-collector, metaphorically rubbing his eyes, felt that this was too good to be true, and he struck the ball sharply into the untenanted off-side and ambled down the wicket with as near an approach to gaiety as a man can achieve who is cut off by the very nature of his profession from the companionship and goodwill of his fellows. He had hardly gone a yard or two when he was paralysed by a hideous yell from the long grass into which the ball had vanished, and still more by the sight of Mr. Harcourt, who, aroused from a deep slumber amid a comfortable couch of grasses and daisies, sprang to his feet and, pulling himself together with miraculous rapidity after a lightning if somewhat bleary glance round the field, seized the ball and unerringly threw down the wicket. Fifty for seven, last man twenty-two. Twenty to win: four wickets to fall.

Mr. Hodge's fifth ball was not a good one, due mainly to the fact that it slipped out of his hand before he was ready, and it went up and came down in a slow-lazy parabola, about seven feet wide of the wicket on the leg-side. The baker had plenty of time to make up his

55

mind. He could either leave it alone and let it count one run as a wide; or he could spring upon it like a panther and, with a terrific six, finish the match sensationally. He could play the part either of a Quintus Fabius Maximus Cunctator, or of a sort of Tarzan. The baker concealed beneath a modest and floury exterior a mounting ambition. Here was his chance to show the village. He chose the sort of Tarzan, sprang like a panther, whirled his bat cyclonically, and missed the ball by about a foot and a half. The wicket-keeping publisher had also had time in which to think and to move, and he also had covered the seven feet. True, his movements were less like the spring of a panther than the sideways waddle of an aldermanic penguin. But nevertheless he got there, and when the ball had passed the flashing blade of the baker, he launched a mighty kick at it – stooping to grab it was out of the question – and by an amazing fluke kicked it on to the wicket. Even the ancient umpire had to give the baker out, for the baker was still lying flat on his face outside the crease.

'I was bowling for that,' observed Mr. Hodge modestly, strolling up the pitch.

'I had plenty of time to use my hands,' remarked the wicket-keeper to the world at large, 'but I preferred to kick it.'

Donald was impressed by the extraordinary subtlety of the game.

Six to win and three wickets to fall.

The next batsman was a schoolboy of about sixteen, an ingenuous youth with pink cheeks and a nervous smile, who quickly fell a victim to Mr. Harcourt, now wideawake and beaming upon everyone. For Mr. Harcourt, poet that he was, understood exactly what the poor, pink child was feeling, and he knew that if he played the ancient dodge and pretended to lose the ball in the long grass, it was a hundred to one that the lad would lose his head. The batsman at the other end played the fourth ball of Mr. Livingston's next over hard in the direction of Mr. Harcourt. Mr. Harcourt rushed towards the spot where it had vanished in the jungle. He groped wildly for it, shouting as he did so, 'Come and help. It's lost.' The pink child scuttered nimbly down the pitch. Six runs to win and two wickets to fall. Mr. Harcourt smiled demoniacally.

The crisis was now desperate. The fieldsmen drew nearer and nearer to the batsmen, excepting the youth in the blue jumper. Livingstone balanced himself on his toes. Mr. Shakespeare Pollock hopped about almost on top of the batsmen, and breathed excitedly and audibly. Even the imperturbable Mr. Southcott discarded the piece of grass which he had been chewing so steadily. Mr. Hodge took himself off and put on the Major, who had by now somewhat lived down the quart and a half.

The batsmen crouched down upon their bats and defended stubbornly. A snick through the slips brought a single. A ball which eluded the publisher's gigantic pads brought a bye. A desperate sweep at a straight half-volley sent the ball off the edge of the bat over third-man's head and in normal circumstances would have certainly scored one, and possibly two. But Mr. Harcourt was on guard at third-man, and the batsmen, by nature cautious men, one being old and the sexton, the other the postman and therefore a Government official, were taking no risks. Then came another single off a mis-hit, and then an interminable period in which no wicket fell and no run was scored. It was broken at last disastrously, for the postman struck the ball sharply at Mr. Pollock, and Mr. Pollock picked it up and, in an ecstasy of zeal, flung it madly at the wicket. Two overthrows resulted.

The scores were level and there were two wickets to fall. Silence fell. The gaffers, victims simultaneously of excitement and senility, could hardly raise their pint pots – for it was past six o'clock, and the front door of the Three Horseshoes was now as wide open officially as the back door had been unofficially all afternoon.

The Major, his red face redder than ever and his chin sticking out almost as far as the Napoleonic Mr. Ogilvy's, bowled a fast half-volley on the leg-stump. The sexton, a man of iron muscle from much digging, hit it fair and square in the middle of the bat, and it flashed like a thunderbolt, waist-high, straight at the youth in the blue jumper. With a shrill scream the youth sprang backwards out of its way and fell over on his back. Immediately behind him, so close were the fieldsmen clustered, stood the mighty Boone. There was no chance of escape for him. Even if he had possessed the figure and the agility to perform back-somersaults, he would have lacked the time. He had been unsighted by the youth in the jumper. The thunderbolt struck him in the midriff like a red-hot cannon-ball upon a Spanish galleon, and with the sound of a drumstick upon an insufficiently stretched drum. With a fearful oath, Boone clapped his hands to his outraged stomach and found that the ball was in the way. He looked at it for a moment in astonishment and then threw it down angrily and started to massage the injured spot while the field rang with applause at the brilliance of the catch.

Donald walked up and shyly added his congratulations. Boone scowled at him.

57

'I didn't want to catch the bloody thing,' he said sourly, massaging away like mad.

'But it may save the side,' ventured Donald.

'Blast the bloody side,' said Boone.

Donald went back to his place.

The scores were level and there was one wicket to fall. The last man in was the blacksmith, leaning heavily upon the shoulder of the baker, who was going to run for him, and limping as if in great pain. He took guard and looked round savagely. He was clearly still in a great rage.

The first ball he received he lashed at wildly and hit straight up in the air to an enormous height. It went up and up and up, until it became difficult to focus it properly against the deep, cloudless blue of the sky, and it carried with it the hopes and fears of an English village. Up and up it went and then at the top it seemed to hang motionless in the air, poised like a hawk, fighting, as it were, a heroic but forlorn battle against the chief invention of Sir Isaac Newton, and then it began its slow descent.

In the meanwhile things were happening below, on the terrestrial sphere. Indeed, the situation was rapidly becoming what the French call *mouvementé*. In the first place, the blacksmith forgot his sprained ankle and set out at a capital rate for the other end, roaring in a great voice as he went, 'Come on, Joe!' The baker, who was running on behalf of the invalid, also set out, and he also roared 'Come on, Joe!' and side by side, like a pair of high-stepping hackneys, the pair cantered along. From the other end Joe set out on his mission, and he roared 'Come on, Bill!' So all three came on. And everything would have been all right, so far as the running was concerned, had it not been for the fact that Joe, very naturally, ran with his head thrown back and his eyes goggling at the hawk-like cricket-ball. And this in itself would not have mattered if it had not been for the fact that the blacksmith and the baker, also very naturally, ran with their heads turned not only upwards but also backwards as well, so that they too gazed at the ball, with an alarming sort of squint and a truly terrific kink in their necks. Half-way down the pitch the three met with a magnificent clang, reminiscent of early, happy days in the tournament-ring at Ashby-de-la-Zouche, and the hopes of the village fell with the resounding fall of their three champions.

But what of the fielding side? Things were not so well with them. If there was doubt and confusion among the warriors of Fordenden, there was also uncertainty and disorganization among the ranks of the invaders. Their main trouble was the excessive concentration of their forces in the neighbourhood of the wicket. Napoleon laid it down that it was impossible to have too many men upon a battlefield, and he used to do everything in his power to call up every available man for a battle. Mr. Hodge, after a swift glance at the ascending ball and a swift glance at the disposition of his troops, disagreed profoundly with the Emperor's dictum. He had too many men, far too many. And all except the youth in the blue silk jumper, and the mighty Boone, were moving towards strategical positions underneath the ball, and not one of them appeared to be aware that any of the others existed. Boone had not moved because he was more or less in the right place, but then Boone was not likely to bring off the catch, especially after the episode of the last ball. Major Hawker, shouting 'Mine, mine!' in a magnificently self-confident voice, was coming up from the bowler's end like a battle-cruiser. Mr. Harcourt had obviously lost sight of the ball altogether, if indeed he had ever seen it, for he was running round and round Boone and giggling foolishly. Livingstone and Southcott, the two cracks, were approaching competently. Either of them would catch it easily. Mr. Hodge had only to choose between them and, coming to a swift decision, he yelled above the din, 'Yours, Livingstone!' Southcott, disciplined cricketer, stopped dead Then Mr. Hodge made a fatal mistake. He remembered Livingstone's two missed sitters, and he reversed his decision and roared 'Yours, Bobby!' Mr. Southcott obediently started again, while Livingstone, who had not heard the second order, went straight on. Captain Hodge had restored the *status quo*.

In the meantime the professor of ballistics had made a lightning calculation of angles, velocities, density of the air, barometer-readings and temperatures, and had arrived at the conclusion that the critical point, the spot which ought to be marked in the photographs with an X, was one yard to the north-east of Boone, and he proceeded to take up station there, colliding on the way with Donald and knocking him over. A moment later Bobby Southcott came racing up and tripped over the recumbent Donald and was shot head first into the Abraham-like bosom of Boone. Boone stepped back a yard under the impact and came down with his spiked boot, surmounted by a good eighteen stone of flesh and blood, upon the professor's toe. Almost simultaneously the portly wicket-keeper, whose movements were a positive triumph of the spirit over the body, bumped the professor from behind. The learned man was thus neatly sandwiched between Tweedledum and Tweedledee, and the sandwich was instantly converted into a ragout by Livingstone, who made up for his lack of extra weight

– for he was always in perfect training – by his extra momentum. And all the time Mr. Shakespeare Pollock hovered alertly upon the outskirts like a Rugby scrum-half, screaming American University cries in a piercingly high tenor voice.

At last the ball came down. To Mr. Hodge it seemed a long time before the invention of Sir Isaac Newton finally triumphed. And it was a striking testimony to the mathematical and ballistical skill of the professor that the ball landed with a sharp report upon the top of his head. Thence it leapt up into the air a foot or so, cannoned on to Boone's head, and then trickled slowly down the colossal expanse of the wicket-keeper's back, bouncing slightly as it reached the massive lower portions. It was only a foot from the ground when Mr. Shakespeare Pollock sprang into the vortex with a last ear-splitting howl of victory and grabbed it off the seat of the wicket-keeper's trousers. The match was a tie. And hardly anyone on the field knew it except Mr. Hodge, the youth in the blue jumper, and Mr. Pollock himself. For the two batsmen and the runner, undaunted to the last, had picked themselves up and were bent on completing the single that was to give Fordenden the crown of victory. Unfortunately, dazed with their falls, with excitement, and with the noise, they all three ran for the same, wicket, simultaneously realized their error, and all three turned and ran for the other – the blacksmith, ankle and all, in the centre, and leading by a yard, so that they looked like pictures of the Russian *troika*. But their effort was in vain, for Mr. Pollock had grabbed the ball and the match was a tie.

And both teams spent the evening at The Three Horseshoes, and Mr. Harcourt made a speech in Italian about the glories of England and afterwards fell asleep in a corner, and Donald got home to Royal Avenue at 1 o'clock in the morning, feeling that he had not learnt very much about the English from his experience of their national game.

KATHERINE MANSFIELD
(1888–1923)

A New Zealander by birth, Katherine Mansfield Beauchamp spent nearly all her adult life in Europe. She has often been compared with Chekov for her expertise with the short story form. Katherine Mansfield is not known for humorous stories, but the following piece, taken from her first collection, *In a German Pension*, shows a wonderfully waspish satirical touch. Her life's output of short stories is available in *The Collected Stories of Katherine Mansfield*.

The Modern Soul

'GOOD EVENING,' said the Herr Professor, squeezing my hand; 'wonderful weather! I have just returned from a party in the wood. I have been making music for them on my trombone. You know, these pine trees provide most suitable accompaniment for a trombone! They are sighing delicacy against sustained strength, as I remarked once in a lecture on wind instruments in Frankfort. May I be permitted to sit beside you on this bench, gnädige Frau?'

He sat down, tugging at a white paper package in the tail pocket of his coat.

'Cherries,' he said, nodding and smiling. 'There is nothing like cherries for producing free saliva after trombone playing, especially after Grieg's "Ich Liebe Dich." Those sustained blasts on "liebe" make my throat as dry as a railway tunnel. Have some?' He shook the bag at me.

'I prefer watching you eat them.'

'Ah, ha!' He crossed his legs, sticking the cherry bag between his knees, to leave both hands free. 'Psychologically I understood your refusal. It is your innate feminine delicacy in preferring etherealised sensations. . . . Or perhaps you do not care to eat the worms. All cherries contain worms. Once I made a very interesting experiment with a colleague of mine at the university. We bit into four pounds of the best cherries and did not find one specimen without a worm. But what would you? As I remarked to him afterwards – dear friend, it amounts to this: if one wishes to satisfy the desires of nature one must be strong enough to ignore the facts of nature. . . . The conversation is not out of your depth? I have so seldom the time or opportunity to open my heart to a woman that I am apt to forget.'

I looked at him brightly.

'See what a fat one!' cried the Herr Professor. 'That is almost a mouthful in itself; it is beautiful enough to hang from a watch-chain.' He chewed it up and spat the stone an incredible distance – over the garden path into the flower bed. He was proud of the feat. I saw it. 'The quantity of fruit I have eaten on this bench,' he sighed; 'apricots, peaches and cherries. One day that garden bed will become an orchard grove, and I shall allow you to pick as much as you please, without paying me anything.'

He was proud of the feat. I saw it

I was grateful, without showing undue excitement.

'Which reminds me' – he hit the side of his nose with one finger – 'the manager of the pension handed me my weekly bill after dinner this evening. It is almost impossible to credit. I do not expect you to believe me – he has charged me extra for a miserable little glass of milk I drink in bed at night to prevent insomnia. Naturally, I did not pay.

But the tragedy of the story is this: I cannot expect the milk to produce somnolence any longer; my peaceful attitude of mind towards it is completely destroyed. I know I shall throw myself into a fever in attempting to plumb this want of generosity in so wealthy a man as the manager of a pension. Think of me to-night' – he ground the empty bag under his heel – 'think that the worst is happening to me as your head drops asleep on your pillow.'

Two ladies came on the front steps of the pension and stood, arm in arm, looking over the garden. The one, old and scraggy, dressed almost entirely in black bead trimming and a satin reticule; the other, young and thin, in a white gown, her yellow hair tastefully garnished with mauve sweet-peas.

The Professor drew in his feet and sat up sharply, pulling down his waistcoat.

'The Godowskas,' he murmured. 'Do you know them? A mother and daughter from Vienna. The mother has an internal complaint and the daughter is an actress. Fräulein Sonia is a very modern soul. I think you would find her most sympathetic. She is forced to be in attendance on her mother just now. But what a temperament! I have once described her in her autograph album as tigress with a flower in the hair. Will you excuse me? Perhaps I can persuade them to be introduced to you.'

I said, 'I am going up to my room.' But the Professor rose and shook a playful finger at me. 'Na,' he said, 'we are friends, and, therefore, I shall speak quite frankly to you. I think they would consider it a little "marked" if you immediately retired to the house at their approach, after sitting here alone with me in the twilight. You know this world. Yes, you know it as I do.'

I shrugged my shoulders, remarking with one eye that while the Professor had been talking the Godowskas had trailed across the lawn towards us. They confronted the Herr Professor as he stood up.

'Good evening,' quavered Frau Godowska. 'Wonderful weather! It has given me quite a touch of hay fever!' Fraulein Godowska said nothing. She swooped over a rose growing in the embryo orchard, then stretched out her hand with a magnificent gesture to the Herr Professor. He presented me.

'This is my little English friend of whom I have spoken. She is the stranger in our midst. We have been eating cherries together.'

'How delightful,' sighed Frau Godowska. 'My daughter and I have often observed you through the bedroom window. Haven't we, Sonia?'

Sonia absorbed my outward and visible form with an inward and spiritual glance, then repeated the magnificent gesture for my benefit. The four of us sat on the bench, with that faint air of excitement of passengers established in a railway carriage on the qui vive for the train whistle. Frau Godowska sneezed. 'I wonder if it is hay fever,' she remarked, worrying the satin reticule for her handkerchief, 'or would it be the dew. Sonia, dear, is the dew falling?'

Fräulein Sonia raised her face to the sky and half closed her eyes. 'No, mamma, my face is quite warm. Oh, look, Herr Professor, there are swallows in flight; they are like a little flock of Japanese thoughts – nicht wahr?'

'Where?' cried the Herr Professor. 'Oh yes, I see, by the kitchen chimney. But why do you say "Japanese"? Could you not compare them with equal veracity to a little flock of German thoughts in flight?' He rounded on me. 'Have you swallows in England?'

'I believe there are some at certain seasons. But doubtless they have not the same symbolical value for the English. In Germany –'

'I have never been to England,' interrupted Fräulein Sonia, 'but I have many English acquaintances. They are so cold!' She shivered.

'Fish-blooded,' snapped Frau Godowska. 'Without soul, without heart, without grace. But you cannot equal their dress materials. I spent a week in Brighton twenty years ago, and the travelling cape I bought there is not yet worn out – the one you wrap the hot-water bottle in, Sonia. My lamented husband, your father, Sonia, knew a great deal about England. But the more he knew about it the oftener he remarked to me, "England is merely an island of beef flesh swimming in a warm gulf sea of gravy." Such a brilliant way of putting things. Do you remember, Sonia?'

'I forget nothing, mamma,' answered Sonia.

Said the Herr Professor: 'That is the proof of your calling, gnädiges Fräulein. Now I wonder – and this is a very interesting speculation – is memory a blessing or – excuse the word – a curse?'

Frau Godowska looked into the distance, then the corners of her mouth dropped and her skin puckered. She began to shed tears.

'Ach Gott! Gracious lady, what have I said?' exclaimed the Herr Professor.

Sonia took her mother's hand. 'Do you know,' she said, 'to-night it is stewed carrots and nut tart for supper. Suppose we go in and take our places,' her sidelong, tragic stare accusing the Professor and me the while.

I followed them across the lawn and up the steps. Frau Godowska was murmuring, 'Such a wonderful, beloved man'; with her disengaged hand Fräulein Sonia was arranging the sweet pea 'garniture.'

*   *   *

'A concert for the benefit of afflicted Catholic infants will take place in the salon at eight-thirty p.m. Artists: Fräulein Sonia Godowska, from Vienna; Herr Professor Windberg and his trombone; Frau Oberlehrer Weidel and others.'

This notice was tied round the neck of the melancholy stag's head in the dining-room. It graced him like a red and white dinner bib for days before the event, causing the Herr Professor to bow before it and say 'good appetite' until we sickened of his pleasantry and left the smiling to be done by the waiter, who was paid to be pleasing to the guests.

On the appointed day the married ladies sailed about the pension dressed like upholstered chairs, and the unmarried ladies like draped muslin dressing-table covers. Frau Godowska pinned a rose in the centre of her reticule; another blossom was tucked in the mazy folds of a white antimacassar thrown across her breast. The gentlemen wore black coats, white silk ties and ferny buttonholes tickling the chin.

The floor of the salon was freshly polished, chairs and benches arranged, and a row of little flags strung across the ceiling – they flew and jigged in the draught with all the enthusiasm of family washing. It was arranged that I should sit beside Frau Godowska, and that the Herr Professor and Sonia should join us when their share of the concert was over.

'That will make you feel quite one of the performers,' said the Herr Professor genially. 'It is a great pity that the English nation is so unmusical. Never mind! To-night you shall hear something – we have discovered a nest of talent during the rehearsals.'

'What do you intend to recite, Fräulein Sonia?'

She shook back her hair. 'I never know until the last moment. When I come on the stage I wait for one moment and then I have the sensation as though something struck me here,' – she placed her hand upon her collar brooch – 'and . . . words come!'

'Bend down a moment,' whispered her mother. 'Sonia, love, your skirt safety-pin is showing at the back. Shall I come outside and fasten it properly for you, or will you do it yourself?'

'Oh, mamma, please don't say such things.' Sonia flushed and grew very angry. 'You know how sensitive I am to the slightest unsympathetic impression at a time like this. . . . I would rather my skirt dropped off my body –'

'Sonia – my heart!'

A bell tinkled.

The waiter came in and opened the piano. In the heated excitement of the moment he entirely forgot what was fitting, and flicked the keys with the grimy table napkin he carried over his arm. The Frau Oberlehrer tripped on the platform followed by a very young gentleman, who blew his nose twice before he hurled his handkerchief into the bosom of the piano.

> 'Yes, I know you have no love for me,
> And no forget-me-not.
> No love, no heart, and no forget-me-not,'

sang the Frau Oberlehrer, in a voice that seemed to issue from her forgotten thimble and have nothing to do with her.

'Ach, how sweet, how delicate,' we cried, clapping her soothingly. She bowed as though to say. 'Yes, isn't it?' and retired, the very young gentleman dodging her train and scowling.

The piano was closed, an arm-chair was placed in the centre of the platform. Fräulein Sonia drifted towards it. A breathless pause. Then, presumably, the winged shaft struck her collar brooch. She implored us not to go into the woods in trained dresses, but rather as lightly draped as possible, and bed with her among the pine needles. Her loud, slightly harsh voice filled the salon. She dropped her arms over the back of the chair, moving her lean hands from the wrists. We were thrilled and silent. The Herr Professor, beside me, abnormally serious, his eyes bulging, pulled at his moustache ends. Frau Godowska adopted that peculiarly detached attitude of the proud parent. The only soul who remained untouched by her appeal was the waiter, who leaned idly against the wall of the salon and cleaned his nails with the edge of a programme. He was 'off duty' and intended to show it.

'What did I say?' shouted the Herr Professor under cover of tumultuous applause, 'tem-per-ament! There you have it. She is a flame in the heart of a lily. I know I am going to play well. It is my turn now. I am inspired. Fräulein Sonia' – as that lady returned to us, pale and draped in a large shawl – 'you are my inspiration. To-night you shall be the soul of my trombone. Wait only.'

To right and left of us people bent over and whispered admiration down Fräulein Sonia's neck. She bowed in the grand style.

'I am always successful,' she said to me. 'You see, when I act I *am*. In Vienna, in the plays of Ibsen we had so many bouquets that the cook had three in the kitchen. But it is difficult here. There is so little magic. Do you not feel it? There is none of that mysterious perfume which floats almost as a visible thing from the souls of the Viennese audiences. My spirit starves for want of that.' She leaned forward, chin on hand. 'Starves,' she repeated.

The Professor appeared with his trombone, blew into it, held it up to one eye, tucked back his shirt cuffs and wallowed in the soul of Sonia Godowska. Such a sensation did he create that he was recalled to play a Bavarian dance, which he acknowledged was to be taken as a breathing exercise rather than an artistic achievement. Frau Godowska kept time to it with a fan.

Followed the very young gentleman who piped in a tenor voice that he loved somebody, 'with blood in his heart and a thousand pains.' Fräulein Sonia acted a poison scene with the assistance of her mother's pill vial and the arm-chair replaced by a *chaise longue*; a young girl scratched a lullaby on a young fiddle; and the Herr Professor performed the last sacrificial rites on the altar of the afflicted children by playing the National Anthem.

'Now I must put mamma to bed,' whispered Fräulein Sonia. 'But afterwards I must take a walk. It is imperative that I free my spirit in the open air for a moment. Would you come with me as far as the railway station and back?'

'Very well, then, knock on my door when you're ready.'

Thus the modern soul and I found ourselves together under the stars.

'What a night!' she said. 'Do you know that poem of Sappho about her hands in the stars. . . . I am curiously sapphic. And this is so remarkable – not only am I sapphic, I find in all the works of all the greatest writers, especially in their unedited letters, some touch, some sign of myself – some resemblance, some part of myself, like a thousand reflections of my own hands in a dark mirror.'

'But what a bother,' said I.

'I do not know what you mean by "bother"; is it rather the curse of my genius. . . .' She paused suddenly, staring at me. 'Do you know my tragedy?' she asked.

I shook my head.

'My tragedy is my mother. Living with her I live with the coffin of my unborn aspirations. You heard that about the safety-pin to-night. It may seem to you a little thing, but it ruined my three first gestures.

They were –'

'Impaled on a safety-pin,' I suggested.

'Yes, exactly that. And when we are in Vienna I am the victim of moods, you know. I long to do wild, passionate things. And mamma says, "Please pour out my mixture first." Once I remember I flew into a rage and threw a wash-stand jug out of the window. Do you know what she said? "Sonia, it is not so much throwing things out of windows, if only you would –"'

'Choose something smaller?' said I.

'No . . . "tell me about it beforehand." Humiliating! And I do not see any possible light out of this darkness.'

'Why don't you join a touring company and leave your mother in Vienna?'

'What! Leave my poor, little, sick, widowed mother in Vienna! Sooner than that I would drown myself. I love my mother as I love nobody else in the world – nobody and nothing! Do you think it is impossible to love one's tragedy? "Out of my great sorrows I make my little songs," that is Heine or myself.'

'Oh, well, that's all right,' I said cheerfully.

'But it is not all right!'

I suggested we should turn back. We turned.

'Sometimes I think the solution lies in marriage,' said Fräulein Sonia. 'If I find a simple, peaceful man who adores me and will look after mamma – a man who would be for me a pillow – for genius cannot hope to mate – I shall marry him. . . . You know the Herr Professor has paid me very marked attentions.'

'Oh, Fräulein Sonia,' I said, very pleased with myself, 'why not marry him to your mother?' We were passing the hairdresser's shop at the moment. Fräulein Sonia clutched my arm.

'You, you,' she stammered. 'The cruelty. I am going to faint. Mamma to marry again before I marry – the indignity. I am going to faint here and now.'

I was frightened. 'You can't,' I said, shaking her. 'Come back to the pension and faint as much as you please. But you can't faint here. All the shops are closed. There is nobody about. Please don't be so foolish.'

'Here and here only!' She indicated the exact spot and dropped quite beautifully, lying motionless.

'Very well,' I said, 'faint away; but please hurry over it.'

She did not move. I began to walk home, but each time I looked behind me I saw the dark form of the modern soul prone before the hairdresser's window. Finally I ran, and rooted out the Herr Professor from his room. 'Fräulein Sonia has fainted,' I said crossly.

'Du lieber Gott! Where? How?'

'Outside the hairdresser's shop in the Station Road.'

'Jesus and Maria! Has she no water with her?' – he seized his carafe – 'nobody beside her?'

'Nothing.'

'Where is my coat? No matter, I shall catch a cold on the chest. Willingly, I shall catch one. . . . You are ready to come with me?'

'No,' I said; 'you can take the waiter.'

'But she must have a woman. I cannot be so indelicate as to attempt to loosen her stays.'

'Modern souls oughtn't to wear them,' said I. He pushed past me and clattered down the stairs.

*　　*　　*

When I came down to breakfast next morning there were two places vacant at table. Fräulein Sonia and the Herr Professor had gone off for a day's excursion in the woods.

I wondered.

FLANN O'BRIEN
(1910–1966)

Flann O'Brien is a pseudonym for Brian O'Nolan. O'Nolan was born in County Tyrone and had a brilliant career at University College, Dublin. After further study in Germany he joined the Irish Civil Service. In 1939, he published *At Swim-Two-Birds*, a comic masterpiece of which Dylan Thomas said: 'Just the book to give your sister, if she's a loud, dirty, boozy girl.'

The pieces reprinted here are from his column in the *Irish Times* called *Cruiskeen Lawn* (under yet another pen-name, Myles na Gopaleen). 'The Brother' is a subject that appeared intermittently in the column, and represents certain Dublin characters rather nicely.

Other works include: *The Third Policeman, The Poor Mouth*, and *The Best of Myles* (from which the excerpts are taken).

The Brother

THE BROTHER is making a great job of the landlady.

I beg your pardon?

Says he'll have her on her feet in another week.

I do not understand.

She was laid up, you know.

Is that a fact?

Ah, yes, she got a very bad attack on New Year's Day. The rheumatism was at her for a long time. The brother ordered her to bed, but bedamn but she'd fight it on her feet. The brother took a very poor view and said she'd be a sorry woman. And, sure enough, so she was. On New Year's Day she got an attack that was something fierce, all classes of stabbing pains down the back. Couldn't move a hand to help herself. Couldn't walk, sit or stand.

I see.

Of course, the brother took command as quick as you'd order a pint. Ordered the whole lot out of the digs for the night, sent for the married sister and had the landlady put to bed. A very strict man for doing things the right way, you know, although he's not a married man himself. O, very strict.

That is satisfactory.

'The brother is making a great job of the landlady'

Well, the next day she was worse. She was in a fierce condition. All classes of pains in the knees, knuckles swollen out and all this class of thing. Couldn't get her breath right, either, wheezing and moaning there inside in the bed. O, a desperate breakdown altogether.

No doubt a doctor was sent for?

Sure that's what I'm coming to man. The unfortunate woman was all on for calling in Doctor Dan. A son of the father, you know, round the corner, a nice young fellow with all classes of degrees after his name. Well, I believe the brother kicked up a fierce row. Wouldn't hear of it at any price. Of course, the brother was always inclined to take a poor view of the doctors, never had any time for them at all.

I see.

If you want to hear the pay given out in right style, get the brother on to the doctors. Fierce language he uses sometimes. Says half of those lads never wash their hands. Now say there's some ould one down the road laid up with a bad knee. Right. She sends for the

71

doctor. Right. But where are you in the meantime? You're laid up, too. You're inside in your bed with a bad cold. Right. You send for the doctor, too. Right. In he comes and takes your pulse and gives you some class of a powder. Next morning you're feeling grand. The cold is gone. Fair enough. You think you'll get up. You hop out of bed like a young one. The next minute you're on your back on the floor roaring out of you with all classes of pains. What's happened?

I fear I have no idea what's happened.

The knee is gone, of course. Your man has cured the cold, but given you a knee that's worse than the knee the ould one had. Be your own doctor, that's what the brother says, or get a good layman that understands first principles. That 'flu that was going round at the Christmas, the brother blames the doctors for that, too.

What happened the landlady?

O the brother started treatment right away. Stuck above in the bedroom half the day working away at her. Running up and down stairs with big basins of scalding water. Of course the brother believes that the whole secret is in the circulation. It's the blood all the time. Well do you know, the third day the landlady was very much improved.

That is remarkable.

Very . . . much . . . improved. But did the brother let her up?

I should not imagine so.

Not on your life man. O no. He still keeps working away at her and puts her on a special diet, milk and nuts and all this class of thing. And now she's nearly cured. The brother is going to let her up for a while on Sunday.

That is very satisfactory.

Of course the married sister was under the roof all the time, if you know what I mean.

I understand.

Ah yes, the brother has fixed up harder cases than that. Weren't you telling me that you had some class of a stiffness in one of your fingers?

I had.

Would you like to show it to the brother?

Thank you very much but the trouble has since cleared up.

I see. Well, any time you think you're not feeling right, you've only to say the word. No trouble at all. Begob, here's me 'bus.

Good-bye and thank you again.

Cheers now.

* * *

I'VE A QUARE bit of news for you. The brother's nose is out of order.

What?

A fact. Some class of a leak somewhere.

I do not understand.

Well do you see it's like this. Listen till I tell you. Here's the way he's fixed. He starts suckin the wind in be the mouth. That's OK, there's no damper there. But now he comes along and shuts the mouth. That leaves him the nose to work with or he's a dead man. Fair enough. He starts suckin in through the nose. AND THEN DO YOU KNOW WHAT?

What?

THE – WIND GOES ASTRAY SOMEWHERE. Wherever it goes it doesn't go down below. Do you understand me? There's some class of a leak above in the head somewhere. There's what they call a valve there. The brother's valve is banjaxed.

I see.

The air does leak up into the head, all up around the brother's brains. How would you like that? Of course, his only man is to not use the nose at all and keep workin' on the mouth. O be gob it's no joke to have the valve misfirin'. And I'll tell you a good one.

Yes?

The brother is a very strict man for not treatin himself. He does have crowds of people up inside in the digs every night lookin for all classes of cures off him, maternity cases and all the rest of it. But he wouldn't treat himself. Isn't that funny? HE WOULDN'T TREAT HIMSELF.

He is at one there with orthodox medical practice.

So he puts his hat on his head and takes a walk down to Charley's. Charley is a man like himself – not a doctor, of course, but a layman that understands first principles. Charley and the brother do have consultations when one or other has a tough case do you understand me. Well anyway the brother goes in and is stuck inside in Charley's place for two hours. And listen till I tell you.

Yes?

When the brother leaves he has your man Charley in bed with strict orders not to make any attempt to leave it. Ordered to bed and told to stop there. The brother said he wouldn't be responsible if Charley stayed on his feet. What do you think of that?

It is very odd to say the least of it.

Of course Charley was always very delicate and a man that never minded himself. The brother takes a very poor view of Charley's kidneys. Between yourself, meself and Jack Mum, Charley is a little bit given to the glawsheen. Charley's little finger is oftener in the air than annywhere else, shure wasn't he in the hands of doctors for years man. They had him nearly destroyed when somebody put him on to the brother. And the brother'll make a job of him yet, do you know that?

No doubt.

Ah yes. Everybody knows that it's the brother that's keepin Charley alive. But begob the brother'll have to look out for himself now with the nose valve out of gear and your man Charley on his hands into the bargain.

Is there any other person to whom your relative could have recourse?

Ah, well, of course, at the latter end he'll have to do a job on himself. HAVE TO, man, sure what else can he do? The landlady was telling me that he's thinkin of openin himself some night.

What?

You'll find he'll take the razor to the nose before you're much older. He's a man that would understand valves, you know. He wouldn't be long puttin it right if he could get his hands at it. Begob there'll be blood in the bathroom anny night now.

He will probably kill himself.

The brother? O trust him to look after Number One. You'll find he'll live longer than you or me. Shure he opened Charley in 1934.

He did?

He gave Charley's kidneys a thorough overhaul, and that's a game none of your doctors would try their hand at. He had Charley in the bathroom for five hours. Nobody was let in, of course, but the water was goin all the time and all classes of cutthroats been sharpened, you could hear your man workin at the strap. O a great night's work. Begob here's me 'bus!

Bye bye.

*   *   *

THE BROTHER can't look at an egg.

Is that so?

Can't stand the sight of an egg at all. Rashers, ham, fish, anything you like to mention – he'll eat them all and ask for more. But he can't go the egg. Thanks very much all the same but no eggs. The egg is barred.

I see.

I do often hear him talking about the danger of eggs. You can get all classes of disease from eggs, so the brother says.

That is disturbing news.

The trouble is that the egg never dies. It is full of all classes of microbes and once the egg is down below in your bag, they do start moving around and eating things, delighted with themselves. No trouble to them to start some class of an ulcer on the sides of the bag.

I see.

Just imagine all your men down there walking up and down your stomach and maybe breeding families, chawing and drinking and feeding away there, it's a wonder we're not all in our graves man, with all them hens in the country.

I must remember to avoid eggs.

I chance an odd one meself but one of these days I'll be a sorry man. Here's me Drimnagh 'bus, I'll have to lave yeh, don't do anything when your uncle's with you, as the man said.

Good bye.

*　　*　　*

Do YOU know what it is, the brother's an extraordinary genius.

I do not doubt it.

Begob he had them all in a right state above in the digs.

Is that a fact?

Comes in wan night there, puts the bike in the hall and without takin off coat, cap or clips walks into the room, takes up the tea-pot, marches out with it without a word and pours the whole issue down the sink. You should see the face of her nibs the landlady, her good black market tay at fifteen bob a knock!

An extraordinary incident.

But then does your man come back and explain?

I should be astonished if he did.

O not a bit of it. Marches upstairs leavin the lot of them sitting there with the eyes out on pins. They do be easily frightened by the brother.

A natural reaction to this unusual personality.

Well annyway the brother is upstairs for half an hour washin and scrubbin himself and smokin fags in the bathroom. And the crowd below sitting there afraid to look at wan another, certain sure they were all poisoned and not knowin which was going to pass out first.

I see.

Well after a while the brother marches downstairs and gives strict orders that nobody is to drink any more water. Gives instructions to the landlady that there's to be no more tea made until further notice. The brother then goes out to the kitchen and makes a dose of stuff with milk and some white powder he had in the pocket and makes them all drink it. The whole lot might be dead only for the brother.

Your relative will no doubt be compensated elsewhere for his selfless conduct.

Well next mornin he's off on the bicycle up to the waterworks at Stillorgan and comes home with bottles full of water. He was above in the waterworks carrying out surveys and colloguin with the turncocks – never lettin on who he was, of course, just chattin and keepin th'oul eye open.

I understand.

And the crowd in the digs livin on custard and cocoa made with milk, the unfortunate landlady crucified for a cup of tea but afraid of her life to make a drop or even take wan look at the tap.

Quite.

Well annyway up with the brother to the bathroom with the bottles of water and he's stuck inside there for hours with the door locked. The brother was carryin out tests, d'y'understand.

I do.

Down he comes at eight o'clock, puts on the hat and coat and begob you should see the face. The brother was gravely concerned. Very gravely concerned. He doesn't look at anyone, just says, 'I'll have to see Hernon to-morrow.' Then out with him.

A most ominous pronouncement.

The next mornin the brother comes down in the blue suit and gives orders that if anybody calls he's above in the City Hall with Hernon and that he'll be back late and to take any message. Well do you know I never seen the digs so quiet after the brother left. And that night at tea-time there wasn't two words said be anybody. The whole crowd was sittin there waitin for the brother to come back from Hernon. Seven o'clock and he wasn't back. Eight, Nine. Begob the suspense was brutal. BRUTAL.

I can quite imagine.

At half nine the door opens and in comes the brother. I never seen a man lookin as tired. And would you blame him, fifteen hours non-stop stuck up in the City Hall?

Undoubtedly a most arduous exertion in the public interest.

Well annyway the brother sits down and starts takin of the boots. And then without liftin the head, he says: 'From tomorrow on,' says he, 'yez can have your tea.'

Indeed.

Well begob there was nearly a cheer. But the brother just goes upstairs without another word, tired to the world. He was after fixin the whole thing and puttin Hernon right about the water.

Undoubtedly a most useful day's work.

*   *   *

THINGS IS movin in great style above in the digs. The brother has the landlady humped down to Skerries.

This is scarcely the season for seaside holidays.

Wait till you hear what happened man. This night, d'y'see, the landlady is for the pictures. Has the black hat and the purple coat on and is standin in the hall havin a screw at the glass and puttin on the gloves. The shoes polished and shinin like an eel's back, of course. All set.

I understand.

Then the key is heard in the hall door and in comes the brother. He's half turnin into the room when he gives a look at her nibs. Then he stops and comes back and starts starin like a man that was seein things. The landlady gets red, of course.

A not unnatural reaction in the circumstances.

Well annyway the brother orders the landlady into the room where he can see her in the light. He puts the finger on the landlady's eye and starts pullin the lids out of her to get a decko at th'inside. Begob the poor landlay gets the windup in right style. Then the brother starts tappin her chest and givin her skelps on the neck. Inside ten minutes he has her stuffed into bed upstairs with himself below in the kitchen makin special feeds of beef-tea and the crowd in the digs told off to take turns sittin up with the landlady all night. That's a quare one for you.

It is undoubtedly a very queer one for you.

An th'unfortunate woman all set for the pictures thinkin' she was as right as rain. Wasn't it the mercy of God the brother put his nose in at that particular minute?

The coincidence has that inscrutable felicity that is usually associated with the more benevolent manifestations of Providence.

Well the next day the brother gives orders for the landlady's things to be packed. What she wanted, the brother said, was a COMPLETE REST, The brother said he wouldn't be responsible if the landlady didn't get a complete rest.

I see.

So what would do him only pack the landlady down to the married sister in Skerries. With strict orders that she was to stop in bed when she got there. And that's where she is since.

The Brother

To be confined to bed in midwinter in that somewhat remote hamlet is not the happiest of destinies.

Of course the brother does things well, you know. Before he packs the landlady off in a cab for the station, he rings up Foley. And of course Foley puts the landlady on the train and sees her right t'oblige the brother.

I see.

A great man for lookin after other people, the brother. Ah yes. Yes, certainly . . .

I quite agree. And now I fear I must be off.

Ah yes . . . I'll tell you another funny thing that happened. Queer things always happen in pairs. I was goin home late wan night and I was certain sure I was the last in. I'm lying there in the bed when I hear the door been opened below. Then the light is switched on in the sittinroom. Next thing begob I think I hear voices. So not knowin what's goin on, I hop out of bed and run down in me peejamas.

A very proper precaution in these queer times.

I whip open the sittin-room door and march in. What do I see only the brother leppin up to meet me with the face gettin a little bit red. This, says he, is Miss Doy-ull.

A lady?

The brother was with a dame on the sofa. I suppose he was chattin her about banks and money and that class of thing. But . . . do you know . . . if the landlady was there . . . not that it's my place to say annything . . . but her nibs would take a very poor view of women been brought into the digs after lights out. Wouldn't fancy that at all.

That is the fashion with all landladies.

Well the brother does have Miss Doy-ull in every night since. They do work very late into the night at the bankin questions. I couldn't tell you when she leaves. A very hard-workin' genius, the brother. I was askin' him when he's goin to let the landlady get up below in Skerries. A thing like this, says he, will take a long time, but I might let her up for half an hour a Sunday.

Care is necessary in these delicate illnesses, of course.

You're right there, but it's not the first breakdown the brother pulled the landlady through. Begob here's me bus!

Good-bye.

*   *   *

I'LL TELL you a good wan.

Indeed?

78

I'll give you a laugh.

How very welcome.

The brother's studyin the French. The brother has the whole digs in a right state and the nerves of half of the crowd up there is broke down.

How truly characteristic of your relative.

The brother comes down to breakfast there about a fortnight back, ten minutes late. And I'll tell you a good wan. What be all the powers had the brother up here at the neck.

I do not know.

A bow tie begob.

I see.

A bow tie with spots on it. Well luckit. I nearly passed out. I didn't know where to look when I seen the bow tie. You couldn't . . . say anythin, you know. The brother wouldn't like that. The brother takes a very poor view of personal remarks. Did you not know that? Shure that's well-known.

I did not know that.

Well anyway the crowd tries to pretend to be goin on with the breakfast and pay no attention to your man but of course there wasn't wan there but was shook in the nerves be the appearance of the brother. Gob now the atmosphere was fierce. What does your man do? Does he sit down and start eatin?

I should be astonished to learn that he did.

Not at all man, over with him to the mantelpiece and starts workin and pokin and foosterin at the clock, he was squintin and peerin and peepin' there for five minutes and then he comes along and starts lightin matches to see better, manipulatin and cavortin there for further orders, you'd swear he was searching for the hallmark on it. He was openin the glass . . . and shuttin it . . . and opening it . . . and slammin it shut again – you'd need the nerves of an iron man to sit there and swally the grub. It was fierce.

I have no doubt.

There we were the whole crowd of us sittin waitin for the blow to fall, the landlady changin colour like something you'd see in a circus. The only man that wasn't sweatin there was meself. Bar meself, the nerves of the crowd was in flitters.

Pray proceed to the dénouement.

At last begob the blow fell. Without turnin round at all, the brother speaks in a very queer voice. I don't see any Hair Dev, says he. *I don't see any Hair Dev.* Well luckit. Do you know what it is?

The Brother

What is it?

The crowd nearly passed out. The poor ould landlady – there was tears in her eyes. What's that, says she. But the brother doesn't pretend to hear, sits down very cross-lookin and starts swallyin tea, you could see the bow tie waggin every time your man swallied a mouthful. There wasn't another thing said that fine morning.

I see.

Next thing off with the poor landlady down town to Moore Street, tried every shop in the street lookin for the brother's fancy feed but it was no use, she didn't know whether it was sold loose or in a bag or in a tin. The nearest French stuff she could get was the French beans. So what does she do only have a feed of them things laid out for the brother's breakfast next mornin. What's this, says the brother. Them's French garden vegetables, says the landlady. *The land of France*, says the brother, *never seen them things*.

That is what one would call 'a quare one'.

Thing's is gone from bad to worse. The brother now had a jug of Hair Dev bought be himself above in the bedroom. Breakfast in bed *and drinkin tay out of a glass!* And the bow tie never offa the neck!

And one assumes that is only a beginning.

The brother says he doesn't know why he lives in this country at all. Takes a very poor view. Here's me bus! Cheers!

Cheers!

*   *   *

YOURSELF, is it? Fit an' well you're lookin. I'll tell you a good one. I'll give you a laugh.

Do.

I'll give you a laugh. The digs was in the front line for near on a fortnight. Martial law, begob. It was a . . . thremendious business. Fierce.

One divines a domestic crisis of unexampled gravity.

Some was for handin in the gun after the first week and runnin off on holidays, muryaa, off down to Skerries or Arklow where they were sleepin five in a bed and not a place to be had for love or money. All hands was losin weight be the pound. It was a . . . most . . . thremendious . . . war of nerves.

No doubt your relative was the author of this tension?

Tuesday fortnight was D-Day. The brother comes down to breakfast without the mark of a shavin-razor on the jaw. The brother – !

Indeed?

A man . . . a man . . . that was never known to put the nose out of the room of a mornin without everything just so – the handkerchief right, the tie right, and never without a fierce smell of shavin-soap off him. An' the hair-oil standin out on the head like diamonds!

One cannot always maintain such an attitude neque semper tendit arcum Apollo.

Of course the crowd starts eatin an' takin no notice. There would be no question of anybody passin remarks, you know. There was very ferocious eatin goin on that morning. The brother just reads the paper and then off to work. He only opens the beak once. Goin out he says to the landlady 'Pardon me but I may be delayed to-night and there is no necessity for you to defer retiring.'

A most considerate thought.

The next mornin the crowd is sittin at the table as white as a sheet, all waitin for the brother to come down. Begob you would think they were all for the firin-squad. And down comes the brother. Do you know what I'm goin to tell you?

I do not.

The face was as black as a black-faced goat. I never seen a more ferocious-lookin sight. Begob there was hair on him from the ears to the neck. The crowd begins to feed like prisoners given thirty second to swally their stew. The landlady's face gets red and out she comes in a big loud voice with a lot of chat about the war. The secret was out! He was tryin to raise wan.

Trying to raise what?

To raise a whisker. Your man was puttin up a beaver!

Curious that any activity so ancient should be considered reprehensible!

I couldn't tell you how the crowd in the digs lived through the next ten days. You wouldn't know your man to look at him. A fierce lookin sight, comin in and sittin down as bold as bedamned. Starts enlargin the bridgehead from wan day to the next. An' not a word out of him but Pardon me this an' Pardon me that. O a very cool customer, say what you like. And no remarks passed, of course. Do you know what it is?

I do not.

If the brother came down without a face on him at all, there wouldn't be wan that would pass a remark. The heads would go down, the chawin and aytin would go on and the landlady would pass the brother the paper. A nice crowd begob.

A remarkable character.

After a fortnight the brother got himself into a condition I never

seen a man in in me life. There was hair hangin out of him behind the
ears an' there was hair growin into the eyes. The strain was terrible.
The digs was about to crack. It was H-Hour. Then begob the big
thing happened. Next mornin the brother comes down with his face as
smooth as a baby's, sits down and says Parding me, ma'am, but I
think that clock is four minutes slow be the Ballast Office. Well luckit.

I am looking.

The crowd in the digs goes off their heads. They all start chattin an'
talkin and roarin out of them about the time and peepin at their
watches and laughin and cavortin for further orders. I think we'll need
more tea, the landlady says, gettin up to go out. Do you know what it
is?

I do not.

I'll give you a laugh. Her nibs was cryin.

Not unusual in such an emotional crisis.

I never put in such a fortnight in me life. Begob here's a 52. Cheers!

Cheers!

*　　*　　*

I'LL TELL you another man that the brother fixed up – Jamesie D. Now
there was a man that wasn't getting his health at all. When he came to
the brother he was a cripple. And look at him now.

In what condition is he now?

Sure wasn't he picked for a trial with Rovers Seconds and couldn't
turn out because the ould mother beyond in Stepaside was taken bad
on the Friday. A great big gorilla of a man.

And what was his trouble?

Arthreetus, so the brother said. It was a very poor glass of water,
I'm telling you. But the brother got it in time.

That was fortunate.

Ah yes, if you don't put it off too long the brother can work wonders.
He does be often giving out about people that don't come to him in
time.

And what happened in connexion with that gentleman you mentioned?

Jamesie D.? Ah poor Jamesie had a bad time. The joint of the elbow
went out of order with his arthreetus. He could no more lift a pint than
he could lift a fog. The poor man took it very badly, hardly ever came
down to the smoker of a Friday. A man remember that could play Ave
Maria on the piana to bring the tears to your eyes. To tell you the
truth he was half poisoned by the doctors. All classes of pills and
bottles. And one doctor gave him the machine.

I beg your pardon?

As true as I'm here, strapped him down to some class of an electric chair and turned on the juice. Poor Jamesie thought it was the end. He thought your man was a maniac, you know, passing himself off as a doctor. Begob, what the chair did for him was to give him a bad ankle. It was after that that he went to the brother.

I see.

Well do you know what I'm going to tell you. The brother got that arthreetus at the elbow, he chased it up the arm to the shoulder, then down the back, over across to the other leg and down the thighs. He got it just above the knee. It took him two years but he got it in the end. He killed it just above the knee. And it never came back.

I see.

No, it never came back. Well, here's me wagon. Good luck now and back no horses, as the man said.

Farewell, friend.

FRANK O'CONNOR (Michael O'Donovan)
(1903–1966)

Born in Cork, O'Connor was almost entirely self-educated.
He worked as translator and journalist, and was for a time
one of the directors of the Abbey Theatre, Dublin. He published many volumes of short stories, the first of which, and
probably the best known, was *Guests of the Nation*.

Song Without Words

EVEN if there were only two men left in the world and both of them
saints they wouldn't be happy. One of them would be bound to try
and improve the other. That is the nature of things.

I am not, of course, suggesting that either Brother Arnold or
Brother Michael was a saint. In private life Brother Arnold was a
postman, but as he had a great name as a cattle doctor they had put
him in charge of the monastery cows. He had the sort of face you
would expect to see advertising somebody's tobacco; a big, innocent,
contented face with a pair of blue eyes that were always twinkling. According to the rule he was supposed to look sedate and go about in a
composed and measured way, but he could not keep his eyes down-
cast for any length of time and wherever his eyes glanced they twink-
led, and his hands slipped out of his long white sleeves and dropped
some remark in sign language. Most of the monks were good at the
deaf and dumb language; it was their way of getting round the rule of
silence, and it was remarkable how much information they managed
to pick up and pass on.

Now, one day it happened that Brother Arnold was looking for a
bottle of castor oil and he remembered that he had lent it to Brother
Michael, who was in charge of the stables. Brother Michael was a
man he did not get on too well with; a dour, dull sort of man who kept
to himself. He was a man of no great appearance, with a mournful
wizened little face and a pair of weak red-rimmed eyes – for all the
world the sort of man who, if you shaved off his beard, clapped a
bowler hat on his head and a cigarette in his mouth, would need no
other reference to get a job in a stable.

There was no sign of him about the stable yard, but this was only natural because he would not be wanted till the other monks returned from the fields, so Brother Arnold pushed in the stable door to look for the bottle himself. He did not see the bottle, but he saw something which made him wish he had not come. Brother Michael was hiding in one of the horse-boxes; standing against the partition with something hidden behind his back and wearing the look of a little boy who has been caught at the jam. Something told Brother Arnold that at that moment he was the most unwelcome man in the world. He grew red, waved his hand to indicate that he did not wish to be involved, and returned to his own quarters.

It came as a shock to him. It was plain enough that Brother Michael was up to some shady business, and Brother Arnold could not help wondering what it was. It was funny, he had noticed the same thing when he was in the world; it was always the quiet, sneaky fellows who were up to mischief. In chapel he looked at Brother Michael and got the impression that Brother Michael was looking at him, a furtive look to make sure he would not be noticed. Next day when they met in the yard he caught Brother Michael glancing at him and gave back a cold look and a nod.

The following day Brother Michael beckoned him to come over to the stables as though one of the horses was sick. Brother Arnold knew it wasn't that; he knew he was about to be given some sort of explanation and was curious to know what it would be. He was an inquisitive man; he knew it, and blamed himself a lot for it.

Brother Michael closed the door carefully after him and then leaned back against the jamb of the door with his legs crossed and his hands behind his back, a foxy pose. Then he nodded in the direction of the horse-box where Brother Arnold had almost caught him in the act, and raised his brows inquiringly. Brother Arnold nodded gravely. It was not an occasion he was likely to forget. Then Brother Michael put his hand up his sleeve and held out a folded newspaper. Brother Arnold shrugged his shoulders as though to say the matter had nothing to do with him, but the other man nodded and continued to press the newspaper on him.

He opened it without any great curiosity, thinking it might be some local paper Brother Michael smuggled in for the sake of the news from home and was now offering as the explanation of his own furtive behaviour. He glanced at the name and then a great light broke on him. His whole face lit up as though an electric torch had been switched on behind, and finally he burst out laughing. He couldn't help himself.

Brother Michael did not laugh but gave a dry little cackle which was as near as he ever got to laughing. The name of the paper was the *Irish Racing News*.

Now that the worst was over Brother Michael grew more relaxed. He pointed to a heading about the Curragh and then at himself. Brother Arnold shook his head, glancing at him expectantly as though he were hoping for another laugh. Brother Michael scratched his head for some indication of what he meant. He was a slow-witted man and had never been good at the sign talk. Then he picked up the sweeping brush and straddled it. He pulled up his skirts, stretched out his left hand holding the handle of the brush, and with his right began flogging the air behind him, a grim look on his leathery little face. Inquiringly he looked again and Brother Arnold nodded excitedly and put his thumbs up to show he understood. He saw now that the real reason Brother Michael had behaved so queerly was that he read racing papers on the sly and he did so because in private life he had been a jockey on the Curragh.

Brother Arnold nodded excitedly and put his thumbs up

He was still laughing like mad, his blue eyes dancing, wishing only for an audience to tell it to, and then he suddenly remembered all the things he had thought about Brother Michael and bowed his head and beat his breast by way of asking pardon. Then he glanced at the paper again. A mischievous twinkle came into his eyes and he pointed the paper at himself. Brother Michael pointed back, a bit puzzled. Brother Arnold chuckled and stowed the paper up his sleeve. Then Brother Michael winked and gave the thumbs-up sign. In that slow cautious way of his he went down the stable and reached to the top of the wall where the roof sloped down on it. This, it seemed, was his hiding-hole. He took down several more papers and gave them to Brother Arnold.

For the rest of the day Brother Arnold was in the highest spirits. He winked and smiled at everyone till they all wondered what the joke was. He still pined for an audience. All that evening and long after he had retired to his cubicle he rubbed his hands and giggled with delight whenever he thought of it; it was like a window let into his loneliness; it gave him a warm, mellow feeling, as though his heart had expanded to embrace all humanity.

It was not until the following day that he had a chance of looking at the papers himself. He spread them on a rough desk under a feeble electric-light bulb high in the roof. It was four years since he had seen a paper of any sort, and then it was only a scrap of local newspaper which one of the carters had brought wrapped about a bit of bread and butter. But Brother Arnold had palmed it, hidden it in his desk, and studied it as if it were a bit of a lost Greek play. He had never known until then the modern appetite for words – printed words, regardless of their meaning. This was merely a County Council wrangle about the appointment of seven warble-fly inspectors, but by the time he was done with it he knew it by heart.

So he did not just glance at the racing papers as a man would in the train to pass the time. He nearly ate them. Blessed words like fragments of tunes coming to him out of a past life; paddocks and point-to-points and two-year-olds, and again he was in the middle of a race-course crowd on a spring day with silver streamers of light floating down the sky like heavenly bunting. He had only to close his eyes and he could see the refreshment tent again with the golden light leaking like spilt honey through the rents in the canvas, and the girl he had been in love with sitting on an upturned lemonade box. 'Ah, Paddy,' she had said, 'sure there's bound to be racing in heaven!' She was fast, too fast for Brother Arnold, who was a steady-going fellow and had never got over the shock of discovering that all the time she had been running another man. But now all he could remember of her was her smile and the tone of her voice as she spoke the words which kept running through his head, and afterwards whenever his eyes met Brother Michael's he longed to give him a hearty slap on the back and say: 'Michael, boy, there's bound to be racing in heaven.' Then he grinned and Brother Michael, though he didn't hear the words or the tone of voice, without once losing his casual melancholy air, replied with a wall-faced flicker of the horny eyelid, a tick-tack man's signal, a real, expressionless, horsy look of complete understanding.

One day Brother Michael brought in a few papers. On one he pointed to the horses he had marked, on the other to the horses who had won. He showed no signs of his jubilation. He just winked, a leathery sort of wink, and Brother Arnold gaped as he saw the list of winners. It filled him with wonder and pride to think that when so many rich and clever people had lost, a simple little monk living hundreds of miles away could work it all out. The more he thought of it the more excited he grew. For one wild moment he felt it might be his duty to tell the Abbot, so that the monastery could have the full advantage of Brother Michael's intellect, but he realised that it wouldn't do. Even if Brother Michael could restore the whole abbey from top to bottom with his winnings, the ecclesiastical authorities would disapprove of it. But more than ever he felt the need of an audience.

He went to the door, reached up his long arm, and took down a loose stone from the wall above it. Brother Michael shook his head several times to indicate how impressed he was by Brother Arnold's ingenuity. Brother Arnold grinned. Then he took down a bottle and handed it to Brother Michael. The ex-jockey gave him a questioning look as though he were wondering if this wasn't cattle-medicine; his face did not change but he took out the cork and sniffed. Still his face did not change. All at once he went to the door, gave a quick glance up and a quick glance down and then raised the bottle to his lips. He reddened and coughed; it was good beer and he wasn't used to it. A shudder as of delight went through him and his little eyes grew moist as he watched Brother Arnold's throttle working on well-oiled hinges. The big man put the bottle back in its hiding-place and indicated by signs that Brother Michael could go there himself whenever he wanted a drink. Brother Michael shook his head doubtfully, but Brother Arnold nodded earnestly. His fingers moved like lightning while he explained how a farmer whose cow he had cured had it left in for him every week.

The two men were now fast friends. They no longer had any secrets from one another. Each knew the full extent of the other's little weakness and liked him the more for it. Though they couldn't speak to one another they sought out one another's company and whenever other things failed they merely smiled. Brother Arnold felt happier than he had felt for years. Brother Michael's successes made him want to try his hand, and whenever Brother Michael gave him a racing paper with his own selections marked, Brother Arnold gave it back with his, and they waited impatiently till the results turned up three or four days late. It was also a new lease of life to Brother Michael, for what comfort is it to a man if he has all the winners when not a soul in the world can ever know whether he has or not. He felt now that if only he could have a bob each way on a horse he would ask no more of life.

It was Brother Arnold, the more resourceful of the pair, who solved that difficulty. He made out dockets, each valued for so many Hail Marys, and the loser had to pay up in prayers for the other man's intention. It was an ingenious scheme and it worked admirably. At first Brother Arnold had a run of luck. But it wasn't for nothing that Brother Michael had had the experience; he was too tough to make a fool of himself even over a few Hail Marys, and everything he did was carefully planned. Brother Arnold began by imitating him, but the moment he struck it lucky he began to gamble wildly. Brother Michael had often seen it happen on the Curragh and remembered the fate of those it had happened to. Men he had known with big houses and cars were now cadging drinks in the streets of Dublin. It struck him that God had been very good to Brother Arnold in calling him to a monastic life where he could do no harm to himself or to his family.

And this, by the way, was quite uncalled for, because in the world Brother Arnold's only weakness had been for a bottle of stout and the only trouble he had ever caused his family was the discomfort of having to live with a man so good and gentle, but Brother Michael was rather given to a distrust of human nature, the sort of man who goes looking for a moral in everything even when there is no moral in it. He tried to make Brother Arnold take an interest in the scientific side of betting but the man seemed to treat it all as a great joke. A flighty sort of fellow! He bet more and more wildly with that foolish good-natured grin on his face, and after a while Brother Michael found himself being owed a deuce of a lot of prayers, which his literal mind insisted on translating into big houses and cars. He didn't like that either. It gave him scruples of conscience and finally turned him against betting altogether. He tried to get Brother Arnold to drop it, but as became an inventor, Brother Arnold only looked hurt and indignant, like a child who has been told to stop his play. Brother Michael had that weakness on his conscience too. It suggested that he was getting far too attached to Brother Arnold, as in fact he was. It would have been very difficult not to. There was something warm and friendly about the man which you couldn't help liking.

Then one day he went in to Brother Arnold and found him with a pack of cards in his hand. They were a very old pack which had more than served their time in some farmhouse, but Brother Arnold was looking at them in rapture. The very sight of them gave Brother Michael a turn. Brother Arnold made the gesture of dealing, half playfully, and the other shook his head sternly. Brother Arnold blushed and bit his lip but he persisted, seriously enough now. All the doubts Brother Michael had been having for weeks turned to conviction. This was the primrose path with a vengeance, one thing leading to another. Brother Arnold grinned and shuffled the deck; Brother Michael, biding his time, cut for deal and Brother Arnold won. He dealt two hands of five and showed the five of hearts as trump. He wanted to play twenty-five. Still waiting for a sign, Brother Michael looked at his own hand. His face grew grimmer. It was not the sort of sign he had expected but it was a sign all the same; four hearts in a bunch; the ace, jack, two other trumps, and the three of spades. An unbeatable hand. Was that luck? Was that coincidence, or was it the Adversary himself, taking a hand and trying to draw him deeper in the mire.

He liked to find a moral in things, and the moral in this was plain, though it went to his heart to admit it. He was a lonesome, melancholy man and the horses had meant a lot to him in his bad spells. At times it had seemed as if they were the only thing that kept him sane. How could he face twenty, perhaps thirty, years more of life, never knowing what horses were running or what jockeys were up – Derby Day, Punchestown, Leopardstown, and the Curragh all going by while he knew no more of them than if he were already dead?

'O Lord,' he thought bitterly, 'a man gives up the whole world for You, his chance of a wife and kids, his home and his family, his friends and his job, and goes off to a bare mountain where he can't even tell his troubles to the man alongside him; and still he keeps something back, some little thing to remind him of what he gave up. With me 'twas the horses and with this man 'twas the sup of beer, and I dare say there are fellows inside who have a bit of a girl's hair hidden some-

where they can go and look at it now and again. I suppose we all have
our little hiding-hole if the truth was known, but as small as it is, the
whole world is in it, and bit by bit it grows on us again till the day You
find us out.'

Brother Arnold was waiting for him to play. He sighed and put his
hand on the desk. Brother Arnold looked at it and at him. Brother
Michael idly took away the spade and added the heart and still
Brother Arnold couldn't see. Then Brother Michael shook his head
and pointed to the floor. Brother Arnold bit his lip again as though he
were on the point of crying, then threw down his own hand and
walked to the other end of the cow-house. Brother Michael left him so
for a few moments. He could see the struggle going on in the man,
could almost hear the Devil whisper in his ear that he (Brother
Michael) was only an old woman – Brother Michael had heard that
before; that life was long and a man might as well be dead and buried
as not have some little innocent amusement – the sort of plausible
whisper that put many a man on the gridiron. He knew, however hard
it was now, that Brother Arnold would be grateful to him in the other
world. 'Brother Michael,' he would say, 'I don't know what I'd ever
have done without your example.'

Then Brother Michael went up and touched him gently on the
shoulder. He pointed to the bottle, the racing paper, and the cards.
Brother Arnold fluttered his hands despairingly but he nodded. They
gathered them up between them, the cards, the bottle, and the papers,
hid them under their habits to avoid all occasion of scandal, and went
off to confess their guilt to the Prior.

EDGAR ALLAN POE
(1809–1849)

Poe may at first seem out of place among the humorists, but a look at even the creepiest of his stories will show a wonderful gift for irony and sense of the ridiculous. He wrote a number of humorous stories, most of which were parodies of the popular fiction of his day. *The System of Dr Tarr and Professor Fether*, however, is a superb piece of black humour which easily stands comparison with Poe's better-known tales of terror.

The System of Doctor Tarr and Professor Fether

DURING the autumn of 18 –, while on a tour through the extreme southern provinces of France, my route led me within a few miles of a certain *Maison de Santé* or private mad-house, about which I had heard much, in Paris, from my medical friends. As I had never visited a place of the kind, I thought the opportunity too good to be lost; and so proposed to my travelling companion (a gentleman with whom I had made casual acquaintance a few days before), that we should turn aside, for an hour or so, and look through the establishment. To this he objected – pleading haste, in the first place, and, in the second, a very usual horror at the sight of a lunatic. He begged of me, however, not to let any mere courtesy toward himself interfere with the gratification of my curiosity, and said that he would ride on leisurely so that I might overtake him during the day, or, at all events, during the next. As he bade me good-by, I bethought me that there might be some difficulty in obtaining access to the premises, and mentioned my fears on this point. He replied that, in fact, unless I had personal knowledge of the superintendent, Monsieur Maillard, or some credential in the way of a letter, a difficulty might be found to exist, as the regulations of these private mad-houses were more rigid than the public hospital laws. For himself, he added, he had, some years since, made the acquaintance of Maillard, and would so far assist me as to ride up to the door and introduce me; although his feelings on the subject of lunacy would not permit of his entering the house.

I thanked him, and, turning from the main road, we entered a grass grown by-path, which, in half an hour, nearly lost itself in a dense forest, clothing the base of a mountain. Through this dank and gloomy wood we rode some two miles, when the *Maison de Santé* came in view. It was a fantastic *château*, much dilapidated, and indeed scarcely tenantable through age and neglect. Its aspect inspired me with absolute dread, and, checking my horse, I half resolved to turn back. I soon, however, grew ashamed of my weakness, and proceeded.

As we rode up to the gate-way, I perceived it slightly open, and the visage of a man peering through. In an instant afterward, this man came forth, accosted my companion by name, shook him cordially by the hand, and begged him to alight. It was Monsieur Maillard him-self. He was a portly, fine-looking gentleman of the old school, with a polished manner, and a certain air of gravity, dignity, and authority which was very impressive.

My friend, having presented me, mentioned my desire to inspect the establishment, and received Monsieur Maillard's assurance that he would show me all attention, now took leave, and I saw him no more.

When he had gone, the superintendent ushered me into a small and exceedingly neat parlor, containing, among other indications of re-fined taste, many books, drawings, pots of flowers, and musical instruments. A cheerful fire blazed upon the hearth. At a piano, sing-ing an aria from Bellini, sat a young and very beautiful woman, who, at my entrance, paused in her song, and received me with graceful courtesy. Her voice was low, and her whole manner subdued. I thought, too, that I perceived the traces of sorrow in her countenance, which was excessively, although to my taste, not unpleasingly, pale. She was attired in deep mourning, and excited in my bosom a feeling of mingled respect, interest, and admiration.

I had heard, at Paris, that the institution of Monsieur Maillard was managed upon what is vulgarly termed the 'system of soothing' – that all punishments were avoided – that even confinement was seldom resorted to – that the patients, while secretly watched, were left much apparent liberty, and that most of them were permitted to roam about the house and grounds in the ordinary apparel of persons in right mind.

Keeping these impressions in view, I was cautious in what I said before the young lady; for I could not be sure that she was sane; and, in fact, there was a certain restless brilliancy about her eyes which half led me to imagine she was not. I confined my remarks, therefore, to general topics, and to such as I thought would not be displeasing or exciting even to a lunatic. She replied in a perfectly rational manner to all that I said; and even her original observations were marked with the soundest good sense; but a long acquaintance with the metaphysics of *mania*, had taught me to put no faith in such evidence of sanity, and I continued to practise, throughout the interview, the caution with which I commenced it.

Presently a smart footman in livery brought in a tray with fruit, wine, and other refreshments, of which I partook, the lady soon afterward leaving the room. As she departed I turned my eyes in an inquiring manner toward my host.

'No,' he said, 'oh, no – a member of my family – my niece, and a most accomplished woman.'

'I beg a thousand pardons for the suspicion,' I replied, 'but of course you will know how to excuse me. The excellent administration of your affairs here is well understood in Paris, and I thought it just possible, you know – '

'Yes, yes – say no more – or rather it is myself who should thank you for the commendable prudence you have displayed. We seldom find so much of forethought in young men; and, more than once, some unhappy *contre-temps* has occurred in consequence of thoughtlessness on the part of our visitors. While my former system was in operation, and my patients were permitted the privilege of roaming to and fro at will, they were often aroused to a dangerous frenzy by injudicious persons who called to inspect the house. Hence I was obliged to enforce a rigid system of exclusion; and none obtained access to the premises upon whose discretion I could not rely.'

'While your *former* system was in operation!' I said, repeating his words – 'do I understand you, then, to say that the "soothing system" of which I have heard so much is no longer in force?'

'It is now,' he replied, 'several weeks since we have concluded to renounce it forever.'

'Indeed! you astonish me!'

'We found it, sir,' he said, with a sigh, 'absolutely necessary to return to the old usages. The *danger* of the soothing system was, at all times, appalling; and its advantages have been much overrated. I believe, sir, that in this house it has been given a fair trial, if ever in any. We did everything that rational humanity could suggest. I am sorry that you could not have paid us a visit at an earlier period, that you might have judged for yourself. But I presume you are conversant with the soothing practice – with its details.'

'Not altogether. What I have heard has been at third or fourth hand.'

'I may state the system, then, in general terms, as one in which the patients were *ménagés* – humored. We contradicted *no* fancies which entered the brains of the mad. On the contrary, we not only indulged but encouraged them; and many of our most permanent cures have been thus effected. There is no argument which so touches the feeble reason of the madman as the *reductio ad absurdum*. We have had men, for example, who fancied themselves chickens. The cure was, to insist upon the thing as a fact – to accuse the patient of stupidity in not sufficiently perceiving it to be a fact – and thus to refuse him any other diet for a week than that which properly appertains to a chicken. In this manner a little corn and gravel were made to perform wonders.'

'But was this species of acquiescence all?'

'By no means. We put much faith in amusements of a simple kind, such as music, dancing, gymnastic exercises generally, cards, certain classes of books, and so forth. We affected to treat each individual as if for some ordinary physical disorder; and the word 'lunacy' was never employed. A great point was to set each lunatic to guard the actions of all the others. To repose confidence in the understanding or discretion of a madman, is to gain him body and soul. In this way we were enabled to dispense with an expensive body of keepers.'

'And you had no punishments of any kind?'

'None.'

'And you never confined your patients?'

'Very rarely. Now and then, the malady of some individual growing to a crisis, or taking a sudden turn of fury, we conveyed him to a secret cell, lest his disorder should infect the rest, and there kept him until we could dismiss him to his friends – for with the raging maniac we have nothing to do. He is usually removed to the public hospitals.'

'And you have now changed all this – and you think for the better?'

'Decidedly. The system had its disadvantages, and even its dangers. It is now, happily, exploded throughout all the *Maisons de Santé* of France.'

'I am very much surprised,' I said, 'at what you tell me; for I made sure that, at this moment, no other method of treatment for mania existed in any portion of the country.'

'You are young yet, my friend,' replied my host, 'but the time will arrive when you will learn to judge for yourself of what is going on in the world, without trusting to the gossip of others. Believe nothing you hear, and only one half that you see. Now about our *Maisons de Santé*, it is clear that some ignoramus has misled you. After dinner, however, when you have sufficiently recovered from the fatigue of your ride, I will be happy to take you over the house, and introduce to you a

system which, in my opinion, and in that of every one who has witnessed its operation, is incomparably the most effectual as yet
devised.'

'Your own?' I inquired – 'one of your own invention?'

'I am proud,' he replied, 'to acknowledge that it is – at least in some
measure.'

In this manner I conversed with Monsieur Maillard for an hour or
two, during which he showed me the gardens and conservatories of
the place.

'I cannot let you see my patients,' he said, 'just at present. To a
sensitive mind there is always more or less of the shocking in such exhibitions; and I do not wish to spoil your appetite for dinner. We will
dine. I can give you some veal *à la St. Meneboult*, with cauliflowers in
velouté sauce – after that a glass of *Clos de Vougeôt* – then your nerves will
be sufficiently steadied.'

At six, dinner was announced; and my host conducted me into a
large *salle à manger*, where a very numerous company were assembled
– twenty-five or thirty in all. They were, apparently, people of rank –
certainly of high breeding – although their habiliments, I thought,
were extravagantly rich, partaking somewhat too much of the osten-
tatious finery of the *ville cour*. I noticed that at least two thirds of these
guests were ladies; and some of the latter were by no means accoutred
in what a Parisian would consider good taste at the present day.
Many females, for example, whose age could not have been less than
seventy, were bedecked with a profusion of jewelry, such as rings,
bracelets, and ear-rings, and wore their bosoms and arms shamefully
bare. I observed, too, that very few of the dresses were well made – or,
at least, that very few of them fitted the wearers. In looking about, I
discovered the interesting girl to whom Monsieur Maillard had presented me in the little parlor; but my surprise was great to see her
wearing a hoop and farthingale, with high-heeled shoes, and a dirty
cap of Brussels lace, so much too large for her that it gave her face a
ridiculously diminutive expression. When I had first seen her, she was
attired, most becomingly, in deep mourning. There was an air of
oddity, in short, about the dress of the whole party, which, at first,
caused me to recur my original idea of the 'soothing system,' and to
fancy that Monsieur Maillard had been willing to deceive me until
after dinner, that I might experience no uncomfortable feelings
during the repast, at finding myself dining with lunatics; but I
remembered having been informed, in Paris, that the southern pro-
vincialists were a peculiarly eccentric people, with a vast number of

antiquated notions; and then, too, upon conversing with several members of the company, my apprehensions were immediately and fully dispelled.

The dining-room itself, although perhaps sufficiently comfortable and of good dimensions, had nothing too much of elegance about it. For example, the floor was uncarpeted; in France, however, a carpet is frequently dispensed with. The windows, too, were without curtains; the shutters, being shut, were securely fastened with iron bars, applied diagonally, after the fashion of our shop-shutters. The apartment, I observed, formed, in itself, a wing of the *château*, and thus the windows were on three sides of the parallelogram, the door being at the other. There were no less than ten windows in all.

The table was superbly set out. It was loaded with plate, and more than loaded with delicacies. The profusion was absolutely barbaric. There were meats enough to have feasted the Anakim. Never, in all my life, had I witnessed so lavish, so wasteful an expenditure of the good things of life. There seemed very little taste, however, in the arrangements; and my eyes, accustomed to quiet lights, were sadly offended by the prodigious glare of a multitude of wax candles, which, in silver *candelabra*, were deposited upon the table, and all about the room, wherever it was possible to find a place. There were several active servants in attendance; and, upon a large table, at the farther end of the apartment, were seated seven or eight people with fiddles, fifes, trombones, and a drum. These fellows annoyed me very much, at intervals, during the repast, by an infinite variety of noises, which were intended for music, and which appeared to afford much entertainment to all present, with the exception of myself.

Upon the whole, I could not help thinking that there was much of the *bizarre* about everything I saw – but then the world is made up of all kinds of persons, with all modes of thought, and all sorts of conventional customs. I had travelled, too, so much, as to be quite an adept at the *nil admirari;* so I took my seat very coolly at the right hand of my host, and, having an excellent appetite, did justice to the good cheer set before me.

The conversation, in the meantime, was spirited and general. The ladies, as usual, talked a great deal. I soon found that nearly all the company were well educated; and my host was a world of good-humored anecdote in himself. He seemed quite willing to speak of his position as superintendent of a *Maison de Santé*; and, indeed, the topic of lunacy was, much to my surprise, a favorite one with all present. A great many amusing stories were told, having reference to the *whims* of the patients.

'We had a fellow here once,' said a fat little gentleman, who sat at my right, – 'a fellow that fancied himself a tea-pot; and by the way, is it not especially singular how often this particular crotchet has entered the brain of the lunatic? There is scarcely an insane asylum in France which cannot supply a human tea-pot. *Our* gentleman was a Britannia-ware tea-pot, and was careful to polish himself every morning with buckskin and whiting.'

'And then,' said a tall man just opposite, 'we had here, not long ago, a person who had taken it into his head that he was a donkey – which, allegorically speaking, you will say, was quite true. He was a troublesome patient; and we had much ado to keep him within bounds. For a long time he would eat nothing but thistles; but of this idea we soon cured him by insisting upon his eating nothing else. Then he was perpetually kicking out his heels – so – so –'

'Mr. De Kock! I will thank you to behave yourself!' here interrupted an old lady, who sat next to the speaker. 'Please keep your feet to yourself! You have spoiled my brocade! Is it necessary, pray, to illustrate a remark in so practical a style? Our friend here can surely comprehend you without all this. Upon my word, you are nearly as great a donkey as the poor unfortunate imagined himself. Your acting is very natural, as I live.'

'*Mille pardons! Ma'm'selle!*' replied Monsieur De Kock, thus addressed – 'a thousand pardons! I had no intention of offending. Ma'm'selle Laplace – Monsieur De Kock will do himself the honor of taking wine with you.'

Here Monsieur De Kock bowed low, kissed his hand with much ceremony, and took wine with Ma'm'selle Laplace.

'Allow me, *mon ami*,' now said Monsieur Maillard, addressing myself, 'allow me to send you a morsel of this veal *à la St. Meneboult* – you will find it particularly fine.'

At this instant three sturdy waiters had just succeeded in depositing safely upon the table an enormous dish, or trencher, containing what I supposed to be the '*monstrum, borrendum, informe, ingens, cui lumen ademptum.*' A closer scrutiny assured me, however, that it was only a small calf roasted whole, and set upon its knees, with an apple in its mouth, as is the English fashion of dressing a hare.

'Thank you, no,' I replied; 'to say the truth, I am not particularly partial to veal *à la St.*—what is it? – for I do not find that it altogether agrees with me. I will change my plate, however, and try some of the rabbit.'

There were several side-dishes on the table, containing what appeared to be the ordinary French rabbit – a very delicious *morceau*, which I can recommend.

'Pierre,' cried the host, 'change this gentleman's plate, and give him a side-piece of this rabbit *au-chat*.'

'This what?' said I.

'This rabbit *au-chat*.'

'Why, thank you – upon second thoughts, no. I will just help myself to some of the ham.'

There is no knowing what one eats, thought I to myself, at the tables of these people of the province. I will have none of their rabbit *au-chat* – and, for the matter of that, none of their *cat-au-rabbit* either.

'And then,' said a cadaverous-looking personage, near the foot of the table, taking up the thread of the conversation where it had been broken off, – 'and then, among other oddities, we had a patient, once upon a time, who very pertinaciously maintained himself to be a Cordova cheese, and went about, with a knife in his hand, soliciting his friends to try a small slice from the middle of his leg.'

'He was a great fool, beyond doubt,' interposed some one, 'but not to be compared with a certain individual whom we all know, with the exception of this strange gentleman. I mean the man who took himself for a bottle of champagne, and always went off with a pop and a fizz, in this fashion.'

Here the speaker, very rudely, as I thought, put his right thumb in his left cheek, withdrew it with a sound resembling the popping of a cork, and then, by a dexterous movement of the tongue upon the teeth, created a sharp hissing and fizzing, which lasted for several minutes, in imitation of the frothing of champagne. This behavior, I saw plainly, was not very pleasing to Monsieur Maillard; but that gentleman said nothing, and the conversation was resumed by a very lean little man in a big wig.

'And then there was an ignoramus,' said he, 'who mistook himself for a frog; which, by the way, he resembled in no little degree. I wish you could have seen him, sir,' – here the speaker addressed myself, – 'it would have done your heart good to see the natural airs that he put on. Sir, if that man was *not* a frog, I can only observe that it is a pity he was not. His croak thus – o-o-o-o-gh – o-o-o-o-gh! was the finest note in the world – B flat; and when he put his elbows upon the table thus – after taking a glass or two of wine – and distended his mouth, thus, and rolled up his eyes, thus, and winked them with excessive rapidity, thus, why then, sir, I take it upon myself to say, positively, that you would have been lost in admiration of the genius of the man.'

'I have no doubt of it,' I said.

'And then,' said somebody else, 'then there was Petit Gaillard, who thought himself a pinch of snuff, and was truly distressed because he could not take himself between his own finger and thumb.'

'And then there was Jules Desoulieres, who was a very singular genius, indeed, and went mad with the idea that he was a pumpkin. He persecuted the cook to make him up into pies – a thing which the cook indignantly refused to do. For my part, I am by no means sure that a pumpkin pie *à la Desoulières* would not have been very capital eating indeed!'

'You astonish me!' said I; and I looked inquisitively at Monsieur Maillard.

'Ha! ha! ha!' said that gentleman – 'he! he! he! – hi! hi! hi! – ho! ho! ho! – hu! hu! hu! – very good indeed! You must not be astonished, *mon ami*; our friend here is a wit – *a drôle* – you must not understand him to the letter.'

'And then,' said some other one of the party, – 'then there was Bouffon Le Grand – another extraordinary personage in his way. He grew deranged through love, and fancied himself possessed of two heads. One of these he maintained to be the head of Cicero; the other he imagined a composite one, being Demosthenes' from the top of the forehead to the mouth, and Lord Brougham's from the mouth to the chin. It is not impossible that he was wrong; but he would have convinced you of his being in the right; for he was a man of great eloquence. He had an absolute passion for oratory, and could not refrain from display. For example, he used to leap upon the dinner-table thus, and – and –'

Here a friend, at the side of the speaker, put a hand upon his shoulder and whispered a few words in his ear; upon which he ceased talking with great suddenness, and sank back within his chair.

'And then,' said the friend who had whispered, 'there was Boullard, the tee-totum. I call him the tee-totum because, in fact, he was seized with the droll, but not altogether irrational, crotchet, that he had been converted into a tee-totum. You would have roared with laughter to see him spin. He would turn round upon one heel by the hour, in this manner – so –'

Here the friend whom he had just interrupted by a whisper, performed an exactly similar office for himself.

'But then,' cried an old lady, at the top of her voice, 'your Monsieur Boullard was a madman, and a very silly madman at best; for who, allow me to ask you, ever heard of a human tee-totum? The thing is absurd. Madame Joyeuse was a more sensible person, as you know. She had a crotchet, but it was instinct with common sense, and gave pleasure to all who had the honor of her acquaintance. She found, upon mature deliberation, that, by some accident, she had been turned into a chicken-cock; but, as such, she behaved with propriety. She flapped her wings with prodigious effect – so – so – so – and, as for her crow, it was delicious! Cock-a-doodle-doo! – cock-a-doodle-doo! – cock-a-dodle-de-doo-doo-dooo-do-o-o-o-o-o-o!'

'Cock-a-doodle-doo! -cock-a-dodle-de-doo-doo-dooo-do-o-o-o-o-o-o!

'Madame Joyeuse, I will thank you to behave yourself!' here interrupted our host, very angrily. 'You can either conduct yourself as a lady should do, or you can quit the table forthwith – take your choice.'

The lady (whom I was much astonished to hear addressed as Madame Joyeuse, after the description of Madame Joyeuse she had just given) blushed up to the eyebrows, and seemed exceedingly abashed at the reproof. She hung down her head, and said not a syllable in reply. But another and younger lady resumed the theme. It was my beautiful girl of the little parlor.

'Oh, Madame Joyeuse *was* a fool!' she exclaimed, 'but there was really much sound sense, after all, in the opinion of Eugenie Salsafette. She was a very beautiful and painfully modest young lady, who thought the ordinary mode of habiliment indecent, and wished to dress herself, always, by getting outside instead of inside of her clothes. It is a thing very easily done, after all. You have only to do so – and then so – so – so – and then so – so – so – and then – '

'*Mon dieu*! Ma'm'selle Salsafette!' here cried a dozen voices at once. 'What are you about? – forbear! – that is sufficient! – we see, very plainly, how it is done! – hold! hold!' and several persons were already leaping from their seats to withhold Ma'm'selle Salsafette from putting herself upon a par with the Medicean Venus, when the point was very effectually and suddenly accomplished by a series of loud screams, or yells, from some portion of the main body of the *chateâu*.

My nerves were very much affected, indeed, by these yells; but the rest of the company I really pitied. I never saw any set of reasonable people so thoroughly frightened in my life. They all grew as pale as so many corpses, and, shrinking within their seats, sat quivering and gibbering with terror, and listening for a repetition of the sound. It came again – louder and seemingly nearer – and then a third time *very* loud, and then a fourth time with a vigor evidently diminished. At this apparent dying away of the noise, the spirits of the company were immediately regained, and all was life and anecdote as before. I now ventured to inquire the cause of the disturbance.

'A mere *bagatelle*,' said Monsieur Maillard. 'We are used to these things, and care really very little about them. The lunatics, every now and then, get up a howl in concert; one starting another, as is sometimes the case with a bevy of dogs at night. It occasionally happens, however, that the *concerto* yells are succeeded by a simultaneous effort at breaking loose; when, of course, some little danger is to be apprehended.'

'And how many have you in charge?'

'At present we have not more than ten, all together.'

'Principally females, I presume?'

'Oh, no – every one of them men, and stout fellows, too, I can tell you.'

'Indeed! I have always understood that the majority of lunatics were of the gentler sex.'

'It is generally so, but not always. Some time ago, there were about twenty-seven patients here; and, of that number, no less than eighteen were women; but lately, matters have changed very much, as you see.'

'Yes – have changed very much, as you see,' here interrupted the gentleman who had broken the shins of Ma'm'selle Laplace.

'Yes – have changed very much, as you see!' chimed in the whole company at once.

'Hold your tongues, every one of you!' said my host, in a great rage. Whereupon the whole company maintained a dead silence for nearly a minute. As for one lady, she obeyed Monsieur Maillard to the letter, and thrusting out her tongue, which was an excessively long one, held it very resignedly, with both hands, until the end of the entertainment.

'And this gentlewoman,' said I, to Monsieur Maillard, bending over and addressing him in a whisper – 'this good lady who has just spoken, and who gives us the cock-a-doodle-de-doo – she, I presume, is harmless – quite harmless, eh?'

'Harmless!' ejaculated he, in unfeigned surprise, 'why – why, what *can* you mean?'

'Only slightly touched?' said I, touching my head. 'I take it for granted that she is not particularly – not dangerously affected, eh?'

'*Mon dieu!* what *is* it you imagine? This lady, my particular old friend, Madame Joyeuse, is as absolutely sane as myself. She has her little eccentricities, to be sure – but then, you know, all old women – all *very* old women – are more or less eccentric!'

'To be sure,' said I, – 'to be sure – and then the rest of these ladies and gentlemen – '

'Are my friends and keepers,' interrupted Monsieur Maillard, drawing himself up with hauteur, – 'my very good friends and assistants.'

'What! all of them?' I asked, – 'the women and all?'

'Assuredly,' he said, – 'we could not do at all without the women; they are the best lunatic nurses in the world; they have a way of their own, you know; their bright eyes have a marvellous effect – something like the fascination of the snake, you know.'

'To be sure,' said I – 'to be sure! They behave a little odd, eh? – they are a little *queer*, eh? – don't you think so?'

'Odd! – queer! – why, do you *really* think so? We are not very prudish, to be sure, here in the South – do pretty much as we please – enjoy life, and all that sort of thing, you know – '

'To be sure,' said I, – 'to be sure.'

'And then, perhaps, this *Clos de Vougeôt* is a little heady, you know –

a little *strong* – you understand, eh?'

'To be sure,' said I, – 'to be sure. By the by, Monsieur, did I understand you to say that the system you have adopted, in place of the celebrated soothing system, was one of very rigorous severity?'

'By no means. Our confinement is necessarily close; but the treatment – the medical treatment, I mean – is rather agreeable to the patients than otherwise.'

'And the new system is one of your own invention?'

'Not altogether. Some portions of it are referable to Doctor Tarr, of whom you have, necessarily, heard; and, again, there are modifications in my plan which I am happy to acknowledge as belonging of right to the celebrated Fether, with whom, if I mistake not, you have the honor of an intimate acquaintance.'

'I am quite ashamed to confess,' I replied, 'that I have never even heard the names of either gentleman before.'

'Good heavens!' ejaculated my host, drawing back his chair abruptly, and uplifting his hands. 'I surely do not hear you aright! You did not intend to say, eh? that you had never *heard* either of the learned Doctor Tarr, or of the celebrated Professor Fether?'

'I am forced to acknowledge my ignorance,' I replied; 'but the truth should be held inviolate above all things. Nevertheless, I feel humbled to the dust, not to be acquainted with the works of these, no doubt, extraordinary men. I will seek out their writings forthwith, and peruse them with deliberate care. Monsieur Maillard, you have really – I must confess it – you have *really* – made me ashamed of myself!'

And this was the fact.

'Say no more, my good friend,' he said kindly, pressing my hand, – 'join me now in a glass of Sauterne.'

We drank. The company followed our example without stint. They chatted – they jested – they laughed – they perpetrated a thousand absurdities – the fiddles shrieked – the drum row-de-dowed – the trombones bellowed like so many brazen bulls of Phalaris – and the whole scene, growing gradually worse and worse, as the wines gained the ascendancy, became at length a sort of pandemonium *in petto*. In the meantime, Monsieur Maillard and myself, with some bottles of Sauterne and Vougeôt between us, continued our conversation at the top of the voice. A word spoken in an ordinary key stood no more chance of being heard than the voice of a fish from the bottom of Niagara Falls.

'And, sir,' said I, screaming in his ear, 'you mentioned something before dinner about the danger incurred in the old system of soothing.

How is that?'

'Yes,' he replied, 'there was, occasionally, very great danger indeed. There is no accounting for the caprices of madmen; and, in my opinion, as well as in that of Dr. Tarr and Professor Fether, it is *never* safe to permit them to run at large unattended. A lunatic may be 'soothed,' as it is called, for a time, but, in the end, he is very apt to become obstreperous. His cunning, too, is proverbial and great. If he has a project in view, he conceals his design with a marvellous wisdom; and the dexterity with which he counterfeits sanity, presents, to the metaphysician, one of the most singular problems in the study of mind. When a madman appears *thoroughly* sane, indeed, it is high time to put him in a strait-jacket.'

'But the *danger*, my dear sir, of which you were speaking – in your own experience – during your control of this house – have you had practical reason to think liberty hazardous in the case of a lunatic?'

'Here? – in my own experience? – why, I may say, yes. For example: – not *very* long ago, a singular circumstance occurred in this very house. The "soothing system," you know, was then in operation, and the patients were at large. They behaved remarkably well – especially so, – any one of sense might have known that some devilish scheme was brewing from that particular fact, that the fellows behaved so *remarkably* well. And, sure enough, one fine morning the keepers found themselves pinioned hand and foot, and thrown into the cells, where they were attended, as if *they* were the lunatics, by the lunatics themselves, who had usurped the offices of the keepers.'

'You don't tell me so! I never heard of anything so absurd in my life!'

'Fact – it all came to pass by means of a stupid fellow – a lunatic – who, by some means, had taken it into his head that he had invented a better system of government than any ever heard of before – of lunatic government, I mean. He wished to give his invention a trial, I suppose, and so he persuaded the rest of the patients to join him in a conspiracy for the overthrow of the reigning powers.'

'And he really succeeded?'

'No doubt of it. The keepers and kept were soon made to exchange places. Not that exactly either, for the madmen had been free, but the keepers were shut up in the cells forthwith, and treated, I am sorry to say, in a very cavalier manner.'

'But I presume a counter-revolution was soon effected. This condition of things could not have long existed. The country people in the neighborhood – visitors coming to see the establishment – would have given the alarm.'

'There you are out. The head rebel was too cunning for that. He admitted no visitors at all – with the exception, one day, of a very stupid-looking young gentleman of whom he had no reason to be afraid. He let him in to see the place – just by way of variety, – to have a little fun with him. As soon as he had gammoned him sufficiently, he let him out, and sent him about his business.'

'And *how* long, then, did the madmen reign?'

'Oh, a very long time, indeed – a month certainly – how much longer I can't precisely say. In the meantime, the lunatics had a jolly season of it – that you may swear. They doffed their own shabby clothes, and made free with the family wardrobe and jewels. The cellars of the *château* were well stocked with wine; and these madmen are just the devils that know how to drink it. They lived well, I can tell you.'

'And the treatment – what was the particular species of treatment which the leader of the rebels put into operation?'

'Why, as for that, a madman is not necessarily a fool, as I have already observed; and it is my honest opinion that his treatment was a much better treatment than that which it superseded. It was a very capital system indeed – simple – neat – no trouble at all – in fact it was delicious – it was –'

Here my host's observations were cut short by another series of yells, of the same character as those which had previously disconcerted us. This time, however, they seemed to proceed from persons rapidly approaching.

'Gracious heavens!' I ejaculated – 'the lunatics have most undoubtedly broken loose.'

'I very much fear it is so,' replied Monsieur Maillard, now becoming excessively pale. He had scarcely finished the sentence, before loud shouts and imprecations were heard beneath the windows; and, immediately afterward, it became evident that some persons outside were endeavoring to gain entrance into the room. The door was beaten with what appeared to be a sledge-hammer, and the shutters were wrenched and shaken with prodigious violence.

A scene of the most terrible confusion ensued. Monsieur Maillard, to my excessive astonishment, threw himself under the sideboard. I had expected more resolution at his hands. The members of the orchestra, who, for the last fifteen minutes, had been seemingly too much intoxicated to do duty, now sprang all at once to their feet and to their instruments, and, scrambling upon their table, broke out, with one accord, into, 'Yankee Doodle,' which they performed, if not exactly in tune, at least with an energy superhuman, during the whole of the uproar.

Meantime, upon the main dining-table, among the bottles and glasses, leaped the gentleman who, with such difficulty, had been restrained from leaping there before. As soon as he fairly settled himself, he commenced an oration, which, no doubt, was a very capital one, if it could only have been heard. At the same moment, the man with the tee-totum predilection, set himself to spinning around the apartment, with immense energy, and with arms outstretched at right angles with his body; so that he had all the air of a tee-totum in fact, and knocked everybody down that happened to get in his way. And now, too, hearing an incredible popping and fizzing of champagne, I discovered at length, that it proceeded from the person who performed the bottle of that delicate drink during dinner. And then, again, the frog-man croaked away as if the salvation of his soul depended upon every note that he uttered. And, in the midst of all this, the continuous braying of a donkey arose over all. As for my old friend, Madame Joyeuse, I really could have wept for the poor lady, she appeared so terribly perplexed. All she did, however, was to stand up in a corner, by the fireplace, and sing out incessantly at the top of her voice, 'Cock-a-doodle-de-dooooooh!'

And now came the climax – the catastrophe of the drama. As no resistance, beyond whooping and yelling and cock-a-doodling, was offered to the encroachments of the party without, the ten windows were very speedily, and almost simultaneously, broken in. But I shall never forget the emotions of wonder and horror with which I gazed, when, leaping through these windows, and down among us *pêle-mêle*, fighting, stamping, scratching, and howling, there rushed a perfect army of what I took to be chimpanzees, ourang-outangs, or big black baboons of the Cape of Good Hope.

I received a terrible beating – after which I rolled under a sofa and lay still. After lying there some fifteen minutes, however, during which time I listened with all my ears to what was going on in the room, I came to some satisfactory *dénouement* of this tragedy. Monsieur Maillard, it appeared, in giving me the account of the lunatic who had excited his fellows to rebellion, had been merely relating his own exploits. This gentleman had, indeed, some two or three years before, been the superintendent of the establishment; but grew crazy himself, and so became a patient. This fact was unknown to the travelling companion who introduced me. The keepers, ten in number, having been suddenly overpowered, were first well tarred, then carefully fea-thered, and then shut up in underground cells. They had been so im-prisoned for more than a month, during which period Monsieur Maillard had generously allowed them not only the tar and feathers (which constituted his 'system'), but some bread and abundance of water. The latter was pumped on them daily. At length, one escaping through a sewer, gave freedom to all the rest.

The 'soothing system,' with important modifications, has been resumed at the *château*; yet I cannot help agreeing with Monsieur Maillard, that his own 'treatment' was a very capital one of its kind. As he justly observed, it was 'simple – neat – and gave no trouble at all – not the least.'

I have only to add that, although I have searched every library in Europe for the works of Doctor *Tarr* and Professor *Fether*, I have, up to the present day, utterly failed in my endeavors to procure a copy.

DAMON RUNYON
(1884–1946)

Runyon was born in Kansas, and had a long career as a
journalist in America and Europe. His style, mimicking the
slang of pre-war Broadway, and remaining constantly in the
present tense, is quite individual. The world of Runyon is
peopled by such soft-centred tough guys as Harry the Horse,
Nathan Detroit and The Lemon Drop Kid. The following
two stories are from *Runyon on Broadway*.

Blood Pressure

IT is maybe eleven-thirty of a Wednesday night, and I am standing at
the corner of Forty-eighth Street and Seventh Avenue, thinking about
my blood pressure, which is a proposition I never before think much
about.

In fact, I never hear of my blood pressure before this Wednesday
afternoon when I go around to see Doc Brennan about my stomach,
and he puts a gag on my arm and tells me that my blood pressure is
higher than a cat's back, and the idea is for me to be careful about
what I eat, and to avoid excitement, or I may pop off all of a sudden
when I am least expecting it.

'A nervous man such as you with a blood pressure away up in the
paint cards must live quietly,' Doc Brennan says. 'Ten bucks, please,'
he says.

Well, I am standing there thinking it is not going to be so tough to
avoid excitement the way things are around this town right now, and
wishing I have my ten bucks back to bet it on Sun Beau in the fourth
race at Pimlico the next day, when all of a sudden I look up, and who is
in front of me but Rusty Charley.

Now if I have any idea Rusty Charley is coming my way, you can go
and bet all the coffee in Java I will be somewhere else at once, for
Rusty Charley is not a guy I wish to have any truck with whatever. In
fact, I wish no part of him. Furthermore, nobody else in this town
wishes to have any part of Rusty Charley, for he is a hard guy indeed.
In fact, there is no harder guy anywhere in the world. He is a big wide
guy with two large hard hands and a great deal of very bad disposition, and he thinks nothing of knocking people down and stepping on
their kissers if he feels like it.

109

In fact, this Rusty Charley is what is called a gorill, because he is known to often carry a gun in his pants pocket, and sometimes to shoot people down as dead as door-nails with it if he does not like the way they wear their hats – and Rusty Charley is very critical of hats. The chances are Rusty Charley shoots many a guy in this man's town, and those he does not shoot he sticks with his shiv – which is a knife – and the only reason he is not in jail is because he just gets out of it, and the law does not have time to think up something to put him back in again for.

Anyway, the first thing I know about Rusty Charley being in my neighbourhood is when I hear him saying: 'Well, well, well, here we are!'

Then he grabs me by the collar, so it is no use of me thinking of taking it on the lam away from there, although I greatly wish to do so.

'Hello, Rusty,' I say, very pleasant. 'What is the score?'

'Everything is about even,' Rusty says. 'I am glad to see you, because I am looking for company. I am over in Philadelphia for three days on business.'

'I hope and trust that you do all right for yourself in Philly, Rusty,' I say; but his news makes me very nervous, because I am a great hand for reading the papers and I have a pretty good idea what Rusty's business in Philly is. It is only the day before that I see a little item from Philly in the papers about how Gloomy Gus Smallwood, who is a very large operator in the alcohol business there, is guzzled right at his front door.

Of course, I do not know that Rusty Charley is the party who guzzles Gloomy Gus Smallwood, but Rusty Charley is in Philly when Gus is guzzled, and I can put two and two together as well as anybody. It is the same thing as if there is a bank robbery in Cleveland, Ohio, and Rusty Charley is in Cleveland, Ohio, or near there. So I am very nervous, and I figure it is a sure thing my blood pressure is going up every second.

'How much dough do you have on you?' Rusty says. 'I am plumb broke.'

'I do not have more than a couple of bobs, Rusty,' I say. 'I pay a doctor ten bucks to-day to find out my blood pressure is very bad. But of course you are welcome to what I have.'

'Well, a couple of bobs is no good to high-class guys like you and me,' Rusty says. 'Let us go to Nathan Detroit's crap game and win some money.'

Now, of course, I do not wish to go to Nathan Detroit's crap game;

and if I do wish to go there I do not wish to go with Rusty Charley, because a guy is sometimes judged by the company he keeps, especially around crap games, and Rusty Charley is apt to be considered bad company. Anyway, I do not have any dough to shoot craps with, and if I do have dough to shoot craps with, I will not shoot craps with it at all, but will bet it on Sun Beau, or maybe take it home and pay off some of the overhead around my joint, such as rent.

Furthermore, I remember what Doc Brennan tells me about avoiding excitement, and I know there is apt to be excitement around Nathan Detroit's crap game if Rusty Charley goes there, and maybe run my blood pressure up and cause me to pop off very unexpected. In fact, I already feel my blood jumping more than somewhat inside me, but naturally I am not going to give Rusty Charley any argument, so we go to Nathan Detroit's crap game.

This crap game is over a garage in Fifty-second Street this particular night, though sometimes it is over a restaurant in Forty-seventh Street, or in back of a cigar store in Forty-fourth Street. In fact, Nathan Detroit's crap game is apt to be anywhere, because it moves around every night, as there is no sense in a crap game staying in one spot until the coppers find out where it is.

So Nathan Detroit moves his crap game from spot to spot, and citizens wishing to do business with him have to ask where he is every night; and of course almost everybody on Broadway knows this, as Nathan Detroit has guys walking up and down, and around and about, telling the public his address, and giving out the password for the evening.

Well, Jack the Beefer is sitting in an automobile outside the garage in Fifty-second Street when Rusty Charley and I come along, and he says 'Kansas City,' very low, as we pass, this being the password for the evening; but we do not have to use any password whatever when we climb the stairs over the garage, because the minute Solid John, the doorman, peeks out through his peephole when we knock, and sees Rusty Charley with me, he opens up very quick indeed, and gives us a big castor-oil smile, for nobody in this town is keeping doors shut on Rusty Charley very long.

It is a very dirty room over the garage, and full of smoke, and the crap game is on an old pool table; and around the table, and packed in so close you cannot get a knitting-needle between any two guys with a mawl, are all the high shots in town, for there is plenty of money around at this time, and many citizens are very prosperous. Furthermore, I wish to say there are some very tough guys around the table, too, including guys who will shoot you in the head, or maybe the stomach, and think nothing whatever about the matter.

In fact, when I see such guys as Harry the Horse, from Brooklyn, and Sleepout Sam Levinsky, and Lone Louie, from Harlem, I know this is a bad place for my blood pressure, for these are very tough guys indeed, and are known as such to one and all in this town.

But there they are wedged up against the table with Nick the Greek, Big Nig, Grey John, Okay Okun, and many other high shots, and they all have big coarse G notes in their hands which they are tossing around back and forth as if these G notes are nothing but pieces of waste paper.

On the outside of the mob at the table are a lot of small operators who are trying to cram their fists in between the high shots now and then to get down a bet, and there are also guys present who are called Shylocks, because they will lend you dough when you go broke at the table, on watches or rings, or maybe cuff-links, at very good interest.

Well, as I say, there is no room at the table for as many as one more very thin guy when we walk into the joint, but Rusty Charley lets out a big hello as we enter, and the guys all look around, and the next minute there is space at the table big enough not only for Rusty Charley but for me, too. It really is quite magical the way there is suddenly room for us when there is no room whatever for anybody when we come in.

'Who is the gunner?' Rusty Charley asks, looking all around.

'Why, you are, Charley,' Big Nig, the stick man in the game, says very quick, handing Charley a pair of dice, although afterward I hear that his pal is right in the middle of a roll trying to make nine when we step up to the table. Everybody is very quiet, just looking at Charley. Nobody pays any attention to me, because I am known to one and all as a guy who is just around, and nobody figures me in on any part of Charley, although Harry the Horse looks at me once in a way that I know is no good for my blood pressure, or for anybody else's blood pressure as far as this goes.

Well, Charley takes the dice and turns to a little guy in a derby hat who is standing next to him scrooching back so Charley will not notice him, and Charley lifts the derby hat off the little guy's head, and rattles the dice in his hand and chucks them into the hat and goes 'Hah!' like crap shooters always do when they are rolling the dice. Then Charley peeks into the hat and says 'Ten,' although he does not let anybody else look in the hat, not even me, so nobody knows if Charley throws a ten, or what.

But, of course, nobody around is going to up and doubt that Rusty Charley throws a ten, because Charley may figure it is the same thing as calling him a liar, and Charley is such a guy as is apt to hate being called a liar.

Now Nathan Detroit's crap game is what is called a head-and-head game, although some guys call it a fading game, because the guys bet against each other rather than against the bank, or house. It is just the same kind of game as when two guys get together and start shooting craps against each other, and Nathan Detroit does not have to bother with a regular crap table and a layout such as they have in gambling houses. In fact, about all Nathan Detroit has to do with the game is to find a spot, furnish the dice and take his percentage, which is by no means bad.

In such a game as this there is no real action until a guy is out on a point, and then the guys around commence to bet he makes this point, or that he does not make this point, and the odds in any country in the world that a guy does not make a ten with a pair of dice before he rolls seven, is 2 to 1.

Well, when Charley says he rolls ten in the derby hat nobody opens their trap, and Charley looks all around the table, and all of a sudden he sees Jew Louie at one end, although Jew Louie seems to be trying to shrink himself up when Charley's eyes light on him.

'I will take the odds for five C's,' Charley says, 'and Louie, you get it' – meaning he is letting Louie bet him $1000 to $500 that he does not make his ten.

Now Jew Louie is a small operator at all times and more of a Shylock than he is a player, and the only reason he is up there against the table at all at this moment is because he moves up to lend Nick the Greek some dough; and ordinarily there is no more chance of Jew Louie betting a thousand to five hundred on any proposition whatever than there is of him giving his dough to the Salvation Army, which is no chance at all. It is a sure thing he will never think of betting a thousand to five hundred a guy will not make ten with the dice, and when Rusty Charley tells Louie he has such a bet, Louie starts trembling all over.

The others around the table do not say a word, and so Charley rattles the dice again in his duke, blows on them, and chucks them into the derby hat and says 'Hah!' But, of course, nobody can see in the derby hat except Charley, and he peeks in at the dice and says 'Five.' He rattles the dice once more and chucks them into the derby and says 'Hah!' and then after peeking into the hat at the dice he says

'Eight.' I am commencing to sweat for fear he may heave a seven in the hat and blow his bet, and I know Charley has no five C's to pay off with, although, of course, I also know Charley has no idea of paying off, no matter what he heaves.

On the next chuck, Charley yells 'Money!' – meaning he finally makes his ten, although nobody sees it but him; and he reaches out his hand to Jew Louie, and Jew Louie hands him a big fat G note, very, very slow. In all my life I never see a sadder-looking guy than Louie when he is parting with his dough. If Louie has any idea of asking Charley to let him see the dice in the hat to make sure about the ten, he does not speak about the matter, and as Charley does not seem to wish to show the ten around, nobody else says anything either, probably figuring Rusty Charley isn't a guy who is apt to let anybody question his word, especially over such a small matter as a ten.

'Well,' Charley says, putting Louie's G note in his pocket, 'I think this is enough for me to-night,' and he hands the derby hat back to the little guy who owns it and motions me to come on, which I am glad to do, as the silence in the joint is making my stomach go up and down inside me, and I know this is bad for my blood pressure. Nobody as much as opens his face from the time we go in until we start out, and you will be surprised how nervous it makes you to be in a big crowd with everybody dead still, especially when you figure it a spot that is liable to get hot any minute. It is only just as we get to the door that anybody speaks, and who is it but Jew Louie, who pipes up and says to Rusty Charley like this:

'Charley,' he says, 'do you make it the hard way?'

Well, everybody laughs, and we go on out, but I never hear myself whether Charley makes his ten with a six and a four, or with two fives – which is the hard way to make a ten with the dice – although I often wonder about the matter afterward.

I am hoping that I can now get away from Rusty Charley and go on home, because I can see he is the last guy in the world to have around a blood pressure, and, furthermore, that people may get the wrong idea of me if I stick around with him, but when I suggest going to Charley, he seems to be hurt.

'Why,' Charley says, 'you are a fine guy to be talking of quitting a pal just as we are starting out. You will certainly stay with me because I like company, and we will go down to Ikey the Pig's and play stuss. Ikey is an old friend of mine, and I owe him a complimentary play.'

Now, of course, I do not wish to go to Ikey the Pig's, because it is a place away downtown, and I do not wish to play stuss, because this is a game which I am never able to figure out myself, and, furthermore, I remember Doc Brennan says I ought to get a little sleep now and then; but I see no use in hurting Charley's feelings, especially as he is apt to do something drastic to me if I do not go.

So he calls a taxi, and we start downtown for Ikey the Pig's, and the jockey who is driving the short goes so fast that it makes my blood pressure go up a foot to a foot and a half from the way I feel inside, although Rusty Charley pays no attention to the speed. Finally I stick my head out the window and ask the jockey to please take it a little easy, as I wish to get where I am going all in one piece, but the guy only keeps busting along.

We are at the corner of Nineteenth and Broadway when all of a sudden Rusty Charley yells at the jockey to pull up a minute, which the guy does. Then Charley steps out of the cab and says to the jockey like this:

'When a customer asks you to take it easy, why do you not be nice and take it easy? Now see what you get.'

And Rusty Charley hauls off and clips the jockey a punch on the chin that knocks the poor guy right off the seat into the street, and then Charley climbs into the seat himself and away we go with Charley driving, leaving the guy stretched out as stiff as a board. Now Rusty Charley once drives a short for a living himself, until the coppers get an idea that he is not always delivering his customers to the right address, especially such as may happen to be drunk when he gets them, and he is a pretty fair driver, but he only looks one way, which is straight ahead.

Personally, I never wish to ride with Charley in a taxicab under any circumstances, especially if he is driving, because he certainly drives very fast. He pulls up a block from Ikey the Pig's, and says we will leave the short there until somebody finds it and turns it in, but just as we are walking away from the short up steps a copper in uniform and claims we cannot park the short in this spot without a driver.

Well, Rusty Charley just naturally hates to have coppers give him any advice, so what does he do but peek up and down the street to see if anybody is looking, and then haul off and clout the copper on the chin, knocking him bow-legged. I wish to say I never see a more accurate puncher than Rusty Charley, because he always connects with that old button. As the copper tumbles, Rusty Charley grabs me by the arm and starts me running up a side street, and after we go about a block we dodge into Ikey the Pig's.

It is what is called a stuss house, and many prominent citizens of

He hauls off and clouts the copper on the chin

the neighbourhood are present playing stuss. Nobody seems any too glad to see Rusty Charley, although Ikey the Pig lets on he is tickled half to death. This Ikey the Pig is a short fat-necked guy who will look very natural at New Year's, undressed, and with an apple in his mouth, but it seems he and Rusty Charley are really old-time friends, and think fairly well of each other in spots.

But I can see that Ikey the Pig is not so tickled when he finds Charley is there to gamble, although Charley flashes his G note at once, and says he does not mind losing a little dough to Ikey just for old time's sake. But I judge Ikey the Pig knows he is never going to handle Charley's G note, because Charley puts it back in his pocket and it never comes out again even though Charley gets off loser playing stuss right away.

Well, at five o'clock in the morning, Charley is stuck one hundred and thirty G's, which is plenty of money even when a guy is playing on his muscle, and of course Ikey the Pig knows there is no chance of getting one hundred and thirty cents off of Rusty Charley, let alone that many thousands. Everybody else is gone by this time and Ikey wishes to close up. He is willing to take Charley's marker for a million if necessary to get Charley out, but the trouble is in stuss a guy is entitled to get back a percentage of what he loses, and Ikey figures Charley is sure to wish this percentage even if he gives a marker, and the percentage will wreck Ikey's joint.

Furthermore, Rusty Charley says he will not quit loser under such circumstances because Ikey is his friend, so what happens but Ikey finally sends out and hires a cheater by the name of Dopey Goldberg, who takes to dealing the game and in no time he has Rusty Charley even by cheating in Rusty Charley's favour.

Personally, I do not pay much attention to the play, but grab myself a few winks of sleep in a chair in a corner, and the rest seems to help my blood pressure no little. In fact, I am not noticing my blood pressure at all when Rusty Charley and I get out of Ikey the Pig's, because I figure Charley will let me go home and I can go to bed. But although it is six o'clock, and coming on broad daylight when we leave Ikey's, Charley is still full of zing, and nothing will do him but we must go to a joint that is called the Bohemian Club.

Well, this idea starts my blood pressure going again, because the Bohemian Club is nothing but a deadfall where guys and dolls go when there is positively no other place in town open, and it is run by a guy by the name of Knife O'Halloran, who comes from down around Greenwich Village and is considered a very bad character. It is well known to one and all that a guy is apt to lose his life in Knife O'Halloran's any night, even if he does nothing more than drink Knife O'Halloran's liquor.

But Rusty Charley insists on going there, so naturally I go with him; and at first everything is very quiet and peaceful, except that a lot of guys and dolls in evening clothes, who wind up there after being in the night clubs all night, are yelling in one corner of the joint. Rusty Charley and Knife O'Halloran are having a drink together out of a bottle which Knife carries in his pocket, so as not to get it mixed up with the liquor he sells his customers, and are cutting up old touches of the time when they run with the Hudson Dusters together, when all of a sudden in comes four coppers in plain clothes.

Now these coppers are off duty and are meaning no harm to anybody, and are only wishing to have a dram or two before going home, and the chances are they will pay no attention to Rusty Charley if he minds his own business, although of course they know who he is very well indeed and will take great pleasure in putting the old sleeve on him if they only have a few charges against him, which they do not. So they do not give him a tumble. But if there is one thing Rusty Charley hates it is a copper, and he starts eyeing them from the moment they sit down at a table, and by and by I hear him say to Knife O'Halloran like this:

'Knife,' Charley says, 'what is the most beautiful sight in the world?'

'I do not know, Charley,' Knife says. 'What is the most beautiful sight in the world?'

'Four dead coppers in a row,' Charley says.

Well, at this I personally ease myself over toward the door, because I never wish to have any trouble with coppers and especially with four coppers, so I do not see everything that comes off. All I see is Rusty Charley grabbing at the big foot which one of the coppers kicks at him, and then everybody seems to go into a huddle, and the guys and dolls in evening dress start squawking, and my blood pressure goes up to maybe a million.

I get outside the door, but I do not go away at once as anybody with any sense will do, but stand there listening to what is going on inside, which seems to be nothing more than a loud noise like ker-bump, ker-bump, ker-bump. I am not afraid there will be any shooting, because as far as Rusty Charley is concerned he is too smart to shoot any coppers, which is the worst thing a guy can do in this town, and the coppers are not likely to start any blasting because they will not wish it to come out that they are in a joint such as the Bohemian Club off duty. So I figure they will all just take it out in pulling and hauling.

Finally the noise inside dies down, and by and by the door opens and out comes Rusty Charley, dusting himself off here and there with his hands and looking very much pleased indeed, and through the door before it flies shut again I catch a glimpse of a lot of guys stretched out on the floor. Furthermore, I can still hear guys and dolls hollering.

'Well, well,' Rusty Charley says, 'I am commencing to think you take the wind on me, and am just about to get mad at you, but here you are. Let us go away from this joint, because they are making so much noise inside you cannot hear yourself think. Let us go to my joint and make my old woman cook us up some breakfast, and then we can catch some sleep. A little ham and eggs will not be bad to take right now.'

Well, naturally ham and eggs are appealing to me no little at this time, but I do not care to go to Rusty Charley's joint. As far as I am personally concerned, I have enough of Rusty Charley to do me a long, long time, and I do not care to enter into his home life to any extent whatever, although to tell the truth I am somewhat surprised to learn he has any such life. I believe I do once hear that Rusty Charley marries one of the neighbours' children, and that he lives somewhere over on Tenth Avenue in the Forties, but nobody really knows much about this, and everybody figures if it is true his wife must lead a terrible dog's life.

But while I do not wish to go to Charley's joint, I cannot very well refuse a civil invitation to eat ham and eggs, especially as Charley is looking at me in a very much surprised way because I do not seem so glad, and I can see that it is not everyone that he invites to his joint. So I thank him, and say there is nothing I will enjoy more than ham and eggs such as his old woman will cook for us, and by and by we are walking along Tenth Avenue up around Forty-fifth Street.

It is still fairly early in the morning, and business guys are opening up their joints for the day, and little children are skipping along the sidewalks going to school and laughing tee-hee, and old dolls are shaking bedclothes and one thing and another out of the windows of the tenement houses, but when they spot Rusty Charley and me everybody becomes very quiet indeed, and I can see that Charley is greatly respected in his own neighbourhood. The business guys hurry into their joints, and the little children stop skipping and tee-heeing and go tip-toeing along, and the old dolls yank in their noodles, and a great quiet comes to the street. In fact, about all you can hear is the heels of Rusty Charley and me hitting on the sidewalk.

There is an ice wagon with a couple of horses hitched to it standing in front of a store, and when he sees the horses Rusty Charley seems to get a big idea. He stops and looks the horses over very carefully, although as far as I can see they are nothing but horses, and big and fat, and sleepy-looking horses, at that. Finally Rusty Charley says to me like this:

'When I am a young guy,' he says, 'I am a very good puncher with my right hand, and often I hit a horse on the skull with my fist and knock it down. I wonder,' he says, 'if I lose my punch. The last copper I hit back there gets up twice on me.'

Then he steps up to one of the ice-wagon horses and hauls off and biffs it right between the eyes with a right-hand smack that does not travel more than four inches, and down goes old Mister Horse to his knees looking very much surprised indeed. I see many a hard puncher

in my day including Dempsey when he really can punch, but I never
see a harder punch than Rusty Charley gives this horse.

Well, the ice-wagon driver comes busting out of the store all heated
up over what happens to his horse, but he cools out the minute he sees
Rusty Charley, and goes on back into the store leaving the horse still
taking a count, while Rusty Charley and I keep walking. Finally we
come to the entrance of a tenement house that Rusty Charley says is
where he lives, and in front of this house is a wop with a push-cart
loaded with fruit and vegetables and one thing and another, which
Rusty Charley tips over as we go into the house, leaving the wop yelling very loud, and maybe cussing us in wop for all I know. I am very
glad, personally, we finally get somewhere, because I can feel that my
blood pressure is getting worse every minute I am with Rusty
Charley.

We climb two flights of stairs, and then Charley opens a door and
we step into a room where there is a pretty little red-headed doll about
knee high to a flivver, who looks as if she may just get out of the hay,
because her red hair is flying around every which way on her head,
and her eyes seem still gummed up with sleep. At first I think she is a
very cute sight indeed, and then I see something in her eyes that tells
me this doll, whoever she is, is feeling very hostile to one and all.

'Hello, tootsie,' Rusty Charley says. 'How about some ham and
eggs for me and my pal here? We are all tired out going around and
about.'

Well, the little red-headed doll just looks at him without saying a
word. She is standing in the middle of the floor with one hand behind
her, and all of a sudden she brings this hand around, and what does
she have in it but a young baseball bat, such as kids play ball with, and
which cost maybe two bits; and the next thing I know I hear something go ker-bap, and I can see she smacks Rusty Charley on the side
of the noggin with the bat.

Naturally I am greatly horrified at this business, and figure Rusty
Charley will kill her at once, and then I will be in a jam for witnessing
the murder and will be held in jail several years like all witnesses to
anything in this man's town; but Rusty Charley only falls into a big
rocking-chair in a corner of the room and sits there with one hand to
his head, saying, 'Now hold on, tootsie,' and 'Wait a minute there,
honey.' I recollect hearing him say, 'We have company for breakfast,'
and then the little red-headed doll turns on me and gives me a look
such as I will always remember, although I smile at her very pleasant
and mention it is a nice morning.

120

Finally she says to me like this:

'So you are the trambo who keeps my husband out all night, are you, you trambo?' she says, and with this she starts for me, and I start for the door; and by this time my blood pressure is all out of whack, because I can see Mrs. Rusty Charley is excited more than somewhat. I get my hand on the knob and just then something hits me alongside the noggin, which I afterward figure must be the baseball bat, although I remember having a sneaking idea the roof caves in on me.

How I get the door open I do not know, because I am very dizzy in the head and my legs are wobbling, but when I think back over the situation I remember going down a lot of steps very fast, and by and by the fresh air strikes me, and I figure I am in the clear. But all of a sudden I feel another strange sensation back of my head and something goes plop against my noggin, and I figure at first that maybe my blood pressure runs up so high that it squirts out the top of my bean. Then I peek around over my shoulder just once to see that Mrs. Rusty Charley is standing beside the wop peddler's cart snatching fruit and vegetables of one kind and another off the cart and chucking them at me.

But what she hits me with back of the head is not an apple, or a peach, or a rutabaga, or a cabbage, or even a casaba melon, but a brickbat that the wop has on his cart to weight down the paper sacks in which he sells his goods. It is this brickbat which makes a lump on the back of my head so big that Doc Brennan thinks it is a tumour when I go to him the next day about my stomach, and I never tell him any different.

'But,' Doc Brennan says, when he takes my blood pressure again, 'your pressure is down below normal now, and as far as it is concerned you are in no danger whatever. It only goes to show what just a little bit of quiet living will do for a guy,' Doc Brennan says. 'Ten bucks, please,' he says.

Romance in the Roaring Forties

ONLY a rank sucker will think of taking two peeks at Dave the Dude's doll, because while Dave may stand for the first peek, figuring it is a mistake, it is a sure thing he will get sored up at the second peek, and Dave the Dude is certainly not a man to have sored up at you.

But this Waldo Winchester is one hundred per cent. sucker, which is why he takes quite a number of peeks at Dave's doll. And what is more, she takes quite a number of peeks right back at him. And there you are. When a guy and a doll get to taking peeks back and forth at each other, why, there you are indeed.

This Waldo Winchester is a nice-looking young guy who writes pieces about Broadway for the *Morning Item*. He writes about the goings-on in night clubs, such as fights, and one thing and another, and also about who is running around with who, including guys and dolls.

Sometimes this is very embarrassing to people who may be married and are running around with people who are not married, but of course Waldo Winchester cannot be expected to ask one and all for their marriage certificates before he writes his pieces for the paper.

The chances are if Waldo Winchester knows Miss Billy Perry is Dave the Dude's doll, he will never take more than his first peek at her, but nobody tips him off until his second or third peek, and by this time Miss Billy Perry is taking her peeks back at him and Waldo Winchester is hooked.

In fact, he is plumb gone, and being a sucker, like I tell you, he does not care whose doll she is. Personally, I do not blame him much, for Miss Billy Perry is worth a few peeks, especially when she is out on the floor of Miss Missouri Martin's Sixteen Hundred Club doing her tap dance. Still, I do not think the best tap-dancer that ever lives can make me take two peeks at her if I know she is Dave the Dude's doll, for Dave somehow thinks more than somewhat of his dolls.

He especially thinks plenty of Miss Billy Perry, and sends her fur coats, and diamond rings, and one thing and another, which she sends back to him at once, because it seems she does not take presents from guys. This is considered most surprising all along Broadway, but people figure the chances are she has some other angle.

Anyway, this does not keep Dave the Dude from liking her just the same, and so she is considered his doll by one and all, and is respected accordingly until this Waldo Winchester comes along.

It happens that he comes along while Dave the Dude is off in the Modoc on a little run down to the Bahamas to get some goods for his business, such as Scotch and champagne, and by the time Dave gets back Miss Billy Perry and Waldo Winchester are at the stage where they sit in corners between her numbers and hold hands.

Of course nobody tells Dave the Dude about this, because they do not wish to get him excited. Not even Miss Missouri Martin tells him, which is most unusual because Miss Missouri Martin, who is sometimes called 'Mizzoo' for short, tells everything she knows as soon as she knows it, which is very often before it happens.

You see, the idea is when Dave the Dude is excited he may blow somebody's brains out, and the chances are it will be nobody's brains but Waldo Winchester's, although some claim that Waldo Winchester has no brains or he will not be hanging around Dave the Dude's doll.

I know Dave is very, very fond of Miss Billy Perry, because I hear him talk to her several times, and he is most polite to her and never gets out of line in her company by using cuss words, or anything like this. Furthermore, one night when One-eyed Solly Abrahams is a little stewed up he refers to Miss Billy Perry as a broad, meaning no harm whatever, for this is the way many of the boys speak of the dolls.

But right away Dave the Dude reaches across the table and bops One-eyed Solly right in the mouth, so everybody knows from then on that Dave thinks well of Miss Billy Perry. Of course Dave is always thinking fairly well of some doll as far as this goes, but it is seldom he gets to bopping guys in the mouth over them.

Well, one night what happens but Dave the Dude walks into the Sixteen Hundred Club, and there in the entrance, what does he see but this Waldo Winchester and Miss Billy Perry kissing each other

123

back and forth friendly. Right away Dave reaches for the old equaliser to shoot Waldo Winchester, but it seems Dave does not happen to have the old equaliser with him, not expecting to have to shoot anybody this particular evening.

So Dave the Dude walks over and, as Waldo Winchester hears him coming and lets go his strangle-hold on Miss Billy Perry, Dave nails him with a big right hand on the chin. I will say for Dave the Dude that he is a fair puncher with his right hand, though his left is not so good, and he knocks Waldo Winchester bow-legged. In fact, Waldo folds right up on the floor.

Well, Miss Billy Perry lets out a screech you can hear clear to the Battery and runs over to where Waldo Winchester lights, and falls on top of him squalling very loud. All anybody can make out of what she says is that Dave the Dude is a big bum, although Dave is not so big, at that, and that she loves Waldo Winchester.

Dave walks over and starts to give Waldo Winchester the leather, which is considered customary in such cases, but he seems to change his mind, and instead of booting Waldo around, Dave turns and walks out of the joint looking very black and mad, and the next anybody hears of him he is over in the Chicken Club doing plenty of drinking.

This is regarded as a very bad sign indeed, because while everybody goes to the Chicken Club now and then to give Tony Bertazzola, the owner, a friendly play, very few people care to do any drinking there, because Tony's liquor is not meant for anybody to drink except the customers.

Well, Miss Billy Perry gets Waldo Winchester on his pegs again, and wipes his chin off with her handkerchief, and by and by he is all okay except for a big lump on his chin. And all the time she is telling Waldo Winchester what a big bum Dave the Dude is, although afterwards Miss Missouri Martin gets hold of Miss Billy Perry and puts the blast on her plenty for chasing a two-handed spender such as Dave the Dude out of the joint.

'You are nothing but a little sap,' Miss Missouri Martin tells Miss Billy Perry. 'You cannot get the right time off this newspaper guy, while everybody knows Dave the Dude is a very fast man with a dollar.'

'But I love Mr. Winchester,' says Miss Billy Perry. 'He is so romantic. He is not a bootlegger and a gunman like Dave the Dude. He puts lovely pieces in the paper about me, and he is a gentleman at all times.'

Now of course Miss Missouri Martin is not in a position to argue about gentlemen, because she meets very few in the Sixteen Hundred Club and anyway, she does not wish to make Waldo Winchester mad as he is apt to turn around and put pieces in his paper that will be a knock to the joint, so she lets the matter drop.

Miss Billy Perry and Waldo Winchester go on holding hands between her numbers, and maybe kissing each other now and then, as young people are liable to do, and Dave the Dude plays the chill for the Sixteen Hundred Club and everything seems to be all right. Naturally we are all very glad there is no more trouble over the proposition, because the best Dave can get is the worst of it in a jam with a newspaper guy.

Personally, I figure Dave will soon find himself another doll and forget all about Miss Billy Perry, because now that I take another peek at her, I can see where she is just about the same as any other tap-dancer, except that she is redheaded. Tap-dancers are generally blackheads, but I do not know why.

Moosh, the doorman at the Sixteen Hundred Club, tells me Miss Missouri Martin keeps plugging for Dave the Dude with Miss Billy Perry in a quiet way, because he says he hears Miss Missouri Martin make the following crack one night to her: 'Well, I do not see any Simple Simon on your lean and linger.'

This is Miss Missouri Martin's way of saying she sees no diamond on Miss Billy Perry's finger, for Miss Missouri Martin is an old experienced doll, who figures if a guy loves a doll he will prove it with diamonds. Miss Missouri Martin has many diamonds herself, though how any guy can ever get himself heated up enough about Miss Missouri Martin to give her diamonds is more than I can see.

I am not a guy who goes around much, so I do not see Dave the Dude for a couple of weeks, but late one Sunday afternoon little Johnny McGowan, who is one of Dave's men, comes and says to me like this: 'What do you think? Dave grabs the scribe a little while ago and is taking him out for an airing!'

Well, Johnny is so excited it is some time before I can get him cooled out enough to explain. It seems that Dave the Dude gets his biggest car out of the garage and sends his driver, Wop Joe, over to the *Item* office where Waldo Winchester works, with a message that Miss Billy Perry wishes to see Waldo right away at Miss Missouri Martin's apartment on Fifty-ninth Street.

Of course this message is nothing but the phonus bolonus, but Waldo drops in for it and gets in the car. Then Wop Joe drives him up to Miss Missouri Martin's apartment, and who gets in the car there but Dave the Dude. And away they go.

Now this is very bad news indeed, because when Dave the Dude takes a guy out for an airing the guy very often does not come back. What happens to him I never ask, because the best a guy can get by asking questions in this man's town is a bust in the nose.

But I am much worried over this proposition, because I like Dave the Dude, and I know that taking a newspaper guy like Waldo Winchester out for an airing is apt to cause talk, especially if he does not come back. The other guys that Dave the Dude takes out for airings do not mean much in particular, but here is a guy who may produce trouble, even if he is a sucker, on account of being connected with a newspaper.

I know enough about newspapers to know that by and by the editor or somebody will be around wishing to know where Waldo Winchester's pieces about Broadway are, and if there are no pieces from Waldo Winchester, the editor will wish to know why. Finally it will get around to where other people will wish to know, and after a while many people will be running around saying: 'Where is Waldo Winchester?'

And if enough people in this town get to running around saying where is So-and-so, it becomes a great mystery and the newspapers hop on the cops and the cops hop on everybody, and by and by there is so much heat in town that it is no place for a guy to be.

But what is to be done about this situation I do not know. Personally, it strikes me as very bad indeed, and while Johnny goes away to do a little telephoning, I am trying to think up some place to go where people will see me, and remember afterwards that I am there in case it is necessary for them to remember.

Finally Johnny comes back, very excited, and says: 'Hey, the Dude is up at the Woodcock Inn on the Pelham Parkway, and he is sending out the word for one and all to come at once. Good Time Charley Bernstein just gets the wire and tells me. Something is doing. The rest of the mob are on their way, so let us be moving.'

But here is an invitation which does not strike me as a good thing at all. The way I look at it, Dave the Dude is no company for a guy like me at this time. The chances are he either does something to Waldo Winchester already, or is getting ready to do something to him which I wish no part of.

Personally, I have nothing against newspaper guys, not even the ones who write pieces about Broadway. If Dave the Dude wishes to do something to Waldo Winchester, all right, but what is the sense of

126

bringing outsiders into it? But the next thing I know, I am in Johnny McGowan's roadster, and he is zipping along very fast indeed, paying practically no attention to traffic lights or anything else.

As we go busting out the Concourse, I get to thinking the situation over, and I figure that Dave the Dude probably keeps thinking about Miss Billy Perry, and drinking liquor such as they sell in the Chicken Club, until finally he blows his topper. The way I look at it, only a guy who is off his nut will think of taking a newspaper guy out for an airing over a doll, when dolls are a dime a dozen in this man's town.

Still, I remember reading in the papers about a lot of different guys who are considered very sensible until they get tangled up with a doll, and maybe loving her, and the first thing anybody knows they hop out of windows, or shoot themselves, or somebody else, and I can see where even a guy like Dave the Dude may go daffy over a doll.

I can see that little Johnny McGowan is worried, too, but he does not say much, and we pull up in front of the Woodcock Inn in no time whatever, to find a lot of other cars there ahead of us, some of which I recognise as belonging to different parties.

The Woodcock Inn is what is called a road house, and is run by Big Nig Skolsky, a very nice man indeed, and a friend of everybody's. It stands back a piece off the Pelham Parkway and is a very pleasant place to go to, what with Nig having a good band and a floor show with a lot of fair-looking dolls, and everything else a man can wish for a good time. It gets a nice play from nice people, although Nig's liquor is nothing extra.

Personally, I never go there much, because I do not care for road houses, but it is a great spot for Dave the Dude when he is pitching parties, or even when he is only drinking single-handed. There is a lot of racket in the joint as we drive up, and who comes out to meet us but Dave the Dude himself with a big hello. His face is very red, and he seems heated up no little, but he does not look like a guy who is meaning any harm to anybody, especially a newspaper guy.

'Come in, guys!' Dave the Dude yells. 'Come right in!'

So we go in, and the place is full of people sitting at tables, or out on the floor dancing, and I see Miss Missouri Martin with all her diamonds hanging from her in different places, and Good Time Charley Bernstein, and Feet Samuels, and Tony Bertazzola, and Skeets Boliver, and Nick the Greek, and Rochester Red, and a lot of other guys and dolls from around and about.

In fact, it looks as if everybody from all the joints on Broadway are present, including Miss Billy Perry, who is all dressed up in white and

127

is lugging a big bundle of orchids and so forth, and who is giggling and smiling and shaking hands and going on generally. And finally I see Waldo Winchester, the scribe, sitting at a ringside table all by himself, but there is nothing wrong with him as far as I can see. I mean, he seems to be all in one piece so far.

'Dave,' I say to Dave the Dude, very quiet, 'what is coming off here? You know a guy cannot be too careful what he does around this town, and I will hate to see you tangled up in anything right now.'

'Why,' Dave says, 'what are you talking about? Nothing is coming off here but a wedding, and it is going to be the best wedding anybody on Broadway ever sees. We are waiting for the preacher now.'

'You mean somebody is going to be married?' I ask, being now somewhat confused.

'Certainly,' Dave the Dude says. 'What do you think? What is the idea of a wedding, anyway?'

'Who is going to be married?' I ask.

'Nobody but Billy and the scribe,' Dave says. 'This is the greatest thing I ever do in my life. I run into Billy the other night and she is crying her eyes out because she loves this scribe and wishes to marry him, but it seems the scribe has nothing he can use for money. So I tell Billy to leave it to me, because you know I love her myself so much I wish to see her happy at all times, even if she has to marry to be that way.

'So I frame this wedding party, and after they are married I am going to stake them to a few G's so they can get a good running start,' Dave says. 'But I do not tell the scribe and I do not let Billy tell him as I wish it to be a big surprise to him. I kidnap him this afternoon and bring him out here and he is scared half to death thinking I am going to scrag him.

'In fact,' Dave says. 'I never see a guy so scared. He is still so scared nothing seems to cheer him up. Go over and tell him to shake himself together, because nothing but happiness for him is coming off here.'

Well, I wish to say I am greatly relieved to think that Dave intends doing nothing worse to Waldo Winchester than getting him married up, so I go over to where Waldo is sitting. He certainly looks somewhat alarmed. He is all in a huddle with himself, and he has what you call a vacant stare in his eyes. I can see that he is indeed frightened, so I give him a jolly slap on the back and I say: 'Congratulations, pal! Cheer up, the worst is yet to come!'

'You bet it is,' Waldo Winchester says, his voice so solemn I am greatly surprised.

'You are a fine-looking bridegroom,' I say. 'You look as if you are at a funeral instead of a wedding. Why do you not laugh ha-ha, and maybe take a dram or two and go to cutting up some?'

'Mister,' says Waldo Winchester, 'my wife is not going to care for me getting married to Miss Billy Perry.'

'Your wife?' I say, much astonished. 'What is this you are speaking of? How can you have any wife except Miss Billy Perry? This is great foolishness.'

'I know,' Waldo says, very sad. 'I know. But I got a wife just the same, and she is going to be very nervous when she hears about this. My wife is very strict with me. My wife does not allow me to go around marrying people. My wife is Lola Sapola, of the Rolling Sapolas, the acrobats, and I am married to her for five years. She is the strong lady who juggles the other four people in the act. My wife just gets back from a year's tour of the Interstate time, and she is at the Marx Hotel right this minute. I am upset by this proposition.'

'Does Miss Billy Perry know about this wife?' I ask.

'No,' he says. 'No. She thinks I am single-o.'

'But why do you not tell Dave the Dude you are already married when he brings you out here to marry you off to Miss Billy Perry?' I ask. 'It seems to me a newspaper guy must know it is against the law for a guy to marry several different dolls unless he is a Turk, or some such.'

'Well,' Waldo says, 'if I tell Dave the Dude I am married after taking his doll away from him, I am quite sure Dave will be very much excited, and maybe do something harmful to my health.'

Now there is much in what the guy says, to be sure. I am inclined to think, myself, that Dave will be somewhat disturbed when he learns of this situation, especially when Miss Billy Perry starts in being unhappy about it. But what is to be done I do not know, except maybe to let the wedding go on, and then when Waldo is out of reach of Dave, to put in a claim that he is insane, and that the marriage does not count. It is a sure thing I do not wish to be around when Dave the Dude hears Waldo is already married.

I am thinking that maybe I better take it on the lam out of there, when there is a great row at the door and I hear Dave the Dude yelling that the preacher arrives. He is a very nice-looking preacher, at that, though he seems somewhat surprised by the goings-on, especially when Miss Missouri Martin steps up and takes charge of him. Miss Missouri Martin tells him she is fond of preachers, and is quite used to them, because she is twice married by preachers, and twice by justices

129

of the peace, and once by a ship's captain at sea.

By this time one and all present, except maybe myself and Waldo Winchester, and the preacher and maybe Miss Billy Perry, are somewhat corned. Waldo is still sitting at his table looking very sad and saying 'Yes' and 'No' to Miss Billy Perry whenever she skips past him, for Miss Billy Perry is too much pleasured up with happiness to stay long in one spot.

Dave the Dude is more corned than anybody else, because he has two or three days' running start on everybody. And when Dave the Dude is corned I wish to say that he is a very unreliable guy as to temper, and he is apt to explode right in your face any minute. But he seems to be getting a great bang out of the doings.

Well, by and by Nig Skolsky has the dance floor cleared, and then he moves out on the floor a sort of arch of very beautiful flowers. The idea seems to be that Miss Billy Perry and Waldo Winchester are to be married under this arch. I can see that Dave the Dude must put in several days planning this whole proposition, and it must cost him plenty of the old do-re-mi, especially as I see him showing Miss Missouri Martin a diamond ring as big as a cough drop.

'It is for the bride,' Dave the Dude says. 'The poor loogan she is marrying will never have enough dough to buy her such a rock, and she always wishes a big one. I get it off a guy who brings it in from Los Angeles. I am going to give the bride away myself in person, so how do I act, Mizzoo? I want Billy to have everything according to the book.'

Well, while Miss Missouri Martin is trying to remember back to one of her weddings to tell him, I take another peek at Waldo Winchester to see how he is making out. I once see two guys go to the old warm squativoo up in Sing Sing, and I wish to say both are laughing heartily compared to Waldo Winchester at this moment.

Miss Billy Perry is sitting with him and the orchestra leader is calling his men dirty names because none of them can think of how 'Oh, Promise Me' goes, when Dave the Dude yells: 'Well, we are all set! Let the happy couple step forward!'

Miss Billy Perry bounces up and grabs Waldo Winchester by the arm and pulls him up out of his chair. After a peek at his face I am willing to lay 6 to 5 he does not make the arch. But he finally gets there with everybody laughing and clapping their hands, and the preacher comes forward, and Dave the Dude looks happier than I ever see him look before in his life as they all get together under the arch of flowers.

Well, all of a sudden there is a terrible racket at the front door of the Woodcock Inn, with some doll doing a lot of hollering in a deep voice

'Let the happy couple step forward!'

that sounds like a man's, and naturally everybody turns and looks
that way. The doorman, a guy by the name of Slugsy Sachs, who is a
very hard man indeed, seems to be trying to keep somebody out, but
pretty soon there is a heavy bump and Slugsy Sachs falls down, and in
comes a doll about four feet high and five feet wide.

In fact, I never see such a wide doll. She looks all hammered down.
Her face is almost as wide as her shoulders, and makes me think of a
great big full moon. She comes in bounding-like, and I can see that she
is all churned up about something. As she bounces in, I hear a gurgle,
and I look around to see Waldo Winchester slumping down to the
floor, almost dragging Miss Billy Perry with him.

Well, the wide doll walks right up to the bunch under the arch and
says in a large bass voice: 'Which one is Dave the Dude?'

'I am Dave the Dude,' says Dave the Dude, stepping up. 'What do
you mean by busting in here like a walrus and gumming up our wedding?'

131

'So you are the guy who kidnaps my ever-loving husband to marry him off to this little red-headed pancake here, are you?' the wide doll says, looking at Dave the Dude, but pointing at Miss Billy Perry.

Well now, calling Miss Billy Perry a pancake to Dave the Dude is a very serious proposition, and Dave the Dude gets very angry. He is usually rather polite to dolls, but you can see he does not care for the wide doll's manner whatever.

'Say, listen here,' Dave the Dude says, 'you better take a walk before somebody clips you. You must be drunk,' he says. 'Or daffy,' he says. 'What are you talking about, anyway?'

'You will see what I am talking about,' the wide doll yells. 'The guy on the floor there is my lawful husband. You probably frighten him to death, the poor dear. You kidnap him to marry this red-headed thing, and I am going to get you arrested as sure as my name is Lola Sapola, you simple-looking tramp!'

Naturally, everybody is greatly horrified at a doll using such language to Dave the Dude, because Dave is known to shoot guys for much less, but instead of doing something to the wide doll at once, Dave says: 'What is this talk I hear? Who is married to who? Get out of here!' Dave says, grabbing the wide doll's arm.

Well, she makes out as if she is going to slap Dave in the face with her left hand, and Dave naturally pulls his kisser out of the way. But instead of doing anything with her left, Lola Sapola suddenly drives her right fist smack-dab into Dave the Dude's stomach, which naturally comes forward as his face goes back.

I wish to say I see many a body punch delivered in my life, but I never see a prettier one than this. What is more, Lola Sapola steps in with the punch, so there is plenty on it.

Now a guy who eats and drinks like Dave the Dude does cannot take them so good in the stomach, so Dave goes 'oof,' and sits down very hard on the dance floor, and as he is sitting there he is fumbling in his pants pocket for the old equaliser, so everybody around tears for cover except Lola Sapola, and Miss Billy Perry, and Waldo Winchester.

But before he can get his pistol out, Lola Sapola reaches down and grabs Dave by the collar and hoists him to his feet. She lets go her hold on him, leaving Dave standing on his pins, but teetering around somewhat, and then she drives her right hand to Dave's stomach a second time.

The punch drops Dave again, and Lola steps up to him as if she is going to give him the foot. But she only gathers up Waldo Winchester from off the floor and slings him across her shoulder like he is a sack of oats, and starts for the door. Dave the Dude sits up on the floor again and by this time he has the old equaliser in his dùke.

'Only for me being a gentleman I will fill you full of slugs,' he yells.

Lola Sapola never even looks back, because by this time she is petting Waldo Winchester's head and calling him loving names and saying what a shame it is for bad characters like Dave the Dude to be abusing her precious one. It all sounds to me as if Lola Sapola thinks well of Waldo Winchester.

Well, after she gets out of sight, Dave the Dude gets up off the floor and stands there looking at Miss Billy Perry, who is out to break all crying records. The rest of us come out from under cover, including the preacher, and we are wondering how mad Dave the Dude is going to be about the wedding being ruined. But Dave the Dude seems only disappointed and sad.

'Billy,' he says to Miss Billy Perry, 'I am mighty sorry you do not get your wedding. All I wish for is your happiness, but I do not believe you can ever be happy with this scribe if he also has to have his lion tamer around. As Cupid I am a total bust. This is the only nice thing I ever try to do in my whole life, and it is too bad it does not come off. Maybe if you wait until he can drown her, or something –'

'Dave,' says Miss Billy Perry, dropping so many tears that she seems to finally wash herself right into Dave the Dude's arms, 'I will never, never be happy with such a guy as Waldo Winchester. I can see now you are the only man for me.'

'Well, well, well,' Dave the Dude says, cheering right up. 'Where is the preacher? Bring on the preacher and let us have our wedding anyway.'

I see Mr. and Mrs. Dave the Dude the other day, and they seem very happy. But you never can tell about married people, so of course I am never going to let on to Dave the Dude that I am the one who telephones Lola Sapola at the Marx Hotel, because maybe I do not do Dave any too much of a favour, at that.

SAKI (HECTOR HUGH MUNRO)
(1870–1916)

Saki was born in Burma, son of the Inspector General of the Burma Police. He was educated in England, and after a short spell in the Military Police back in Burma, settled in London to pursue a career as a writer. He published a number of volumes of short stories, all characterized by a witty, urbane style and biting satiric edge.

Saki was killed in France in 1916 while serving in the Royal Fusiliers. The name Saki was taken from the Rubáiyát of Omar Khayyám.

The Lost Sanjak

THE prison Chaplain entered the condemned's cell for the last time, to give such consolation as he might.

'The only consolation I crave for,' said the condemned, 'is to tell my story in its entirety to some one who will at least give it a respectful hearing.'

'We must not be too long over it,' said the Chaplain, looking at his watch.

The condemned repressed a shiver and commenced.

'Most people will be of opinion that I am paying the penalty of my own violent deeds. In reality I am a victim to a lack of specialization in my education and character.'

'Lack of specialization!' said the Chaplain.

'Yes. If I had been known as one of the few men in England familiar with the fauna of the Outer Hebrides, or able to repeat stanzas of Camoëns' poetry in the original, I should have had no difficulty in proving my identity in the crisis when my identity became a matter of life and death for me. But my education was merely a moderately good one, and my temperament was of the general order that avoids specialization. I know a little in a general way about gardening and history and old masters, but I could never tell you off-hand whether 'Stella van der Loopen' was a chrysanthemum or a heroine of the American War of Independence, or something by Romney in the Louvre.'

The Chaplain shifted uneasily in his seat. Now that the alternatives had been suggested they all seemed dreadfully possible.

'I fell in love, or thought I did, with the local doctor's wife,' con-

134

tinued the condemned. 'Why I should have done so, I cannot say, for I do not remember that she possessed any particular attractions of mind or body. On looking back at past events it seems to me that she must have been distinctly ordinary, but I suppose the doctor had fallen in love with her once, and what man has done man can do. She appeared to be pleased with the attentions which I paid her, and to that extent I suppose I might say she encouraged me, but I think she was honestly unaware that I meant anything more than a little neighbourly interest. When one is face to face with Death one wishes to be just.'

The Chaplain murmured approval. 'At any rate, she was genuinely horrified when I took advantage of the doctor's absence one evening to declare what I believed to be my passion. She begged me to pass out of her life, and I could scarcely do otherwise than agree, though I hadn't the dimmest idea of how it was to be done. In novels and plays I knew it was a regular occurrence, and if you mistook a lady's sentiments or intentions you went off to India and did things on the frontier as a matter of course. As I stumbled along the doctor's carriage-drive I had no very clear idea as to what my line of action was to be, but I had a vague feeling that I must look at the *Times* Atlas before going to bed. Then, on the dark and lonely highway, I came suddenly on a dead body.'

The Chaplain's interest in the story visibly quickened.

'Judging by the clothes it wore the corpse was that of a Salvation Army captain. Some shocking accident seemed to have struck him down, and the head was crushed and battered out of all human semblance. Probably, I thought, a motor-car fatality; and then, with a sudden overmastering insistence came another thought, that here was a remarkable opportunity for losing my identity and passing out of the life of the doctor's wife for ever. No tiresome and risky voyage to distant lands, but a mere exchange of clothes and identity with the unknown victim of an unwitnessed accident. With considerable difficulty I undressed the corpse, and clothed it anew in my own garments. Any one who has valeted a dead Salvation Army captain in an uncertain light will appreciate the difficulty. With the idea, presumably, of inducing the doctor's wife to leave her husband's roof-tree for some habitation which would be run at my expense, I had crammed my pockets with a store of banknotes, which represented a good deal of my immediate worldly wealth. When, therefore, I stole away into the world in the guise of a nameless Salvationist, I was not without resources which would easily support so humble a rôle for a con-

135

siderable period. I tramped to a neighbouring market-town, and, late as the hour was, the production of a few shillings procured me supper and a night's lodging in a cheap coffee-house. The next day I started forth on an aimless course of wandering from one small town to another. I was already somewhat disgusted with the upshot of my sudden freak; in a few hours' time I was considerably more so. In the contents-bill of a local news sheet I read the announcement of my own murder at the hands of some person unknown; on buying a copy of the paper for a detailed account of the tragedy, which at first had aroused in me a certain grim amusement, I found that the deed was ascribed to a wandering Salvationist of doubtful antecedents, who had been seen lurking in the roadway near the scene of the crime. I was no longer amused. The matter promised to be embarrassing. What I had mistaken for a motor accident was evidently a case of savage assault and murder, and, until the real culprit was found, I should have much difficulty in explaining my intrusion into the affair. Of course I could establish my own identity; but how, without disagreeably involving the doctor's wife, could I give any adequate reason for changing clothes with the murdered man? While my brain worked feverishly at this problem, I subconsciously obeyed a secondary instinct – to get as far away as possible from the scene of the crime, and to get rid at all costs of my incriminating uniform. There I found a difficulty. I tried two or three obscure clothes shops, but my entrance invariably aroused an attitude of hostile suspicion in the proprietors, and on one excuse or another they avoided serving me with the now ardently desired change of clothing. The uniform that I had so thoughtlessly donned seemed as difficult to get out of as the fatal shirt of – You know, I forget the creature's name.'

'Yes, yes,' said the Chaplain hurriedly. 'Go on with your story.'

'Somehow, until I could get out of those compromising garments, I felt it would not be safe to surrender myself to the police. The thing that puzzled me was why no attempt was made to arrest me, since there was no question as to the suspicion which followed me, like an inseparable shadow, wherever I went. Stares, nudgings, whisperings, and even loud-spoken remarks of 'that's 'im' greeted my every appearance, and the meanest and most deserted eating-house that I patronized soon became filled with a crowd of furtively watching customers. I began to sympathize with the feelings of Royal personages trying to do a little private shopping under the unsparing scrutiny of an irrepressible public. And still, with all this inarticulate shadowing, which weighed on my nerves almost worse than open hostility would have done, no attempt was made to interfere with my liberty. Later on I discovered the reason. At the time of the murder on the lonely highway a series of important blood-hound trials had been taking place in the near neighbourhood, and some dozen and a half couples of trained animals had been put on the track of the supposed murderer – on my track. One of our most public-spirited London dailies had offered a princely prize to the owner of the pair that should first track me down, and betting on the chances of the respective competitors became rife throughout the land. The dogs ranged far and wide over about thirteen counties, and though my own movements had become by this time perfectly well known to police and public alike, the sporting instincts of the nation stepped in to prevent my premature arrest. 'Give the dogs a chance,' was the prevailing sentiment, whenever some ambitious local constable wished to put an end to my drawn-out evasion of justice. My final capture by the winning pair was not a very dramatic episode, in fact, I'm not sure that they would have taken any notice of me if I hadn't spoken to them and patted them, but the event gave rise to an extraordinary amount of partisan excitement. The owner of the pair who were next nearest up at the finish was an American, and he lodged a protest on the ground that an otterhound had married into the family of the winning pair six generations ago, and that the prize had been offered to the first pair of bloodhounds to capture the murderer, and that a dog that had one sixty-fourth part of otterhound blood in it couldn't technically be considered a bloodhound. I forget how the matter was ultimately settled, but it aroused a tremendous amount of acrimonious discussion on both sides of the Atlantic. My own contribution to the controversy consisted in pointing out that the whole dispute was beside the mark, as the actual murderer had not yet been captured; but I soon discovered that on this point there was not the least divergence of public or expert opinion. I had looked forward apprehensively to the proving of my identity and the establishment of my motives as a disagreeable necessity; I speedily found out that the most disagreeable part of the business was that it couldn't be done. When I saw in the glass the haggard and hunted expression which the experiences of the past few weeks had stamped on my erstwhile placid countenance, I could scarcely feel surprised that the few friends and relations I possessed refused to recognize me in my altered guise, and persisted in their obstinate but widely shared belief that it was I who had been done to death on the highway. To make matters worse, infinitely worse, an aunt of the really murdered man, an appalling female of an obviously

The prize had been offered to the first pair of bloodhounds to capture the murderer

low order of intelligence, identified me as her nephew, and gave the authorities a lurid account of my depraved youth and of her laudable but unavailing efforts to spank me into a better way. I believe it was even proposed to search me for finger-prints.'

'But,' said the Chaplain, 'surely your educational attainments –'

'That was just the crucial point,' said the condemned; 'that was where my lack of specialization told so fatally against me. The dead Salvationist, whose identity I had so lightly and so disastrously adopted, had possessed a veneer of cheap modern education. It should have been easy to demonstrate that my learning was on altogether another plane to his, but in my nervousness I bungled miserably over test after test that was put to me. The little French I had ever known deserted me; I could not render a simple phrase about the gooseberry of the gardener into that language, because I had forgotten the French for gooseberry.'

The Chaplain again wriggled uneasily in his seat. 'And then,' resumed the condemned, 'came the final discomfiture. In our village we had a modest little debating club, and I remembered having promised, chiefly, I suppose, to please and impress the doctor's wife, to give a sketchy kind of lecture on the Balkan Crisis. I had relied on being able to get up my facts from one or two standard works, and the back-numbers of certain periodicals. The prosecution had made a careful note of the circumstance that the man whom I claimed to be – and actually was – had posed locally as some sort of second-hand authority on Balkan affairs, and, in the midst of a string of questions on indifferent topics, the examining counsel asked me with a diabolical suddenness if I could tell the court the whereabouts of Novibazar. I felt the question to be a crucial one; something told me that the answer was St. Petersburg or Baker Street. I hesitated, looked helplessly round at the sea of tensely expectant faces, pulled myself together, and chose Baker Street. And then I knew that everything was lost. The prosecution had no difficulty in demonstrating that an individual, even moderately versed in the affairs of the Near East, could never have so unceremoniously dislocated Novibazar from its accustomed corner of the map. It was an answer which the Salvation Army captain might conceivably have made – and I had made it. The circumstantial evidence connecting the Salvationist with the crime was overwhelmingly convincing, and I had inextricably identified myself with the Salvationist. And thus it comes to pass that in ten minutes' time I shall be hanged by the neck until I am dead in expiation of the murder of myself, which murder never took place, and of which, in any case, I am necessarily innocent.'

When the Chaplain returned to his quarters, some fifteen minutes later, the black flag was floating over the prison tower. Breakfast was waiting for him in the dining-room, but he first passed into his library, and, taking up the *Times* Atlas, consulted a map of the Balkan Peninsula. 'A thing like that,' he observed, closing the volume with a snap, 'might happen to any one.'

The Mouse

THEODORIC VOLER had been brought up, from infancy to the confines
of middle age, by a fond mother whose chief solicitude had been to
keep him screened from what she called the coarser realities of life.
When she died she left Theodoric alone in a world that was as real as
ever, and a good deal coarser than he considered it had any need to be.
To a man of his temperament and upbringing even a simple railway
journey was crammed with petty annoyances and minor discords,
and as he settled himself down in a second-class compartment one
September morning he was conscious of ruffled feelings and general
mental discomposure. He had been staying at a country vicarage, the
inmates of which had been certainly neither brutal nor bacchanalian,
but their supervision of the domestic establishment had been of that
lax order which invites disaster. The pony carriage that was to take
him to the station had never been properly ordered, and when the
moment for his departure drew near the handyman who should have
produced the required article was nowhere to be found. In this emergency Theodoric, to his mute but very intense disgust, found himself
obliged to collaborate with the vicar's daughter in the task of harnessing the pony, which necessitated groping about in an ill-lighted
outhouse called a stable, and smelling very like one – except in
patches where it smelt of mice. Without being actually afraid of mice,
Theodoric classed them among the coarser incidents of life, and considered that Providence, with a little exercise of moral courage, might
long ago have recognised that they were not indispensable, and have
withdrawn them from circulation. As the train glided out of the station Theodoric's nervous imagination accused himself of exhaling a

weak odour of stableyard, and possibly of displaying a mouldy straw or two on his usually well-brushed garments. Fortunately the only other occupant of the compartment, a lady of about the same age as himself, seemed inclined for slumber rather than scrutiny; the train was not due to stop till the terminus was reached, in about an hour's time, and the carriage was of the old-fashioned sort, that held no communication with a corridor, therefore no further travelling companions were likely to intrude on Theodoric's semi-privacy. And yet the train had scarcely attained its normal speed before he became reluctantly but vividly aware that he was not alone with the slumbering lady; he was not even alone in his own clothes. A warm, creeping movement over his flesh betrayed the unwelcome and highly resented presence, unseen but poignant, of a strayed mouse, that had evidently dashed into its present retreat during the episode of the pony harnessing. Furtive stamps and shakes and wildly directed pinches failed to dislodge the intruder, whose motto, indeed, seemed to be Excelsior; and the lawful occupant of the clothes lay back against the cushions and endeavoured rapidly to evolve some means for putting an end to the dual ownership. It was unthinkable that he should continue for the space of a whole hour in the horrible position of a Rowton House for vagrant mice (already his imagination had at least doubled the numbers of the alien invasion). On the other hand, nothing less drastic than partial disrobing would ease him of his tormentor, and to undress in the presence of a lady, even for so laudable a purpose, was an idea that made his eartips tingle in a blush of abject shame. He had never been able to bring himself even to the mild exposure of open-work socks in the presence of the fair sex. And yet – the lady in this case was to all appearances soundly and securely asleep; the mouse, on the other hand, seemed to be trying to crowd a Wanderjahr into a few strenuous minutes. If there is any truth in the theory of transmigration, this particular mouse must certainly have been in a former state a member of the Alpine Club. Sometimes in its eagerness it lost its footing and slipped for half an inch or so; and then, in fright, or more probably temper, it bit. Theodoric was goaded into the most audacious undertaking of his life. Crimsoning to the hue of a beetroot and keeping an agonised watch on his slumbering fellow-traveller, he swiftly and noiselessly secured the ends of his railway-rug to the racks on either side of the carriage, so that a substantial curtain hung athwart the compartment. In the narrow dressing-room that he had thus improvised he proceeded with violent haste to extricate himself partially and the mouse entirely from the surrounding casings of tweed and half-wool. As the unravelled mouse gave a wild leap to the floor, the rug, slipping its fastening at either end, also came down with a heart-curdling flop, and almost simultaneously the awakened sleeper opened her eyes. With a movement almost quicker than the mouse's, Theodoric pounced on the rug, and hauled its ample folds chin-high over his dismantled person as he collapsed into the further corner of the carriage. The blood raced and beat in the veins of his neck and forehead, while he waited dumbly for the communication-cord to be pulled. The lady, however, contented herself with a silent stare at her strangely muffled companion. How much had she seen, Theodoric queried to himself, and in any case what on earth must she think of his present posture?

The lady, however, contented herself with a silent stare

'I think I have caught a chill,' he ventured desperately.

'Really, I'm sorry,' she replied. 'I was just going to ask you if you would open this window.'

'I fancy it's malaria,' he added, his teeth chattering slightly, as much from fright as from a desire to support his theory.

'I've got some brandy in my hold-all, if you'll kindly reach it down for me,' said his companion.

'Not for worlds – I mean, I never take anything for it,' he assured her earnestly.

'I suppose you caught it in the Tropics?'

Theodoric, whose acquaintance with the Tropics was limited to an annual present of a chest of tea from an uncle in Ceylon, felt that even the malaria was slipping from him. Would it be possible, he wondered, to disclose the real state of affairs to her in small instalments?

'Are you afraid of mice?' he ventured, growing, if possible, more scarlet in the face.

'Not unless they came in quantities, like those that ate up Bishop Hatto. Why do you ask?'

'I had one crawling inside my clothes just now,' said Theodoric in a voice that hardly seemed his own. 'It was a most awkward situation.'

'It must have been, if you wear your clothes at all tight,' she observed; 'but mice have strange ideas of comfort.'

'I had to get rid of it while you were asleep,' he continued; then, with a gulp, he added, 'it was getting rid of it that brought me to – to this.'

'Surely leaving off one small mouse wouldn't bring on a chill,' she exclaimed, with a levity that Theodoric accounted abominable.

Evidently she had detected something of his predicament, and was enjoying his confusion. All the blood in his body seemed to have mobilised in one concentrated blush, and an agony of abasement, worse than a myriad mice, crept up and down over his soul. And then, as reflection began to assert itself, sheer terror took the place of humiliation. With every minute that passed the train was rushing nearer to the crowded and bustling terminus where dozens of prying eyes would be exchanged for the one paralysing pair that watched him from the further corner of the carriage. There was one slender despairing chance, which the next few minutes must decide. His fellow-traveller might relapse into a blessed slumber. But as the minutes throbbed by that chance ebbed away. The furtive glance which Theodoric stole at her from time to time disclosed only an unwinking wakefulness.

'I think we must be getting near now,' she presently observed.

Theodoric had already noted with growing terror the recurring stacks of small, ugly dwellings that heralded the journey's end. The words acted as a signal. Like a hunted beast breaking cover and dashing madly towards some other haven of momentary safety he threw aside his rug, and struggled frantically into his dishevelled garments. He was conscious of dull suburban stations racing past the window, of a choking, hammering sensation in his throat and heart, and of an icy silence in that corner towards which he dared not look. Then as he sank back in his seat, clothed and almost delirious, the train slowed down to a final crawl, and the woman spoke.

'Would you be so kind,' she asked, 'as to get me a porter to put me into a cab? It's a shame to trouble you when you're feeling unwell, but being blind makes one so helpless at a railway station.'

SOMERVILLE AND ROSS

Somerville and Ross is the combined pen-name of Edith
Somerville (1858–1949) and Violet Martin (1862–1915).
The ladies were cousins, Somerville from County Cork and
Martin from Galway. The following story is from their best-
known work, *Some Experiences of an Irish R M*, (Resident
Magistrate). The plot concerns a battle of wits between the
authorities and the residents of a small Irish town over the fu-
ture of a large quantity of rum.

The Holy Island

FOR three days of November a white fog stood motionless over the
country. All day and all night smothered booms and bangs away to
the south-west told that the Fastnet gun was hard at work, and the
sirens of the American liners uplifted their monstrous female voices as
they felt their way along the coast of Cork. On the third afternoon the
wind began to whine about the windows of Shreelane, and the baro-
meter fell like a stone. At 11 P.M. the storm rushed upon us with the
roar and the suddenness of a train; the chimneys bellowed, the tall old
house quivered, and the yelling wind drove against it, as a man puts
his shoulder against a door to burst it in.

We none of us got much sleep, and if Mrs. Cadogan is to be believed
– which experience assured me she is not – she spent the night in devo-
tional exercises, and in ministering to the panic-stricken kitchen-
maid by the light of a Blessed candle. All that day the storm screamed
on, dry-eyed; at nightfall the rain began, and next morning, which
happened to be Sunday, every servant in the house was a messenger of
Job, laden with tales of leakages, floods, and fallen trees, and inflated
with the ill-concealed glory of their kind in evil tidings. To Peter
Cadogan, who had been to early Mass, was reserved the crowning satisfaction of reporting that a big vessel had gone on the rocks at Yokahn
Point the evening before, and was breaking up fast; it was rumoured
that the crew had got ashore, but this feature, being favourable and
uninteresting, was kept as much as possible in the background. Mrs.
Cadogan, who had been to America in an ocean liner, became at once
the latest authority on shipwrecks, and was of opinion that 'whoever
would be dhrownded, it wouldn't be thim lads o' sailors. Sure wasn't

145

there the greatest storm ever was in it the time meself was on the say, and what'd thim fellows do but to put us below entirely in the ship, and close down the doors on us, the way theirselves'd leg it when we'd be dhrownding!'

This view of the position was so startlingly novel that Philippa withdrew suddenly from the task of ordering dinner, and fell up the kitchen stairs in unsuitable laughter. Philippa has not the most rudimentary capacity for keeping her countenance.

That afternoon I was wrapped in the slumber, balmiest and most profound, that follows on a wet Sunday luncheon, when Murray, our D.I. of police, drove up in uniform, and came into the house on the top of a gust that set every door banging and every picture dancing on the walls. He looked as if his eyes had been blown out of his head, and he wanted something to eat very badly.

'I've been down at the wreck since ten o'clock this morning,' he said, 'waiting for her to break up, and once she does there'll be trouble. She's an American ship, and she's full up with rum, and bacon, and butter, and all sorts. Bosanquet is there with all his coast-guards, and there are five hundred country people on the strand at this moment, waiting for the fun to begin. I've got ten of my fellows there, and I wish I had as many more. You'd better come back with me, Yeates, we may want the Riot Act before all's done!'

The heavy rain had ceased, but it seemed as if it had fed the wind instead of calming it, and when Murray and I drove out of Shreelane, the whole dirty sky was moving, full sailed, in from the south-west, and the telegraph wires were hanging in a loop from the post outside the gate. Nothing except a Skebawn car-horse would have faced the whooping charges of the wind that came at us across Corran Lake; stimulated mysteriously by whistles from the driver, Murray's yellow hireling pounded woodenly along against the blast, till the smell of the torn sea-weed was borne upon it, and we saw the Atlantic waves come towering into the bay of Tralagough.

The ship was, or had been, a three-masted barque; two of her masts were gone, and her bows stood high out of water on the reef that forms one of the shark-like jaws of the bay. The long strand was crowded with black groups of people, from the bank of heavy shingle that had been hurled over on to the road, down to the slope where the waves pitched themselves and climbed and fought and tore the gravel back with them, as though they had dug their fingers in. The people were nearly all men, dressed solemnly and hideously in their Sunday clothes; most of them had come straight from Mass without any dinner, true to that Irish instinct that places its fun before its food. That the wreck was regarded as a spree of the largest kind was sufficiently obvious. Our car pulled up at a public-house that stood askew between the road and the shingle; it was humming with those whom Irish publicans are pleased to call 'Bonâ feeds,' and sundry of the same class were clustered round the door. Under the wall on the leeside was seated a bagpiper, droning out 'The Irish Washerwoman' with nodding head and tapping heel, and a young man was cutting a few steps of a jig for the delectation of a group of girls.

So far Murray's constabulary had done nothing but exhibit their imposing chest measurement and spotless uniforms to the Atlantic, and Bosanquet's coastguards had only salvaged some spars, the débris of a boat, and a dead sheep, but their time was coming. As we stumbled down over the shingle, battered by the wind and pelted by clots of foam, some one beside me shouted, 'She's gone!' A hill of water had smothered the wreck, and when it fell from her again nothing was left but the bows, with the bowsprit hanging from them in a tangle of rigging. The clouds, bronzed by an unseen sunset, hung low over her; in that greedy pack of waves, with the remorseless rocks above and below her, she seemed the most lonely and tormented of creatures.

About half-an-hour afterwards the cargo began to come ashore on the top of the rising tide. Barrels were plunging and diving in the trough of the waves, like a school of porpoises; they were pitched up the beach in waist-deep rushes of foam; they rolled down again, and were swung up and shouldered by the next wave, playing a kind of Tom Tiddler's ground with the coast-guards. Some of the barrels were big and dangerous, some were small and nimble like young pigs, and the bluejackets were up to their middles as their prey dodged and ducked, and the police lined out along the beach to keep back the people. Ten men of the R.I.C. can do a great deal, but they cannot be in more than twenty or thirty places at the same instant; therefore they could hardly cope with a scattered and extremely active mob of four or five hundred, many of whom had taken advantage of their privileges as 'bona-fide travellers,' and all of whom were determined on getting at the rum.

As the dusk fell the thing got more and more out of hand; the people had found out that the big puncheons held the rum, and had succeeded in capturing one. In the twinkling of an eye it was broached, and fifty backs were shoving round it like a football scrummage. I have heard many rows in my time: I have seen two Irish regiments – one of them Militia – at each other's throats in Fermoy barracks; I have heard Phillippa's water spaniel and two fox-terriers hunting a strange cat round the dairy; but never have I known such untrammelled bedlam as that which yelled round the rum-casks on Tralagough strand. For it was soon not a question of one broached cask, or even of two. The barrels were coming in fast, so fast that it was impossible for the representatives of law and order to keep on any sort of terms with them. The people, shouting with laughter, stove in the casks, and drank rum at 34° above proof, out of their hands, out of their hats, out of their boots. Women came fluttering over the hillsides through the twilight, carrying jugs, milk-pails, anything that would hold the liquor; I saw one of them, roaring with laughter, tilt a filthy zinc bucket to an old man's lips.

With the darkness came anarchy. The rising tide brought more and yet more booty: great spars came lunging in on the lap of the waves, mixed up with cabin furniture, seamen's chests, and the black and slippery barrels, and the country people continued to flock in, and the drinking became more and more unbridled. Murray sent for more men and a doctor, and we slaved on hopelessly in the dark; collaring half-drunken men, shoving pig-headed casks up hills of shingle, hustling in among groups of roaring drinkers – we rescued perhaps one barrel in half-a-dozen. I began to know that there were men there who were not drunk and were not idle; I was also aware, as the strenuous hours of darkness passed, of an occasional rumble of cart wheels on the road. It was evident that the casks which were broached were the least part of the looting, but even they were beyond our control. The most that Bosanquet, Murray, and I could do was to concentrate our forces on the casks that had been secured, and to organise charges upon the swilling crowds in order to upset the casks that they had broached. Already men and boys were lying about, limp as leeches, motionless as the dead.

'They'll kill themsleves before morning, at this rate!' shouted Murray to me. 'They're drinking it by the quart! Here's another barrel; come on!'

We rallied our small forces, and after a brief but furious struggle succeeded in capsizing it. It poured away in a flood over the stones, over the prostrate figures that sprawled on them, and a howl of reproach followed.

'If ye pour away any more o' that, Major,' said an unctuous voice in my ear, 'ye'll intoxicate the stones and they'll be getting up and knocking us down!'

I had been aware of a fat shoulder next to mine in the throng as we heaved the puncheon over, and I now recognised the ponderous wit and Falstaffian figure of Mr. James Canty, a noted member of the Skebawn Board of Guardians, and the owner of a large farm near at hand.

'I never saw worse work on this strand,' he went on. 'I considher these debaucheries a disgrace to the counthry.'

Mr. Canty was famous as an orator, and I presume that it was from long practice among his fellow P.L.G.'s that he was able, without apparent exertion, to out-shout the storm.

At this juncture the long-awaited reinforcements arrived, and along with them came Dr. Jerome Hickey, armed with a black bag. Having mentioned that the bag contained a pump – not one of the common or garden variety – and that no pump on board a foundering ship had more arduous labours to perform, I prefer to pass to other themes. The wreck, which had at first appeared to be as inexhaustible and as variously stocked as that in the 'Swiss Family Robinson,' was beginning to fail in its supply. The crowd were by this time for the most part incapable from drink, and the fresh contingent of police tackled their work with some prospect of success by the light of a tar barrel, contributed by the owner of the public-house. At about the same time I began to be aware that I was aching with fatigue, that my clothes hung heavy and soaked upon me, that my face was stiff with the salt spray and the bitter wind, and that it was two hours past dinner-time. The possibility of fried salt herrings and hot whisky and water at the public-house rose dazzlingly before my mind, when Mr. Canty again crossed my path.

'In my opinion ye have the whole cargo under conthrol now, Major,' he said, 'and the police and the sailors should be able to account for it all now by the help of the light. Wasn't I the finished fool that I didn't think to send up to my house for a tar barrel before now! Well – we're all foolish sometimes! But indeed it's time for us to give over, and that's what I'm after saying to the Captain and Mr. Murray. You're exhausted now the three of ye, and if I might make so bold, I'd suggest that ye'd come up to my little place and have what'd warm ye before ye'd go home. It's only a few perches up the road.'

The tide had turned, the rain had begun again, and the tar barrel illumined the fact that Dr. Hickey's dreadful duties alone were pressing. We held a council and finally followed Mr. Canty, picking our way through wreckage of all kinds, including the human variety. Near the public-house I stumbled over something that was soft and had a squeak in it; it was the piper, with his head and shoulders in an over-turned rum-barrel, and the bagpipes still under his arm.

I knew the outward appearance of Mr. Canty's house very well. It was a typical southern farmhouse, with dirty whitewashed walls, a slated roof, and small, hermetically-sealed windows staring at the morass of manure which constituted the yard. We followed Mr. Canty up the filthy lane that led to it, picked our way round vague and squelching spurs of the manure heap, and were finally led through the kitchen into a stifling best parlour. Mrs. Canty, a vast and slatternly matron, had evidently made preparations for us; there was a newly-lighted fire pouring flame up the chimney from layers of bogwood, there were whisky and brandy on the table, and a plateful of biscuits sugared in white and pink. Upon our hostess was a black silk dress which indifferently concealed the fact that she was short of boot-laces, and that the boots themselves had made many excursions to the yard and none to the blacking-bottle. Her manners, however, were admirable, and while I live I shall not forget her potato cakes. They came in hot and hot from a pot-oven, they were speckled with caraway seeds, they swam in salt butter, and we ate them shamelessly and greasily, and washed them down with hot whisky and water; I knew to a nicety how ill I should be next day, and heeded not.

'Well, gentlemen,' remarked Mr. Canty later on, in his best Board of Guardians' manner, 'I've seen many wrecks between this and the Mizen Head, but I never witnessed a scene of more disgraceful ex-cess than what was in it to-night.'

'Hear, hear!' murmured Bosanquet with unseemly levity.

'I should say,' went on Mr. Canty, 'there was at one time to-night upwards of one hundhred men dead dhrunk on the strand, or anyway so dhrunk that if they'd attempt to spake they'd foam at the mouth.'

'The craytures!' interjected Mrs. Canty sympathetically.

'But if they're dhrunk to-day,' continued our host, 'it's nothing at all to what they'll be to-morrow and afther to-morrow, and it won't be on the strand they'll be dhrinkin' it.'

'Why, where will it be?' said Bosanquet, with his disconcerting English way of asking a point-blank question.

Mr. Canty passed his hand over his red cheeks.

'There'll be plenty asking that before all's said and done, Captain,' he said, with a compassionate smile, 'and there'll be plenty that could give the answer if they'll like, but by dam I don't think ye'll be apt to get much out of the Yokahn boys!'

'The Lord save us, 'twould be better to keep out from the likes o' thim!' put in Mrs. Canty, sliding a fresh avalanche of potato cakes on to the dish; 'didn't they pull the clothes off the gauger and pour potheen down his throath till he ran screeching through the streets o' Skebawn!'

James Canty chuckled.

'I remember there was a wreck here one time, and the undherwriters put me in charge of the cargo. Brandy it was – cases of the best Frinch brandy. The people had a song about it, what's this the first verse was –

'One night to the rocks of Yokahn
Came the barque *Isabella* so dandy,
To pieces she went before dawn,
Herself and her cargo of brandy.
And all met a wathery grave
Excepting the vessel's car*pen*ther,
Poor fellow, so far from his home.'

Mr. Canty chanted these touching lines in a tuneful if wheezy tenor. 'Well, gentlemen, we're all friends here,' he continued, 'and it's no harm to mention that this man below at the public-house came askin' me would I let him have some of it for a consideration. "Sullivan," says I to him "if ye ran down gold in a cup in place of the brandy, I wouldn't give it to you. Of coorse," says I, "I'm not sayin' but that if a bottle was to get a crack of a stick, and it to be broken, and a man to drink a glass out of it, that would be no more than an accident." "That's no good to me," says he, "but if I had twelve gallons of that brandy in Cork," says he, "by the Holy German!" says he, saying an awful curse, "I'd sell twenty-five out of it!" Well, indeed, it was true for him; it was grand stuff. As the saying is, it would make a horse out of a cow!'

'It appears to be a handy sort of place for keeping a pub,' said Bosanquet.

'Shut to the door, Margaret,' said Mr. Canty with elaborate caution. 'It'd be a queer place that wouldn't be handy for Sullivan!'

A further tale of great length was in progress when Dr. Hickey's Mephistophelian nose was poked into the best parlour.

'Hullo, Hickey! Pumped out? eh?' said Murray.

'If I am, there's plenty more like me,' replied the Doctor enigmatically, 'and some of them three times over! James, did these gentlemen leave you a drop of anything that you'd offer me?'

151

'Maybe ye'd like a glass of rum, Doctor?' said Mr. Canty with a wink at his other guests.

Dr. Hickey shuddered.

I had next morning precisely the kind of mouth that I had anticipated, and it being my duty to spend the better part of the day administering justice in Skebawn, I received from Mr. Flurry Knox and other of my brother magistrates precisely the class of condolences on my 'Monday head' that I found least amusing. It was unavailing to point out the resemblance between hot potato cakes and molten lead, or to dilate on their equal power of solidifying; the collective wisdom of the Bench decided that I was suffering from contraband rum, and rejoiced over me accordingly.

During the next three weeks Murray and Bosanquet put in a time only to be equalled by that of the heroes in detective romances. They began by acting on the hint offered by Mr. Canty, and were rewarded by finding eight barrels of bacon and three casks of rum in the heart of Mr. Sullivan's turf rick, placed there, so Mr. Sullivan explained with much detail, by enemies, with the object of getting his licence taken away. They stabbed potato gardens with crowbars to find the buried barrels, they explored the chimneys, they raided the cow-houses; and in every possible and impossible place they found some of the cargo of the late barque *John D. Williams*, and, as the sympathetic Mr. Canty said, 'For as much as they found, they left five times as much afther them!'

It was a wet, lingering autumn, but towards the end of November the rain dried up, the weather stiffened, and a week of light frosts and blue skies was offered as a tardy apology. Philippa possesses, in common with many of her sex, an inappeasable passion for picnics, and her ingenuity for devising occasions for them is only equalled by her gift for enduring their rigours. I have seen her tackle a moist chicken pie with a splinter of slate and my stylograph pen. I have known her to take the tea-basket to an auction, and make tea in a four-wheeled inside car, regardless of the fact that it was coming under the hammer in ten minutes, and that the kettle took twenty minutes to boil. It will therefore be readily understood that the rare occasions when I was free to go out with a gun were not allowed to pass uncelebrated by the tea-basket.

'You'd much better shoot Corran Lake tomorrow,' my wife said to me one brilliant afternoon. 'We could send the punt over, and I could meet you on Holy Island with –'

The rest of the sentence was concerned with ways, means, and the tea-basket, and need not be recorded.

I had taken the shooting of a long snipe bog that trailed from Corran Lake almost to the sea at Tralagough, and it was my custom to begin to shoot from the seaward end of it, and finally to work round the lake after duck.

To-morrow proved a heavenly morning, touched with frost, gilt with sun. I started early, and the mists were still smoking up from the calm, all-reflecting lake, as the Quaker stepped out along the level road, smashing the thin ice on the puddles with his big feet. Behind the calves of my legs sat Maria, Philippa's brown Irish water-spaniel, assiduously licking the barrels of my gun, as was her custom when the ecstasy of going out shooting was hers. Maria had been given to Philippa as a wedding-present, and since then it had been my wife's ambition that she should conform to the Beth Gelert standard of being 'a lamb at home, a lion in the chase.' Maria did pretty well as a lion: she hunted all dogs unmistakably smaller than herself, and whenever it was reasonably possible to do so she devoured the spoils of the chase, notably jack snipe. It was as a lamb that she failed; objectionable as I have no doubt a lamb would be as a domestic pet, it at least would not snatch the cold beef from the luncheon-table, nor yet, if banished for its crimes, would it spend the night in scratching the paint off the hall door. Maria bit beggars (who valued their disgusting limbs at five shillings the square inch), she bullied the servants, she concealed ducks' claws and fishes' backbones behind the sofa cushions, and yet, when she laid her brown snoud upon my knee, and rolled her blackguard amber eyes upon me, and smote me with her feathered paw, it was impossible to remember her iniquities against her. On shooting mornings Maria ceased to be a buccaneer, a glutton, and a hypocrite. From the moment when I put my gun together her breakfast stood untouched until it suffered the final degradation of being eaten by the cats, and now in the trap she was shivering with excitement, and agonising in her soul lest she should even yet be left behind.

Slipper met me at the cross roads from which I had sent back the trap; Slipper, redder in the nose than anything I had ever seen off the stage, very husky as to the voice, and going rather tender on both feet. He informed me that I should have a grand day's shooting, the head-poacher of the locality having, in a most gentlemanlike manner, refrained from exercising his sporting rights the day before, on hearing that I was coming. I understood that this was to be considered as a mark of high personal esteem, and I set to work at the bog with suitable gratitude.

In spite of Mr. O'Driscoll's magnanimity, I had not a very good morning. The snipe were there, but in the perfect stillness of the weather it was impossible to get near them, and five times out of six they were up, flickering and dodging, before I was within shot. Maria became possessed of seven devils and broke away from heel the first time I let off my gun, ranging far and wide in search of the bird I had missed, and putting up every live thing for half a mile round, as she went splashing and steeple-chasing through the bog. Slipper expressed his opinion of her behaviour in language more appallingly picturesque and resourceful than any I have heard, even in the Ske-bawn Court-house; I admit that at the time I thought he spoke very suitably. Before she was recaptured every remaining snipe within ear-shot was lifted out of it by Slipper's steam-engine whistles and my own infuriated bellows; it was fortunate that the bog was spacious and that there was still a long tract of it ahead, where beyond these voices there was peace.

I worked my way on, jumping treacle-dark drains, floundering through the rustling yellow rushes, circumnavigating the bog-holes, and taking every possible and impossible chance of a shot; by the time I had reached Corran Lake I had got two and a half brace, retrieved by Maria with a perfection that showed what her powers were when the sinuous adroitness of Slipper's woodbine stick was fresh in her mind. But with Maria it was always the unexpected that happened. My last snipe, a jack, fell in the lake, and Maria, bursting through the reeds with kangaroo bounds, and cleaving the water like a tor-pedo-boat, was a model of all the virtues of her kind. She picked up the bird with a snake-like dart of her head, clambered with it on to a tus-sock, and there, well out of reach of the arm of the law, before our in-dignant eyes crunched it twice and bolted it.

'Well,' said Slipper complacently, some ten minutes afterwards, 'divil such a bating ever I gave a dog since the day Prince killed owld Mrs. Knox's paycock! Prince was a lump of a brown tarrier I had one time, and faith I kicked the toes out o' me owld boots on him before I had the owld lady composed!'

However composing Slipper's methods may have been to Mrs. Knox, they had quite the contrary effect upon a family party of duck that had been lying in the reeds. With horrified outcries they broke into flight, and now were far away on the ethereal mirror of the lake, among strings of their fellows that were floating and quacking in preoccupied indifference to my presence.

A promenade along the lake-shore demonstrated the fact that without a boat there was no more shooting for me; I looked across to the island where, some time ago, I had seen Philippa and her punt arrive. The boat was tied to an overhanging tree, but my wife was nowhere to be seen. I was opening my mouth to give a hail, when I saw her emerge precipitately from among the trees and jump into the boat; Philippa had not in vain spent many summers on the Thames, she was under way in a twinkling, sculled a score of strokes at the rate of a finish, then stopped and stared at the peaceful island. I called to her, and in a minute or two the punt had crackled through the reeds, and shoved its blunt nose ashore at the spot where I was standing.

'Sinclair,' said Philippa in awe-struck tones, 'there's something on the island!'

'I hope there's something to eat there,' said I.

'I tell you there *is* something there, alive,' said my wife with her eyes as large as saucers; 'it's making an awful sound like snoring.'

'That's the fairies, ma'am,' said Slipper with complete certainty; 'sure I know them that seen fairies in that island as thick as the grass, and every one o' them with little caps on them.'

Philippa's wide gaze wandered to Slipper's hideous pug face and back to me.

'It was not a human being, Sinclair!' she said combatively, though I had not uttered a word.

Maria had already, after the manner of dogs, leaped, dripping, into the boat: I prepared to follow her example.

'Major,' said Slipper, in a tragic whisper, 'there was a man was a night on that island one time, watching duck, and Thim People cot him, and dhragged him through Hell and through Death, and threw him in the tide –'

'Shove off the boat,' I said, too hungry for argument.

Slipper obeyed, throwing his knee over the gunwale as he did so, and tumbling into the bow; we could have done without him very comfortably, but his devotion was touching.

Holy Island was perhaps a hundred yards long, and about half as many broad; it was covered with trees and a dense growth of rhododendrons; somewhere in the jungle was a ruined fragment of a chapel, smothered in ivy and briars, and in a little glade in the heart of the island there was a holy well. We landed, and it was obviously a sore humiliation to Philippa that not a sound was to be heard in the spell-bound silence of the island, save the cough of a heron on a tree-top.

'It *was* there,' she said, with an unconvinced glance at the surrounding thickets.

'Sure, I'll give a thrawl through the island, ma'am,' volunteered Slipper with unexpected gallantry, 'an' if it's the divil himself is in it, I'll rattle him into the lake!'

He went swaggering on his search, shouting, 'Hi, cock!' and whacking the rhododendrons with his stick, and after an interval returned and assured us that the island was uninhabited. Being provided with refreshments he again withdrew, and Philippa and Maria and I fed variously and at great length, and washed the plates with water from the holy well. I was smoking a cigarette when we heard Slipper addressing the solitudes at the farther end of the island, and ending with one of his whisky-throated crows of laughter.

He presently came lurching towards us through the bushes, and a glance sufficed to show even Philippa – who was as incompetent a judge of such matters as many of her sex – that he was undeniably screwed.

'Major Yeates!' he began, 'and Mrs. Major Yeates, with respex to ye, I'm bastely dhrunk! Me head is light since the 'fluenzy, and the docthor told me I should carry a little bottle-een o' sperrits – '

'Look here,' I said to Philippa, 'I'll take him across, and bring the boat back for you.'

'Sinclair,' responded my wife with concentrated emotion, 'I would rather die than stay on this island alone!'

Slipper was getting drunker every moment, but I managed to stow him on his back in the bows of the punt, in which position he at once began to uplift husky and wandering strains of melody. To this accompaniment we, as Tennyson says,

> 'moved from the brink like some full-breasted swan,
> That, fluting a wild carol ere her death,
> Ruffles her pure cold plume, and takes the flood
> With swarthy web.'

Slipper would certainly have been none the worse for taking the flood, and, as the burden of 'Lannigan's Ball' strengthened and spread along the tranquil lake, and the duck once more fled in justifiable consternation, I felt much inclined to make him do so.

We made for the end of the lake that was nearest Shreelane, and, as we rounded the point of the island, another boat presented itself to our view. It contained my late entertainer, Mrs. Canty, seated bulkily in the stern, while a small boy bowed himself between the two heavy oars.

'It's a lovely evening, Major Yeates,' she called out. 'I'm just going to the island to get some water from the holy well for me daughter that has an impression on her chest. Indeed, I thought 'twas yourself was singing a song for Mrs. Yeates when I heard you coming, but sure Slipper is a great warrant himself for singing.'

'It's a lovely evening, Major Yeates'

'May the divil crack the two legs undher ye!' bawled Slipper in acknowledgment of the compliment.

Mrs. Canty laughed genially, and her boat lumbered away.

I shoved Slipper ashore at the nearest point; Philippa and I paddled to the end of the lake, and abandoning the duck as a bad business, walked home.

A few days afterwards it happened that it was incumbent upon me to attend the funeral of the Roman Catholic Bishop of the diocese. It was what is called in France '*un bel enterrement,*' with inky flocks of tall-hatted priests, and countless yards of white scarves, and a repast of monumental solidity at the Bishop's residence. The actual interment

157

was to take place in Cork, and we moved in long and imposing procession to the railway station, where a special train awaited the cortège. My friend Mr. James Canty was among the mourners: an important and active personage, exchanging condolences with the priests, giving directions to porters, and blowing his nose with a trumpeting mournfulness that penetrated all the other noises of the platform. He was condescending enough to notice my presence, and found time to tell me that he had given Mr. Murray 'a sure word' with regard to some of '*the wreckage*' – this with deep significance, and a wink of an inflamed and tearful eye. I saw him depart in a first-class carriage, and the odour of sanctity; seeing that he was accompanied by seven priests, and that both windows were shut, the latter must have been considerable.

Afterwards, in the town, I met Murray, looking more pleased with himself than I had seen him since he had taken up the unprofitable task of smuggler-hunting.

'Come along and have some lunch,' he said, 'I've got a real good thing on this time! That chap Canty came to me late last night, and told me that he knew for a fact that the island on Corran Lake was just stiff with barrels of bacon and rum, and that I'd better send every man I could spare to-day to get them into the town. I sent the men out at eight o'clock this morning; I think I've gone one better than Bosanquet this time!'

I began to realise that Philippa was going to score heavily on the subject of the fairies that she had heard snoring on the island, and I imparted to Murray the leading features of our picnic there.

'Oh, Slipper's been up to his chin in that rum from the first,' said Murray. 'I'd like to know who his sleeping partner was!'

It was beginning to get dark before the loaded carts of the salvage party came lumbering past Murray's windows and into the yard of the police-barrack. We followed them, and in so doing picked up Flurry Knox, who was sauntering in the same direction. It was a good haul, five big casks of rum, and at least a dozen smaller barrels of bacon and butter, and Murray and his Chief Constable smiled seraphically on one another as the spoil was unloaded and stowed in a shed.

'Wouldn't it be as well to see how the butter is keeping?' remarked Flurry, who had been looking on silently, with, as I had noticed, a still and amused eye. 'The rim of that small keg there looks as if it had been shifted lately.'

The sergeant looked hard at Flurry; he knew as well as most people that a hint from Mr. Knox was usually worth taking. He turned to Murray.

'Will I open it, sir?'

'Oh! open it if Mr. Knox wishes,' said Murray, who was not famous for appreciating other people's suggestions.

The keg was opened.

'Funny butter,' said Flurry.

The sergeant said nothing. The keg was full of black bog-mould. Another was opened, and another, all with the same result.

'Damnation!' said Murray, suddenly losing his temper. 'What's the use of going on with those? Try one of the rum casks.'

A few moments passed in total silence while a tap and a spigot were sent for and applied to the barrel. The sergeant drew off a mugful and put his nose to it with the deliberation of a connoisseur.

'Water, sir,' he pronounced, 'dirty water, with a small indication of sperrits.'

A junior constable tittered explosively, met the light blue glare of Murray's eye, and withered away.

'Perhaps it's holy water!' said I, with a wavering voice.

Murray's glance pinned me like an assegaii, and I also faded into the background.

'Well,' said Flurry in dulcet tones, 'if you want to know where the stuff is that was in those barrels, I can tell you, for I was told it myself half-an-hour ago. It's gone to Cork with the Bishop by special train!'

Mr. Canty was undoubtedly a man of resource. Mrs. Canty had mistakenly credited me with an intelligence equal to her own, and on receiving from Slipper a highly coloured account of how audibly Mr. Canty had slept off his potations, had regarded the secret of Holy Island as having been given away. That night and the two succeeding ones were spent in the transfer of the rum to bottles, and the bottles and the butter to fish boxes; these were, by means of a slight lubrication of the railway underlings loaded into a truck as 'Fresh Fish, Urgent,' and attached to the Bishop's funeral train, while the police, decoyed far from the scene of action, were breaking their backs over barrels of bog-water. 'I suppose,' continued Flurry pleasantly, 'you don't know the pub that Canty's brother has in Cork. Well, I do. I'm going to buy some rum there next week, cheap.'

'I shall proceed against Canty!' said Murray, with fateful calm.

'You won't proceed far,' said Flurry; 'you'll not get as much evidence out of the whole country as'd hang a cat.'

'Who was your informant?' demanded Murray.

Flurry laughed. 'Well, by the time the train was in Cork, yourself and the Major were the only two men in the town that weren't talking about it.'

JAMES THURBER
(1894–1961)

Thurber was born in Columbus, Ohio, and his family of mid-western eccentrics strongly influenced his humour. He was connected with the *New Yorker* from 1933 until his death and was a central force in its development as a vehicle for modern American humour. The small, downtrodden man, large domineering woman and world-weary dogs of Thurber's stories are so well observed that one still hears phrases like: 'X's wife is a typical "Thurber" woman', or 'Have you ever seen such a "Thurber" dog?'.

The Dog That Bit People

PROBABLY no one man should have as many dogs in his life as I have had, but there was more pleasure than distress in them for me except in the case of an Airedale named Muggs. He gave me more trouble than all the other fifty-four or five put together, although my moment of keenest embarrassment was the time a Scotch terrier named Jeannie, who had just had six puppies in the clothes closet of a fourth floor apartment in New York, had the unexpected seventh and last at the corner of Eleventh Street and Fifth Avenue during a walk she had insisted on taking. Then, too, there was the prize-winning French poodle, a great big black poodle – none of your little, untroublesome white miniatures – who got sick riding in the rumble seat of a car with me on her way to the Greenwich Dog Show. She had a red rubber bib tucked around her throat and, since a rain storm came up when we were half way through the Bronx, I had to hold over her a small green umbrella, really more of a parasol. The rain beat down fearfully and suddenly the driver of the car drove into a big garage, filled with mechanics. It happened so quickly that I forgot to put the umbrella down and I will always remember, with sickening distress, the look of incredulity mixed with hatred that came over the face of the particular hardened garage man that came over to see what we wanted, when he took a look at me and the poodle. All garage men, and people of that intolerant stripe, hate poodles with their curious hair cut, especially the pom-poms that you got to leave on their hips if you expect the dogs to win a prize.

But the Airedale, as I have said, was the worst of all my dogs. He really wasn't my dog, as a matter of fact: I came home from a vacation one summer to find that my brother Roy had bought him while I was away. A big, burly, choleric dog, he always acted as if he thought I wasn't one of the family. There was a slight advantage in being one of the family, for he didn't bite the family as often as he bit strangers. Still, in the years that we had him he bit everybody but mother, and he made a pass at her once but missed. That was during the month when we suddenly had mice, and Muggs refused to do anything about them. Nobody ever had mice exactly like the mice we had that month. They acted like pet mice, almost like mice somebody had trained. They were so friendly that one night when mother entertained at dinner the Friraliras, a club she and my father had belonged to for twenty years, she put down a lot of little dishes with food in them on the pantry floor so that the mice would be satisfied with that and wouldn't come into the dining room. Muggs stayed out in the pantry with the mice, lying on the floor, growling to himself – not at the mice, but about all the people in the next room that he would have liked to get at. Mother slipped out into the pantry once to see how everything was going. Everything was going fine. It made her so mad to see Muggs lying there, oblivious of the mice – they came running up to her – that she slapped him and he slashed at her, but didn't make it. He was sorry immediately, mother said. He was always sorry, she said, after he bit someone, but we could not understand how she figured this out. He didn't act sorry.

Mother used to send a box of candy every Christmas to the people the Airedale bit. The list finally contained forty or more names. Nobody could understand why we didn't get rid of the dog. I didn't understand it very well myself, but we didn't get rid of him. I think that one or two people tried to poison Muggs – he acted poisoned once in a while – and old Major Moberly fired at him once with his service revolver near the Seneca Hotel in East Broad Street – but Muggs lived to be almost eleven years old and even when he could hardly get around he bit a Congressman who had called to see my father on business. My mother had never liked the Congressman – she said the signs of his horoscope showed he couldn't be trusted (he was Saturn with the moon in Virgo) – but she sent him a box of candy that Christmas. He sent it right back, probably because he suspected it was trick candy. Mother persuaded herself it was all for the best that the dog had bitten him, even though father lost an important business association because of it. 'I wouldn't be associated with such a man,' mother said, 'Muggs could read him like a book.'

We used to take turns feeding Muggs to be on his good side, but

Nobody knew exactly what was the matter with him

that didn't always work. He was never in a very good humour, even after a meal. Nobody knew exactly what was the matter with him, but whatever it was it made him irascible, especially in the mornings. Roy never felt very well in the morning, either, especially before breakfast, and once when he came downstairs and found that Muggs had moodily chewed up the morning paper he hit him in the face with a grapefruit and then jumped up on the dining room table, scattering dishes and silverware and spilling the coffee. Muggs' first free leap carried him all the way across the table and into a brass fire screen in front of the gas grate but he was back on his feet in a moment and in the end he got Roy and gave him a pretty vicious bite in the leg. Then he was all over it; he never bit anyone more than once at a time. Mother always mentioned that as an argument in his favour; she said he had a quick temper but that he didn't hold a grudge. She was forever defending him. I think she liked him because he wasn't well. 'He's not strong,' she would say, pityingly, but that was inaccurate; he may not have been well but he was terribly strong.

One time my mother went to the Chittenden Hotel to call on a woman mental healer who was lecturing in Columbus on the subject of 'Harmonious Vibrations.' She wanted to find out if it was possible

163

to get harmonious vibrations into a dog. 'He's a large tan-coloured Airedale,' mother explained. The woman said that she had never treated a dog but she advised my mother to hold the thought that he did not bite and would not bite. Mother was holding the thought the very next morning when Muggs got the iceman but she blamed that slip-up on the iceman. 'If you didn't think he would bite you, he wouldn't,' mother told him. He stomped out of the house in a terrible jangle of vibrations.

One morning when Muggs bit me slightly, more or less in passing, I reached down and grabbed his short stumpy tail and hoisted him into the air. It was a foolhardy thing to do and the last time I saw my mother, about six months ago, she said she didn't know what possessed me. I don't either, except that I was pretty mad. As long as I held the dog off the floor by his tail he couldn't get at me, but he twisted and jerked so, snarling all the time, that I realized I couldn't hold him that way very long. I carried him to the kitchen and flung him onto the floor and shut the door on him just as he crashed against

Lots of people reported our Airedale to the police

it. But I forgot about the backstairs. Muggs went up the backstairs and down the frontstairs and had me cornered in the living room. I managed to get up onto the mantelpiece above the fireplace, but it gave way and came down with a tremendous crash throwing a large marble clock, several vases, and myself heavily to the floor. Muggs was so alarmed by the racket that when I picked myself up he had disappeared. We couldn't find him anywhere, although we whistled and shouted, until old Mrs. Detweiler called after dinner that night. Muggs had bitten her once, in the leg, and she came into the living room only after we assured her that Muggs had run away. She had just seated herself when, with a great growling and scratching of claws, Muggs emerged from under a davenport where he had been quietly hiding all the time, and bit her again. Mother examined the bite and put arnica on it and told Mrs. Detweiler that it was only a bruise. 'He just bumped you,' she said. But Mrs. Detweiler left the house in a nasty state of mind.

Lots of people reported our Airedale to the police but my father held a municipal office at the time and was on friendly terms with the police. Even so, the cops had been out a couple of times – once when Muggs bit Mrs. Rufus Sturtevant and again when he bit Lieutenant-Governor Malloy – but mother told them that it hadn't been Muggs' fault but the fault of the people who were bitten. 'When he starts for them, they scream,' she explained, 'and that excites him.' The cops suggested that it might be a good idea to tie the dog up, but mother said that it mortified him to be tied up and that he wouldn't eat when he was tied up.

Muggs at his meals was an unusual sight. Because of the fact that if you reached toward the floor he would bite you, we usually put his food plate on top of an old kitchen table with a bench alongside the table. Muggs would stand on the bench and eat. I remember that my mother's Uncle Horatio, who boasted that he was the third man up Missionary Ridge, was splutteringly indignant when he found out that we fed the dog on a table because we were afraid to put his plate on the floor. He said he wasn't afraid of any dog that ever lived and that he would put the dog's plate on the floor if we would give it to him. Roy said that if Uncle Horatio had fed Muggs on the ground just before the battle he would have been the first man up Missionary Ridge. Uncle Horatio was furious. 'Bring him in! Bring him in now!' he shouted. 'I'll feed the –– on the floor!' Roy was all for giving him a chance, but my father wouldn't hear of it. He said that Muggs had already been fed. 'I'll feed him again!' bawled

165

Muggs at his meals was an unusual sight

Uncle Horatio. We had quite a time quieting him.

In his last year Muggs used to spend practically all of his time outdoors. He didn't like to stay in the house for some reason or other – perhaps it held too many unpleasant memories for him. Anyway, it was hard to get him to come in and as a result the garbage man, the iceman, and the laundryman wouldn't come near the house. We had to haul the garbage down to the corner, take the laundry out and bring it back, and meet the iceman a block from home. After this had gone on for some time we hit on an ingenious arrangement for getting the dog in the house so that we could lock him up while the gas meter was read, and so on. Muggs was afraid of only one thing, an electrical storm. Thunder and lightning frightened him out of his senses (I think he thought a storm had broken the day the mantelpiece fell). He would rush into the house and hide under a bed or in a clothes closet. So we fixed up a thunder machine out of a long narrow

166

piece of sheet iron with a wooden handle on one end. Mother would shake this vigorously when she wanted to get Muggs into the house. It made an excellent imitation of thunder, but I suppose it was the most round-about system for running a household that was ever devised. It took a lot out of mother.

A few months before Muggs died, he got to 'seeing things.' He would rise slowly from the floor, growling low, and stalk stiff-legged and menacing toward nothing at all. Sometimes the Thing would be just a little to the right or left of a visitor. Once a Fuller Brush salesman got hysterics. Muggs came wandering into the room like Hamlet following his father's ghost. His eyes were fixed on a spot just to the left of the Fuller Brush man, who stood it until Muggs was about three slow, creeping paces from him. Then he shouted. Muggs wavered on past him into the hallway grumbling to himself but the Fuller man went on shouting. I think mother had to throw a pan of cold water on him before he stopped. That was the way she used to stop us boys when we got into fights.

Muggs died quite suddenly one night. Mother wanted to bury him in the family lot under a marble stone with some such inscription as 'Flights of angels sing thee to thy rest' but we persuaded her it was against the law. In the end we just put up a smooth board above his grave along a lonely road. On the board I wrote with an indelible pencil 'Cave Canem.' Mother was quite pleased with the simple classic dignity of the old Latin epitaph.

The Remarkable Case Of Mr. Bruhl

SAMUEL O. BRUHL was just an ordinary-looking citizen, like you and me, except for a curious, shoe-shaped scar on his left cheek, which he got when he fell against a wagon-tongue in his youth. He had a good job as treasurer for a syrup-and-fondant concern, a large, devout wife, two tractable daughters, and a nice home in Brooklyn. He worked from nine to five, took in a show occasionally, played a bad, complacent game of golf, and was usually in bed by eleven o'clock. The Bruhls had a dog named Bert, a small circle of friends, and an old sedan. They had made a comfortable, if unexciting, adjustment to life.

There was no reason in the world why Samuel Bruhl shouldn't have lived along quietly until he died of some commonplace malady. He was a man designed by Nature for an uneventful life, an inexpensive but respectable funeral, and a modest stone marker. All this you would have predicted had you observed his colourless comings and goings, his mild manner, the small stature of his dreams. He was, in brief, the sort of average citizen that observers of Judd Gray thought Judd Gray was. And precisely as that mild little family man was abruptly hurled into an incongruous tragedy, so was Samuel Bruhl suddenly picked out of the hundreds of men just like him and marked for an extravagant and unpredictable end. Oddly enough it was the shoe-shaped scar on his left cheek which brought to his heels a Nemesis he had never dreamed of. A blemish on his heart, a tic in his soul would have been different; one would have blamed Bruhl for whatever anguish an emotional or spiritual flaw laid him open to, but it is ironical indeed when the Furies ride down a man who has been guilty of nothing worse than an accident in his childhood.

168

Samuel O. Bruhl looked very much like George ('Shoescar') Clinigan. Clinigan had that same singular shoe-shaped scar on his left cheek. There was also a general resemblance in height, weight, and complexion. A careful study would have revealed very soon that Clinigan's eyes were shifty and Bruhl's eyes were clear, and that the syrup-and-fondant company's treasurer had a more pleasant mouth and a higher forehead than the gangster and racketeer, but at a glance the similarity was remarkable.

Had Clinigan not become notorious, this prank of Nature would never have been detected, but Clinigan did become notorious and dozens of persons observed that he looked like Bruhl. They saw Clinigan's picture in the papers the day he was shot, and the day after, and the day after that. Presently someone in the syrup-and-fondant concern mentioned to someone else that Clinigan looked like Mr. Bruhl, remarkably like Mr. Bruhl. Soon everybody in the place had commented on it, among themselves, and to Mr. Bruhl.

Mr. Bruhl rather laughed it off at first, but one day when Clinigan had been in the hospital a week, a cop peered closely at Mr. Bruhl when he was on his way home from work. After that, the little treasurer noticed a number of other strangers staring at him with mingled surprise and alarm. One small, dark man hastily thrust a hand into his coat pocket and paled slightly.

Mr. Bruhl began to worry. He began to imagine things. 'I hope this fellow Clinigan doesn't pull through,' he said one morning at breakfast. 'He's a bad actor. He's better off dead.'

'Oh, he'll pull through,' said Mrs. Bruhl, who had been reading the morning paper. 'It says here he'll pull through. But it says they'll shoot him again. It says they're sure to shoot him again.'

The morning after the night that Clinigan left the hospital, secretly, by a side door, and disappeared into the town, Bruhl decided not to go to work. 'I don't feel so good today,' he said to his wife. 'Would you call up the office and tell them I'm sick?'

'You don't look well,' said his wife. 'You really don't look well. Get down, Bert,' she added, for the dog had jumped upon her lap and whined. The animal knew that something was wrong.

That evening Bruhl, who had mooned about the house all day, read in the papers that Clinigan had vanished, but was believed to be somewhere in the city. His various rackets required his presence, at least until he made enough money to skip out with; he had left the hospital penniless. Rival gangsters, the papers said, were sure to seek him out, to hunt him down, to give it to him again. 'Give him what again?' asked Mrs. Bruhl when she read this. 'Let's talk about something else,' said her husband.

It was little Joey, the office-boy at the syrup-and-fondant company, who first discovered that Mr. Bruhl was afraid. Joey, who went about with tennis shoes on, entered the treasurer's office suddenly – flung open the door and started to say something. 'Good God!' cried Mr. Bruhl, rising from his chair. 'Why, what's the matter, Mr. Bruhl?' asked Joey. Other little things happened. The switchboard girl phoned Mr. Bruhl's desk one afternoon and said there was a man waiting to see him, a Mr. Globe. 'What's he look like?' asked Bruhl, who didn't know anybody named Globe. 'He's small and dark,' said the girl. 'A small, dark man?' said Bruhl. 'Tell him I'm out. Tell him I've gone to California.' The personnel, comparing notes, decided at length that the treasurer was afraid of being mistaken for Shoescar and put on the spot. They said nothing to Mr. Bruhl about this, because they were forbidden to by Ollie Breithofter, a fattish clerk who was a tireless and inventive practical joker and who had an idea.

As the hunt went on for Clinigan and he still wasn't found and killed, Mr. Bruhl lost weight and grew extremely fidgety. He began to figure out new ways of getting to work, one requiring the use of two different ferry lines; he ate his lunch in, he wouldn't answer bells, he cried out when anyone dropped anything, and he ran into stores or banks when cruising taxidrivers shouted at him. One morning, in setting the house to rights, Mrs. Bruhl found a revolver under his pillow. 'I found a revolver under your pillow,' she told him that night. 'Burglars are bad in this neighbourhood,' he said. 'You oughtn't to have a revolver,' she said. They argued about it, he irritably, she uneasily, until time for bed. As Bruhl was undressing, after locking and bolting all the doors, the telephone rang. 'It's for you, Sam,' said Mrs. Bruhl. Her husband went slowly to the phone, passing Bert on the way. 'I wish I was you,' he said to the dog, and took up the receiver. 'Get this, Shoescar,' said a husky voice. 'We trailed you where you are, see? You're cooked.' The receiver at the other end was hung up. Bruhl shouted. His wife came running. 'What is it, Sam, what is it?' she cried. Bruhl, pale, sick-looking, had fallen into a chair. 'They got me,' he moaned. 'They got me.' Slowly, deviously, Minnie Bruhl got it out of her husband that he had been mistaken for Clinigan and that he was cooked. Mrs. Bruhl was not very quick mentally, but she had a certain intuition and this intuition told her, as she trembled there in her nightgown above her broken husband, that this was the work of Ollie Breithofter. She instantly phoned Ollie Breithofter's wife and, before she hung up, had got the truth out of Mrs. Breithofter. It was Ollie who had called.

The treasurer of the Maskonsett Syrup & Fondant Company, Inc., was so relieved to know that the gangs weren't after him that he admitted frankly at the office next day that Ollie had fooled him for a minute. Mr. Bruhl even joined in the laughter and wisecracking, which went on all day. After that, for almost a week, the mild little man had comparative peace of mind. The papers said very little about Clinigan now. He had completely disappeared. Gang warfare had died down for the time being.

One Sunday morning Mr. Bruhl went for an automobile ride with his wife and daughters. They had driven about a mile through Brooklyn streets when, glancing in the mirror above his head, Mr. Bruhl observed a blue sedan just behind him. He turned off into the next side street, and the sedan turned off too. Bruhl made another turn, and the sedan followed him. 'Where are you going, dear?' asked

Mrs. Bruhl. Mr. Bruhl didn't answer her, he speeded up, he drove terrifically fast, he turned corners so wildly that the rear wheels swung around. A traffic cop shrilled at him. The younger daughter screamed. Bruhl drove right on, weaving in and out. Mrs. Bruhl began to berate him wildly. 'Have you lost your mind, Sam?' she shouted. Mr. Bruhl looked behind him. The sedan was no longer to be seen. He slowed up. 'Let's go home,' he said. 'I've had enough of this.'

A month went by without incident (thanks largely to Mrs. Breithofter) and Samuel Bruhl began to be himself again. On the day that he was practically normal once more, sluggy Pensiotta, alias Killer Lewis, alias Stranger Koetschke, was shot. Sluggy was the leader of the gang that had sworn to get Shoescar Clinigan. The papers instantly took up the gang-war story where they had left off. Pictures of Clinigan were published again. The slaying of Pensiotta, said the papers, meant but one thing: it meant that Shoescar Clinigan was cooked. Mr. Bruhl, reading this, went gradually to pieces once more.

After another week of sulking about, starting at every noise, and once almost fainting when an automobile backfired near him, Samuel Bruhl began to take on a remarkable new appearance. He talked out of the corner of his mouth, his eyes grew shifty. He looked more and more like Shoescar Clinigan. He snarled at his wife. Once he called her 'Babe,' and he had never called her anything but Minnie. He kissed her in a strange, new way, acting rough, almost brutal. At the office he was mean and overbearing. He used peculiar language. One night when the Bruhls had friends in for bridge – old Mr. Creegan and his wife – Bruhl suddenly appeared from upstairs with a pair of scarlet pyjamas on, smoking a cigarette, and gripping his revolver. After a few loud and incoherent remarks of a boastful nature, he let fly at a clock on the mantel, and hit it squarely in the middle. Mrs. Bruhl screamed. Mr. Creegan fainted. Bert, who was in the kitchen, howled. 'What's the matta you?' snarled Bruhl. 'Ya bunch of softies.'

Quite by accident, Mrs. Bruhl discovered, hidden away in a closet, eight or ten books on gangs and gangsters, which Bruhl had put there. They included 'Al Capone,' 'You Can't Win,' '10,000 Public Enemies' and a lot of others; and they were all well thumbed. Mrs. Bruhl realized that it was high time something was done, and she determined to have a doctor for her husband. For two or three days Bruhl had not gone to work. He lay around in his bedroom, in his red pyjamas, smoking cigarettes. The office phoned once or twice. When Mrs. Bruhl urged him to get up and dress and go to work, he laughed and patted her roughly on the head. 'It's a knockover, kid,' he said. 'We'll be sitting pretty. To hell with it.'

The doctor who finally came and slipped into Bruhl's bedroom was very grave when he emerged. 'This is a psychosis,' he said, 'a definite psychosis. Your husband is living in a world of fantasy. He has built up a curious defence mechanism against something or other.' The doctor suggested that a psychiatrist be called in, but after he had gone Mrs. Bruhl decided to take her husband out of town on a trip. The Maskonsett Syrup & Fondant Company, Inc., was very fine about it. Mr. Scully said of course. 'Sam is very valuable to us, Mrs. Bruhl,' said Mr. Scully, 'and we all hope he'll be all right.' Just the same he had Mr. Bruhl's accounts examined, when Mrs. Bruhl had gone.

Oddly enough, Samuel Bruhl was amenable to the idea of going away. 'I need a rest,' he said. 'You're right. Let's get the hell out of here.' He seemed normal up to the time they set out for the Grand Central and then he insisted on leaving from the 125th Street station. Mrs. Bruhl took exception to this, as being ridiculous, whereupon her doting husband snarled at her. 'God, what a dumb moll *I* picked,' he said to Minnie Bruhl, and he added bitterly that if the heat was put to him it would be his own babe who was to blame. 'And what do you think of *that*?' he said, pushing her to the floor of the cab.

They went to a little inn in the mountains. It wasn't a very nice place, but the rooms were clean and the meals were good. There was no form of entertainment, except a Tom Thumb golf course and an uneven tennis court, but Mr. Bruhl didn't mind. He said it was too cold outdoors, anyway. He stayed indoors, reading and smoking. In the evening he played the mechanical piano in the dining-room. He liked to play 'More Than You Know' over and over again. One night, about nine o'clock, he was putting in his seventh or eighth nickel when four men walked into the dining-room. They were silent men, wearing overcoats, and carrying what appeared to be cases for musical instruments. They took out various kinds of guns from their cases, quickly, expertly, and walked over toward Bruhl, keeping step. He turned just in time to see them line up four abreast and aim at him. Nobody else was in the room. There was a cumulative roar and a series of flashes. Mr. Bruhl fell and the men walked out in single file, rapidly, nobody having said a word.

Mrs. Bruhl, state police, and the hotel manager tried to get the wounded man to talk. Chief Witznitz of the nearest town's police force tried it. It was no good. Bruhl only snarled and told them to go away and let him alone. Finally, Commissioner O'Donnell of the New York City Police Department arrived at the hospital. He asked Bruhl what the men looked like. 'I don't know what they looked like,' snarled Bruhl, 'and if I did know I wouldn't tell you.' He was silent a moment, then: 'Cop!' he added, bitterly. The Commissioner sighed and turned away. 'They're all like that,' he said to the others in the room. 'They never talk.' Hearing this, Mr. Bruhl smiled, a pleased smile, and closed his eyes.

The Day The Dam Broke

MY MEMORIES of what my family and I went through during the 1913 flood in Ohio I would gladly forget. And yet neither the hardships we endured nor the turmoil and confusion we experienced can alter my feeling toward my native state and city. I am having a fine time now and wish Columbus were here, but if anyone ever wished a city was in hell it was during that frightful and perilous afternoon in 1913 when the dam broke, or, to be more exact, when everybody in town *thought* that the dam broke. We were both ennobled and demoralized by the experience. Grandfather especially rose to magnificent heights which can never lose their splendour for me, even though his reactions to the flood were based upon a profound misconception; namely, that Nathan Bedford Forrest's cavalry was the menace we were called upon to face. The only possible means of escape for us was to flee the house, a step which grandfather sternly forbade, brandishing his old army sabre in his hand. 'Let the sons – come!' he roared. Meanwhile hundreds of people were streaming by our house in wild panic, screaming 'Go east! Go east!' We had to stun grandfather with the ironing board. Impeded as we were by the inert form of the old gentleman – he was taller than six feet and weighed almost a hundred and seventy pounds – we were passed, in the first half-mile, by practically everybody else in the city. Had grandfather not come to, at the corner of Parsons Avenue and Town Street, we would unquestionably have been overtaken and engulfed by the roaring waters – that is, if there had *been* any roaring waters. Later, when the panic had died down and people had gone rather sheepishly back to their homes and their offices, minimizing the distances they had run and offering various

175

reasons for running, city engineers pointed out that even if the dam had broken, the water level would not have risen more than two additional inches in the West Side. The West Side was, at the time of the dam scare, under thirty feet of water – as, indeed, were all Ohio river towns during the great spring floods of twenty years ago. The East Side (where we lived and where all the running occurred) had never been in any danger at all. Only a rise of some ninety-five feet could have caused the flood waters to flow over High Street – the thoroughfare that divided the east side of town from the west – and engulf the East Side.

The fact that we were all as safe as kittens under a cookstove did not, however, assuage in the least the fine despair and the grotesque desperation which seized upon the residents of the East Side when the cry spread like a grass fire that the dam had given way. Some of the most dignified, staid, cynical, and clear-thinking men in town abandoned their wives, stenographers, homes, and offices and ran east. There are few alarms in the world more terrifying than 'The dam has broken!' There are few persons capable of stopping to reason when that clarion cry strikes upon their ears, even persons who live in towns no nearer than five hundred miles to a dam.

The Columbus, Ohio, broken-dam rumour began, as I recall it, about noon of March 12, 1913. High Street, the main canyon of trade, was loud with the placid hum of business and the buzzing of placid businessmen arguing, computing, wheedling, offering, refusing, compromising. Darius Conningway, one of the foremost corporation lawyers in the Middle-West, was telling the Public Utilities Commission in the language of Julius Caesar that they might as well try to move the Northern star as to move him. Other men were making their little boasts and their little gestures. Suddenly somebody began to run. It may be that he had simply remembered, all of a moment, an engagement to meet his wife, for which he was now frightfully late. Whatever it was, he ran east on Broad Street (probably toward the Maramor Restaurant, a favourite place for a man to meet his wife). Somebody else began to run, perhaps a newsboy in high spirits. Another man, a portly gentleman of affairs, broke into a trot. Inside of ten minutes, everybody on High Street, from the Union Depot to the Courthouse, was running. A loud mumble gradually crystallized into the dread word 'dam.' 'The dam has broke!' The fear was put into words by a little old lady in an electric, or by a traffic cop, or by a small boy: nobody knows who, nor does it now really matter. Two thousand people were abruptly in full flight. 'Go east!' was the cry

176

Two thousand people were in full flight

that arose – east away from the river, east to safety. 'Go east! Go east! Go east!'

Black streams of people flowed eastward down all the streets leading in that direction; these streams, whose headwaters were in the dry-goods stores, office buildings, harness shops, movie theatres, were fed by trickles of housewives, children, cripples, servants, dogs, and cats, slipping out of the houses past which the main streams flowed, shouting and screaming. People ran out leaving fires burning and food cooking and doors wide open. I remember, however, that my mother turned out all the fires and that she took with her a dozen eggs and two loaves of bread. It was her plan to make Memorial Hall, just two blocks away, and take refuge somewhere in the top of it, in one of the dusty rooms where war veterans met and where old battle flags and stage scenery were stored. But the seething throngs, shouting 'Go east!' drew her along and the rest of us with her. When grandfather regained full consciousness, at Parsons Avenue, he turned upon the retreating mob like a vengeful prophet and exhorted the men to form ranks and stand off the Rebel dogs, but at length he, too, got the idea

177

that the dam had broken and, roaring 'Go east!' in his powerful voice, he caught up in one arm a small child and in the other a slight clerkish man of perhaps forty-two and we slowly began to gain on those ahead of us.

A scattering of firemen, policemen, and army officers in dress uniforms – there had been a review at Fort Hayes, in the northern part of town – added colour to the surging billows of people. 'Go east!' cried a little child in a piping voice, as she ran past a porch on which drowsed a lieutenant-colonel of infantry. Used to quick decisions, trained to immediate obedience, the officer bounded off the porch and, running at full tilt, soon passed the child, bawling 'Go east!' The two of them emptied rapidly the houses of the little street they were on. 'What is it? What is it?' demanded a fat, waddling man who intercepted the colonel. The officer dropped behind and asked the little child what it was. 'The dam has broke!' gasped the girl. 'The dam has broke!' roared the colonel. 'Go east! Go east! Go east!' He was soon leading, with the exhausted child in his arms, a fleeing company of three hundred persons who had gathered around him from living-rooms, shops, garages, backyards, and basements.

Nobody has ever been able to compute with any exactness how many people took part in the great rout of 1913, for the panic, which extended from the Winslow Bottling Works in the south end to Clintonville, six miles north, ended as abruptly as it began and the bobtail and rag-tag and velvet-gowned groups of refugees melted away and slunk home, leaving the streets peaceful and deserted. The shouting, weeping, tangled evacuation of the city lasted not more than two hours in all. Some few people got as far east as Reynoldsburg, twelve miles away; fifty or more reached the Country Club, eight miles away; most of the others gave up, exhausted, or climbed trees in Franklin Park, four miles out. Order was restored and fear dispelled finally by means of militiamen riding about in motor lorries bawling through megaphones: 'The dam has *not* broken!' At first this tended only to add to the confusion and increase the panic, for many stampeders thought the soldiers were bellowing 'The dam has now broken!' thus setting an official seal of authentication on the calamity.

All the time, the sun shone quietly and there was nowhere any sign of oncoming waters. A visitor in an airplane, looking down on the straggling, agitated masses of people below, would have been hard put to it to divine a reason for the phenomenon. It must have inspired, in such an observer, a peculiar kind of terror, like the sight of the *Marie Celeste*, abandoned at sea, its galley fires peacefully burning, its tranquil decks bright in the sunlight.

An aunt of mine, Aunt Edith Taylor, was in a movie theatre on High Street when, over and above the sound of the piano in the pit (a W. S. Hart picture was being shown), there rose the steadily increasing tromp of running feet. Persistent shouts rose above the tromping. An elderly man, sitting near my aunt, mumbled something, got out of his seat, and went up the aisle at a dogtrot. This started everybody. In an instant the audience was jamming the aisles. 'Fire!' shouted a woman who always expected to be burned up in a theatre; but now the shouts outside were louder and coherent. 'The dam has broke!' cried somebody. 'Go east!' screamed a small woman in front of my aunt. And east they went, pushing and shoving and clawing, knocking women and children down, emerging finally into the street, torn and sprawling. Inside the theatre, Bill Hart was calmly calling some desperado's bluff and the brave girl at the piano played 'Row! Row! Row!' loudly and then 'In My Harem.' Outside, men were streaming across the Statehouse yard, others were climbing trees, a woman managed to get up onto the 'These Are My Jewels' statue, whose bronze figures of Sherman, Stanton, Grant, and Sheridan watched with cold unconcern the going to pieces of the capital city.

'I ran south to State Street, east on State to Third, south on Third to Town, and out east on Town,' my Aunt Edith has written me. 'A tall spare woman with grim eyes and a determined chin ran past me down the middle of the street. I was still uncertain as to what was the matter, in spite of all the shouting. I drew up alongside the woman with some effort, for although she was in her late fifties, she had a beautiful easy running form and seemed to be in excellent condition "What is it?" I puffed. She gave me a quick glance and then looked ahead again, stepping up her pace a trifle. "Don't ask me, ask God!" she said.

'When I reached Grant Avenue, I was so spent that Dr. H. R. Mallory – you remember Dr. Mallory, the man with the white beard who looks like Robert Browning? – well, Dr. Mallory, whom I had drawn away from at the corner of Fifth and Town, passed me. "It's got us!" he shouted, and I felt sure that whatever it was *did* have us, for you know what conviction Dr. Mallory's statements always carried. I didn't know at the time what he meant, but I found out later. There was a boy behind him on roller-skates, and Dr. Mallory mistook the swishing of the skates for the sound of rushing water. He eventually reached the Columbus School for Girls, at the corner of Parsons Avenue and Town Street, where he collapsed, expecting the cold fro-

179

'It's got us!' he shouted

thing waters of the Scioto to sweep him into oblivion. The boy on the skates swirled past him and Dr. Mallory realized for the first time what he had been running from. Looking back up the street, he could see no signs of water, but nevertheless, after resting a few minutes, he jogged on east again. He caught up with me at Ohio Avenue, where we rested together. I should say that about seven hundred people passed us. A funny thing was that all of them were on foot. Nobody seemed to have had the courage to stop and start his car; but as I remember it, all cars had to be cranked in those days, which is probably the reason.'

The next day, the city went about its business as if nothing had happened, but there was no joking. It was two years or more before you dared treat the breaking of the dam lightly. And even now, twenty years after, there are a few persons, like Dr. Mallory, who will shut up like a clam if you mention the Afternoon of the Great Run.

MARK TWAIN (Samuel Clemens)
(1835–1910)

Twain was born in Missouri, and his childhood along the Mississippi provided much of the material for his writing. Indeed, the pen-name 'Mark Twain' is taken from river-boat slang for two fathoms deep. After early careers as printer, steam boat pilot, and lecturer, he made his reputation as a writer with the publication of *The Innocents Abroad*. His better-known works include *Huckleberry Finn, Tom Sawyer, Life on the Mississippi*, and *The Man that Corrupted Hadleyburg*.

The Notorious Jumping Frog Of Calaveras County

In compliance with the request of a friend of mine, who wrote me from the East, I called on good-natured, garrulous old Simon Wheeler, and inquired after my friend's friend, Leonidas W. Smiley, as requested to do, and I hereunto append the result. I have a lurking suspicion that *Leonidas W.* Smiley is a myth; that my friend never knew such a personage; and that he only conjectured that if I asked old Wheeler about him, it would remind him of his infamous *Jim* Smiley, and he would go to work and bore me to death with some exasperating reminiscence of him as long and as tedious as it should be useless to me. If that was the design, it succeeded.

I found Simon Wheeler dozing comfortably by the bar-room stove of the dilapidated tavern in the decayed mining camp of Angel's, and I noticed that he was fat and bald-headed, and had an expression of winning gentleness and simplicity upon his tranquil countenance. He roused up and gave me good day. I told him a friend of mine had commissioned me to make some inquiries about a cherished companion of his boyhood, named *Leonidas W.* Smiley – *Rev. Leonidas W.* Smiley – a young minister of the gospel, who he had heard was at one time a resident of Angel's Camp. I added that if Mr. Wheeler could tell me anything about this *Rev. Leonidas W.* Smiley, I would feel under many obligations to him.

Simon Wheeler backed me into a corner and blockaded me there with his chair, and then sat down and reeled off the monotonous narrative which follows this paragraph. He never smiled, he never frowned, he never changed his voice from the gentle-flowing key to which he tuned his initial sentence, he never betrayed the slightest suspicion of enthusiasm; but all through the interminable narrative there ran a vein of impressive earnestness and sincerity which showed me plainly that, so far from his imagining that there was anything ridiculous or funny about his story, he regarded it as a really important matter, and admired its two heroes as men of transcendent genius in *finesse*. I let him go on in his own way, and never interrupted him once.

'Rev. Leonidas W. – H'm, Reverend Le – well, there was a feller here once by the name of *Jim* Smiley, in the winter of '49, or maybe it was the spring of '50 – I don't recollect exactly, somehow, though what makes me think it was one or the other, is because I remember the big flume warn't finished when he first come to the camp; but anyway, he was the curiousest man about, always betting on anything that turned up you ever see, if he could get anybody to bet on the other side; and if he couldn't, he'd change sides. Any way that suited the other side would suit *him* – any way, just so's he got a bet, *he* was satisfied. But still he was lucky, uncommon lucky; he most always come out winner. He was always ready, and laying for a chance; there couldn't be no solit'ry thing mentioned but that feller'd offer to bet on it, and take ary side you please, as I was just telling you. If there was a horse-race, you'd find him flush or you'd find him busted at the end of it; if there was a dog-fight, he'd bet on it; if there was a cat-fight, he'd bet on it; if there was a chicken-fight, he'd bet on it; why, if there was two birds setting on a fence, he would bet you which one would fly first; or if there was a camp-meeting, he would be there reg'lar to bet on Parson Walker, which he judged to be the best exhorter about here; and so he was, too, and a good man. If he even see a straddle-bug start to go anywheres, he would bet you how long it would take him to get to – to wherever he was going to; and if you took him up, he would foller that straddle-bug to Mexico, but what he would find out where he was bound for, and how long he was on the road. Lots of the boys here has seen that Smiley, and can tell you about him. Why, it never made no difference to *him* – he'd bet *any* thing – the dangdest feller. Parson Walker's wife laid very sick once for a good while, and it seemed as if they warn't going to save her; but one morning he come in, and Smiley up and asked him how she was, and he said she was considable better – thank the Lord for his inf'nit mercy! – and coming on so smart that, with the blessing of Prov'dence, she'd get well yet; and Smiley, before he thought, says, "Well, I'll resk two-and-a-half she don't, anyway."

'This-yer Smiley had a mare – the boys called her the fifteen-minute nag, but that was only in fun, you know, because of course she was faster than that – and he used to win money on that horse, for all she was so slow and always had the asthma, or the distemper, or the consumption, or something of that kind. They used to give her two or three hundred yards' start, and then pass her under way; but always at the fag-end of the race she'd get excited and desperate-like, and come cavorting and straddling up, and scattering her legs around limber, sometimes in the air, and sometimes out to one side amongst the fences, and kicking up m-o-r-e dust and raising m-o-r-e racket with her coughing and sneezing and blowing her nose – and *always* fetch up at the stand just about a neck ahead, as near as you could cipher it down.

'And he had a little small bull-pup, that to look at him you'd think he warn't worth a cent but to set around and look ornery, and lay for a chance to steal something. But as soon as money was up on him he was a different dog; his under-jaw'd begin to stick out like the fo'castle of a steamboat, and his teeth would uncover and shine like the furnaces. And a dog might tackle him and bullyrag him, and bite him, and throw him over his shoulder two or three times, and Andrew Jackson – which was the name of the pup – Andrew Jackson would never let on but what *he* was satisfied, and hadn't expected nothing else – and the bets being doubled and doubled on the other side all the time, till the money was all up; and then all of a sudden he would grab the other dog jest by the j'int of his hind leg and freeze to it – not chaw, you understand, but only just grip and hang on till they throwed up the sponge, if it was a year. Smiley always come out winner on that pup, till he harnessed a dog once that didn't have no hind legs, because they'd been sawed off in a circular saw, and when the thing had gone along far enough, and the money was all up, and he come to make a snatch for his pet holt, he see in a minute how he'd been imposed on, and how the other dog had him in the door, so to speak, and he 'peared surprised, and then he looked sorter discouraged-like, and didn't try no more to win the fight, and so he got shucked out bad. He give Smiley a look, as much as to say his heart was broke, and it was *his* fault, for putting up a dog that hadn't no hind legs for him to take holt of, which was his main dependence in a fight, and then he limped off a piece and laid down and died. It was a good pup, was that Andrew Jackson, and would have made a name for hisself if he'd lived, for the stuff was in him and he had genius – I know it, because he hadn't no opportunities to speak of, and it don't stand to reason that a dog could make such a fight as he could under them circumstances if he hadn't no talent. It always makes me feel sorry when I think of that last fight of his'n, and the way it turned out.

'Well, this-yer Smiley had rat-tarriers, and chicken cocks, and tomcats and all them kind of things, till you couldn't rest, and you couldn't fetch nothing for him to bet on but he'd match you. He ketched a frog one day, and took him home, and said he cal'lated to educate him; and so he never done nothing for three months but set in his back yard and learn that frog to jump. And you bet you he *did* learn him, too. He'd give him a little punch behind, and the next minute you'd see that frog whirling in the air like a doughnut – see him turn one summerset, or maybe a couple, if he got a good start, and come down flat-footed and all right, like a cat. He got him up so in the matter of ketching flies, and kep' him in practice so constant, that he'd nail a fly every time as fur as he could see him. Smiley said all a frog wanted was education, and he could do 'most anything – and I believe him. Why, I've seen him set Dan'l Webster down here on this floor – Dan'l Webster was the name of the frog – and sing out, "Flies, Dan'l, flies!" and quicker'n you could wink he'd spring straight up and snake a fly off'n the counter there, and flop down on the floor ag'in as solid as a gob of mud, and fall to scratching the side of his head with his hind foot as indifferent as if he hadn't no idea he'd been doin' any more'n any frog might do. You never see a frog so modest and straightfor'ard as he was, for all he was so gifted. And when it come to fair and square jumping on a dead level, he could get over more ground at one straddle than any animal of his breed you ever see. Jumping on a dead level was his strong suit, you understand; and when it come to that, Smiley would ante up money on him as long as he had a red. Smiley was monstrous proud of his frog, and well he might be, for fellers that had travelled and been everywheres, all said he laid over any frog that ever *they* see.

'Well, Smiley kep' the beast in a little latice box, and he used to fetch him down-town sometimes and lay for a bet. One day a feller – a stranger in the camp, he was – come acrost him with his box, and says:–

'"What might it be that you've got in the box?"

'And Smiley says, sorter indifferent-like, "It might be a parrot, or it might be a canary, maybe, but it ain't – it's only just a frog."

'And the feller took it, and looked at it careful, and turned it round this way and that, and says, "H'm – so 'tis. Well, what's *he* good for?"

'"Well," Smiley says, easy and careless, "he's good enough for *one* thing, I should judge – he can outjump any frog in Calaveras County."

You never see a frog so modest and straightfor'ard as he was

'The feller took the box again, and took another long, particular look, and give it back to Smiley, and says, very deliberate, "Well," he says, "I don't see no p'ints about that frog that's any better'n any other frog."

'"Maybe you don't," Smiley says. "Maybe you understand frogs, and maybe you don't understand 'em; maybe you've had experience, and maybe you ain't only a amature, as it were. Anyways, I've got *my* opinion, and I'll resk forty dollars that he can outjump any frog in Calaveras County."

'And the feller studied a minute, and then says, kinder sad like, "Well, I'm only a stranger here, and I ain't got no frog; but if I had a frog, I'd bet you."

'And then Smiley says, "That's all right – that's all right – if you'll hold my box a minute, I'll go and get you a frog." And so the feller took the box, and put up his forty dollars along with Smiley's, and set down to wait.

'So he set there a good while thinking and thinking to hisself, and then he got the frog out and prized his mouth open, and took a tea-spoon and filled him full of quail shot – filled him pretty near up to his chin – and set him on the floor. Smiley he went to the swamp and slopped around in the mud for a long time, and finally he ketched a frog, and fetched him in, and give him to this feller, and says:–

'"Now, if you're ready, set him alongside of Dan'l, with his fore-paws just even with Dan'l's, and I'll give the word." Then he says, "One – two – three – *git!*" and him and the feller touched up the frogs from behind, and the new frog hopped off lively, but Dan'l give a heave, and hysted up his shoulders – so – like a Frenchman, but it warn't no use – he couldn't budge; he was planted as solid as a church, and he couldn't no more stir than if he was anchored out. Smiley was a good deal surprised, and he was disgusted too, but he didn't have no idea what the matter was, of course.

'The feller took the money and started away; and when he was going out at the door, he sorter jerked his thumb over his shoulder – so – at Dan'l, and says again, very deliberate, "Well," he says, "I don't see no p'ints about that frog that's any better'n any other frog."

'Smiley he stood scratching his head and looking down at Dan'l a long time, and at last he says, "I do wonder what in the nation that frog throw'd off for – I wonder if there ain't something the matter with him – he 'pears to look mighty baggy, somehow.'– And he ketched Dan'l by the nap of the neck, and hefted him, and says, "Why, blame my cats if he don't weigh five pound!" and turned him upside down, and he belched out a double handful of shot. And then he see how it was, and he was the maddest man – he set the frog down and took out after the feller, but he never ketched him. And – '

[Here Simon Wheeler heard his name called from the front yard, and got up to see what was wanted.] 'A-turning to me as he moved away, he said: "Just set where you are, stranger, and rest easy – I ain't going to be gone a second."'

But, by your leave, I did not think that a continuation of the history of the enterprising vagabond *Jim* Smiley would be likely to afford me much information concerning the Rev. *Leonidas W.* Smiley, and so I started away.

At the door I met the sociable Wheeler returning, and he botton-holed me and recommenced:-

'Well, this-yer Smiley had a yaller one-eyed cow that didn't have no tail, only jest a short stump like a bannanner, and – '

However, lacking both time and inclination, I did not wait to hear about the afflicted cow, but took my leave.

Blue-Jays

ANIMALS talk to each other, of course. There can be no question about that; but I suppose there are very few people who can understand them. I never knew but one man who could. I knew he could, however, because he told me so himself. He was a middle-aged, simple-hearted miner, who had lived in a lonely corner of California, among the woods and mountains, a good many years, and had studied the ways of his only neighbours, the beasts and the birds, until he believed he could accurately translate any remark which they made. This was Jim Baker. According to Jim Baker, some animals have only a limited education and use only very simple words, and scarcely ever a comparison or a flowery figure; whereas, certain other animals have a large vocabulary, a fine command of language, and a ready and fluent delivery; consequently these latter talk a great deal; they like it; they are conscious of their talent, and they enjoy 'showing off.' Baker said that, after long and careful observation, he had come to the conclusion that the blue-jays were the best talkers he had found among birds and beasts. Said he:

'There's more *to* a blue-jay than any other creature. He has got more moods and more different kinds of feelings than other creatures; and, mind you, whatever a blue-jay feels, he can put into language. And no mere commonplace language either, but rattling, out-and-out book talk – and bristling with metaphor too – just bristling! And as for command of language – why, *you* never see a blue jay get stuck for a word. No man ever did. They just boil out of him! And another thing: I've noticed a good deal, and there's no bird, or cow, or anything that uses as good grammar as a blue-jay. You may say a cat uses good

187

grammar. Well, a cat does – but you let a cat get excited, once; you let a cat get to pulling fur with another cat on a shed, nights, and you'll hear grammar that will give you the lockjaw. Ignorant people think it's the *noise* which fighting cats make that is so aggravating, but it ain't so; it's the sickening grammar they use. Now I've never heard a jay use bad grammar but very seldom; and when they do, they are as ashamed as a human; they shut right down and leave.

'You may call a jay a bird. Well, so he is, in a measure – because he's got feathers on him, and don't belong to no church, perhaps; but otherwise he is just as much a human as you be. And I'll tell you for why. A jay's gifts, and instincts, and feelings, and interests, cover the whole ground. A jay hasn't got any more principle than a Congressman. A jay will lie, a jay will steal, a jay will deceive, a jay will betray; and, four times out of five, a jay will go back on his solemnest promise. The sacredness of an obligation is a thing which you can't cram into no blue-jay's head. Now, on top of all this, there's another thing: a jay can out-swear any gentleman in the mines. You think a cat can swear. Well, a cat can; but you give a blue-jay a subject that calls for his reserve powers, and where is your cat? Don't talk to *me* – I know too much about this thing. And there's yet another thing: in the one little particular of scolding – just good, clean, out-and-out scolding – a blue-jay can lay over anything, human or divine. Yes, sir, a jay is everything that a man is. A jay can cry, a jay can laugh, a jay can feel shame, a jay can reason and plan and discuss, a jay likes gossip and scandal, a jay has got a sense of humour, a jay knows when he is an ass just as well as you do – maybe better. If a jay ain't human, he better take in his sign, that's all. Now I am going to tell you a perfectly true fact about some blue-jays.

'When I first begun to understand jay language correctly, there was a little incident happened here. Seven years ago, the last man in this region but me moved away. There stands his house – been empty ever since; a log house, with a plank roof – just one big room, and no more; no ceiling – nothing between the rafters and the floor. Well, one Sunday morning I was sitting out here in front of my cabin, with my cat, taking the sun, and looking at the blue hills, and listening to the leaves rustling so lonely in the trees, and thinking of the home away yonder in the States, that I hadn't heard from in thirteen years, when a blue-jay lit on that house, with an acorn in his mouth, and says, "Hello, I reckon I've struck something!" When he spoke, the acorn fell out of his mouth and rolled down the roof, of course, but he didn't care; his mind was all on the thing he had struck. It was a knot-hole in the roof. He cocked his head to one side, shut one eye and put the other one to the hole, like a 'possum looking down a jug, then he glanced up with his bright eyes, gave a wink or two with his wings – which signifies gratification, you understand – and says, "It looks like a hole, it's located like a hole – blamed if I don't believe it *is* a hole!"

'Blamed if I don't believe it is *a hole!'*

'Then he cocked his head down and took another look; he glances up perfectly joyful this time; winks his wings and his tail both, and says, "Oh no, this ain't no fat thing, I reckon! If I ain't in luck! – why, it's a perfectly elegant hole!" So he flew down and got that acorn, and fetched it up and dropped it in, and was just tilting his head back with the heavenliest smile on his face, when all of a sudden he was paralysed into a listening attitude, and that smile faded gradually out of his countenance like breath off'n a razor, and the queerest look of surprise took its place. Then he says, "Why, I didn't hear it fall!" He cocked his eye at the hole again and took a long look; raised up and shook his head; stepped around to the other side of the hole, and took another look from that side; shook his head again. He studied a while, then he just went into the *de*tails – walked round and round the hole, and spied into it from every point of the compass. No use. Now he took a thinking attitude on the comb of the roof, and scratched the back of his head with his right foot a minute, and finally says, "Well, it's too many for *me*, that's certain; must be a mighty long hole; however, I ain't got no time to fool around here; I got to 'tend to business; I reckon it's all right – chance it, anyway!"

'So he flew off and fetched another acorn and dropped it in, and tried to flirt his eye to the hole quick enough to see what become of it, but he was too late. He held his eye there as much as a minute; then he raised up and sighed, and says, "Confound it, I don't seem to understand this thing, no way; however, I'll tackle her again." He fetched another acorn, and done his level best to see what become of it, but he couldn't. He says, "Well, *I* never struck no such a hole as this before; I'm of the opinion it's a totally new kind of a hole." Then he begun to get mad. He held in for a spell, walking up and down the comb of the roof, and shaking his head and muttering to himself; but his feelings got the upper hand of him presently, and he broke loose and cussed himself black in the face. I never see a bird take on so about a little thing. When he got through, he walks to the hole and looks in again for a half a minute; then he says, "Well, you're a long hole, and a deep hole, and a mighty singular hole altogether – but I've started in to fill you, and I'm d——d if I *don't* fill you, if it takes a hundred years!"

'And with that, away he went. You never see a bird work so since you was born. He laid into his work like a nigger, and the way he hove acorns into that hole for about two hours and a half was one of the most exciting and astonishing spectacles I ever struck. He never stopped to take a look any more – he just hove 'em in, and went for more. Well, at last he could hardly flop his wings, he was so tuckered out. He comes a-drooping down, once more, sweating like an ice-pitcher, drops his acorn in and says, "*Now* I guess I've got the bulge on you by this time!" So he bent down for a look. If you'll believe me, when his head come up again he was just pale with rage. He says, "I've shovelled acorns enough in there to keep the family thirty years, and if I can see a sign of one of 'em, I wish I may land in a museum with a belly full of sawdust in two minutes!"

'He just had strength enough to crawl up on to the comb and lean his back agin the chimbly, and then he collected his impressions and begun to free his mind. I see in a second that what I had mistook for profanity in the mines was only just the rudiments, as you may say.

'Another jay was going by, and heard him doing his devotions, and stops to inquire what was up. The sufferer told him the whole circumstance, and says, "Now yonder's the hole, and if you don't believe me, go and look for yourself." So this fellow went and looked, and comes back and says, "How many did you say you put in there?" "Not any less than two tons," says the sufferer. The other jay went and looked again. He couldn't seem to make it out, so he raised a yell, and three more jays come. They all examined the hole, they all made the sufferer tell it over again, then they all discussed it, and got off as many leather-headed opinions about it as an average crowd of humans could have done.

'They did call in more jays; then more and more, till pretty soon this whole region 'peared to have a blue flush about it. There must have been five thousand of them; and such another jawing and disputing and ripping and cussing, you never heard. Every jay in the whole lot put his eye to the hole, and delivered a more chuckle-headed opinion about the mystery than the jay that went there before him. They examined the house all over, too. The door was standing half-open, and at last one old jay happened to go and light on it and look in. Of course, that knocked the mystery galley-west in a second. There lay the acorns, scattered all over the floor. He flopped his wings and raised a whoop. "Come here!" he says; "come here, everybody; hang'd if this fool hasn't been trying to fill up a house with acorns!" They all came a-swooping down like a blue cloud, and as each fellow lit on the door and took a glance, the whole absurdity of the contract that that first jay had tackled hit him home, and he fell over backwards suffocating with laughter, and the next jay took his place and done the same.

'Well, sir, they roosted around here on the house-top and the trees for an hour, and guffawed over that thing like human beings. It ain't no use to tell me a blue-jay hasn't got a sense of humour, because I know better. And memory too. They brought jays here from all over the United States to look down that hole, every summer for three years. Other birds too. And they could all see the point, except an owl that come from Nova Scotia to visit the Yo Semite, and he took this thing in on his way back. He said he couldn't see anything funny in it. But then, he was a good deal disappointed about Yo Semite, too.'

EVELYN WAUGH
(1903–1966)

Waugh's writing career is similar to that of Mark Twain in that he started out producing light-hearted social satires, poking gentle fun at his contemporaries and ended up writing sharp-edged, moralizing tales as his attitudes became increasingly bitter. Better-known works include: *Decline and Fall*, *Vile Bodies*, and *Brideshead Revisited*. The following two stories are from *Mr Loveday's Little Outing and Other Stories*.

Mr. Loveday's Little Outing

'YOU will not find your father greatly changed,' remarked Lady Moping, as the car turned into the gates of the County Asylum.

'Will he be wearing a uniform?' asked Angela.

'No, dear, of course not. He is receiving the very best attention.'

It was Angela's first visit and it was being made at her own suggestion.

Ten years had passed since the showery day in late summer when Lord Moping had been taken away; a day of confused but bitter memories for her; the day of Lady Moping's annual garden party, always bitter, confused that day by the caprice of the weather which, remaining clear and brilliant with promise until the arrival of the first guests, had suddenly blackened into a squall. There had been a scuttle for cover; the marquee had capsized; a frantic carrying of cushions and chairs; a table-cloth lofted to the boughs of the monkey-puzzler, fluttering in the rain; a bright period and the cautious emergence of guests onto the soggy lawns; another squall; another twenty minutes of sunshine. It had been an abominable afternoon, culminating at about six o'clock in her father's attempted suicide.

Lord Moping habitually threatened suicide on the occasion of the garden party; that year he had been found black in the face, hanging by his braces in the orangery; some neighbours, who were sheltering there from the rain, set him on his feet again, and before dinner a van had called for him. Since then Lady Moping had paid seasonal calls at the asylum and returned in time for tea, rather reticent of her experience.

Many of her neighbours were inclined to be critical of Lord

192

Moping's accommodation. He was not, of course, an ordinary inmate. He lived in a separate wing of the asylum, specially devoted to the segregation of wealthier lunatics. These were given every consideration which their foibles permitted. They might choose their own clothes (many indulged in the liveliest fancies), smoke the most expensive brands of cigars and, on the anniversaries of their certification entertain any other inmates for whom they had an attachment, to private dinner parties.

Many indulged in the liveliest fancies

The fact remained, however, that it was far from being the most expensive kind of institution; the uncompromising address, 'COUNTY HOME FOR MENTAL DEFECTIVES' stamped across the notepaper, worked on the uniforms of their attendants, painted, even, upon a prominent hoarding at the main entrance, suggested the lowest associations. From time to time, with less or more tact, her friends attempted to bring to Lady Moping's notice particulars of seaside nursing homes, of 'qualified practitioners with large private grounds suitable for the charge of nervous or difficult cases', but she accepted them lightly; when her son came of age he might make any changes that he thought fit; meanwhile she felt no inclination to relax her economical régime; her husband had betrayed her basely on the one day in the year when she looked for loyal support, and was far better off than he deserved.

A few lonely figures in great-coats were shuffling and loping about the park.

'Those are the lower class lunatics,' observed Lady Moping. 'There is a very nice little flower garden for people like your father. I sent them some cuttings last year.'

They drove past the blank, yellow brick façade to the doctor's private entrance and were received by him in the 'visitors room', set aside for interviews of this kind. The window was protected on the inside by bars and wire netting; there was no fireplace; when Angela nervously attempted to move her chair further from the radiator, she found that it was screwed to the floor.

'Lord Moping is quite ready to see you,' said the doctor.

'How is he?'

'Oh, very well, very well indeed, I'm glad to say. He had rather a nasty cold some time ago, but apart from that his condition is excellent. He spends a lot of his time in writing.'

They heard a shuffling, skipping sound approaching along the flagged passage. Outside the door a high peevish voice, which Angela recognized as her father's, said: 'I haven't the time, I tell you. Let them come back later.'

A gentler tone, with a slight rural burr, replied, 'Now come along. It is a purely formal audience. You need stay no longer than you like.'

Then the door was pushed open (it had no lock or fastening) and Lord Moping came into the room. He was attended by an elderly little man with full white hair and an expression of great kindness.

'That is Mr. Loveday who acts as Lord Moping's attendant.'

'Secretary,' said Lord Moping. He moved with a jogging gait and shook hands with his wife.

'This is Angela. You remember Angela, don't you?'

'No, I can't say that I do. What does she want?'

'We just came to see you.'

'Well, you have come at an exceedingly inconvenient time. I am very busy. Have you typed out that letter to the Pope yet, Loveday?'

'No, my lord. If you remember, you asked me to look up the figures

194

about the Newfoundland fisheries first?'

'So I did. Well, it is fortunate, as I think the whole letter will have to be redrafted. A great deal of new information has come to light since luncheon. A great deal . . . You see, my dear, I am fully occupied.' He turned his restless, quizzical eyes upon Angela. 'I suppose you have come about the Danube. Well, you must come again later. Tell them it will be all right, quite all right, but I have not had time to give my full attention to it. Tell them that.'

'Very well, Papa.'

'Anyway,' said Lord Moping rather petulantly, 'it is a matter of secondary importance. There is the Elbe and the Amazon and the Tigris to be dealt with first, eh, Loveday? . . . *Danube* indeed. Nasty little river. I'd only call it a stream myself. Well, can't stop, nice of you to come. I would do more for you if I could, but you see how I'm fixed. Write to me about it. That's it. *Put it in black and white.*'

And with that he left the room.

'You see,' said the doctor, 'he is in excellent condition. He is putting on weight, eating and sleeping excellently. In fact, the whole tone of his system is above reproach.'

The door opened again and Loveday returned.

'Forgive my coming back, sir, but I was afraid that the young lady might be upset at his Lordship's not knowing her. You mustn't mind him, miss. Next time he'll be very pleased to see you. It's only to-day he's put out on account of being behindhand with his work. You see, sir, all this week I've been helping in the library and I haven't been able to get all his Lordship's reports typed out. And he's got muddled with his card index. That's all it is. He doesn't mean any harm.'

'What a nice man,' said Angela, when Loveday had gone back to his charge.

'Yes. I don't know what we should do without old Loveday. Everybody loves him, staff and patients alike.'

'I remember him well. It's a great comfort to know that you are able to get such good warders,' said Lady Moping; 'people who don't know, say such foolish things about asylums.'

'Oh, but Loveday isn't a warder,' said the doctor.

'You don't mean he's cuckoo, too?' said Angela.

The doctor corrected her.

'He is an *inmate*. It is rather an interesting case. He has been here for thirty-five years.'

'But I've never seen anyone saner,' said Angela.

'He certainly has that air,' said the doctor, 'and in the last twenty years we have treated him as such. He is the life and soul of the place. Of course he is not one of the private patients, but we allow him to mix freely with them. He plays billiards excellently, does conjuring tricks at the concert, mends their gramophones, valets them, helps them in their crossword puzzles and various – er – hobbies. We allow them to give him small tips for services rendered, and he must by now have amassed quite a little fortune. He has a way with even the most troublesome of them. An invaluable man about the place.'

'Yes, but why is he here?'

'Well, it is rather sad. When he was a very young man he killed somebody – a young woman quite unknown to him, whom he knocked off her bicycle and then throttled. He gave himself up immediately afterwards and has been here ever since.'

'But surely he is perfectly safe now. Why is he not let out?'

'Well, I suppose if it was to anyone's interest, he would be. He has no relatives except a step-sister who lives in Plymouth. She used to visit him at one time, but she hasn't been for years now. He's perfectly happy here and I can assure you *we* aren't going to take the first steps in turning him out. He's far too useful to us.'

'But it doesn't seem fair,'said Angela.

Look at your father,' said the doctor. 'He'd be quite lost without Loveday to act as his secretary.'

'It doesn't seem fair.'

Angela left the asylum, oppressed by a sense of injustice. Her mother was unsympathetic.

'Think of being locked up in a looney bin all one's life.'

'He attempted to hang himself in the orangery,' replied Lady Moping, '*in front of the Chester-Martins.*'

'I don't mean Papa. I mean Mr. Loveday.'

'I don't think I know him.'

'Yes, the looney they have put to look after papa.'

'Your father's secretary. A very decent sort of man, I thought, and eminently suited to his work.'

Angela left the question for the time, but returned to it again at luncheon on the following day.

'Mums, what does one have to do to get people out of the bin?'

'The bin? God gracious, child, I hope that you do not anticipate your father's return *here*.'

'No, no. Mr. Loveday.'

'Angela, you seem to me to be totally bemused. I see it was a mistake to take you with me on our little visit yesterday.'

After luncheon Angela disappeared to the library and was soon immersed in the lunacy laws as represented in the encyclopædia.

She did not re-open the subject with her mother, but a fortnight later, when there was a question of taking some pheasants over to her father for his eleventh Certification Party she showed an unusual willingness to run over with them. Her mother was occupied with other interests and noticed nothing suspicious.

Angela drove her small car to the asylum, and after delivering the game, asked for Mr. Loveday. He was busy at the time making a crown for one of his companions who expected hourly to be anointed Emperor of Brazil, but he left his work and enjoyed several minutes' conversation with her. They spoke about her father's health and spirits. After a time Angela remarked, 'Don't you ever want to get away?'

Mr. Loveday looked at her with his gentle, blue-grey eyes. 'I've got very well used to the life, miss. I'm fond of the poor people here, and I think that several of them are quite fond of me. At least, I think they would miss me if I were to go.'

'But don't you ever think of being free again?'

'Oh yes, miss, I think of it – almost all the time I think of it.'

'What would you do if you got out? There must be *something* you would sooner do than stay here.'

The old man fidgeted uneasily. 'Well, miss, it sounds ungrateful, but I can't deny I should welcome a little outing, once, before I get too old to enjoy it. I expect we all have our secret ambitions, and there *is* one thing I often wish I could do. You mustn't ask me what. . . It wouldn't take long. But I do feel that if I had done it, just for a day, an afternoon even, then I would die quiet. I could settle down again easier, and devote myself to the poor crazed people here with a better heart. Yes, I do feel that.'

There were tears in Angela's eyes that afternoon as she drove away. 'He *shall* have his little outing, bless him,' she said.

From that day onwards for many weeks Angela had a new purpose in life. She moved about the ordinary routine of her home with an abstracted air and an unfamiliar, reserved courtesy which greatly disconcerted Lady Moping.

'I believe the child's in love. I only pray that it isn't that uncouth Egbertson boy.'

197

She read a great deal in the library, she cross-examined any guests who had pretensions to legal or medical knowledge, she showed extreme goodwill to old Sir Roderick Lane-Foscote, their Member. The names 'alienist,' 'barrister' or 'government official' now had for her the glamour that formerly surrounded film actors and professioal wrestlers. She was a woman with a cause, and before the end of the hunting season she had triumphed. Mr. Loveday achieved his liberty.

The doctor at the asylum showed reluctance but no real opposition. Sir Roderick wrote to the Home Office. The necessary papers were signed, and at last the day came when Mr. Loveday took leave of the home where he had spent such long and useful years.

His departure was marked by some ceremony. Angela and Sir Roderick Lane-Foscote sat with the doctors on the stage of the gymnasium. Below them were assembled everyone in the institution who was thought to be stable enough to endure the excitement.

Lord Moping, with a few suitable expressions of regret, presented Mr. Loveday on behalf of the wealthier lunatics with a gold cigarette case; those who supposed themselves to be emperors showered him with decorations and titles of honour. The warders gave him a silver watch and many of the non-paying inmates were in tears on the day of the presentation.

The doctor made the main speech of the afternoon. 'Remember,' he remarked, 'that you leave behind you nothing but our warmest good wishes. You are bound to us by ties that none will forget. Time will only deepen our sense of debt to you. If at any time in the future you should grow tired of your life in the world, there will always be a welcome for you here. Your post will be open.'

A dozen or so variously afflicted lunatics hopped and skipped after him down the drive until the iron gates opened and Mr. Loveday stepped into his freedom. His small trunk had already gone to the station; he elected to walk. He had been reticent about his plans, but he was well provided with money, and the general impression was that he would go to London and enjoy himself a little before visiting his step-sister in Plymouth.

It was to the surprise of all that he returned within two hours of his liberation. He was smiling whimsically, a gentle, self-regarding smile of reminiscence.

'I have come back,' he informed the doctor. 'I think that now I shall be here for good.'

'But, Loveday, what a short holiday. I'm afraid that you have hardly enjoyed yourself at all.'

'Oh yes, sir, thank you, sir, I've enjoyed myself *very much*. I'd been promising myself one little treat, all these years. It was short, sir, but *most* enjoyable. Now I shall be able to settle down again to my work here without any regrets.'

Half a mile up the road from the asylum gates, they later discovered an abandoned bicycle. It was a lady's machine of some antiquity. Quite near it in the ditch lay the strangled body of a young woman, who, riding home to her tea, had chanced to overtake Mr. Loveday, as he strode along, musing on his opportunities.

Period Piece

LADY AMELIA had been educated in the belief that it was the height of impropriety to read a novel in the morning. Now, in the twilight of her days, when she had singularly little to occupy the two hours between her appearance downstairs at quarter past eleven, hatted and fragrant with lavender water, and the announcement of luncheon, she adhered rigidly to this principle. As soon as luncheon was over, however, and coffee had been served in the drawing room; before the hot milk in his saucer had sufficiently cooled for Manchu to drink it; while the sunlight, in summer, streamed through the Venetian blinds of the round-fronted Regency windows; while, in winter, the carefully stacked coal-fire glowed in its round-fronted grate; while Manchu sniffed and sipped at his saucer, and Lady Amelia spread out on her knees the various shades of coarse wool with which her failing eyesight now compelled her to work; while the elegant Regency clock ticked off the two and a half hours to tea time – it was Miss Myers' duty to read a novel aloud to her employer.

With the passing years Lady Amelia had grown increasingly fond of novels, and of novels of a particular type. They were what the assistant in the circulating library termed 'strong meat' and kept in a hidden place under her desk. It was Miss Myers' duty to fetch and return them. 'Have you anything of the kind Lady Amelia likes?' she would ask sombrely.

'Well, there's this just come in,' the assistant would answer, fishing up a volume from somewhere near her feet.

At one time Lady Amelia had enjoyed love stories about the irresponsible rich; then she had had a psychological phase; at the

Fond of novels, and of novels of a particular type

moment her interests were American, in the school of brutal realism and gross slang. 'Something else like *Sanctuary* or *Bessie Cotter*,' Miss Myers was reluctantly obliged to demand. And as the still afternoon was disturbed by her delicately modulated tones enunciating page by page, in scarcely comprehensible idiom, the narratives of rape and betrayal, Lady Amelia would occasionally chuckle a little over her woolwork.

'Women of my age always devote themselves either to religion or novels,' she said. 'I have remarked among my few surviving friends that those who read novels enjoy far better health.'

The story they were reading came to an end at half-past four.

'Thank you,' said Lady Amelia. 'That was *most* entertaining. Make a note of the author's name, please, Miss Myers. You will be able to go to the library after tea and see whether they have another. I hope you enjoyed it.'

'Well, it was very sad, wasn't it?'

'Sad?'

'I mean the poor young man who wrote it must come from a terrible home.'

'Why do you say that, Miss Myers?'

'Well, it was so far fetched.'

'It is odd you should think so. I invariably find modern novels painfully reticent. Of course until lately I never read novels at all. I cannot say what they were like formerly. I was far too busy in the old days living my own life and sharing the lives of my friends – all people who came from anything but terrible homes,' she added with a glance at her companion; a glance sharp and smart as a rap on the knuckles with an ivory ruler.

There was half-an-hour before tea; Manchu was asleep on the hearth rug, before the fireless grate; the sun streamed in through the blinds, casting long strips of light on the Aubusson carpet. Lady Amelia fixed her eyes on the embroidered, heraldic firescreen; and proceeded dreamily. 'I suppose it would not do. You couldn't write about the things which actually happen. People are so used to novels that they would not believe them. The poor writers are constantly at pains to make the truth seem probable. Dear me, I often think, as you sit, *so kindly*, reading to me, "If one was just to write down quite simply the events of a few years in *any* household one knows . . . No one would believe it." I can hear you yourself, dear Miss Myers, saying, "Perhaps these things *do* happen, very occasionally, once in a century, in terrible homes"; instead of which they are constantly happening, every day, all round us – or at least, they were in my young days.

'Take for example the extremely ironic circumstances of the succession of the present Lord Cornphillip:

'I used to know the Cornphillips very well in the old days,' said Lady Amelia – 'Etty was a cousin of my mother's – and when we were first married my husband and I used to stay there every autumn for the pheasant shooting. Billy Cornphillip was a *very* dull man – very dull indeed. He was in my husband's regiment. I used to know a great many dull people at the time when I was first married, but Billy Cornphillip was notorious for dullness even among my husband's friends. Their place is in Wiltshire. I see the boy is trying to sell it now. I am not surprised. It was very ugly and very unhealthy. I used to dread our visits there.

'Etty was entirely different, a lively little thing with very nice eyes. People thought her fast. Of course it was a *very* good match for her; she was one of seven sisters and her father was a younger son, poor dear.

202

Billy was twelve years older. She had been after him for years. I remember crying with pleasure when I received her letter telling me of the engagement . . . It was at the breakfast table . . . she used a very artistic kind of writing paper with pale blue edges and bows of blue ribbon at the corner . . .

'Poor Etty was always being artistic; she tried to do something with the house – put up peacocks' feathers and painted tambourines and some very modern stencil work – but the result was always depressing. She made a little garden for herself at some distance from the house, with a high wall and a padlocked door, where she used to retire to think – or so she said – for hours at a time. She called it the Garden of Her Thoughts. I went in with her once, as a great privilege, after one of her quarrels with Billy. Nothing grew very well there – because of the high walls, I suppose, and her doing it all herself. There was a mossy seat in the middle. I suppose she used to sit on it while she thought. The whole place had a nasty dank smell . . .

'Well we were all delighted at Ett's luck and I think she quite liked Billy at first and was prepared to behave well to him, in spite of his dullness. You see it came just when we had all despaired. Billy had been the friend of Lady Instow for a long time and we were all afraid she would never let him marry but they had a quarrel at Cowes that year and Billy went up to Scotland in a bad temper and little Etty was staying in the house; so everything was arranged and I was one of her bridesmaids.

'The only person who was not pleased was Ralph Bland. You see he was Billy's nearest relative and would inherit if Billy died without children and he had got very hopeful as time went on.

'He came to a very sad end – in fact I don't know *what* became of him – but at the time of which I am speaking he was extremely popular, especially with women . . . Poor Viola Chasm was terribly in love with him. Wanted to run away. She and Lady Anchorage were very jealous of each other about him. It became quite disagreeable, particularly when Viola found that Lady Anchorage was paying her maid five pounds a week to send on all Ralph's letters to her – *before* Viola had read them, that was what she minded. He really had a most agreeable manner and said such ridiculous things . . . The marriage was a great disappointment to Ralph; he was married himself and had two children. She had a little money at one time, but Ralph ran through it. Billy did not get on with Ralph – they had very little in common, of course – but he treated him quite well and was always getting him out of difficulties. In fact he made him a regular allowance at one time, and what with that and what he got from Viola and Lady Anchorage he was really quite comfortable. But, as he said, he had his children's future to consider, so that Billy's marriage *was* a *great* disappointment to him. He even talked of emigrating and Billy advanced him a large sum of money to purchase a sheep farm in New Zealand, but nothing came of that because Ralph had a Jewish friend in the city who made away with the entire amount. It all happened in a very unfortunate manner because Billy had given him this lump sum on the understanding that he should not expect an allowance. And then Viola and Lady Anchorage were greatly upset at his talk of leaving and made other arrangements so that in one way and another Ralph found himself in very low water, poor thing.

'However he began to recover his spirits when, after two years, there was no sign of an heir. People had babies very much more regularly when I was young. Everybody expected that Etty would have a baby – she was a nice healthy little thing – and when she did not, there was a great deal of ill natured gossip. Ralph himself behaved very wrongly in the matter. He used to make jokes about it, my husband told me, quite openly at his club in the worst possible taste.

'I well remember the last time that Ralph stayed with the Cornphillips; it was a Christmas party and he came with his wife and his two children. The eldest boy was about six at the time and there was a very painful scene. I was not there myself, but we were staying nearby with the Lockejaws and of course we heard all about it. Billy seems to have been in his most pompous mood and was showing off the house when Ralph's little boy said solemnly and very loudly, "Daddy says that when I step into your shoes I can pull the whole place down. The only thing worth worrying about is the money."

'It was towards the end of a large and rather old-fashioned Christmas party, so no one was feeling in a forgiving mood. There was a final breach between the two cousins. Until then, in spite of the New Zealand venture, Billy had been reluctantly supporting Ralph. Now the allowance ceased once for all and Ralph took it in very bad part.

'You know what it is – or perhaps, dear Miss Myers, you are so fortunate as not to know what it is – when near relatives begin to quarrel. There is no limit to the savagery to which they will resort. I should be ashamed to indicate the behaviour of these two men towards each other during the next two or three years. No one had any sympathy with either.

'For example, Billy, of course, was a Conservative. Ralph came down and stood as a Radical in the General Election in his own county and got in.

'This, you must understand, was in the days before the lower classes began going into politics. It was customary for the candidates on both sides to be men of means and, in the circumstances, there was considerable expenditure involved. Much more in fact than Ralph could well afford, but in those days Members of Parliament had many opportunities for improving their position, so we all thought it a very wise course of Ralph's – the first really sensible thing we had known him do. What followed was *very* shocking.

'Billy of course had refused to lend his interest – that was only to be expected – but when the election was over, and everybody perfectly satisfied with the result, he did what I always consider a *Very Wrong Thing*. He made an accusation against Ralph of corrupt practices. It was a matter of three pounds which Ralph had given to a gardener whom Billy had discharged for drunkenness. I daresay that all that kind of thing has ceased nowadays, but at the time to which I refer, it was universally customary. No one had any sympathy with Billy but he pressed the charge and poor Ralph was unseated.

'Well, after this time, I really think that poor Ralph became a little unsettled in his mind. It is a very sad thing, Miss Myers, when a middle-aged man becomes obsessed by a grievance. You remember how difficult it was when the Vicar thought that Major Etheridge was persecuting him. He actually informed me that Major Etheridge put water in the petrol tank of his motor-cycle and gave sixpences to the choir boys to sing out of tune – well it was like that with poor Ralph. He made up his mind that Billy had deliberately ruined him. He took a cottage in the village and used to embarrass Billy terribly by coming to all the village fêtes and staring at Billy fixedly. Poor Billy was always embarrassed when he had to make a speech. Ralph used to laugh ironically at the wrong places but never so loudly that Billy could have him turned out. And he used to go to public houses and drink far too much. They found him asleep on the terrace twice. And of course no one on the place liked to offend him, because at any moment he might become Lord Cornphillip.

'It must have been a very trying time for Billy. He and Etty were not getting on at all well together, poor things, and she spent more and more time in the Garden of Her Thoughts and brought out a very silly little book of sonnets, mostly about Venice and Florence, though she could never induce Billy to take her abroad. He used to think that foreign cooking upset him.

205

'Billy forbade her to speak to Ralph, which was very awkward as they were always meeting one another in the village and had been great friends in the old days. In fact Ralph used often to speak very contemptuously of his cousin's manliness and say it was time someone took Etty off his hands. But that was only one of Ralph's jokes, because Etty had been getting terribly thin and dressing in the *most* artistic way, and Ralph *always* liked people who were chic and plump – like poor Viola Chasm. Whatever her faults – ' said Lady Amelia, 'Viola was always chic and plump.

'It was at the time of the Diamond Jubilee that the crisis took place. There was a bonfire and a great deal of merry making of a rather foolish kind and Ralph got terribly drunk. He began threatening Billy in a very silly way and Billy had him up before the magistrates and they made an order against him to keep the peace and not to reside within ten miles of Cornphillip. "All right," Ralph said, in front of the whole Court, "I'll go away, but I won't go alone." And will you believe it, Miss Myers, he and Etty went off to Venice together that very afternoon.

'Poor Etty, she had always wanted to go to Venice and had written so many poems about it, but it was a great surprise to us all. Apparently she had been meeting Ralph for some time in the Garden of Her Thoughts.

'I don't think Ralph ever cared about her, because, as I say, she was not at all his type, but it seemed to him a very good revenge on Billy.

'Well, the elopement was far from successful. They took rooms in a very insanitary palace, and had a gondola and ran up a great many bills. Then Etty got a septic throat as a result of the sanitation and while she was laid up Ralph met an American woman who was *much* more his type. So in less than six weeks poor Etty was back in England. Of course she did not go back to Billy at once. She wanted to stay with us, but, naturally, that wasn't possible. It was very awkward for everyone. There was never, I think, any talk of a divorce. It was long before that became fashionable. But we all felt it would be very inconsiderate to Billy if we had her to stay. And then, this is what will surprise you, Miss Myers, the next thing we heard was that Etty was back at Cornphillip and about to have a baby. It was a son. Billy was very pleased about it and I don't believe that the boy ever knew, until quite lately, at luncheon with Lady Metroland, when my nephew Simon told him, in a rather ill-natured way.

'As for poor Ralph's boy, I am afraid he has come to very little good.

He must be middle aged by now. No one ever seems to hear anything of him. Perhaps he was killed in war. I cannot remember.

'And here comes Ross with the tray; and I see that Mrs. Samson has made more of those little scones which you always seem to enjoy so much. I am sure, dear Miss Myers, you would suffer much less from your *migraine* if you avoided them. But you take so little care of yourself, dear Miss Myers . . . Give one to Manchu.'

OSCAR WILDE
(1854–1900)

Wilde.is, of course, best known for his plays, especially *The Importance of Being Earnest*. Nevertheless the polished wit of Wilde the playwright is equally evident in his stories. *The Canterville Ghost* first appeared in 1891 in a small volume entitled *Lord Arthur Savile's Crime and other Stories*.

The Canterville Ghost
A Hylo-Idealistic Romance

1

WHEN Mr. Hiram B. Otis, the American minister, bought Canterville Chase, every one told him he was doing a very foolish thing, as there was no doubt at all that the place was haunted. Indeed, Lord Canterville himself, who was a man of the most punctilious honour, had felt it his duty to mention the fact to Mr. Otis, when they came to discuss terms.

'We have not cared to live in the place ourselves,' said Lord Canterville, 'since my grand-aunt, the Dowager Duchess of Bolton, was frightened into a fit, from which she never really recovered, by two skeleton hands being placed on her shoulders as she was dressing for dinner, and I feel bound to tell you, Mr. Otis, that the ghost has been seen by several living members of my family, as well as by the rector of the parish, the Rev. Augustus Dampier, who is a fellow of King's College, Cambridge. After the unfortunate accident to the Duchess, none of our younger servants would stay with us, and Lady Canterville often got very little sleep at night, in consequence of the mysterious noises that came from the corridor and the library.'

'My lord,' answered the Minister, 'I will take the furniture and the ghost at a valuation. I come from a modern country, where we have everything that money can buy; and with all our spry young fellows painting the Old World red, and carrying off your best actresses and prima-donnas, I reckon that if there were such a thing as a ghost in Europe, we'd have it at home in a very short time in one of our public museums, or on the road as a show.'

'I fear that the ghost exists,' said Lord Canterville, smiling, 'though it may have resisted the overtures of your enterprising impresarios. It has been well known for three centuries, since 1584 in fact, and always makes its appearance before the death of any member of our family.

'Well, so does the family doctor for that matter, Lord Canterville. But there is no such thing, sir, as a ghost, and I guess the laws of nature are not going to be suspended for the British aristocracy.'

'You are certainly very natural in America,' answered Lord Canterville, who did not quite understand Mr. Otis's last observation, 'and if you don't mind a ghost in the house, it is all right. Only you must remember I warned you.'

A few weeks after this, the purchase was completed, and at the close of the season the Minister and his family went down to Canterville Chase. Mrs. Otis, who, as Miss Lucretia R. Tappan, of West 53rd Street, had been a celebrated New York belle, was now a very handsome middle-aged woman, with fine eyes, and a superb profile. Many American ladies on leaving their native land adopt an appearance of chronic ill-health, under the impression that it is a form of European refinement, but Mrs. Otis had never fallen into this error. She had a magnificent constitution, and a really wonderful amount of animal spirits. Indeed, in many respects, she was quite English, and was an excellent example of the fact that we have really everything in common with America nowadays, except, of course, language. Her eldest son, christened Washington by his parents in a moment of patriotism, which he never ceased to regret, was a fair-haired, rather good-looking young man, who had qualified himself for American diplomacy by leading the German at the Newport Casino for three successive seasons, and even in London was well known as an excellent dancer. Gardenias and the peerage were his only weaknesses. Otherwise he was extremely sensible. Miss Virginia E. Otis was a little girl of fifteen, lithe and lovely as a fawn, and with a fine freedom in her large blue eyes. She was a wonderful amazon, and had once raced old Lord Bilton on her pony twice round the park, winning by a length and a half, just in front of Achilles statue, to the huge delight of the young Duke of Cheshire, who proposed to her on the spot, and was sent back to Eton that very night by his guardians, in floods of tears. After Virginia came the twins, who were usually called 'The Stars and Stripes' as they were always getting swished. They were delightful boys, and with the exception of the worthy Minister the only true republicans of the family.

As Canterville Chase is seven miles from Ascot, the nearest railway station, Mr. Otis had telegraphed for a waggonette to meet them, and they started on their drive in high spirits. It was a lovely July evening, and the air was delicate with the scent of the pinewoods. Now and then they heard a wood pigeon brooding over its own sweet voice, or saw, deep in the rustling fern, the burnished breast of the pheasant. Little squirrels peered at them from the beech-trees as they went by, and the rabbits scudded away through the brushwood and over the mossy knolls, with their white tails in the air. As they entered the avenue of Canterville Chase, however, the sky became suddenly overcast with clouds, a curious stillness seemed to hold the atmosphere, a great flight of rooks passed silently over their heads, and, before they reached the house, some big drops of rain had fallen.

Standing on the steps to receive them was an old woman, neatly dressed in black silk, with a white cap and apron. This was Mrs. Umney, the housekeeper, whom Mrs. Otis, at Lady Canterville's earnest request, had consented to keep on in her former position. She made them each a low curtsey as they alighted, and said in a quaint, old-fashioned manner, 'I bid you welcome to Canterville Chase.' Following her, they passed through the fine Tudor hall into the library, a long, low room, panelled in black oak, at the end of which was a large stained-glass window. Here they found tea laid out for them, and, after taking off their wraps, they sat down and began to look round, while Mrs. Umney waited on them.

Suddenly Mrs. Otis caught sight of a dull red stain on the floor just by the fireplace and, quite unconscious of what it really signified, said to Mrs. Umney, 'I am afraid something has been spilt there.'

'Yes, madam,' replied the old housekeeper in a low voice, 'blood has been spilt on that spot.'

'How horrid,' cried Mrs. Otis; 'I don't at all care for bloodstains in a sitting-room. It must be removed at once.'

The old woman smiled, and answered in the same low, mysterious voice, 'It is the blood of Lady Eleanore de Canterville, who was murdered on that very spot by her own husband, Sir Simon de Canterville, in 1575. Sir Simon survived her nine years, and disappeared suddenly under very mysterious circumstances. His body has never been discovered, but his guilty spirit still haunts the Chase. The blood-stain has been much admired by tourists and others, and cannot be removed.'

'That is all nonsense,' cried Washington Otis; 'Pinkerton's Champion Stain Remover and Paragon Detergent will clean it up in no time,' and before the terrified housekeeper could interfere he had fallen upon his knees, and was rapidly scouring the floor with a small

stick of what looked like a black cosmetic. In a few moments no trace
of the blood-stain could be seen.

'I knew Pinkerton would do it,' he exclaimed triumphantly, as he
looked round at his admiring family; but no sooner had he said these
words than a terrible flash of lightning lit up the sombre room, a fearful peal of thunder made them all start to their feet, and Mrs. Umney
fainted.

'What a monstrous climate!' said the American Minister calmly, as
he lit a long cheroot. 'I guess the old country is so overpopulated that
they have not enough decent weather for everybody. I have always
been of opinion that emigration is the only thing for England.'

'My dear Hiram,' cried Mrs. Otis, 'what can we do with a woman
who faints?'

'Charge it to her like breakages,' answered the Minister; 'she won't
faint after that'; and in a few moments Mrs. Umney certainly came to.
There was no doubt, however, that she was extremely upset, and she
sternly warned Mr. Otis to beware of some trouble coming to the
house.

'I have seen things with my own eyes, sir,' she said, 'that would
make any Christian's hair stand on end, and many and many a night I
have not closed my eyes in sleep for the awful things that are done
here.' Mr. Otis, however, and his wife warmly assured the honest soul
that they were not afraid of ghosts, and, after invoking the blessings of
Providence on her new master and mistress, and making arrangements for an increase of salary, the old housekeeper tottered off to her
own room.

2

THE storm raged fiercely all that night, but nothing of particular note
occurred. The next morning, however, when they came down to
breakfast, they found the terrible stain of blood once again on the
floor. 'I don't think it can be the fault of the Paragon Detergent,' said
Washington, 'for I have tried it with everything. It must be the ghost.'
He accordingly rubbed out the stain a second time, but the second
morning it appeared again. The third morning also it was there,
though the library had been locked up at night by Mr. Otis himself,
and the key carried upstairs. The whole family were now quite interested; Mr. Otis began to suspect that he had been too dogmatic in his
denial of the existence of ghosts, Mrs. Otis expressed her intention of
joining the Psychical Society, and Washington prepared a long letter
to Messrs. Myers and Podmore on the subject of the Permanence of

Sanguineous Stains when connected with crime. That night all doubts about the objective existence of phantasmata were removed for ever.

The day had been warm and sunny; and, in the cool of the evening, the whole family went out for a drive. They did not return home till nine o'clock, when they had a light supper. The conversation in no way turned upon ghosts, so there were not even those primary conditions of receptive expectation which so often precede the presentation of psychical phenomena. The subjects discussed, as I have since learned from Mr. Otis, were merely such as form the ordinary conversation of cultured Americans of the better class, such as the immense superiority of Miss Fanny Davenport over Sarah Bernhardt as an actress; the difficulty of obtaining green corn, buckwheat cakes, and hominy, even in the best English houses; the importance of Boston in the development of the world-soul; the advantages of the baggage check system in railway travelling; and the sweetness of the New York accent as compared to the London drawl. No mention at all was made of the supernatural, nor was Sir Simon de Canterville alluded to in any way. At eleven o'clock the family retired and by half-past all the lights were out. Some time after, Mr. Otis was awakened by a curious noise in the corridor, outside his room. It sounded like the clank of metal, and seemed to be coming nearer every moment. He got up at once, struck a match, and looked at the time. It was exactly one o'clock. He was quite calm, and felt his pulse, which was not at all feverish. The strange noise still continued, and with it he heard distinctly the sound of footsteps. He put on his slippers, took a small oblong phial out of his dressing-case, and opened the door. Right in front of him he saw, in the wan moonlight, an old man of terrible aspect. His eyes were as red as burning coals; long grey hair fell over his shoulders in matted coils; his garments, which were of antique cut, were soiled and ragged, and from his wrists and ankles hung heavy manacles and rusty gyves.

'My dear sir,' said Mr. Otis, 'I really must insist on your oiling those chains, and have brought you for that purpose a small bottle of the Tammany Rising Sun Lubricator. It is said to be completely efficacious upon one application, and there are several testimonials to that effect on the wrapper from some of our most eminent native divines. I shall leave it here for you by the bedroom candles, and will be happy to supply you with more should you require it.' With these words the United States Minister laid the bottle down on a marble table, and, closing his door, retired to rest.

212

'I really must insist on your oiling those chains!'

For a moment the Canterville ghost stood quite motionless in natural indignation; then, dashing the bottle violently upon the polished floor, he fled down the corridor, uttering hollow groans, and emitting a ghastly green light. Just, however, as he reached the top of the great oak staircase, a door was flung open, two little white-robed figures appeared, and a large pillow whizzed past his head! There was evidently no time to be lost, so, hastily adopting the Fourth Dimension of Space as a means of escape, he vanished through the wainscoting, and the house became quite quiet.

On reaching a small secret chamber in the left wing, he leaned up against a moonbeam to recover his breath, and began to try and realise his position. Never, in a brilliant and uninterrupted career of three hundred years, had he been so grossly insulted. He thought of the Dowager Duchess, whom he had frightened into a fit as she stood before the glass in her lace and diamonds; of the four housemaids, who had gone off into hysterics when he merely grinned at them through the curtains of one of the spare bedrooms; of the rector of the parish, whose candle he had blown out as he was coming late one night from the library, and who had been under the care of Sir William Gull ever since, a perfect martyr to nervous disorders; and of old Madame de Tremouillac, who, having wakened up one morning early and seen a skeleton seated in an arm-chair by the fire reading her diary had been confined to her bed for six weeks with an attack of brain fever, and, on her recovery, had become reconciled to the Church, and had broken off her connection with that notorious sceptic Monsieur de Voltaire. He remembered the terrible night when the wicked Lord Canterville was found choking in his dressing-room, with the knave of diamonds half-way down his throat, and confessed, just before he died, that he had cheated Charles James Fox out of £50,000 at Crockford's by means of that very card, and swore that the ghost had made him swallow it. All his great achievements came back to him again, from the butler who had shot himself in the pantry because he had seen a green hand tapping at the window pane, to the beautiful Lady Stutfield, who was always obliged to wear a black velvet band round her throat to hide the mark of five fingers burnt upon her white skin, and who drowned herself at last in the carp-pond at the end of the King's Walk. With the enthusiastic egotism of the true artist he went over his most celebrated performances, and smiled bitterly to himself as he recalled to mind his last appearance as 'Red Ruben, or the Strangled Babe,' his *début* as 'Gaunt Gibeon, the Bloodsucker of Bexley Moor,' and the *furore* he had excited one lonely June evening by merely playing ninepins with his own bones upon the lawn-tennis ground. And after all this, some wretched modern Americans were to come and offer him the Rising Sun Lubricator, and throw pillows at his head! It was quite unbearable. Besides, no ghosts in history had ever been treated in this manner. Accordingly, he determined to have vengeance, and remained till daylight in an attitude of deep thought.

3

THE next morning when the Otis family met at breakfast, they discussed the ghost at some length. The United States Minister was naturally a little annoyed to find that his present had not been accepted. 'I have no wish,' he said, 'to do the ghost any personal injury, and I must say that, considering the length of time he has been in the house, I don't think it is at all polite to throw pillows at him' – a very just remark, at which, I am sorry to say, the twins burst into shouts of laughter. 'Upon the other hand,' he continued, 'if he really declines to use the Rising Sun Lubricator, we shall have to take his chains from him. It would be quite impossible to sleep, with such a noise going on outside the bedrooms.'

For the rest of the week, however, they were undisturbed, the only thing that excited any attention being the continual renewal of the blood-stain on the library floor. This certainly was very strange, as the door was always locked at night by Mr. Otis, and the windows kept closely barred. The chameleon-like colour, also, of the stain excited a good deal of comment. Some mornings it was a dull (almost Indian) red, then it would be vermilion, then a rich purple, and once when they came down for family prayers, according to the simple rites of the Free American Reformed Episcopalian Church, they found it a bright emerald-green. These kaleidoscopic changes naturally amused the party very much, and bets on the subject were freely made every evening. The only person who did not enter into the joke was little Virginia, who, for some unexplained reason, was always a good deal distressed at the sight of the blood-stain, and very nearly cried the morning it was emerald-green.

The second appearance of the ghost was on Sunday night. Shortly after they had gone to bed they were suddenly alarmed by a fearful crash in the hall. Rushing downstairs, they found that a large suit of old armour had become detached from its stand, and had fallen on the stone floor, while, seated in a high-backed chair, was the Canterville ghost, rubbing his knees with an expression of acute agony on his face. The twins, having brought their peashooters with them, at once discharged two pellets on him, with that accuracy of aim which can only be attained by long and careful practice on a writing-master, while the United States Minister covered him with his revolver, and called upon him, in accordance with Californian etiquette, to hold up his hands! The ghost started up with a wild shriek of rage, and swept through them like a mist, extinguishing Washington Otis's candle as he passed, and so leaving them all in total darkness. On reaching the top of the staircase he recovered himself, and determined to give his celebrated peal of demoniac laughter. This he had on more than one occasion found extremely useful. It was said to have turned Lord Raker's wig grey in a single night, and had certainly made three of Lady Canterville's French governesses give warning before their month was up. He accordingly laughed his most horrible laugh, till the old vaulted roof rang and rang again, but hardly had the fearful echo died away when a door opened, and Mrs. Otis came out in a light blue dressing-gown. 'I am afraid you are far from well,' she said, 'and

215

have brought you a bottle of Dr. Dobell's tincture. If it is indigestion, you will find it a most excellent remedy.' The ghost glared at her in fury, and began at once to make preparations for turning himself into a large black dog, an accomplishment for which he was justly renowned, and to which the family doctor always attributed the permanent idiocy of Lord Canterville's uncle, the Hon. Thomas Horton. The sound of approaching footsteps, however, made him hesitate in his fell purpose, so he contented himself with becoming faintly phosphorescent, and vanished with a deep church-yard groan, just as the twins had come up to him.

On reaching his room he entirely broke down, and became a prey to the most violent agitation. The vulgarity of the twins, and the gross materialism of Mrs. Otis, were naturally extremely annoying, but what really distressed him most was, that he had been unable to wear the suit of mail. He had hoped that even modern Americans would be thrilled by the sight of a Spectre In Armour, if for no more sensible reason, at least out of respect for their national poet Longfellow, over whose graceful and attractive poetry he himself had whiled away many a weary hour when the Cantervilles were up in town. Besides, it was his own suit. He had worn it with success at the Kenilworth tournament, and had been highly complimented on it by no less a person than the Virgin Queen herself. Yet when he had put it on, he had been completely overpowered by the weight of the huge breastplate and steel casque, and had fallen heavily on the stone pavement, barking both his knees severely, and bruising the knuckles of his right hand.

For some days after this he was extremely ill, and hardly stirred out of his room at all, except to keep the blood-stain in proper repair. However, by taking great care of himself, he recovered, and resolved to make a third attempt to frighten the United States Minister and his family. He selected Friday, the 17th of August, for his appearance, and spent most of that day in looking over his wardrobe, ultimately deciding in favour of a large slouched hat with a red feather, a winding-sheet frilled at the wrists and neck, and a rusty dagger. Towards evening a violent storm of rain came on, and the wind was so high that all the windows and doors in the old house shook and rattled. In fact, it was just such weather as he loved. His plan of action was this. He was to make his way quietly to Washington Otis's room, gibber at him from the foot of the bed, and stab himself three times in the throat to the sound of slow music. He bore Washington a special grudge, being quite aware that it was he who was in the habit of removing the famous Canterville blood-stain, by means of Pinkerton's Paragon Detergent. Having reduced the reckless and foolhardy youth to a condition of abject terror, he was then to proceed to the room occupied by the United States Minister and his wife, and there to place a clammy hand on Mrs. Otis's forehead, while he hissed into her trembling husband's ear the awful secrets of the charnel-house. With regard to little Virginia, he had not quite made up his mind. She had never insulted him in any way, and was pretty and gentle. A few hollow groans from the wardrobe, he thought, would be more than sufficient, or, if that failed to wake her, he might grabble at the counterpane with palsy-twitching fingers. As for the twins, he was quite determined to teach them a lesson. The first thing to be done was, of course, to sit upon their chests, so as to produce the stifling sensation of nightmare. Then, as their beds were quite close to each other, to stand between them in the form of a green, icy-cold corpse, till they became paralysed with fear, and finally, to throw off the winding-sheet, and crawl round the room, with white bleached bones and one rolling eyeball, in the character of 'Dumb Daniel, or the Suicide's Skeleton,' a *rôle* in which he had on more than one occasion produced a great effect, and which he considered quite equal to his famous part of 'Martin the Maniac, or the Masked Mystery.'

At half-past ten he heard the family going to bed. For some time he was disturbed by wild shrieks of laughter from the twins, who, with the light-hearted gaiety of schoolboys, were evidently amusing themselves before they retired to rest, but at a quarter-past eleven all was still, and, as midnight sounded, he sallied forth. The owl beat against the window panes, the raven croaked from the old yew-tree, and the wind wandered moaning round the house like a lost soul; but the Otis family slept unconscious of their doom, and high above the rain and storm he could hear the steady snoring of the Minister for the United States. He stepped stealthily out of the wainscoting, with an evil smile on his cruel, wrinkled mouth, and the moon hid her face in a cloud as he stole past the great oriel window, where his own arms and those of his murdered wife were blazoned in azure and gold. On and on he glided, like an evil shadow, the very darkness seeming to loathe him as he passed. Once he thought he heard something call, and stopped; but it was only the baying of a dog from the Red Farm, and he went on, muttering strange sixteenth-century curses, and ever and anon brandishing the rusty dagger in the midnight air. Finally he reached the corner of the passage that led to luckless Washington's room. For a moment he paused there, the wind blowing his long grey locks about his head, and twisting into grotesque and fantastic folds the nameless horror of the dead man's shroud. Then the clock struck the quarter, and he felt the time was come. He chuckled to himself, and turned the corner; but no sooner had he done so, than, with a piteous wail of terror, he fell back, and hid his blanched face in his long, bony hands. Right in front of him was standing a horrible spectre, motionless as a carven image, and monstrous as a madman's dream! Its head was bald and burnished; its face round, and fat, and white; and hideous laughter seemed to have writhed its features into an eternal grin. From the eyes streamed rays of scarlet light, the mouth was a wide well of fire, and a hideous garment, like to his own, swathed with its silent snows the Titan form. On its breast was a placard with strange writing in antique characters, some scroll of shame it seemed, some record of wild sins, some awful calendar of crime, and, with its right hand, it bore aloft a falchion of gleaming steel.

Never having seen a ghost before, he naturally was terribly frightened, and, after a second hasty glance at the awful phantom, he fled back to his room, tripping up in his long winding-sheet as he sped down the corridor, and finally dropping the rusty dagger into the Minister's jack-boots, where it was found in the morning by the butler. Once in the privacy of his own apartment, he flung himself down on a small pallet-bed and hid his face under the clothes. After a time, however, the brave old Canterville spirit asserted itself, and he determined to go and speak to the other ghost as soon as it was daylight. Accordingly, just as the dawn was touching the hills with silver, he returned towards the spot where he had first laid eyes on the grisly phantom, feeling that, after all, two ghosts were better than one, and that, by the aid of his new friend, he might safely grapple with the twins. On reaching the spot, however, a terrible sight met his gaze. Something had evidently happened to the spectre, for the light had entirely faded from its hollow eyes, the gleaming falchion had fallen from its hand, and it was leaning up against the wall in a strained and uncomfortable attitude. He rushed forward and seized it in his arms, when, to his horror, the head slipped off and rolled on the floor, the body assumed a recumbent posture, and he found himself clasping a white dimity bed-curtain, with a sweeping-brush, a kitchen cleaver, and a hollow turnip lying at his feet! Unable to understand this curious transformation, he clutched the placard with feverish haste, and there, in the grey morning light, he read these fearful words:

YE OTIS GHOSTE
Ye Onlie True and Originale Spook.
Beware of Ye Imitationes.
All others are Counterfeite.

The whole thing flashed across him. He had been tricked, foiled, and outwitted! The old Canterville look came into his eyes; he ground his toothless gums together; and, raising his withered hands high above his head, swore, according to the picturesque phraseology of the antique school, that when Chanticleer had sounded twice his merry horn, deeds of blood would be wrought, and Murder walk abroad with silent feet.

Hardly had he finished this awful oath when, from the red-tiled roof of a distant homestead, a cock crew. He laughed a long, low, bitter laugh, and waited. Hour after hour he waited, but the cock, for some strange reason, did not crow again. Finally, at half-past seven, the arrival of the housemaids made him give up his fearful vigil, and he stalked back to his room, thinking of his vain hope and baffled purpose. There he consulted several books of ancient chivalry, of which he was exceedingly fond, and found that, on every occasion on which his oath had been used, Chanticleer had always crowed a second time. 'Perdition seize the naughty fowl,' he muttered, 'I have seen the day when, with my stout spear, I would have run him through the gorge, and made him crow for me an 'twere in death!' He then retired to a comfortable lead coffin, and stayed there till evening.

4

THE next day the ghost was very weak and tired. The terrible excitement of the last four weeks was beginning to have its effect. His nerves were completely shattered, and he started at the slightest noise. For five days he kept his room, and at last made up his mind to give up the point of the blood-stain on the library floor. If the Otis family did not want it, they clearly did not deserve it. They were evidently people on a low, material plane of existence, and quite incapable of appreciating the symbolic value of sensuous phenomena. The question of phantasmic apparitions, and the development of astral bodies, was of course quite a different matter, and really not under his control. It was his solemn duty to appear in the corridor once a week, and to gibber from the large oriel window on the first and third Wednesday in every month, and he did not see how he could honourably escape from his

219

obligations. It is quite true that his life had been very evil, but, upon the other hand, he was most conscientious in all things connected with the supernatural. For the next three Saturdays, accordingly, he traversed the corridor as usual between midnight and three o'clock, taking every possible precaution against being either heard or seen. He removed his boots, trod as lightly as possible on the old worm-eaten boards, wore a large black velvet cloak, and was careful to use the Rising Sun Lubricator for oiling his chains. I am bound to acknowledge that it was with a good deal of difficulty that he brought himself to adopt this last mode of protection. However, one night, while the family were at dinner, he slipped into Mr. Otis's bedroom and carried off the bottle. He felt a little humiliated at first, but afterwards was sensible enough to see that there was a great deal to be said for the invention, and, to a certain degree, it served his purpose. Still, in spite of everything, he was not left unmolested. Strings were continually being stretched across the corridor, over which he tripped in the dark, and on one occasion, while dressed for the part of 'Black Isaac, or the Huntsman of Hogley Woods,' he met with a severe fall, through treading on a butter-slide, which the twins had constructed from the entrance of the Tapestry Chamber to the top of the oak staircase. This last insult so enraged him, that he resolved to make one final effort to assert his dignity and social position, and determined to visit the insolent young Etonians the next night in his celebrated character of 'Reckless Rupert, or the Headless Earl.'

He had not appeared in this disguise for more than seventy years; in fact, not since he had so frightened pretty Lady Barbara Modish by means of it, that she suddenly broke off her engagement with the present Lord Canterville's grandfather, and ran away to Gretna Green with handsome Jack Castleton, declaring that nothing in the world would induce her to marry into a family that allowed such a horrible phantom to walk up and down the terrace at twilight. Poor Jack was afterwards shot in a duel by Lord Canterville on Wandsworth Common, and Lady Barbara died of a broken heart at Tunbridge Wells before the year was out, so, in every way, it had been a great success. It was, however, an extremely difficult 'make-up,' if I may use such a theatrical expression in connection with one of the greatest mysteries of the supernatural, or, to employ a more scientific term, the higher-natural world, and it took him fully three hours to make his preparations. At last everything was ready, and he was very pleased with his appearance. The big leather riding-boots that went with the dress were just a little too large for him, and he could only find one of the two horse-pistols, but, on the whole, he was quite satisfied, and at a quarter-past one he glided out of the wainscoting and crept down the corridor. On reaching the room occupied by the twins, which I should mention was called the Blue Bed Chamber, on account of the colour of its hangings, he found the door just ajar. Wishing to make an effective entrance, he flung it wide open, when a heavy jug of water fell right down on him, wetting him to the skin, and just missing his left shoulder by a couple of inches. At the same moment he heard stifled shrieks of laughter proceeding from the four-post bed. The shock to his nervous system was so great that he fled back to his room as hard as he could go, and the next day he was laid up with a severe cold. The only thing that at all consoled him in the whole affair was the fact that he had not brought his head with him, for, had he done so, the consequences might have been very serious.

He now gave up all hope of ever frightening this rude American family, and contented himself, as a rule, with creeping about the passages in list slippers, with a thick red muffler round his throat for fear of draughts, and a small arquebuse, in case he should be attacked by the twins. The final blow he received occurred on the 19th of September. He had gone downstairs to the great entrance-hall, feeling sure that there, at any rate, he would be quite unmolested, and was amusing himself by making satirical remarks on the large Saroni photographs of the United States Minister and his wife, which had now taken the place of the Canterville family pictures. He was simply but neatly clad in a long shroud, spotted with churchyard mould, had tied up his jaw with a strip of yellow linen, and carried a small lantern and a sexton's spade. In fact, he was dressed for the character of 'Jonas the Graveless, or the Corpse-Snatcher of Chertsey Barn,' one of his most remarkable impersonations, and one which the Cantervilles had every reason to remember, as it was the real origin of their quarrel with their neighbour, Lord Rufford. It was about a quarter past two o'clock in the morning, and, as far as he could ascertain, no one was stirring. As he was strolling towards the library, however, to see if there were any traces left of the blood-stain, suddenly there leaped out on him from a dark corner two figures, who waved their arms wildly above their heads, and shrieked out 'BOO!' in his ear.

Seized with a panic, which, under the circumstances, was only natural, he rushed for the staircase, but found Washington Otis waiting for him there with the big garden-syringe; and being thus hemmed in by his enemies on every side, and driven almost to bay, he vanished into the great iron stove, which, fortunately for him, was not lit, and had to make his way home through the flues and chimneys, arriving at his own room in a terrible state of dirt, disorder, and despair.

After this he was not seen again on any nocturnal expedition. The twins lay in wait for him on several occasions, and strewed the passages with nutshells every night to the great annoyance of their parents and the servants, but it was of no avail. It was quite evident that his feelings were so wounded that he would not appear. Mr. Otis consequently resumed his great work on the history of the Democratic Party, on which he had been engaged for some years; Mrs. Otis organised a wonderful clambake, which amazed the whole county; the boys took to lacrosse, euchre, poker, and other American national games; and Virginia rode about the lanes on her pony, accompanied by the young Duke of Cheshire, who had come to spend the last week of his holidays at Canterville Chase. It was generally assumed that the ghost had gone away, and, in fact, Mr. Otis wrote a letter to that effect to Lord Canterville, who, in reply, expressed his great pleasure at the news, and sent his best congratulations to the Minister's worthy wife.

The Otises, however, were deceived, for the ghost was still in the house, and though now almost an invalid, was by no means ready to let matters rest, particularly as he heard that among the guests was the young Duke of Cheshire, whose grand-uncle, Lord Francis Stilton, had once bet a hundred guineas with Colonel Carbury that he would play dice with the Canterville ghost, and was found the next morning lying on the floor of the card-room in such a helpless paralytic state, that though he lived on to a great age, he was never able to say anything again but 'Double Sixes.' The story was well known at the time, though, of course, out of respect to the feelings of the two noble families, every attempt was made to hush it up; and a full account of all the circumstances connected with it will be found in the third volume of Lord Tattle's *Recollections of the Prince Regent and his Friends*. The ghost, then, was naturally very anxious to show that he had not lost his influence over the Stiltons, with whom indeed, he was distantly connected, his own first cousin having been married *en secondes noces*[1] to the Sieur de Bulkeley, from whom, as every one knows, the Dukes of Cheshire are lineally descended. Accordingly, he made arrangements for appearing to Virginia's little lover in his celebrated impersonation of 'The Vampire Monk, or, the Bloodless Benedictine,' a performance so horrible that when old Lady Startup saw it, which she did on one fatal New Year's Eve, in the year 1764, she went off into the most piercing shrieks, which culminated in violent

[1] For the second time.

222

apoplexy, and died in three days, after disinheriting the Cantervilles, who were her nearest relations, and leaving all her money to her London apothecary. At the last moment, however, his terror of the twins prevented his leaving his room, and the little Duke slept in peace under the great feathered canopy in the Royal Bedchamber, and dreamed of Virginia.

5

A FEW days after this, Virginia and her curly-haired cavalier went out riding on Brockley meadows, where she tore her habit so badly in getting through a hedge, that, on her return home, she made up her mind to go up by the back staircase so as not to be seen. As she was running past the Tapestry Chamber, the door of which happened to be opened, she fancied she saw some one inside, and thinking it was her mother's maid, who sometimes used to bring her work there, looked in to ask her to mend her habit. To her immense surprise, however, it was the Canterville Ghost himself! He was sitting by the window, watching the ruined gold of the yellow trees fly through the air, and the red leaves dancing madly down the long avenue. His head was leaning on his hand, and his whole attitude was one of extreme depression. Indeed, so forlorn, and so much out of repair did he look, that little Virginia, whose first idea had been to run away and lock herself in her room, was filled with pity, and determined to try and comfort him. So light was her footfall, and so deep his melancholy, that he was not aware of her presence till she spoke to him.

'I am so sorry for you,' she said, 'but my brothers are going back to Eton to-morrow, and then, if you behave yourself, no one will annoy you.'

'It is absurd asking me to behave myself,' he answered, looking round in astonishment at the pretty little girl who had ventured to address him, 'quite absurd. I must rattle my chains, and groan through keyholes, and walk about at night, if that is what you mean. It is my only reason for existing.'

'It is no reason at all for existing, and you know you have been very wicked. Mrs. Umney told us, the first day we arrived here, that you had killed your wife.'

'Well, I quite admit it,' said the Ghost petulantly, 'but it was a purely family matter, and concerned no one else.'

'It is very wrong to kill any one,' said Virginia, who at times had a sweet Puritan gravity, caught from some old New England ancestor.

'Oh, I hate the cheap severity of abstract ethics! My wife was very

223

plain, never had my ruffs properly starched, and knew nothing about cookery. Why, there was a buck I had shot in Hogley Woods, a magnificent pricket, and do you know how she had it sent up to table? However, it is no matter now, for it is all over, and I don't think it was very nice of her brothers to starve me to death, though I did kill her.'

'Starve you to death? Oh, Mr. Ghost, I mean Sir Simon, are you hungry? I have a sandwich in my case. Would you like it?'

'No, thank you, I never eat anything now; but it is very kind of you, all the same, and you are much nicer than the rest of your horrid, rude, vulgar, dishonest family.'

'Stop!' cried Virginia, stamping her foot, 'it is you who are rude, and horrid, and vulgar; and as for dishonesty, you know you stole the paints out of my box to try and furbish up that ridiculous blood-stain in the library. First you took all my reds, including the vermilion, and I couldn't do any more sunsets, then you took the emerald-green and the chrome-yellow, and finally I had nothing left but indigo and Chinese white, and could only do moonlight scenes, which are always depressing to look at, and not at all easy to paint. I never told on you, though I was very much annoyed, and it was most ridiculous, the whole thing; for who ever heard of emerald-green blood?'

'Well, really,' said the Ghost, rather meekly, 'what was I to do? It is a very difficult thing to get real blood nowadays, and, as your brother began it all with his Paragon Detergent, I certainly saw no reason why I should not have your paints. As for colour, that is always a matter of taste: the Cantervilles have blue blood, for instance, the very bluest in England; but I know you Americans don't care for things of this kind.'

'You know nothing about it, and the best thing you can do is to emigrate and improve your mind. My father will be only too happy to give you a free passage, and though there is a heavy duty on spirits of every kind, there will be no difficulty about the Custom House, as the officers are all Democrats. Once in New York, you are sure to be a great success. I know lots of people there who would give a hundred thousand dollars to have a grandfather, and much more than that to have a family Ghost.'

'I don't think I should like America.'

'I suppose because we have no ruins and no curiosities,' said Virginia satirically.

'No ruins! no curiosities!' answered the Ghost; 'you have your navy and your manners.'

'Good evening; I will go and ask papa to get the twins an extra week's holiday.'

'Please don't go, Miss Virginia,' he cried; 'I am so lonely and so unhappy, and I really don't know what to do. I want to go to sleep and I cannot.'

'That's quite absurd! You have merely to go to bed and blow out the candle. It is very difficult sometimes to keep awake, especially at church, but there is no difficulty at all about sleeping. Why, even babies know how to do that, and they are not very clever.'

'I have not slept for three hundred years,' he said sadly, and Virginia's beautiful blue eyes opened in wonder; 'for three hundred years I have not slept, and I am so tired.'

Virginia grew quite grave, and her little lips trembled like rose-leaves. She came towards him, and kneeling down at his side, looked up into his old withered face.

'Poor, poor Ghost,' she murmured; 'have you no place where you can sleep?'

'Far away beyond the pine-woods,' he answered, in a low dreamy voice, 'there is a little garden. There the grass grows long and deep, there are the great white stars of the hemlock flower, there the nightingale sings all night long. All night long he sings, and the cold, crystal moon looks down, and the yew-tree spreads out its giant arms over the sleepers.'

Virginia's eyes grew dim with tears, and she hid her face in her hands.

'You mean the Garden of Death,' she whispered.

'Yes, Death. Death must be so beautiful. To lie in the soft brown earth, with the grasses waving above one's head, and listen to silence. To have no yesterday, and no to-morrow. To forget time, to forgive life, to be at peace. You can help me. You can open for me the portals of Death's house, for Love is always with you, and Love is stronger than Death is.'

Virginia trembled, a cold shudder ran through her, and for a few moments there was silence. She felt as if she was in a terrible dream.

Then the Ghost spoke again, and his voice sounded like the sighing of the wind.

'Have you ever read the old prophecy on the library window?'

'Oh, often,' cried the little girl, looking up; 'I know it quite well. It is painted in curious black letters, and it is difficult to read. There are only six lines:

> When a golden girl can win
> Prayer from out the lips of sin,

225

When the barren almond bears,
And a little child gives away its tears,
Then shall all the house be still
And peace come to Canterville.

But I don't know what they mean.'

'They mean,' he said sadly, 'that you must weep for me for my sins, because I have no tears, and pray with me for my soul, because I have no faith, and then, if you have always been sweet, and good, and gentle, the Angel of Death will have mercy on me. You will see fearful shapes in darkness, and wicked voices will whisper in your ear, but they will not harm you, for against the purity of a little child the powers of Hell cannot prevail.'

Virginia made no answer, and the Ghost wrung his hands in wild despair as he looked down at her bowed golden head. Suddenly she stood up, very pale, and with a strange light in her eyes. 'I am not afraid,' she said firmly, 'and I will ask the Angel to have mercy on you.'

He rose from his seat with a faint cry of joy, and taking her hand bent over it with old-fashioned grace and kissed it. His fingers were as cold as ice, and his lips burned like fire, but Virginia did not falter, as he led her across the dusky room. On the faded green tapestry were broidered little huntsmen. They blew their tasselled horns and with their tiny hands waved to her to go back. 'Go back! little Virginia,' they cried, 'go back!' but the Ghost clutched her hand more tightly, and she shut her eyes against them. Horrible animals with lizard tails, and goggle eyes, blinked at her from the carven chimney-piece, and murmured 'Beware! little Virginia, beware! we may never see you again,' but the Ghost glided on more swiftly, and Virginia did not listen. When they reached the end of the room he stopped, and muttered some words she could not understand. She opened her eyes, and saw the wall slowly fading away like a mist, and a great black cavern in front of her. A bitter cold wind swept round them, and she felt something pulling at her dress. 'Quick, quick,' cried the Ghost, 'or it will be too late,' and, in a moment, the wainscoting had closed behind them, and the Tapestry Chamber was empty.

6

ABOUT ten minutes later, the bell rang for tea, and, as Virginia did not come down, Mrs. Otis sent up one of the footmen to tell her. After a little time he returned and said that he could not find Miss Virginia anywhere. As she was in the habit of going out to the garden every evening to get flowers for the dinner-table, Mrs. Otis was not at all alarmed at first, but when six o'clock struck, and Virginia did not appear, she became really agitated, and sent the boys out to look for her, while she herself and Mr. Otis searched every room in the house. At half-past six the boys came back and said that they could find no trace of their sister anywhere. They were all now in the greatest state of excitement, and did not know what to do, when Mr. Otis suddenly remembered that, some few days before, he had given a band of gypsies permission to camp in the park. He accordingly at once set off for Blackfell Hollow, where he knew they were, accompanied by his eldest son and two of the farm-servants. The little Duke of Cheshire, who was perfectly frantic with anxiety, begged hard to be allowed to go too, but Mr. Otis would not allow him, as he was afraid there might be a scuffle. On arriving at the spot, however, he found that the gypsies had gone, and it was evident that their departure had been rather sudden, as the fire was still burning, and some plates were lying on the grass. Having sent off Washington and the two men to scour the district, he ran home, and despatched telegrams to all the police inspectors in the county, telling them to look out for a little girl who had been kidnapped by tramps or gypsies. He then ordered his horse to be brought round, and, after insisting on his wife and the three boys sitting down to dinner, rode off down the Ascot Road with a groom. He had hardly, however, gone a couple of miles when he heard somebody galloping after him, and, looking round, saw the little Duke coming up on his pony, with his face very flushed and no hat. 'I'm awfully sorry, Mr. Otis,' gasped out the boy, 'but I can't eat any dinner as long as Virginia is lost. Please, don't be angry with me; if you had let us be engaged last year, there would never have been all this trouble. You won't send me back, will you? I can't go! I won't go!'

The Minister could not help smiling at the handsome young scapegrace, and was a good deal touched at his devotion to Virginia, so leaning down from his horse, he patted him kindly on the shoulders, and said, 'Well, Cecil, if you won't go back I suppose you must come with me, but I must get you a hat at Ascot.'

'Oh, bother my hat! I want Virginia!' cried the little Duke, laughing, and they galloped on to the railway station. There Mr. Otis inquired of the station-master if any one answering the description of Virginia had been seen on the platform, but could get no news of her. The station-master, however, wired up and down the line, and assured him that a strict watch would be kept for her, and, after having bought a hat for the little Duke from a linen-draper, who was just putting up his shutters, Mr. Otis rode off to Bexley, a village about four miles away, which he was told was a well-known haunt of the gypsies, as there was a large common next to it. Here they roused up the rural policeman, but could get no information from him, and, after riding all over the common, they turned their horses' heads homewards, and reached the Chase about eleven o'clock, dead-tired and almost heartbroken. They found Washington and the twins waiting for them at the gate-house with lanterns, as the avenue was very dark. Not the slightest trace of Virginia had been discovered. The gypsies had been caught on Broxley meadows, but she was not with them, and they had explained their sudden departure by saying that they had mistaken the date of Chorton Fair, and had gone off in a hurry for fear they might be late. Indeed, they had been quite distressed at hearing of Virginia's disappearance, as they were very grateful to Mr. Otis for having allowed them to camp in his park, and four of their number had stayed behind to help in the search. The carp-pond had been dragged, and the whole Chase thoroughly gone over, but without any result. It was evident that, for that night at any rate, Virginia was lost to them; and it was in a state of the deepest depression that Mr. Otis and the boys walked up to the house, the groom following behind with the two horses and the pony. In the hall they found a group of frightened servants, and lying on a sofa in the library was poor Mrs. Otis, almost out of her mind with terror and anxiety, and having her forehead bathed with eau-de-Cologne by the old housekeeper. Mr. Otis at once insisted on her having something to eat, and ordered up supper for the whole party. It was a melancholy meal, as hardly any one spoke, and even the twins were awestruck and subdued, as they were very fond of their sister. When they had finished, Mr. Otis, in spite of the entreaties of the little Duke, ordered them all to bed, saying that nothing more could be done that night, and that he would telegraph in the morning to Scotland Yard for some detectives to be sent down immediately. Just as they were passing out of the dining-room, midnight began to boom from the clock tower, and when the last stroke sounded they heard a crash and a sudden shrill cry; a dreadful peal of thunder shook the house, a strain of unearthly music floated through the air, a panel at the top of the staircase flew back with a loud noise, and out on the landing, looking very pale and white, with a little casket in her hand, stepped Virginia. In a moment they had all rushed up to her. Mrs. Otis clasped her passionately in her arms, the Duke smothered her with violent kisses, and the twins executed a wild war-dance round the group.

'Good heavens! child, where have you been?' said Mr. Otis, rather angrily, thinking that she had been playing some foolish trick for them. 'Cecil and I have been riding all over the country looking for you, and your mother has been frightened to death. You must never play these practical jokes any more.'

'Except on the Ghost! except on the Ghost!' shrieked the twins, as they capered about.

'My own darling, thank God you are found; you must never leave my side again,' murmured Mrs. Otis, as she kissed the trembling child, and smoothed the tangled gold of her hair.

'Papa,' said Virginia quietly, 'I have been with the Ghost. He is dead, and you must come and see him. He had been very wicked, but he was really sorry for all that he had done, and he gave me this box of beautiful jewels before he died.'

The whole family gazed at her in mute astonishment, but she was quite grave and serious; and, turning round, she led them through the opening in the wainscoting down a narrow secret corridor, Washington following with a lighted candle, which he had caught up from the table. Finally, they came to a great oak door, studded with rusty nails. When Virginia touched it, it swung back on its heavy hinges, and they found themselves in a little low room, with a vaulted ceiling, and one tiny grated window. Imbedded in the wall was a huge iron ring, and chained to it was a gaunt skeleton, that was stretched out at full length on the stone floor, and seemed to be trying to grasp with its long flesh-less fingers an old-fashioned trencher and ewer, that were placed just out of its reach. The jug had evidently been once filled with water, as it was covered inside with green mould. There was nothing on the trencher but a pile of dust. Virginia knelt down beside the skeleton, and, folding her little hands together, began to pray silently, while the rest of the party looked on in wonder at the terrible tragedy whose secret was now disclosed to them.

'Hallo!' suddenly exclaimed one of the twins, who had been looking out of the window to try and discover in what wing of the house the room was situated. 'Hallo! the old withered almond-tree has blos-somed. I can see the flowers quite plainly in the moonlight.'

'God has forgiven him,' said Virginia gravely, as she rose to her feet, and a beautiful light seemed to illumine her face.

'What an angel you are!' cried the young Duke, and he put his arm round her neck and kissed her.

7

FOUR days after these curious incidents a funeral started from Canterville Chase at about eleven o'clock at night. The hearse was drawn by eight black horses, each of which carried on its head a great tuft of nodding ostrich-plumes, and the leaden coffin was covered by a rich purple pall, on which was embroidered in gold the Canterville coat-of-arms. By the side of the hearse and the coaches walked the servants with lighted torches, and the whole procession was wonderfully impressive. Lord Canterville was the chief mourner, having come up specially from Wales to attend the funeral, and sat in the first carriage along with little Virginia. Then came the United States Minister and his wife, then Washington and the three boys, and in the last carriage was Mrs. Umney. It was generally felt that, as she had been frightened by the ghost for more than fifty years of her life, she had a right to see the last of him. A deep grave had been dug in the corner of the churchyard, just under the old yew-tree, and the service was read in the most impressive manner by the Rev. Augustus Dampier. When the ceremony was over the servants according to an old custom observed in the Canterville family, extinguished their torches, and, as the coffin was being lowered into the grave, Virginia stepped forward and laid on it a large cross made of white and pink almond-blossoms. As she did so, the moon came out from behind a cloud, and flooded with its silent silver the little churchyard, and from a distant copse a nightingale began to sing. She thought of the ghost's description of the Garden of Death, her eyes became dim with tears, and she hardly spoke a word during the drive home.

The next morning, before Lord Canterville went up to town, Mr. Otis had an interview with him on the subject of the jewels the ghost had given to Virginia. They were perfectly magnificent, especially a certain ruby necklace with old Venetian setting, which was really a superb specimen of sixteenth-century work, and their value was so great that Mr. Otis felt considerable scruples about allowing his daughter to accept them.

'My Lord,' he said, 'I know that in this country mortmain is held to apply to trinkets as well as to land, and it is quite clear to me that these jewels are, or should be, heirlooms in your family. I must beg you, accordingly, to take them to London with you, and to regard them simply as a portion of your property which has been restored to you under certain strange conditions. As for my daughter, she is merely a child, and has as yet, I am glad to say, but little interest in such appurtenances of idle luxury. I am also informed by Mrs. Otis, who, I may say, is no mean authority upon Art – having had the privilege of spending several winters in Boston when she was a girl – that these gems are of great monetary worth, and if offered for sale would fetch a tall price. Under these circumstances, Lord Canterville, I feel sure that you will recognise how impossible it would be for me to allow them to remain in the possession of any member of my family; and, indeed, all such vain gauds and toys, however suitable or necessary to the dignity of the British aristocracy, would be completely out of place among those who have been brought up on the severe, and I believe immortal, principles of republican simplicity. Perhaps I should mention that Virginia is very anxious that you should allow her to retain the box as a memento of your unfortunate but misguided ancestor. As it is extremely old, and consequently a good deal out of repair, you may perhaps think fit to comply with her request. For my own part, I confess I am a good deal surprised to find a child of mine expressing sympathy with mediævalism in any form, and can only account for it by the fact that Virginia was born in one of your London suburbs shortly after Mrs. Otis had returned from a trip to Athens.'

Lord Canterville listened very gravely to the worthy Minister's speech, pulling his grey moustache now and then to hide an involuntary smile, and when Mr. Otis had ended, he shook him cordially by the hand, and said, 'My dear sir, your charming little daughter rendered my unlucky ancestor, Sir Simon, a very important service, and I and my family are much indebted to her for her marvellous courage and pluck. The jewels are clearly hers, and, egad, I believe that if I were heartless enough to take them from her, the wicked old fellow would be out of his grave in a fortnight, leading me the devil of a life. As for their being heirlooms, nothing is an heirloom that is not so mentioned in a will or legal document, and the existence of these jewels has been quite unknown. I assure you I have no more claim on them than your butler, and when Miss Virginia grows up I daresay she will be pleased to have pretty things to wear. Besides, you forget, Mr. Otis, that you took the furniture and the ghost at a valuation, and anything that belonged to the ghost passed at once into your possession, as, whatever activity Sir Simon may have shown in the corridor at night, in point of law he was really dead, and you acquired his property by purchase.'

Mr. Otis was a good deal distressed at Lord Canterville's refusal, and begged him to reconsider his decision, but the good-natured peer was quite firm, and finally induced the Minister to allow his daughter to retain the present the ghost had given her, and when, in the spring of 1890, the young Duchess of Cheshire was presented at the Queen's first drawing-room on the occasion of her marriage, her jewels were the universal theme of admiration. For Virginia received the coronet, which is the reward of all good little American girls, and was married to her boy-lover as soon as he came of age. They were both so charming, and they loved each other so much, that every one was delighted at the match, except the old Marchioness of Dumbleton, who had tried to catch the Duke for one of her seven unmarried daughters, and had given no less than three expensive dinner-parties for that purpose, and, strange to say, Mr. Otis himself. Mr. Otis was extremely fond of the young Duke personally, but, theoretically, he objected to titles, and, to use his own words, 'was not without apprehension lest, amid the enervating influences of a pleasure-loving aristocracy, the true principles of republican simplicity should be forgotten.' His objections, however, were completely overruled, and I believe that when he walked up the aisle of St. George's, Hanover Square, with his daughter leaning on his arm, there was not a prouder man in the whole length and breadth of England.

The Duke and Duchess, after the honeymoon was over, went down to Canterville Chase, and on the day after their arrival they walked over in the afternoon to the lonely churchyard by the pine-woods. There had been a great deal of difficulty at first about the inscription on Sir Simon's tombstone, but finally it had been decided to engrave on it simply the initials of the old gentleman's name, and the verse from the library window. The Duchess had brought with her some lovely roses, which she strewed upon the grave, and after they had stood by it for some time they strolled into the ruined chancel of the old abbey. There the Duchess sat down on a fallen pillar, while her husband lay at her feet smoking a cigarette and looking up at her beautiful eyes. Suddenly he threw his cigarette away, took hold of her hand, and said to her, 'Virginia, a wife should have no secrets from her husband.'

'Dear Cecil! I have no secrets from you.'

'Yes, you have,' he answered, smiling, 'you have never told me what happened to you when you were locked up with the ghost.'

'I have never told any one, Cecil,' said Virginia gravely.

'I know that, but you might tell me.'

'Please don't ask me, Cecil, I cannot tell you. Poor Sir Simon! I owe him a great deal. Yes, don't laugh, Cecil, I really do. He made me see what Life is, and what Death signifies, and why Love is stronger than both.'

The Duke rose and kissed his wife lovingly.

'You can have your secret as long as I have your heart,' he mur-mured.

'You have always had that, Cecil.'

'And you will tell our children some day, won't you?'

Virginia blushed.

P G WODEHOUSE
(1881–1975)

Wodehouse began his career as a writer with the publication of serialized stories for *The Captain*, a magazine for boys, while employed as a London bank clerk. These early stories gave birth to Psmith and other favourite characters. His best-loved characters, Jeeves and Bertie Wooster, made their first full-fledged appearance in *The Inimitable Jeeves*, in 1924. Wodehouse was knighted in 1975, shortly before his death.

The Rummy Affair Of Old Biffy

'JEEVES,'' I said, emerging from the old tub, 'rally round.'

'Yes, sir.'

I beamed on the man with no little geniality. I was putting in a week or two in Paris at the moment, and there's something about Paris that always makes me feel fairly full of *espièglerie* and *joie de vivre*.

'Lay out our gent's medium-smart raiment, suitable for Bohemian revels,' I said. 'I am lunching with an artist bloke on the other side of the river.'

'Very good, sir.'

'And if anybody calls for me, Jeeves, say that I shall be back towards the quiet evenfall.'

'Yes, sir. Mr. Biffen rang up on the telephone while you were in your bath.'

'Mr. Biffen? Good heavens!'

Amazing how one's always running across fellows in foreign cities – coves, I mean, whom you haven't seen for ages and would have betted weren't anywhere in the neighbourhood. Paris was the last place where I should have expected to find old Biffy popping up. There was a time when he and I had been lads about town together, lunching and dining together practically everyday; but some eighteen months back his old godmother had died and left him that place in Hereford-shire, and he had retired there to wear gaiters and prod cows in the ribs and generally be the country gentleman and landed proprietor. Since then I had hardly seen him.

'Old Biffy in Paris? What's he doing here?'

'He did not confide in me, sir,' said Jeeves – a trifle frostily, I thought. It sounded somehow as if he didn't like Biffy. And yet they had always been matey enough in the old days.

'Where's he staying?'

'At the Hotel Avenida, Rue du Colisée, sir. He informed me that he was about to take a walk and would call this afternoon.'

'Well, if he comes when I'm out, tell him to wait. And now, Jeeves, *mes gants, mon chapeau, et le whangee de monsieur*. I must be popping.'

It was such a corking day and I had so much time in hand that near the Sorbonne I stopped my cab, deciding to walk the rest of the way. And I had hardly gone three steps and a half when there on the pavement before me stood old Biffy in person. If I had completed the last step I should have rammed him.

'Biffy!' I cried. 'Well, well, well!'

He peered at me in a blinking kind of way, rather like one of his Herefordshire cows prodded unexpectedly while lunching.

'Bertie!' he gurgled, in a devout sort of tone. 'Thank God!' He clutched my arm. 'Don't leave me, Bertie. I'm lost.'

'What do you mean, lost?'

'I came out for a walk and suddenly discovered after a mile or two that I didn't know where on earth I was. I've been wandering round in circles for hours.'

'Why didn't you ask the way?'

'I can't speak a word of French.'

'Well, why didn't you call a taxi?'

'I suddenly discovered I'd left all my money at my hotel.'

'You could have taken a cab and paid it when you got to the hotel.'

'Yes, but I suddenly discovered, dash it, that I'd forgotten its name.'

And there in a nutshell you have Charles Edward Biffen. As vague and woollen-headed a blighter as ever bit a sandwich. Goodness knows – and my Aunt Agatha will bear me out in this – I'm no master-mind myself; but compared with Biffy I'm one of the great thinkers of all time.

'I'd give a shilling,' said Biffy wistfully, 'to know the name of that hotel.'

'You can owe it to me. Hotel Avenida, Rue du Colisée.'

'Bertie! This is uncanny. How the deuce did you know?'

'That was the address you left with Jeeves this morning.'

'So it was. I had forgotten.'

'Well, come along and have a drink, and then I'll put you in a cab and send you home. I'm engaged for lunch, but I've plenty of time.'

'Don't leave me, Bertie. I'm lost.'

We drifted to one of the eleven cafés which jostled each other along the street and I ordered restoratives.

'What on earth are you doing in Paris?' I asked.

'Bertie, old man,' said Biffy solemnly, 'I came here to try and forget.'

'Well, you've certainly succeeded.'

'You don't understand. The fact is, Bertie, old lad, my heart is broken. I'll tell you the whole story.'

'No, I say!' I protested. But he was off.

'Last year,' said Biffy, 'I buzzed over to Canada to do a bit of salmon fishing.'

I ordered another. If this was going to be a fish-story, I needed stimulants.

'On the liner going to New York I met a girl.' Biffy made a sort of curious gulping noise not unlike a bulldog trying to swallow half a cutlet in a hurry so as to be ready for the other half. 'Bertie, old man, I can't describe her. I simply can't describe her.'

This was all to the good.

'She was wonderful! We used to walk on the boat-deck after dinner. She was on the stage. At least, sort of.'

'How do you mean, sort of?'

'Well, she had posed for artists and been a mannequin in a big dressmaker's and all that sort of thing, don't you know. Anyway, she had saved up a few pounds and was on her way to see if she could get a job in New York. She told me all about herself. Her father ran a milk-walk in Clapham. Or it may have been Cricklewood. At least, it was either a milk-walk or a boot-shop.'

'Easily confused.'

'What I'm trying to make you understand,' said Biffy, 'is that she came of good, sturdy, respectable middle-class stock. Nothing flashy about her. The sort of wife any man might have been proud of.'

'Well, whose wife was she?'

'Nobody's. That's the whole point of the story. I wanted her to be mine, and I lost her.'

'Had a quarrel, you mean?'

'No, I don't mean we had a quarrel. I mean I literally lost her. The last I ever saw of her was in the Customs sheds at New York. We were behind a pile of trunks, and I had just asked her to be my wife, and she had just said she would and everything was perfectly splendid, when a most offensive blighter in a peaked cap came up to talk about some cigarettes which he had found at the bottom of my trunk and which I had forgotten to declare. It was getting pretty late by then, for we hadn't docked till about ten-thirty, so I told Mabel to go on to her hotel and I would come round next day and take her to lunch. And since then I haven't set eyes on her.'

'You mean she wasn't at the hotel?'

'Probably she was. But –'

'You don't mean you never turned up?'

'Bertie, old man,' said Biffy, in an overwrought kind of way, 'for Heaven's sake don't keep trying to tell me what I mean and what I don't mean! Let me tell this my own way, or I shall get all mixed up and have to go back to the beginning.'

'Tell it your own way,' I said hastily.

'Well, then, to put it in a word, Bertie, I forgot the name of the hotel. By the time I'd done half an hour's heavy explaining about those cigarettes my mind was a blank. I had an idea I had written the name down somewhere, but I couldn't have done, for it wasn't on any of the papers in my pocket. No, it was no good. She was gone.'

237

'Why didn't you make inquiries?'

'Well, the fact is, Bertie, I had forgotten her name.'

'Oh, no, dash it!' I said. This seemed a bit too thick even for Biffy. 'How could you forget her name? Besides, you told it me a moment ago. Muriel or something.'

'Mabel,' corrected Biffy coldly. 'It was her surname I'd forgotten. So I gave it up and went to Canada.'

'But half a second,' I said. 'You must have told her your name. I mean, if you couldn't trace her, she could trace you.'

'Exactly. That's what makes it all seem so infernally hopeless. She knows my name and where I live and everything, but I haven't heard a word from her. I suppose, when I didn't turn up at the hotel, she took it that that was my way of hinting delicately that I had changed my mind and wanted to call the thing off.'

'I suppose so,' I said. There didn't seem anything else to suppose. 'Well, the only thing to do is to whizz around and try to heal the wound, what? How about dinner tonight, winding up at the Abbaye or one of those places?'

Biffy shook his head.

'It wouldn't be any good. I've tried it. Besides, I'm leaving on the four o'clock train. I have a dinner engagement tomorrow with a man who's nibbling at that house of mine in Herefordshire.'

'Oh, are you trying to sell that place? I thought you liked it.'

'I did. But the idea of going on living in that great, lonely barn of a house after what has happened appals me, Bertie. So when Sir Roderick Glossop came along – '

'Sir Roderick Glossop! You don't mean the loony-doctor?'

'The great nerve specialist, yes. Why, do you know him?'

It was a warm day, but I shivered.

'I was engaged to his daughter for a week or two,' I said, in a hushed voice. The memory of that narrow squeak always made me feel faint.

'Has he a daughter?' said Biffy absently.

'He has. Let me tell you all about – '

'Not just now, old man,' said Biffy, getting up. 'I ought to be going back to my hotel to see about my packing.'

Which, after I had listened to his story, struck me as pretty low-down. However, the longer you live, the more you realise that the good old sporting spirit of give-and-take has practically died out in our midst. So I boosted him into a cab and went off to lunch.

It can't have been more than ten days after this that I received a nasty shock while getting outside my morning tea and toast. The

English papers had arrived, and Jeeves was just drifting out of the room after depositing *The Times* by my bed-side, when, as I idly turned the pages in search of the sporting section, a paragraph leaped out and hit me squarely in the eyeball.

As follows:

FORTHCOMING MARRIAGES
Mr. C. E. Biffen and Miss Glossop

'The engagement is announced between Charles Edward, only son of the late Mr. E. C. Biffen, and Mrs. Biffen, of 11, Penslow Square, Mayfair, and Honoria Jane Louise, only daughter of Sir Roderick and Lady Glossop, of 6b, Harley Street, W.'

'Great Scott!' I exclaimed.

'Sir?' said Jeeves, turning at the door.

'Jeeves, you remember Miss Glossop?'

'Very vividly, sir.'

'She's engaged to Mr. Biffen!'

'Indeed, sir?' said Jeeves. And, with not another word, he slid out. The blighter's calm amazed and shocked me. It seemed to indicate that there must be a horrible streak of callousness in him. I mean to say, it wasn't as if he didn't know Honoria Glossop.

I read the paragraph again. A peculiar feeling it gave me. I don't know if you have ever experienced the sensation of seeing the announcement of the engagement of a pal of yours to a girl whom you were only saved from marrying yourself by the skin of your teeth. It induces a sort of – well, it's difficult to describe it exactly; but I should imagine a fellow would feel much the same if he happened to be strolling through the jungle with a boyhood chum and met a tigress or a jaguar, or what not, and managed to shin up a tree and looked down and saw the friend of his youth vanishing into the undergrowth in the animal's slavering jaws. A sort of profound, prayerful relief, if you know what I mean, blended at the same time with a pang of pity. What I'm driving at is that, thankful as I was that I hadn't had to marry Honoria myself, I was sorry to see a real good chap like old Biffy copping it. I sucked down a spot of tea and began to brood over the business.

Of course, there are probably fellows in the world – tough, hardy blokes with strong chins and glittering eyes – who could get engaged to this Glossop menace and like it; but I knew perfectly well that Biffy was not one of them. Honoria, you see, is one of those robust, dynamic girls with the muscles of a welter-weight and a laugh like a squadron

239

of cavalry charging over a tin bridge. A beastly thing to have to face over the breakfast table. Brainy, moreover. The sort of girl who reduces you to pulp with sixteen sets of tennis and a few rounds of golf, and then comes down to dinner as fresh as a daisy, expecting you to take an intelligent interest in Freud. If I had been engaged to her another week, her old father would have had one more patient on his books; and Biffy is much the same quiet sort of peaceful, inoffensive bird as me. I was shocked, I tell you, shocked.

And, as I was saying, the thing that shocked me most was Jeeves's frightful lack of proper emotion. The man happening to float in at this juncture, I gave him one more chance to show some human sympathy.

'You got the name correctly, didn't you, Jeeves?' I said. 'Mr. Biffen is going to marry Honoria Glossop, the daughter of the old boy with the egg-like head and the eyebrows.'

'Yes, sir. Which suit would you wish me to lay out this morning?'

And this, mark you, from the man who, when I was engaged to the Glossop, strained every fibre in his brain to extricate me. It beat me. I couldn't understand it.

'The blue with the red twill,' I said coldly. My manner was marked, and I meant him to see that he had disappointed me sorely.

About a week later I went back to London, and scarcely had I got settled in the old flat when Biffy blew in. One glance was enough to tell me that the poisoned wound had begun to fester. The man did not look bright. No, there was no getting away from it, not bright. He had that kind of stunned, glassy expression which I used to see on my own face in the shaving-mirror during my brief engagement to the Glossop pestilence. However, if you don't want to be one of the What is Wrong Within This Picture brigade, you must observe the conventions, so I shook his hand as warmly as I could.

'Well, well, old man,' I said. 'Congratulations.'

'Thanks,' said Biffy wanly, and there was rather a weighty silence.

'Bertie,' said Biffy, after the silence had lasted about three minutes.

'Hallo?'

'Is it really true – ?'

'What?'

'Oh, nothing,' said Biffy, and conversation languished again. After about a minute and a half he came to the surface once more.

'Bertie.'

'Still here, old thing. What is it?'

'I say, Bertie, is it really true that you were once engaged to

240

Honoria?'

'It is.'

Biffy coughed.

'How did you get out – I mean, what was the nature of the tragedy that prevented the marriage?'

'Jeeves worked it. He thought out the entire scheme.'

'I think, before I go,' said Biffy thoughtfully, 'I'll just step into the kitchen and have a word with Jeeves.'

I felt that the situation called for complete candour.

'Biffy, old egg,' I said, 'as man to man, do you want to oil out of this thing?'

'Bertie, old cork,' said Biffy earnestly, 'as one friend to another, I do.'

'Then why the dickens did you ever get into it?'

'I don't know. Why did you?'

'I – well, it sort of happened.'

'And it sort of happened with me. You know how it is when your heart's broken. A kind of lethargy comes over you. You get absent-minded and cease to exercise proper precautions, and the first thing you know you're for it. I don't know how it happened, old man, but there it is. And what I want you to tell me is, what's the procedure?'

'You mean, how does a fellow edge out?'

'Exactly. I don't want to hurt anybody's feelings, Bertie, but I can't go through with this thing. The shot is not on the board. For about a day and a half I thought it might be all right, but now – You remember that laugh of hers?'

'I do.'

'Well, there's that, and then all this business of never letting a fellow alone – improving his mind and so forth –'

'I know. I know.'

'Very well, then. What do you recommend? What did you mean when you said that Jeeves worked a scheme?'

'Well, you see, old Sir Roderick, who's a loony-doctor and nothing but a loony-doctor, however much you may call him a nerve special-ist, discovered that there was a modicum of insanity in my family. Nothing serious. Just one of my uncles. Used to keep rabbits in his bedroom. And the old boy came to lunch here to give me the once-over, and Jeeves arranged matters so that he went away firmly con-vinced that I was off my onion.'

'I see,' said Biffy thoughtfully. 'The trouble is there isn't any in-sanity in my family.'

241

'None?'

It seemed to me almost incredible that a fellow could be such a perfect chump as dear old Biffy without a bit of assistance.

'Not a loony on the list,' he said gloomily. 'It's just like my luck. The old boy's coming to lunch with me tomorrow, no doubt to test me as he did you. And I never felt saner in my life.'

I thought for a moment. The idea of meeting Sir Roderick again gave me a cold shivery feeling; but when there is a chance of helping a pal we Woosters have no thought of self.

'Look here, Biffy,' I said, 'I'll tell you what. I'll roll up for that lunch. It may easily happen that when he finds you are a pal of mine he will forbid the banns right away and no more questions asked.'

'Something in that,' said Biffy, brightening. 'Awfully sporting of you, Bertie.'

'Oh, not at all,' I said. 'And meanwhile I'll consult Jeeves. Put the whole thing up to him and ask his advice. He's never failed me yet.'

Biffy pushed off, a good deal braced, and I went into the kitchen.

'Jeeves,' I said, 'I want your help once more. I've just been having a painful interview with Mr. Biffen.'

'Indeed, sir?'

'It's like this,' I said, and told him the whole thing.

It was rummy, but I could feel him freezing from the start. As a rule, when I call Jeeves into conference on one of these little problems, he's all sympathy and bright ideas; but not today.

'I fear, sir,' he said, when I had finished, 'it is hardly my place to intervene in a private matter affecting – '

'Oh, come!'

'No, sir. It would be taking a liberty.'

'Jeeves,' I said, tackling the blighter squarely, 'what have you got against old Biffy?'

'I, sir?'

'Yes, you.'

'I assure you, sir!'

'Oh, well, if you don't want to chip in and save a fellow-creature, I suppose I can't make you. But let me tell you this. I am now going back to the sittingroom, and I am going to put in some very tense thinking. You'll look pretty silly when I come and tell you that I've got Mr. Biffen out of the soup without your assistance. Extremely silly you'll look.'

'Yes, sir. Shall I bring you a whisky-and-soda, sir?'

'No. Coffee! Strong and black. And if anybody wants to see me, tell 'em that I'm busy and can't be disturbed.'

An hour later I rang the bell.

'Jeeves,' I said with hauteur.

'Yes, sir?'

'Kindly ring Mr. Biffen up on the 'phone and say that Mr. Wooster presents his compliments and that he has got it.'

I was feeling more than a little pleased with myself next morning as I strolled round to Biffy's. As a rule the bright ideas you get overnight have a trick of not seeming quite so frightfully fruity when you examine them by the light of day; but this one looked as good at breakfast as it had done before dinner. I examined it narrowly from every angle, and I didn't see how it could fail.

A few days before, my Aunt Emily's son Harold had celebrated his sixth birthday; and, being up against the necessity of weighing in with a present of some kind, I had happened to see in a shop in the Strand a rather sprightly little gadget, well calculated in my opinion to amuse the child and endear him to one and all. It was a bunch of flowers in a sort of holder ending in an ingenious bulb attachment which, when pressed, shot about a pint and a half of pure spring water into the face of anyone who was ass enough to sniff at it. It seemed to me just the thing to please the growing mind of a kid of six, and I had rolled round with it.

But when I got to the house I found Harold sitting in the midst of a mass of gifts so luxurious and costly that I simply hadn't the crust to contribute a thing that had set me back a mere elevenpence-ha'penny; so with rare presence of mind – for we Woosters can think quick on occasion – I wrenched my Uncle James's card off a toy aeroplane, substituted my own, and trousered the squirt, which I took away with me. It had been lying around in my flat ever since, and it seemed to me that the time had come to send it into action.

'Well?' said Biffy anxiously, as I curveted into his sitting-room.

The poor old bird was looking pretty green about the gills. I recognised the symptoms. I had felt much the same myself when waiting for Sir Roderick to turn up and lunch with me. How the deuce people who have anything wrong with their nerves can bring themselves to chat with that man, I can't imagine; and yet he has the largest practice in London. Scarcely a day passes without his having to sit on somebody's head and ring for the attendant to bring the strait-waistcoat: and outlook on life has become so jaundiced through constant association with coves who are picking straws out of their hair that I was convinced that Biffy had merely got to press the bulb and nature would do the rest.

So I patted him on the shoulder and said: 'It's all right, old man!'

'What does Jeeves suggest?' asked Biffy eagerly.

'Jeeves doesn't suggest anything.'

'But you said it was all right.'

'Jeeves isn't the only thinker in the Wooster home, my lad. I have taken over your little problem, and I can tell you at once that I have the situation well in hand.'

'You?' said Biffy.

His tone was far from flattering. It suggested a lack of faith in my abilities, and my view was that an ounce of demonstration would be worth a ton of explanation. I shoved the bouquet at him.

'Are you fond of flowers, Biffy?' I said.

'Eh?'

'Smell these.'

Biffy extended the old beak in a careworn sort of way, and I pressed the bulb as per printed instructions on the label.

I do like getting my money's-worth. Elevenpence-ha'penny the thing had cost me, and it would have been cheap at double. The advertisement on the outside of the box had said that its effects were 'indescribably ludicrous', and I can testify that it was no over-statement. Poor old Biffy leaped three feet in the air and overturned a small table.

'There!' I said.

The old egg was a trifle incoherent at first, but he found words fairly soon, and began to express himself with a good deal of warmth.

'Calm yourself, laddie,' I said, as he paused for breath. 'It was no mere jest to pass an idle hour. It was a demonstration. Take this, Biffy, with an old friend's blessing, refill the bulb, shove it into Sir Roderick's face, press firmly, and leave the rest to him. I'll guarantee that in something under three seconds the idea will have dawned on him that you are not required in his family.'

Biffy stared at me.

'Are you suggesting that I squirt Sir Roderick?'

'Absolutely. Squirt him good. Squirt as you have never squirted before.'

'But –'

He was still yammering at me in a feverish sort of way when there was a ring at the front-door bell.

'Good Lord!' cried Biffy, quivering like a jelly. 'There he is. Talk to

244

him while I go and change my shirt.'

I had just time to refill the bulb and shove it beside Biffy's plate, when the door opened and Sir Roderick came in. I was picking up the fallen table at the moment, and he started talking brightly to my back.

'Good afternoon. I trust I am not – Mr. Wooster!'

I'm bound to say I was not feeling entirely at my ease. There is something about the man that is calculated to strike terror into the stoutest heart. If ever there was a bloke at the very mention of whose name it would be excusable for people to tremble like aspens, that bloke is Sir Roderick Glossop. He has an enormous bald head, all the hair which ought to be on it seeming to have run into his eyebrows, and his eyes go through you like a couple of Death Rays.

'How are you, how are you, how are you?' I said, overcoming a slight desire to leap backwards out of the window. 'Long time since we met, what?'

'Nevertheless, I remember you most distinctly, Mr. Wooster.'

'That's fine,' I said. 'Old Biffy asked me to come and join you in mangling a bit of lunch.'

He waggled the eyebrows at me.

'Are you a friend of Charles Biffen?'

'Oh, rather. Been friends for years and years.'

He drew in his breath sharply, and I could see that Biffy's stock had dropped several points. His eye fell on the floor, which was strewn with things that had tumbled off the upset table.

'Have you had an accident?' he said.

'Nothing serious,' I explained. 'Old Biffy had some sort of fit or seizure just now and knocked over the table.'

'A fit!'

'Or seizure.'

'Is he subject to fits?'

I was about to answer, when Biffy hurried in. He had forgotten to brush his hair, which gave him a wild look, and I saw the old boy direct a keen glance at him. It seemed to me that what you might call the preliminary spade-work had been most satisfactorily attended to and that the success of the good old bulb could be in no doubt whatever.

Biffy's man came in with the nose-bags and we sat down to lunch.

It looked at first as though the meal was going to be one of those complete frosts which occur from time to time in the career of a constant luncher-out. Biffy, a very C_3 host, contributed nothing to the feast of reason and flow of soul beyond an occasional hiccup, and every time I started to pull a nifty, Sir Roderick swung round on me with such a piercing stare that it stopped me in my tracks. Fortunately, however, the second course consisted of a chicken fricassee of such outstanding excellence that the old boy, after wolfing a plateful, handed up his dinner-pail for a second instalment and became almost genial.

'I am here this afternoon, Charles,' he said, with what practically amounted to bonhomie, 'on what I might describe as a mission. Yes, a mission. This is most excellent chicken.'

'Glad you like it,' mumbled old Biffy.

'Singularly toothsome,' said Sir Roderick, pronging another half ounce. 'Yes, as I was saying, a mission. You young fellows nowadays are, I know, content to live in the centre of the most wonderful metropolis the world has seen, blind and indifferent to its many marvels. I should be prepared – were I a betting man, which I am not – to wager a considerable sum that you have never in your life visited even so historic a spot as Westminster Abbey. Am I right?'

Biffy gurgled something about always having meant to.

'Nor the Tower of London?'

No, nor the Tower of London.

'And there exists at this very moment, not twenty minutes by cab from Hyde Park Corner, the most supremely absorbing and educational collection of objects, both animate and inanimate, gathered from the four corners of the Empire, that has ever been assembled in England's history. I allude to the British Empire Exhibition now situated at Wembley.'

'A fellow told me one about Wembley yesterday,' I said, to help on the cheery flow of conversation. 'Stop me if you've heard it before. Chap goes up to deaf chap outside the exhibition and says, 'Is this Wembley?' 'Hey?' says deaf chap. 'Is this Wembley?' says chap. 'Hey?' says deaf chap. 'Is this Wembley?' says chap. 'No, Thursday,' says deaf chap. Ha, ha, I mean, what?'

The merry laughter froze on my lips. Sir Roderick sort of just waggled an eyebrow in my direction and I saw that it was back to the basket for Bertram. I never met a man who had such a knack of making a fellow feel like a waste-product.

'Have you yet paid a visit to Wembley, Charles?' he asked. 'No? Precisely as I suspected. Well, that is the mission on which I am here this afternoon. Honoria wishes me to take you to Wembley. She says it will broaden your mind, in which view I am at one with her. We will start immediately after luncheon.'

Biffy cast an imploring look at me.

'You'll come too, Bertie?'

There was such agony in his eyes that I only hesitated for a second. A pal is a pal. Besides, I felt that, if only the bulb fulfilled the high expectations I had formed of it, the merry expedition would be cancelled in no uncertain manner.

'Oh, rather,' I said.

'We must not trespass on Mr. Wooster's good nature,' said Sir Roderick, looking pretty puff-faced.

'Oh, that's all right,' I said. 'I've been meaning to go to the good old exhibish for a long time. I'll slip home and change my clothes and pick you up here in my car.'

There was a silence. Biffy seemed too relieved at the thought of not having to spend the afternoon alone with Sir Roderick to be capable of speech, and Sir Roderick was registering silent disapproval. And then he caught sight of the bouquet by Biffy's plate.

'Ah, flowers,' he said. 'Sweet peas, if I am not in error. A charming plant, pleasing alike to the eye and the nose.'

I caught Biffy's eye across the table. It was bulging, and a strange light shone in it.

'Are you fond of flowers, Sir Roderick?' he croaked.

'Extremely.'

'Smell these.'

Sir Roderick dipped his head and sniffed. Biffy's fingers closed slowly over the bulb. I shut my eyes and clutched the table.

'Very pleasant,' I heard Sir Roderick say. 'Very pleasant indeed.'

I opened my eyes, and there was Biffy leaning back in his chair with a ghastly look, and the bouquet on the cloth beside him. I realised what had happened. In that supreme crisis of his life, with his whole happiness depending on a mere pressure of the fingers, Biffy, the poor spineless fish, had lost his nerve. My closely-reasoned scheme had gone phut.

Jeeves was fooling about with the geraniums in the sitting-room windowbox when I got home.

'They make a very nice display, sir,' he said, cocking a paternal eye at the things.

'Don't talk to me about flowers,' I said. 'Jeeves, I know now how a general feels when he plans out some great scientific movement and his troops let him down at the eleventh hour.'

'Indeed, sir?'

'Yes,' I said, and told him what had happened.

He listened thoughtfully.

'A somewhat vacillating and changeable young gentleman, Mr. Biffen,' was his comment when I had finished. 'Would you be requiring me for the remainder of the afternoon, sir?'

'No. I'm going to Wembley. I just came back to change and get the car. Produce some fairly durable garments which can stand getting squashed by the many-headed, Jeeves, and then 'phone to the garage.'

'Very good, sir. The grey cheviot lounge will, I fancy, be suitable. Would it be too much if I asked you to give me a seat in the car, sir? I had thought of going to Wembley myself this afternoon.'

'Eh? Oh, all right.'

'Thank you very much, sir.'

I got dressed, and we drove round to Biffy's flat. Biffy and Sir Roderick got in at the back and Jeeves climbed into the front seat next to me. Biffy looked so ill-attuned to an afternoon's pleasure that my heart bled for the blighter and I made one last attempt to appeal to Jeeves's better feelings.

'I must say, Jeeves,' I said, 'I'm dashed disappointed in you.'

'I am sorry to hear that, sir.'

'Well, I am. Dashed disappointed. I do think you might rally round. Did you see Mr. Biffen's face?'

'Yes, sir.'

'Well, then.'

'If you will pardon my saying so, sir, Mr. Biffen has surely only himself to thank if he has entered upon matrimonial obligations which do not please him.'

'You're talking absolute rot, Jeeves. You know as well as I do that Honoria Glossop is an Act of God. You might just as well blame a fellow for getting run over by a truck.'

'Yes, sir?'

'Absolutely yes. Besides, the poor ass wasn't in a condition to resist. He told me all about it. He had lost the only girl he had ever loved, and you know what a man's like when that happens to him.'

'How was that, sir?'

'Apparently he fell in love with some girl on the boat going over to New York, and they parted at the Customs sheds, arranging to meet next day at her hotel. Well, you know what Biffy's like. He forgets his own name half the time. He never made a note of the address, and it passed clean out of his mind. He went about in a sort of trance, and

248

suddenly woke up to find that he was engaged to Honoria Glossop.'

'I did not know of this, sir.'

'I don't suppose anybody knows of it except me. He told me when I was in Paris.'

'I should have supposed it would have been feasible to make inquiries, sir.'

'That's what I said. But he had forgotten her name.'

'That sounds remarkable, sir.'

'I said that, too. But it's a fact. All he remembered was that her Christian name was Mabel. Well, you can't go scouring New York for a girl named Mabel, what?'

'I appreciate the difficulty, sir.'

'Well, there it is, then.'

'I see, sir.'

We had got into a mob of vehicles outside the Exhibition by this time, and, some tricky driving being indicated, I had to suspend the conversation. We parked ourselves eventually and went in. Jeeves drifted away, and Sir Roderick took charge of the expedition. He headed for the Palace of Industry, with Biffy and myself trailing behind.

Well, you know, I have never been much of a lad for exhibitions. The citizenry in the mass always rather puts me off, and after I have been shuffling along with the multitude for a quarter of an hour or so I feel as if I were walking on hot bricks. About this particular binge, too, there seemed to me a lack of what you might call human interest. I mean to say, millions of people, no doubt, are so constituted that they scream with joy and excitement at the spectacle of a stuffed porcupine-fish or a glass jar of seeds from Western Australia – but not Bertram. No; if you will take the word of one who would not deceive you, not Bertram. By the time we had tottered out of the Gold Coast village and were working towards the Palace of Machinery, everything pointed to my shortly executing a quiet sneak in the direction of that rather jolly Planters' Bar in the West Indian section. Sir Roderick had whizzed us past this at a high rate of speed, it touching no chord in him; but I had been able to observe that there was a sprightly sportsman behind the counter mixing things out of bottles and stirring them up with a stick in long glasses that seemed to have ice in them, and the urge came upon me to see more of this man. I was about to drop away from the main body and become a straggler, when something pawed at my coat-sleeve. It was Biffy, and he had the air of one who has had about sufficient.

There are certain moments in life when words are not needed. I looked at Biffy, Biffy looked at me. A perfect understanding linked our two souls.

'?'

'!'

Three minutes later we had joined the Planters.

I have never been in the West Indies, but I am in a position to state that in certain of the fundamentals of life they are streets ahead of our European civilisation. The man behind the counter, as kindly a bloke as I ever wish to meet, seemed to guess our requirements the moment we hove in view. Scarcely had our elbows touched the wood before he was leaping to and fro, bringing down a new bottle with each leap. A planter, apparently, does not consider he has had a drink unless it contains at least seven ingredients, and I'm not saying, mind you, that he isn't right. The man behind the bar told us the things were called Green Swizzles; and, if ever I marry and have a son, Green Swizzle Wooster is the name that will go down on the register, in memory of the day his father's life was saved at Wembley.

After the third, Biffy breathed a contented sigh.

'Where do you think Sir Roderick is?' he said.

'Biffy, old thing,' I replied frankly, 'I'm not worrying.'

'Bertie, old bird,' said Biffy, 'nor am I.'

He sighed again, and broke a long silence by asking the man for a straw.

'Bertie,' he said, 'I've just remembered something rather rummy. You know Jeeves?'

I said I knew Jeeves.

'Well, a rather rummy incident occurred as we were going into this place. Old Jeeves sidled up to me and said something rather rummy. You'll never guess what it was.'

'No. I don't believe I ever shall.'

'Jeeves said,' proceeded Biffy earnestly, 'and I am quoting his very words – Jeeves said, "Mr. Biffen" – addressing me, you understand –'

'I understand.'

'"Mr. Biffen," he said, "I strongly advise you to visit the – "'

'The what?' I asked as he paused.

'Bertie, old man,' said Biffy, deeply concerned, 'I've absolutely forgotten!'

I stared at the man.

'What I can't understand,' I said, 'is how you manage to run that Herefordshire place of yours for a day. How on earth do you remember to milk the cows and give the pigs their dinner?'

'Oh, that's all right. There are divers blokes about the places – hirelings and menials, you know – who look after all that.'

'Ah!' I said. 'Well, that being so, let us have one more Green Swizzle, and then hey for the Amusement Park.'

When I indulged in those few rather bitter words about exhibitions, it must be distinctly understood that I was not alluding to what you might call the more earthy portion of these curious places. I yield to no man in my approval of those institutions where on payment of a shilling you are permitted to slide down a slippery run-way sitting on a mat. I love the Jiggle-Joggle, and I am prepared to take on all and sundry at Skee Ball for money, stamps, or Brazil nuts.

But, joyous reveller as I am on these occasions, I was simply not in it with old Biffy. Whether it was the Green Swizzles or merely the relief of being parted from Sir Roderick. I don't know, but Biffy flung himself into the pastimes of the proletariat with a zest that was almost frightening. I could hardly drag him away from the Whip, and as for the Switchback, he looked like spending the rest of his life on it. I managed to remove him at last, and he was wandering through the crowd at my side with gleaming eyes, hesitating between having his fortune told and taking a whirl at the Wheel of Joy, when he suddenly grabbed my arm and uttered a sharp animal cry.

'Bertie!'

'Now what?'

He was pointing at a large sign over a building.

'Look! Palace of Beauty!'

I tried to choke him off. I was getting a bit weary by this time. Not so young as I was.

'You don't want to go in there,' I said. 'A fellow at the club was telling me about that. It's only a lot of girls. You don't want to see a lot of girls.'

'I do want to see a lot of girls,' said Biffy firmly. 'Dozens of girls, and the more unlike Honoria they are, the better. Besides, I've suddenly remembered that that's the place Jeeves told me to be sure and visit. It all comes back to me. "Mr. Biffen," he said, "I strongly advise you to visit the Palace of Beauty." Now, what the man was driving at or what his motive was, I don't know; but I ask you, Bertie, is it wise, is it safe, is it judicious ever to ignore Jeeves's lightest word? We enter by the door on the left.'

I don't know if you know this Palace of Beauty place? It's a sort of aquarium full of the delicately-nurtured instead of fishes. You go in, and there is a kind of cage with a female goggling out at you through a sheet of plate glass. She's dressed in some weird kind of costume, and over the cage is written 'Helen of Troy'. You pass on to the next, and there's another one doing jiu-jitsu with a snake. Sub-title, Cleopatra. You get the idea – Famous Women Through the Ages and all that. I can't say it fascinated me to any great extent. I maintain that a lovely woman loses a lot of her charm if you have to stare at her in a tank. Moreover, it gave me a rummy sort of feeling of having wandered into the wrong bedroom at a country house, and I was flying past at a fair rate of speed, anxious to get it over, when Biffy suddenly went off his rocker.

At least, it looked like that. He let out a piercing yell, grabbed my arm with a sudden clutch that felt like the bite of a crocodile, and stood there gibbering.

'Wuk!' ejaculated Biffy, or words to that general import.

A large and interested crowd had gathered round. I think they thought the girls were going to be fed or something. But Biffy paid no attention to them. He was pointing in a loony manner at one of the cages. I forget which it was, but the female inside wore a ruff, so it may have been Queen Elizabeth or Boadicea or someone of that period. She was rather a nice-looking girl, and she was staring at Biffy in much the same pop-eyed way as he was staring at her.

'Mabel!' yelled Biffy, going off in my ear like a bomb.

I can't say I was feeling my chirpiest. Drama is all very well, but I hate getting mixed up in it in a public spot; and I had not realised before how dashed public this spot was. The crowd seemed to have doubled itself in the last five seconds, and, while most of them had their eye on Biffy, quite a goodish few were looking at me as if they thought I was an important principal in the scene and might be expected at any moment to give of my best in the way of wholesome entertainment for the masses.

Biffy was jumping about like a lamb in the springtime – and, what is more, a feeble-minded lamb.

'Bertie! It's her! It's she!' He looked about him wildly. 'Where the deuce is the stage-door?' he cried. 'Where's the manager? I want to see the house-manager immediately.'

And then he suddenly bounded forward and began hammering on the glass with his stick.

'I say, old lad!' I began, but he shook me off.

These fellows who live in the country are apt to go in for fairly siza-ble clubs instead of the light canes which your well-dressed man about town considers suitable for metropolitan use; and down in Herefordshire, apparently, something in the nature of a knobkerrie is *de rigueur*. Biffy's first slosh smashed the glass all to a hash. Three more cleared the way for him to go into the cage without cutting himself. And, before the crowd had time to realise what a wonderful bob's-worth it was getting in exchange for its entrance-fee, he was inside, engaging the girl in earnest conversation. And at the same moment two large policemen rolled up.

You can't make policemen take the romantic view. Not a tear did these two blighters stop to brush away. They were inside the cage and out of it and marching Biffy through the crowd before you had time to blink. I hurried after them, to do what I could in the way of soothing Biffy's last moments, and the poor old lad turned a glowing face in my direction.

'Chiswick, 60873,' he bellowed in a voice charged with emotion. 'Write it down, Bertie, or I shall forget it. Chiswick, 60873. Her tele-phone number.'

And then he disappeared, accompanied by about eleven thousand sightseers, and a voice spoke at my elbow.

'Mr. Wooster! What – what – what is the meaning of this?'

Sir Roderick, with bigger eyebrows than ever, was standing at my side.

'It's all right,' I said. 'Poor old Biffy's only gone off his crumpet.'

He tottered.

'What?'

'Had a sort of fit or seizure, you know.'

'Another!' Sir Roderick drew a deep breath. 'And this is the man I was about to allow my daughter to marry!' I heard him mutter.

I tapped him in a kindly spirit on the shoulder. It took some doing, mark you, but I did it.

'If I were you,' I said, 'I should call that off. Scratch the fixture. Wash it out absolutely, is my advice.'

He gave me a nasty look.

'I do not require your advice, Mr. Wooster! I had already arrived independently at the decision of which you speak. Mr. Wooster, you are a friend of this man – a fact which should in itself have been suf-ficient warning to me. You will – unlike myself – be seeing him again. Kindly inform him, when you do see him, that he may consider his engagement at an end.'

'Right-ho,' I said, and hurried off after the crowd. It seemed to me that a little bailing-out might be in order.

It was about an hour later that I shoved my way out to where I had parked the car. Jeeves was sitting in the front seat, brooding over the cosmos. He rose courteously as I approached.

'You are leaving, sir?'

'I am.'

'And Sir Roderick, sir?'

'Not coming. I am revealing no secrets, Jeeves, when I inform you that he and I have parted brass-rags. Not on speaking terms now.'

'Indeed, sir? And Mr. Biffen? Will you wait for him?'

'No. He's in prison.'

'Really, sir?'

'Yes. I tried to bail him out, but they decided on second thoughts to coop him up for the night.'

'What was his offence, sir?'

'You remember that girl of his I was telling you about? He found her in a tank at the Palace of Beauty and went after her by the quickest route, which was *via* a plate-glass window. He was then scooped up and borne off in irons by the constabulary.' I gazed sideways at him. It is difficult to bring off a penetrating glance out of the corner of your eye, but I managed it. 'Jeeves,' I said, 'there is more in this than the casual observer would suppose. You told Mr. Biffen to go to the Palace of Beauty. Did you know the girl would be there?'

'Yes, sir.'

This was most remarkable and rummy to a degree.

'Dash it, do you know everything?'

'Oh, no, sir,' said Jeeves with an indulgent smile. Humouring the young master.

'Well, how did you know that?'

'I happen to be acquainted with the future Mrs. Biffen, sir.'

'I see. Then you knew all about that business in New York?'

'Yes, sir. And it was for that reason that I was not altogether favourably disposed towards Mr. Biffen when you were first kind enough to suggest that I might be able to offer some slight assistance. I mistakenly supposed that he had been trifling with the girl's affections, sir. But when you told me the true facts of the case I appreciated the injustice I had done to Mr. Biffen and endeavoured to make amends.'

'Well, he certainly owes you a lot. He's crazy about her.'

254

'That is very gratifying, sir.'

'And she ought to be pretty grateful to you, too. Old Biffy's got fifteen thousand a year, not to mention more cows, pigs, hens, and ducks than he knows what to do with. A dashed useful bird to have in any family.'

'Yes, sir.'

'Tell me, Jeeves,' I said, 'how did you happen to know the girl in the first place?'

Jeeves looked dreamily out into the traffic.

'She is my niece, sir. If I might make the suggestion, sir, I should not jerk the steering-wheel with quite such suddenness. We very nearly collided with that omnibus.'

Comrade Bingo

THE thing really started in the Park – at the Marble Arch end, where blighters of every description collect on Sunday afternoons and stand on soap-boxes and make speeches. It isn't often you'll find me there, but it so happened that on this particular Sabbath, having a call to pay in Manchester Square, I had taken a short cut through and found myself right in the middle of it. On the prompt side a gang of top-hatted birds were starting an open-air missionary service; on the O.P. side an atheist was hauling up his slacks with a good deal of vim, though handicapped a bit by having no roof to his mouth; a chappie who wanted a hundred million quid to finance him in a scheme for solving the problem of perpetual motion was playing to a thin house up left centre; while in front of me there stood a little group of serious thinkers with a banner labelled 'Heralds Of the Red Dawn'; and as I came up one of the Heralds, a bearded egg in a slouch hat and a tweed suit, was slipping it into the Idle Rich with such breadth and vigour that I paused for a moment to get an earful. While I was standing there somebody spoke to me.

'Mr. Wooster, surely?'

Stout chappie. Couldn't place him for a second. Then I got him. Bingo Little's uncle, the one I had lunch with at the time when young Bingo was in love with that waitress at the Piccadilly bun-shop. No wonder I hadn't recognised him at first. When I had seen him last he had been a rather sloppy old gentleman – coming down to lunch, I remember, in carpet slippers and a velvet smoking-jacket; whereas now dapper simply wasn't the word. He absolutely gleamed in the sunlight in a silk hat, morning coat, lavender spats, and sponge-bag trousers, as now worn. Dressy to a degree.

'Oh, hallo!' I said. 'Going strong?'

'I am in excellent health, I thank you. And you?'

'In the pink. Just been over in France for a change of air. Got back the day before yesterday. Seen anything of Bingo lately?'

'Bingo?'

'Your nephew.'

'Oh, Richard? No, not very recently. Since my marriage a little coolness seems to have sprung up.

'Sorry to hear that. So you've married since I saw you, what? Mrs. Little all right?'

'My wife is happily robust. But – er – *not* Mrs. Little. Since we last met a gracious Sovereign has been pleased to bestow on me a signal mark of his favour in the shape of – ah – a peerage. On the publication of the last Honours List I became Lord Bittlesham.'

'By Jove! Really? I say, heartiest congratulations. Lord Bittlesham?' I said. 'Why, you're the owner of Ocean Breeze.'

'Yes. Marriage has enlarged my horizon in many directions. My wife is interested in horse-racing, and I now maintain a small stable. I understand that Ocean Breeze is fancied, as I am told the expression is, for a race which will take place at the end of the month at Goodwood, the Duke of Richmond's seat in Sussex.'

'The Goodwood Cup. Rather! I've got my chemise on it for one.'

'Indeed? Well, I trust the animal will justify your confidence. I know little of these matters myself, but my wife tells me that it is regarded in knowledgeable circles as what I believe is termed a snip.'

At this moment I suddenly noticed that the audience was gazing in our direction with a good deal of interest, and I saw that the bearded chappie was pointing at us.

'Yes, look at them! Drink them in!' he was yelling, his voice rising above the perpetual-motion fellow's and beating the missionary service all to nothing. 'There you see two typical members of the class which has down-trodden the poor for centuries. Idlers! Non-producers! Look at the tall, thin one with the face like a motor-mascot. Has he ever done an honest day's work in his life? No! A prowler, a trifler, and a blood-sucker! And I bet he still owes his tailor for those trousers!'

He seemed to me to be verging on the personal, and I didn't think a lot of it. Old Bittlesham, on the other hand, was pleased and amused.

'A great gift of expression these fellows have,' he chuckled. 'Very trenchant.'

'And the fat one!' proceeded the chappie. 'Don't miss him. Do you know who that is? That's Lord Bittlesham. One of the worst. What has he ever done except eat four square meals a day? His god is his belly, and he sacrifices burnt-offerings to it till his eyes bubble. If you opened that man now you would find enough lunch to support ten working-class families for a week.'

'You know, that's rather well put,' I said, but the old boy didn't seem to see it. He had turned a brightish magenta and was bubbling like a kettle on the boil.

'Come away, Mr. Wooster,' he said. 'I am the last man to oppose the right of free speech, but I refuse to listen to this vulgar abuse any longer.'

We legged it with quiet dignity, the chappie pursuing us with his foul innuendoes to the last. Dashed embarrassing.

Next day I looked in at the club, and found young Bingo in the smoking-room.

'Hallo, Bingo,' I said, toddling over to his corner full of bonhomie, for I was glad to see the chump. 'How's the boy?'

'Jogging along.'

'I saw your uncle yesterday.'

Young Bingo unleased a grin that split his face in half.

'I know you did, you trifler. Well, sit down, old thing, and suck a bit of blood. How's the prowling these days?'

'Good Lord! You weren't there!'

'Yes, I was.'

'I didn't see you.'

'Yes, you did. But perhaps you didn't recognise me in the shrubbery.'

'The shrubbery?'

'The beard, my boy. Worth every penny I paid for it. Defies detection.'

I goggled at him.

'I don't understand.'

'It's a long story. Have a martini or a small gore-and-soda, and I'll tell you all about it. Before we start, give me your honest opinion. Isn't she the most wonderful girl you ever saw in your puff?'

He had produced a photograph from somewhere, like a conjuror taking a rabbit out of a hat, and was waving it in front of me. It appeared to be a female of sorts, all eyes and teeth.

'Oh, great Scott!' I said. 'Don't tell me you're in love again.'

He seemed aggrieved.

'What do you mean – again?'

'Well, to my certain knowledge you've been in love with at least half-a-dozen girls since the Spring, and it's only July now. There was that waitress and Honoria Glossop and – '

'Oh, tush! Not to say pish! Those girls? Mere passing fancies. This is the real thing.'

'Where did you meet her?'

'On top of a bus. Her name is Charlotte Corday Rowbotham.'

'My God!'

'It's not her fault, poor child. Her father had her christened that because he's all for the Revolution, and it seems that the original Charlotte Corday used to go about stabbing oppressors in their baths, which entitles her to consideration and respect. You must meet old Rowbotham, Bertie. A delightful chap. Wants to massacre the bourgeoisie, sack Park Lane, and disembowel the hereditary aristocracy. Well, nothing could be fairer than that, what? But about Charlotte. We were on top of the bus and it started to rain. I offered her my umbrella, and we chatted of this and that. I fell in love and got her address, and a couple of days later I bought the beard and toddled round and met the family.'

'But why the beard?'

'Well, she had told me all about her father on the bus, and I saw that to get any footing at all in the home I should have to join these Red Dawn blighters; and naturally, if I was to make speeches in the Park, where at any moment I might run into a dozen people I knew, something in the nature of a disguise was indicated. So I bought the beard, and, by Jove, old boy, I've become dashed attached to the thing. When I take it off to come in here, for instance, I feel absolutely nude. It's done me a lot of good with old Rowbotham. He thinks I'm a Bolshevist of sorts who has to go about disguised because of the police. You really must meet old Rowbotham, Bertie. I tell you what, are you doing anything tomorrow afternoon?'

'Nothing special. Why?'

'Good! Then you can have us all to tea at your flat. I had promised to take the crowd to Lyon's Popular Café after a meeting we're holding down in Lambeth, but I can save money this way; and, believe me laddie, nowadays, as far as I'm concerned, a penny saved is a penny earned. My uncle told you he'd got married?'

'Yes. And he said there was a coolness between you.'

'Coolness? I'm down to zero. Ever since he married he's been launching out in every direction and economising on *me*. I suppose

259

that peerage cost the old devil the deuce of a sum. Even baronetcies have gone up frightfully nowadays, I'm told. And he's started a racing-stable. By the way, put your last collar-stud on Ocean Breeze for the Goodwood Cup. It's a cert.'

'I'm going to.'

'It can't lose. I mean to win enough on it to marry Charlotte with. You're going to Goodwood of course?'

'Rather!'

'So are we. We're holding a meeting on Cup day just outside the paddock.'

'But, I say, aren't you taking frightful risks? Your uncle's sure to be at Goodwood. Suppose he spots you? He'll be fed to the gills if he finds out that you're the fellow who ragged him in the Park.'

'How the deuce is he to find out? Use your intelligence, you prowling inhaler of red corpuscles. If he didn't spot me yesterday, why should he spot me at Goodwood? Well, thanks for your cordial invitation for tomorrow, old thing. We shall be delighted to accept. Do us well, laddie, and blessings shall reward you. By the way, I may have misled you by using the word "tea". None of your wafer slices of bread-and-butter. We're good trenchermen, we of the Revolution. What we shall require will be something in the order of scrambled eggs, muffins, jam, ham, cake, and sardines. Expect us at five sharp.'

'But, I say, I'm not quite sure – '

'Yes, you are. Silly ass, don't you see that this is going to do you a bit of good when the Revolution breaks loose? When you see old Rowbotham sprinting up Piccadilly with a dripping knife in each hand, you'll be jolly thankful to be able to remind him that he once ate your tea and shrimps. There will be four of us – Charlotte, self, the old man, and Comrade Butt. I suppose he will insist on coming along.'

'Who the devil's Comrade Butt?'

'Did you notice a fellow standing on my left in our little troupe yesterday? small, shrivelled chap. Looks like a haddock with lung-trouble. That's Butt. My rival, dash him. He's sort of semi-engaged to Charlotte at the moment. Till I came along he was the blue-eyed boy. He's got a voice like a fog-horn, and old Rowbotham thinks a lot of him. But, hang it, if I can't thoroughly encompass this Butt and cut him out and put him where he belongs among the discards – well, I'm not the man I was, that's all. He may have a big voice, but he hasn't my gift of expression. Thank heaven I was once cox of my college boat. Well, I must be pushing now. I say, you don't know how I could raise fifty quid somehow, do you?'

'Why don't you work?'

'Work?' said young Bingo, surprised. 'What, me? No, I shall have to think of some way. I must put at least fifty on Ocean Breeze. Well, see you tomorrow. God bless you, old sport, and don't forget the muffins.'

I don't know why, ever since I first knew him at school, I should have felt a rummy feeling of responsibility for young Bingo. I mean to say, he's not my son (thank goodness) or my brother or anything like that. He's got absolutely no claim on me at all, and yet a large-sized chunk of my existence seems to be spent in fussing over him like a bally old hen and hauling him out of the soup. I suppose it must be some rare beauty in my nature or something. At any rate, this latest affair of his worried me. He seemed to be doing his best to marry into a family of pronounced loonies, and how the deuce he thought he was going to support even a mentally afflicted wife on nothing a year beat me. Old Bittlesham was bound to knock off his allowance if he did anything of the sort; and, with a fellow like young Bingo, if you knocked off his allowance, you might just as well hit him on the head with an axe and make a clean job of it.

'Jeeves,' I said, when I got home, 'I'm worried.'

'Sir?'

'About Mr. Little. I won't tell you about it now, because he's bringing some friends of his to tea tomorrow, and then you will be able to judge for yourself. I want you to observe closely, Jeeves, and form your decision.'

'Very good, sir.'

'And about the tea. Get in muffins.'

'Yes, sir.'

'And some jam, ham, cake, scrambled eggs, and five or six wagonloads of sardines.'

'Sardines, sir?' said Jeeves, with a shudder.

'Sardines.'

There was an awkward pause.

'Don't blame me, Jeeves,' I said. 'It isn't my fault.'

'No sir.'

'Well, that's that.'

'Yes, sir.'

I could see the man was brooding tensely.

I've found, as a general rule in life, that the things you think are going to be the scaliest nearly always turn out not so bad after all; but it wasn't that way with Bingo's tea-party. From the moment he invited himself I felt that the thing was going to be blue round the edges, and it was. And I think the most gruesome part of the whole affair was the fact that, for the first time since I'd known him, I saw Jeeves come very near to being rattled. I suppose there's a chink in everyone's armour, and young Bingo found Jeeves's right at the drop of the flag when he breezed in with six inches or so of brown beard hanging on to his chin. I had forgotten to warn Jeeves about the beard, and it came on him absolutely out of a blue sky. I saw the man's jaw drop, and he clutched at the table for support. I don't blame him, mind you. Few people have ever looked fouler than young Bingo in the fungus. Jeeves paled a little; then the weakness passed and he was himself again. But I could see that he had been shaken.

Young Bingo was too busy introducing the mob to take much notice. They were a very C_3 collection. Comrade Butt looked like one of the things that come out of dead trees after the rain; moth-eaten was the word I should have used to describe old Rowbotham; and as for Charlotte, she seemed to take me straight into another and a dreadful world. It wasn't that she was exactly bad-looking. In fact, if she had knocked off starchy foods and done Swedish exercises for a bit, she might have been quite tolerable. But there was too much of her. Billowy curves. Well-nourished perhaps expresses it best. And, while she may have had a heart of gold, the thing you noticed about her first was that she had a tooth of gold. I knew that young Bingo, when in form, could fall in love with practically anything of the other sex; but this time I couldn't see any excuse for him at all.

'My friend Mr. Wooster,' said Bingo, completing the ceremonial.

Old Rowbotham looked at me and then he looked round the room, and I could see he wasn't particularly braced. There's nothing of absolutely Oriental luxury about the old flat, but I have managed to make myself fairly comfortable, and I suppose the surroundings jarred him a bit.

'Mr. Wooster?' said old Rowbotham. 'May I say Comrade Wooster?'

'I beg your pardon?'

'Are you of the movement?'

'Well – er – '

'Do you yearn for the Revolution?'

'Well, I don't know that I exactly yearn. I mean to say, as far as I can make out, the whole nub of the scheme seems to be to massacre coves like me; and I don't mind owning I'm not frightfully keen on the idea.'

'But I'm talking him round,' said Bingo. 'I'm wrestling with him. A few more treatments ought to do the trick.'

Old Rowbotham looked at me a bit doubtfully.

'Comrade Little has great eloquence,' he admitted.

'I think he talks something wonderful,' said the girl, and young Bingo shot a glance of such succulent devotion at her that I reeled in my tracks. It seemed to depress Comrade Butt a good deal too. He scowled at the carpet and said something about dancing on volcanoes.

'Tea is served, sir,' said Jeeves.

'Tea, pa!' said Charlotte, starting at the word like the old war-horse who hears the bugle; and we got down to it.

Funny how one changes as the years roll on. At school, I remember, I would cheerfully have sold my soul for scrambled eggs and sardines at five in the afternoon; but somehow, since reaching man's estate, I had rather dropped out of the habit; and I'm bound to admit I was appalled to a goodish extent at the way the sons and daughter of the Revolution shoved their heads down and went for the foodstuffs. Even Comrade Butt cast off his gloom for a space and immersed his whole being in scrambled eggs, only coming to the surface at intervals to grab another cup of tea. Presently the hot water gave out, and I turned to Jeeves.

'More hot water.'

'Very good, sir.'

'Hey! what's this? What's this?' Old Rowbotham had lowered his cup and was eyeing us sternly. He tapped Jeeves on the shoulder. 'No servility, my lad; no servility!'

'I beg your pardon, sir?'

'Don't call me "sir". Call me Comrade. Do you know what you are, my lad? You're an obsolete relic of an exploded feudal system.'

'Very good, sir.'

'If there's one thing that makes the blood boil in my veins – '

'Have another sardine,' chipped in young Bingo – the first sensible thing he'd done since I had known him. Old Rowbotham took three and dropped the subject, and Jeeves drifted away. I could see by the look of his back what he felt.

At last, just as I was beginning to feel that it was going on for ever, the thing finished. I woke up to find the party getting ready to leave.

Sardines and about three quarts of tea had mellowed old Rowbotham. There was quite a genial look in his eye as he shook my hand.

263

'Don't call me "sir". Call me Comrade.'

'I must thank you for your hospitality, Comrade Wooster,' he said.
'Oh, not at all! Only too glad –'

'Hospitality!' snorted the man Butt, going off in my ear like a depth-charge. He was scowling in a morose sort of manner at young Bingo and the girl, who were giggling together by the window. 'I wonder the food didn't turn to ashes in our mouths! Eggs! Muffins! Sardines! All wrung from the bleeding lips of the starving poor!'

'Oh, I say! What a beastly idea!'

'I will send you some literature on the subject of the Cause,' said old Rowbotham. 'And soon, I hope, we shall see you at one of our little meetings.'

Jeeves came in to clear away, and found me sitting among the ruins. It was all very well for Comrade Butt to knock the food, but he had pretty well finished the ham; and if you had shoved the remainder of the jam into the bleeding lips of the starving poor it would hardly have made them sticky.

'Well, Jeeves,' I said, 'how about it?'

'I would prefer to express no opinion, sir.'

'Jeeves, Mr. Little is in love with that female.'`

'So I gathered, sir. She was slapping him in the passage.'

I clutched the brow.

'Slapping him?'

'Yes, sir. Roguishly.'

'Great Scott! I didn't know it had got as far as that. How did Comrade Butt seem to be taking it? Or perhaps he didn't see?'

'Yes, sir, he observed the entire proceedings. He struck me as extremely jealous.'

'I don't blame him. Jeeves, what are we to do?'

'I could not say, sir.'

'It's a bit thick.'

'Very much so, sir.'

And that was all the consolation I got from Jeeves.

I had promised to meet young Bingo next day, to tell him what I thought of his infernal Charlotte, and I was mooching slowly up St. James's Street, trying to think how the dickens I could explain to him, without hurting his feelings, that I considered her one of the world's foulest, when who should come toddling out of the Devonshire Club but old Bittlesham and Bingo himself. I hurried on and overtook them.

'What-ho!' I said.

The result of this simple greeting was a bit of a shock. Old Bittlesham quivered from head to foot like a pole-axed blanc-mange. His eyes were popping and his face had gone sort of greenish.

'Mr. Wooster!' He seemed to recover somewhat, as if I wasn't the worst thing that could have happened to him. 'You gave me a severe start.'

'Oh, sorry!'

'My uncle,' said young Bingo in a hushed, bedside sort of voice, 'isn't feeling quite himself this morning. He's had a threatening letter.'

'I go in fear of my life,' said old Bittlesham.

'Threatening letter?'

'Written,' said old Bittlesham, 'in an uneducated hand and couched in terms of uncompromising menace. Mr. Wooster, do you recall a sinister, bearded man who assailed me in no measured terms in Hyde Park last Sunday?'

I jumped, and shot a look at young Bingo. The only expression on his face was one of grave, kindly concern.

'Why – ah – yes,' I said. 'Bearded man. Chap with a beard.'

'Could you identify him, if necessary?'

'Well, I – er – how do you mean?'

'The fact is, Bertie,' said Bingo, 'we think this man with the beard is at the bottom of all this business. I happened to be walking late last night through Pounceby Gardens, where Uncle Mortimer lives, and as I was passing the house a fellow came hurrying down the steps in a furtive sort of way. Probably he had just been shoving the letter in at the front door. I noticed that he had a beard. I didn't think any more of it, however, until this morning, when Uncle Mortimer showed me the letter he had received and told me about the chap in the Park. I'm going to make inquiries.'

'The police should be informed,' said Lord Bittlesham.

'No,' said young Bingo, firmly, 'not at this stage of the proceedings. It would hamper me. Don't you worry, Uncle; I think I can track this fellow down. You leave it all to me. I'll pop you into a taxi now, and go and talk it over with Bertie.'

'You're a good boy, Richard,' said old Bittlesham and we put him in a passing cab and pushed off. I turned and looked young Bingo squarely in the eye ball.

'Did you send that letter?' I said.

'Rather! You ought to have seen it, Bertie! One of the best gent's ordinary threatening letters I ever wrote.'

'But where's the sense of it?'

'Bertie, my lad,' said Bingo, taking me earnestly by the coat-sleeve, 'I had an excellent reason. Posterity may say of me what it will, but one thing it can never say – that I have not a good solid business head. Look here!' He waved a bit of paper in front of my eyes.

'Great Scott!' It was a cheque – an absolute, dashed cheque for fifty of the best, signed Bittlesham and made out to the order of R. Little. 'What's that for?'

'Expenses,' said Bingo, pouching it. 'You don't suppose an investigation like this can be carried on for nothing, do you? I now proceed to the bank and startle them into a fit with it. Later I edge round to my bookie and put the entire sum on Ocean Breeze. What you want in situations of this kind, Bertie, is tact. If I had gone to my uncle and asked him for fifty quid, would I have got it? No! But by exercising tact – Oh! by the way, what do you think of Charlotte?'

'Well – er – '

Young Bingo massaged my sleeve affectionately.

'I know, old man, I know. Don't try to find words. She bowled you over, eh? Left you speechless, what? I know! That's the effect she has on everybody. Well, I leave you here, laddie. Oh, before we part – Butt! What of Butt? Nature's worst blunder, don't you think?'

'I must say I've seen cheerier souls.'

'I think I've got him licked, Bertie. Charlotte is coming to the Zoo with me this afternoon. Alone. And later on to the pictures. That looks like the beginning of the end, what? Well, toodle-oo, friend of my youth. If you've nothing better to do this morning, you might take a stroll along Bond Street, and be picking out a wedding present.'

I lost sight of Bingo after that. I left messages a couple of times at the club, asking him to ring me up, but they didn't have any effect. I took it that he was too busy to respond. The Sons of the Red Dawn also passed out of my life, though Jeeves told me he had met Comrade Butt one evening and had a brief chat with him. He reported Butt as gloomier than ever. In the competition for the bulging Charlotte, Butt had apparently gone right back in the betting.

'Mr. Little would appear to have eclipsed him entirely, sir,' said Jeeves.

'Bad news, Jeeves; bad news!'

'Yes, sir.'

'I suppose what it amounts to, Jeeves, is that, when young Bingo really takes his coat off and starts in, there is no power of God or man that can prevent him making a chump of himself.'

'It would seem so, sir,' said Jeeves.

Then Goodwood came along, and I dug out the best suit and popped down.

I never know, when I'm telling a story, whether to cut the thing down to plain facts or whether to drool and shove in a lot of atmosphere and all that. I mean, many a cove would no doubt edge into the final spasm of this narrative with a long description of Goodwood, featuring the blue sky, the rolling prospects, the joyous crowds of pick-pockets, and the parties of the second part who were having their pockets picked, and – in a word, what not. But better give it a miss, I think. Even if I wanted to go into details about the bally meeting I don't think I'd have the heart to. The thing's too recent. The anguish hasn't had time to pass. You see, what happened was that Ocean Breeze (curse him!) finished absolutely nowhere for the Cup. Believe me, nowhere.

These are the times that try men's souls. It's never pleasant to be caught in the machinery when a favourite comes unstitched and in the case of this particular dashed animal, one had come on the running of the race as a pure formality, a sort of quaint, old-world ceremony to be gone through before one sauntered up to the bookie and collected. I had wandered out of the paddock to try and forget, when I bumped into old Bittlesham; and he looked so rattled and purple, and his eyes were standing out of his head at such an angle, that I simply pushed my hand out and shook his in silence.

'Me, too,' I said. 'Me, too. How much did *you* drop?'

'Drop?'

'On Ocean Breeze.'

'I did not bet on Ocean Breeze.'

'What! You owned the favourite for the Cup, and didn't back it!'

'I never bet on horse-racing. It is against my principles. I am told that the animal failed to win the contest.'

'Failed to win! Why, he was so far behind that he nearly came in first in the next race.'

'Tut!' said old Bittlesham.

'Tut is right,' I agreed. Then the rumminess of the thing struck me. 'But if you haven't dropped a parcel over the race,' I said, 'why are you looking so rattled?'

'That fellow is here!'

'What fellow is here!'

'That bearded man.'

It will show you to what an extent the iron had entered into my soul when I say that this was the first time I had given a thought to young Bingo. I suddenly remembered now that he had told me he would be at Goodwood.

'He is making an inflammatory speech at this very moment, specifically directed at me. Come! Where that crowd is.' He lugged me along and, by using his weight scientifically, got us into the front rank. 'Look! Listen!'

Young Bingo was certainly tearing off some ripe stuff. Inspired by the agony of having put his little all on a stumer that hadn't finished in the first six, he was fairly letting himself go on the subject of the blackness of the hearts of plutocratic owners who allowed a trusting public to imagine a horse was the real goods when it couldn't trot the length of its stable without getting its legs crossed and sitting down to rest. He then went on to draw what I'm bound to say was a most moving picture of the ruin of a working-man's home, due to this dishonesty. He showed us the working-man, all optimism and simple trust, believing every word he read in the papers about Ocean Breeze's form; depriving his wife and children of food in order to back the brute; going without beer so as to be able to cram an extra bob on; robbing the baby's money-box with a hatpin on the eve of the race; and finally getting let down with a thud. Dashed impressive it was. I could see old Rowbotham nodding his head gently, while poor old Butt glowered at the speaker with ill-concealed jealousy. The audience ate it.

'But what does Lord Bittlesham care,' shouted Bingo, 'if the poor working-man loses his hard-earned savings? I tell you, friends and comrades, you may talk, and you may argue, and you may cheer, and you may pass resolutions, but what you need is Action! Action! The world won't be a fit place for honest men to live in till the blood of Lord Bittlesham and his kind flows in rivers down the gutters of Park Lane!'

Roars of approval from the populace, most of whom, I suppose, had had their little bit on blighted Ocean Breeze, and were feeling it deeply. Old Bittlesham bounded over to a large, sad policeman who was watching the proceedings, and appeared to be urging him to rally round. The policeman pulled at his moustache, and smiled gently, but that was as far as he seemed inclined to go; and old Bittlesham came back to me, puffing not a little.

'It's monstrous! The man definitely threatens my personal safety, and that policeman declines to interefere. Said it was just talk. Talk! It's monstrous!'

'Absolutely,' I said, but I can't say it seemed to cheer him up much.

Comrade Butt had taken the centre of the stage now. He had a voice like the Last Trump, and you could hear every word he said, but somehow he didn't seem to be clicking. I suppose the fact was he was too impersonal, if that's the word I want. After Bingo's speech the audience was in the mood for something a good deal snappier than just general remarks about the Cause. They had started to heckle the poor blighter pretty freely when he stopped in the middle of a sentence, and I saw that he was staring at old Bittlesham.

The crowd thought he had dried up.

'Suck a lozenge,' shouted someone.

Comrade Butt pulled himself together with a jerk, and even from where I stood I could see the nasty gleam in his eye.

'Ah,' he yelled, 'you may mock, comrades; you may jeer and sneer; and you may scoff; but let me tell you that the movement is spreading

269

every day and every hour. Yes, even amongst the so-called upper classes it's spreading. Perhaps you'll believe me when I tell you that here today on this very spot we have in our little band one of our most earnest workers, the nephew of that very Lord Bittlesham whose name you were hooting but a moment ago.'

And before poor old Bingo had a notion of what was up, he had reached out a hand and grabbed the beard. It came off all in one piece, and, well as Bingo's speech had gone, it was simply nothing compared with the hit made by this bit of business. I heard old Bittlesham give one short, sharp snort of amazement at my side, and then any remarks he may have made were drowned in thunders of applause.

I'm bound to say that in this crisis young Bingo acted with a good deal of decision and character. To grab Comrade Butt by the neck and try to twist his head off was with him the work of a moment. But before he could get any results the sad policeman, brightening up like magic, had charged in, and the next minute he was shoving his way back through the crowd, with Bingo in his right hand and Comrade Butt in his left.

'Let me pass, sir, please,' he said, civilly, as he came up against old Bittlesham, who was blocking the gangway.

'Eh?' said old Bittlesham, still dazed.

At the sound of his voice young Bingo looked up quickly from under the shadow of the policeman's right hand, and as he did so all the stuffing seemed to go out of him with a rush. For an instant he drooped like a bally lily, and then shuffled brokenly on. His air was the air of a man who has got it in the neck properly.

Sometimes when Jeeves has brought in my morning tea and shoved it on the table beside my bed, he drifts silently from the room, and leaves me to go to it; at other times he sort of shimmies respectfully in the middle of the carpet, and then I know that he wants a word or two. On the day after I had got back from Goodwood I was lying on my back, staring at the ceiling, when I noticed that he was still in my midst.

'Oh, hallo,' I said. 'Yes?'

'Mr. Little called earlier in the morning, sir.'

'Oh, by Jove, what? Did he tell you about what happened?'

'Yes, sir. It was in connexion with that that he wished to see you. He proposes to retire to the country and remain there for some little while.'

'Dashed sensible.'

'That was my opinion also, sir. There was, however, a slight financial difficulty to be overcome. I took the liberty of advancing him ten pounds on your behalf to meet current expenses. I trust that meets with your approval, sir?'

'Oh, of course. Take a tenner off the dressing-table.'

'Very good, sir.'

'Jeeves,' I said.

'Sir?'

'What beats me is how the dickens the thing happened. I mean, how did the chappie Butt ever get to know who he was?'

Jeeves coughed.

'There, sir, I fear I may have been somewhat to blame.'

'You? How?'

'I fear I may carelessly have disclosed Mr. Little's identity to Mr. Butt on the occasion when I had that conversation with him.'

I sat up.

'What!'

'Indeed, now that I recall the incident, sir, I distinctly remember saying that Mr. Little's work for the Cause really seemed to me to deserve something in the nature of public recognition. I greatly regret having been the means of bringing about a temporary estrangement between Mr. Little and his lordship. And I am afraid there is another aspect to the matter. I am also responsible for the breaking-off of relations between Mr. Little and the young lady who came to tea here.'

I sat up again. It's a rummy thing, but the silver lining had absolutely escaped my notice till then.

'Do you mean to say it's off?'

'Completely, sir. I gathered from Mr. Little's remarks that his hopes in the direction may now be looked on as definitely quenched. If there were no other obstacle, the young lady's father, I am informed by Mr. Little, now regards him as a spy and a deceiver.'

'Well, I'm dashed!'

'I appear inadvertently to have caused much trouble, sir.'

'Jeeves!' I said.

'Sir?'

'How much money is there on the dressing-table?'

'In addition to the ten-pound note which you instructed me to take, sir, there are two five-pound notes, three one-pounds, a ten-shillings, two half-crowns, a florin, four shillings, a sixpence, and a halfpenny, sir.'

'Collar it all,' I said. 'You've earned it.'